I0728204

FAITHFUL

LIGHT *in the* EMPIRE

FAITHFUL

CAROL ASHBY

CERRILLO PRESS

FAITHFUL

Copyright 2018 by Carol Ashby

All rights reserved. No portion of this book may be reproduced, stored in a retrieval system, or transmitted in any form or by any means—electronic, mechanical, photocopy, recording, scanning, or other—except for brief quotations in critical reviews or articles, without the prior written permission of the publisher.

Publisher's Note: This novel is a work of fiction. Names, characters, places, and incidents are either products of the author's imagination or used fictitiously. All characters are fictional, and any similarity to people living or dead is purely coincidental.

Scripture quotations marked (KJV) are taken from the Holy Bible, King James Version, 1769 edition.

Scripture quotations marked (NKJV) are taken from the New King James Version. Copyright © 1982 by Thomas Nelson, Inc. All rights reserved. Used by permission.

Scripture quotations marked (NLT) are taken from the Holy Bible, New Living Translation, copyright © 1996, 2004, 2007. Used by permission of Tyndale House Publishers Inc., Carol Stream, Illinois 60188. All rights reserved.

Scripture quotations marked (ESV) are from the Holy Bible, English Standard Version, copyright © 2001, 2007, 2011, 2016 by Crossway Bibles, a division of Good News Publishers. Used by permission. All rights reserved.

Cover and interior design by Roseanna White Designs

Cover images from Shutterstock.com

ISBN: 978-1-946139-06-1 (paperback)
        978-1-946139-07-8 (ebook)
        978-1-946139-15-3 (hardcover)

Cerrillo Press
Edgewood, NM

Bear one another's burdens, and so fulfill the law of
Christ.

Galatians 6:2 (NKJV)

"By this all will know that you are My disciples, if you
have love for one another."

John 13:35 (NKJV)

"Greater love hath no man than this, that a man lay
down his life for his friends."

John 15:13 (KJV)

And we know that for those who love God all things
work together for good, for those who are called accord-
ing to his purpose.

Romans 8:28 (NKJV)

"For I know the plans I have for you," says the LORD.
"They are plans for good and not for disaster, to give you
a future and a hope."

Jeremiah 29:11 (NLT)

To my children, Paul and Lydia,
for their love, support, and encouragement,
and especially to my husband, Jim,
who helps me find the good in everything.

And most of all, to Jesus.

Soli Deo gloria.

A Note from the Author

A faithful friend. Someone who cares enough to warn us before we do something foolish. Someone who will help us dig out of the mess we created after we ignore that advice.

That's something we all long for. It's someone we treasure once we find them. A faithful friend is the living embodiment of the kind of love we're called to share as followers of Jesus.

But Jesus calls us to extend the love we might naturally show a friend to those outside our circle of friendship. Friendship rides atop a shared history, where things we've done have earned the trust and affection of our friends. Agape love extends to those we've barely met and even to those who have declared themselves our enemies.

It's agape love that Jesus meant when He said, "Love one another." He told His followers that the love they showed for each other would declare to all that they were His disciples.

In Roman times, that love shared among the believers was surprising and attracted new followers. The love they showed to strangers and enemies amazed even those who wanted them destroyed. The same is true today.

Obeying the command to love can be challenging. In a world where so many are looking out for themselves at the expense of others, we're called to consider what's better for everyone, not just ourselves. It's not always easy, and it's certainly not natural, but God doesn't call us to live natural lives. He calls us to live lives that please Him.

When we respond faithfully to that call, He gives us His Spirit to help us do it.

When we try, we can expect certain responses. Some will think we're easy targets and try to take advantage of us. Some will think we're fools to make ourselves vulnerable, even though they don't try to hurt us. Some will consider the idea good in theory but not something to try themselves. But some will long to be part of a community that welcomes them without asking anything in return.

Faithful tells the story of a man who is so loyal that he refuses to stop searching until he finds his kidnapped friend and risks dying to save him. When that quest exposes him to a mortal enemy, he's so devoted to Jesus that he's willing to die before denying his Lord.

But it's more than the story of one man's commitment to his friend and his God. It's the story of how living his faith in Jesus rescues a stranger, turns an enemy into a friend, and draws both toward his Lord.

I hope you'll enjoy this story of the power of a faithful life to open others to hearing God's call as much as I've enjoyed writing it. May God give us all the courage and strength to live and love faithfully so we can see others respond to His love.

Carol Ashby

Characters

ADELA'S FAMILY
Adela: (19) daughter of Adalmar
Adalmar: (40) Adela's father, chieftain of the Hermunduri tribe
Hildegard: (34) stepmother of Adela, new wife of Adalmar
Gunda: (13) Hildegard's daughter

LICINIUS CRASSUS FAMILY
Galen: (21) Gaius Licinius Crassus, whose father fled Rome to escape execution as a Christian
Valeria: (27) "Val," German adopted sister of Galen and Rhoda, wife of Decimus
Rhoda: (17) Galen's sister

OTTO'S FAMILY
Otto: (21) "Bjorn," best friend and trading partner of Galen, fourth son of Baldric
Baldric: (54) Otto's father, chieftain of Vangiones tribe
Adolf: (28) third son of Baldric

CORNELIUS LENTULUS FAMILY
Tiberius: (55) former governor of Germania Superior, Decimus's father
Decimus: (33) "Dec," Tiberius's only surviving son, Valeria's husband
Publius: (6) older son of Decimus and Valeria, named for Decimus's mentor
Gaius: (4) younger son of Decimus and Valeria, named for Galen's father
Priscilla: (1) baby daughter of Decimus and Valeria, named for Galen's mother
Graecus: chief steward of the Lentulus properties near Rome

CLAUDIUS DRUSUS FAMILY
Publius: (deceased) Tiberius's best friend, Decimus's mentor; executed for his faith

Other important characters

Silanus: centurion in VIII Augusta Legion based in Argentorate, Germania Superior

Gundahar: German who kidnaps Adela and Otto

Gerlach: German kidnapper, Gundahar's partner

Scaurus: a trainer of gladiators (*lanista*) in Augusta Raurica

Lothar and Baldwin: German gladiators in Octodurus

Marcus Antonius Brutus: owner of gladiator schools in Luca, Florentia, and Roma

Ursus: Thracian lanista who runs Brutus's school in Florentia

Quintus: owner of an inn and stable on the outskirts of Rome

Cities and Towns

Alpes: the Alps, mountains between Italy, Germany, France, and Switzerland

Argentorate: headquarters for VIII Augusta Legion; located on Rhine; present-day Strasbourg

Arretium: Present day Arezzo, Italy

Augusta Praetoria: Present day Aosta, Italy

Augusta Raurica: town on the route from Argentorate to Rome; 20 km east of present-day Basel, Switzerland

Aventicum: town on the route from Argentorate to Rome; present-day Avenches, Switzerland

Borbetomagus: garrison town on the Rhine between Mogontiacum and Argentorate; present-day Worms, Germany

Brigantium: town on Lake Constance in Roman province of Raetia; present-day Bregenz, Austria

Florentia: Present day Florence, Italy

Lacus Brigantinus: Lake Constance, patrolled by a Roman provincial fleet based in Brigantium

Lacus Valsiniensis: Lake Bolsena

Lugdunum: Present day Lyon, France

Mogontiacum: capital of Roman province of Germania Superior, headquarters of XXII Primigenia Legion; located on the Rhine; present-day Mainz, Germany

Nepete: Present day Nepi, Italy

Octodurus: full name Civitas Vallensium Octodurus, location of Forum Claudii Vallensium; provincial capital of Alpes Graiae et Poeninae; present-day Martigny, Switzerland

Parma: Present day Parma, Italy

Ticinum: Present day Pavia

Vivisco: Present day Vevey, Switzerland

Vindonissa: town between Augusta Raurica and Brigantium, former legion headquarters

Volsinii: Present day Bolsena, Italy

Modified excerpt of map by Andrei N. – Wikimedia Commons user: Andrein- Own work, CC BY-SA 3.0, https://commons.wikimedia.org/w/index.php?curid=26047281

Chapter 1

Heading Out

Land of the Hermunduri, two days north of Germania Superior, AD 122

Adela felt the daggers as she hung her horse's bridle on the gatepost and swatted its rump to send it into the corral. When she turned to face the cottage, her father's new wife spun and stomped inside.

She rolled her eyes. It was going to be another one of those days.

It had only been four months since Mother died. Why had Father been in such a hurry to remarry? He had a son, and Adela would marry soon to give him a son-in-law. She'd told him he should take his time. A chieftain of the Hermunduri could have his pick of the maidens whenever he decided to wed.

But had he listened? Maybe if her brother had spoken, Father might have. All she got was a frown and a flick of a hand to shoo her away.

They weren't at war, so why marry the sister of another chieftain to seal an alliance? It made no sense. Especially when Hildegard was meaner than a weasel. She would not call that woman Mother, no matter what Father said.

She cringed at the thought of another day in the company of Hildegard's mousy daughter, Gunda. No Hermunduri girl should jump at her own shadow.

Adela's gaze flipped over her shoulder when she felt the hand.

Gunda was holding two baskets. "The wild strawberries are ripe. Olga had some this morning, and Mother wants us to go gather some, too."

"I didn't see any when I was riding."

Her stepsister hugged herself as her eyes flicked toward the cottage, then returned to Adela. "But Mother said they were ripe where the stream forks."

"That far? We won't be back in time for supper if we go there."

Gunda rubbed her nose and glanced at the cottage again. "I know, but when Mother says go, I'm not going to argue. Neither should you."

She held out a basket and gave it a small shake. "Your father already told you to do what Mother says. Do you want her to tell him you wouldn't go?"

Adela snatched the basket, jerking Gunda toward her when she didn't let go fast enough. "The sooner we go, the sooner we get back."

She set a fast pace as they entered the woods. Gunda had to scurry to keep up, but it wasn't Adela's fault that her stepsister was a scrawny little thing, even though she was thirteen. Hildegard spoiled her precious daughter, and spoiling made a person weak.

Adela squared her shoulders. No one would ever dare call her weak. Father might not value her opinion about remarrying, but she'd heard him brag on her skill with weapons and horses. A daughter fit for a chieftain's son. That's what he'd said, and her heart warmed at the thought.

She was nineteen. Within the year, she would marry, and she knew exactly what kind of man she wanted. Tall, handsome, proud, afraid of nothing and no one—a warrior like Father.

Already Father was talking with the other chieftains with sons ready to take a wife. Adela's lips curved into a satisfied smile. Her marriage couldn't be soon enough to get her out from under Hildegard's aggravating control. After she was wed, she could tell that woman what she thought of her. That thought broadened her smile.

"Slow down, Adela."

Gunda's whining heightened the anticipation. One more thing she'd leave behind when she married her warrior.

When they reached the glade where the stream forked, Adela's brow furrowed. Lush, green...but no sign of red.

"I don't see any ripe strawberries." She spun on Gunda. "Did Olga pick everything already?" Her lips tightened. "Just like your mother to waste my time like this."

Gunda turned in a circle as she scanned the surrounding trees. "But Mother said they were here." Her eyes caught Adela's, then flitted away. "Maybe we need to look among the deep grass and ferns." She pointed across the stream. "You look over there. I'll look on this side."

Adela jumped the stream and shuffled through the grass, pushing it aside with her foot before each step. No strawberries, not even green ones. Her back was to the stream when she heard hoofbeats behind her.

Then Gunda gasped. Adela spun. A man on a bay horse stood between her and Gunda, but she could see Gunda's legs under the horse's belly. She was backing up as the man leaned toward her. He nudged the horse closer and grabbed Gunda's arm.

Adela trotted to the stream bank and leaped across. "Leave her alone!"

The man turned to face her, and his lips twisted into a sneer as Adela moved closer.

Gunda strained to pull free and started to cry. "No. Don't do it."

Adela sprinted toward the horseman as Gunda's tears turned to sobs. A feral laugh escaped his throat as he shoved Gunda away and focused on her.

Her eyes narrowed as she neared his horse's head. The man was brawny, and she had no weapon. But she knew horses. She grasped the loose fabric panel that draped the front of her dress and flicked it into his horse's face.

With a panicky neigh, the horse reared, launching the man into the air. When the flailing hooves returned to earth, Adela was ready. She scooped up the reins, grabbed a handful of mane, and sprang onto its back.

Gunda stood like a statue, eyes enormous and hands over her mouth. Adela held out her hand. "Get up behind me."

Her stepsister started to move...backward.

The man moaned behind her.

"Gunda, now!"

Hoofbeats...two horses...coming up fast from behind. "Gunda!"

Gunda spun and ran into the trees and up the hill. Adela whirled the horse. Two men were coming straight for her.

"Keep running!" Adela bent low on the horse, drove her heels into its flanks, and hurtled forward...toward their attackers.

She shot between them before they could react. If only they would follow her...Gunda was running toward their home. Perhaps she'd get away.

The pounding hooves behind her promised a chance for her stepsister. Adela urged the horse forward. She reached the edge of the clearing and was forced to slow down as she wove between the trees.

The head of a horse moved up on her right side. Too close, but also close enough. Low branches lay straight ahead. As she pulled her reins to the right, she lay flush with her horse's neck. She barely cleared, but the tall man beside her didn't. His yell as the branches swept him from his horse was music to her ears. The trees thickened; the hill grew steeper. Her horse lurched as she pounded her heels into its sides to keep it lunging up the slope.

Hoofbeats behind her...closer...closer...

The front neckline of her dress cut into her throat as a hand grasped the back. The horse leaped forward as her thighs lost their grip. Blue breaks in the green canopy flashed overhead as she was dragged across the horse's rump.

Then all went black.

A hill-country farm in Germania Superior

As Galen tied his bedroll to the saddle, Astrelo turned his head to watch.

"Ready for an adventure, boy?"

Astrelo's bridle jingled as he shook his elegant black head.

Galen slapped the stallion's neck twice. "I'll take that as a yes." A quick rub of the star-shaped blaze drew a contented nicker. "Let's go do some trading."

As he stepped away from his horse, two small boys dropped the sticks they were poking into the mud puddle and ran to him. He scooped up four-year old Gaius and plunked him on his shoulders. Six-year-old Publius bounced at his side.

"I wish I could go with you, Uncle."

Galen tousled the boy's wavy brown hair. "When your mother and father say it's time."

He glanced at his sister, Val, as she walked toward him, a sack containing food and a change of clothes slung across her right shoulder and a giggling baby girl on her left hip. "Better if we ask Dec. He's more likely to say yes sooner." He put his finger across his lips. "Don't tell your mother."

Val reached his side, a smile tugging at the corner of her mouth. "Don't tell me what?"

Galen swung Gaius to the ground and slapped his bottom. "Run, before she gets an answer out of you."

The two boys sprinted away, giggling.

Galen took the sack from her. "Should be a good trip. We'll stop in Borbetomagus first. I already know someone who wants the mare there. Then we'll head south to Argentorate. Roman officers always have more money than they can spend out here, and the colts should bring top money at the legion fortress." He bounced his eyebrows. "I might even get a couple of the tribunes into a bidding war, like last time."

Val pushed a stray lock of hair back from his forehead. He fought the grin. She was always going to see him as her little brother who needed tending.

"My father would be impressed by how good you are at this."

Galen chuckled. "I learned from masters, watching you and Baldric."

"I know you'll only be gone for a week and a half, but be careful. I'll be praying for you."

"Don't worry, Val. I'll have Otto along to advise me."

Her eye-roll pulled another chuckle from him.

She planted her fist on the hip without a baby. "You know Baldric and I are relying on you to keep Otto out of trouble, not the other way around."

A grin split Galen's face. "You can tell Baldric I'll get a good price for his horses. I'll also make sure his young stallion comes home in one piece."

He whistled, and Astrelo trotted over. The sack joined the bedroll at the back of his saddle. As Galen mounted, Val untied the lead rope of the first horse in the string from the corral railing. After he settled into the saddle, she handed it to him.

"May God bless and keep you on the journey."

Galen nodded once. "He always does. We'll head down to the river road as soon as Otto brings Baldric's horses to the village. See you in about ten days."

He nudged Astrelo into a trot and tossed his sister a backhanded wave as he entered the tree-lined wagon track that led to the village. The sunlight made dancing patterns of light and shade as it filtered through the leafy branches. There could be no better way to start a journey of ten days with his best friend.

◆

Valeria shook her head as she smiled. Her brother was always joking, but he had a good head on his shoulders and a heart that wanted to please God. She'd be praying for his safe return, but he and Otto should be fine.

Chapter 2

No Respect

North of the Roman Frontier

Adela awoke with a skull ready to split open. She was lying on her stomach, draped over something that bounced faster than her pounding heart. The bouncing had added new bruises to compound the pain from her fall. Her head throbbed with every bounce. The sack over her eyes shrouded her in darkness. Trying to lift her hands to remove it tugged on her ankles.

Why was she draped like a sack of grain across the back of a horse?

"What is going on here?" No answer. "Untie me right now!" No answer. Just more bouncing, more throbbing, more pain.

She twisted her hands as she struggled to free herself from the ropes binding her wrists together. After several minutes, she stopped. She'd rubbed her skin raw, and nothing had loosened.

The horse finally slowed, then stopped. The stench of someone who reeked of sweat penetrated the bag. Jerks on the ropes tying her hands to her feet made her chafed wrists sting. Rough hands gripped her shoulders and shoved her backward to slide off the horse. She lost her balance and sat down hard on the uneven ground.

Her hands were still tied, but the rope around her neck that held the bag on loosened. When the bag was jerked off, the bright light momentarily blinded her. When her eyes adjusted, the leering face of a tall, blond man with filthy hair and a scraggly beard was inches from her own.

She squared her shoulders and raised her chin. "What do you think you're doing? I am the daughter of Adalmar, chieftain of the Hermunduri. You will release me right now. If you don't, when my father catches you, he'll make you sorry you were ever born."

A vicious grin split the kidnapper's face, and a cruel laugh erupted from deep within him. "Take a look at yourself, daughter of Adalmar. I see no chieftain's daughter. I see a slave."

Adela didn't want to break eye contact, but her eyes were irresistibly drawn to the shabby slave tunic someone had put her in. When had they taken her clothes? Who had put her in this? She swallowed hard, then fought against showing any fear.

His face moved closer to hers. Foul breath made her head recoil. "Forget about being a chieftain's daughter. You're never going back there. You're nothing but my slave now, and the sooner you start acting like one, the better for you."

She forced herself to keep her eyes on his. "Where is Gunda? What have you done with my stepsister?"

Another laugh rumbled out of his leering mouth. He stood and motioned for his companion to give her some water before he sauntered away.

Adela fought against the panic that drove in upon her. Something horrible must have happened to Gunda, or she'd be there, too. Adela had tried to save her but...

As she held the cup of water, her hands trembled. Her vision blurred as tears tried to escape. *No! I am a chieftain's daughter. I will not let them see my fear. I will not show weakness. I will escape, and my father will make them pay for this.*

She forced herself to take slow breaths, to push the panic back as she looked around. There were three of them. Too many eyes were watching her now. They would let down their guard if she acted like a helpless woman too stupid to know how to escape. Her heart rate slowed. *Wait for the right time, and then they'll be sorry.*

The leader strolled back and picked up the bag. "Enough water and freedom for you, daughter of Adalmar." He pulled the bag over her head and tied the rope around her neck.

Someone dragged her to the horse and hoisted her onto its back. Her bound hands were tied loosely to the saddle. She bent over to put the neck rope within reach of her fingers.

A hand gripped her shoulder and jerked her back to an upright position. "You don't need to see to ride. Stop trying, or..." Adela fought the shudder that his chuckle triggered and straightened her spine.

A finger traced down her bare arm, followed by a cruel laugh. "I hope you're ready for a three-day ride, chieftain's daughter. We have a long way to go before you get to your new master's house."

The horse started trotting, and Adela settled into the saddle. She'd practically lived on horseback since she was a small child. A three-day ride would be no problem. When the kidnappers let down their guard, she would be ready.

Argentorate, three days later

The gray stone walls of the legion fortress cast a shadow across Otto's path as he and Galen rode toward the double-arched gate with two strings of horses behind them. The eyes of the sentry narrowed, and his hand settled on the hilt of his sword as they approached. It was the response Otto expected.

He was tall, muscular, armed, and German, a combination that guaranteed a Roman sentry would assume the worst.

They reined in ten feet from the sentry, and Galen raised his hands in a peaceful gesture. "*Salve.* We've come to see Centurion Junius Silanus. He's expecting us. I would appreciate you sending him word that Gaius Licinius Crassus is back with the horses he wanted to see."

When Galen's polished Latin announced the three-part name that declared his Roman citizenship, the sentry relaxed. He turned to another legionary standing behind him under the archway. "Find Centurion Silanus."

As the soldier disappeared behind the wall, Otto's mouth turned down. Roman officers had the money to pay what his father's horses were worth, but to get the money...

His eyebrows lowered. To get the money, he had to deal with the Romans. His father laughed at the Roman air of superiority, but it galled Otto.

He glanced at Galen's profile. The Roman nose and wavy, dark brown hair declared his Italian origin even before his first Latin word. His best friend since childhood was more German than Roman, but that wasn't what the soldiers saw. They only saw one of their own.

Otto's father complained that he didn't get as much money for their horses as his brother Adolf had. But Adolf had always been quick with a joke and full of stories. Maybe that let Adolf cajole the Romans into accepting him and paying more than they had to. Otto couldn't play that game.

Galen didn't either, but he still got good money, no matter what he was selling. Father had ordered Otto to do whatever Galen said on this trading trip. Galen was to negotiate the sale of their horses, and Otto was to watch him and learn.

His frown deepened. He and Galen had both celebrated twenty-one birthdays. But Otto was more than a foot taller, and more than once he'd picked Galen up and held him over his head until Galen begged him to put him down. Galen was his best friend, and Otto would defend him against anyone who insulted him. But Otto would be the first to admit that his friend was a runt in a world of big men. For Father to imply Galen was a better man and he had to obey him, that rankled.

Two centurions came through the gate: Silanus and another whom Otto hadn't seen before. They sported the standard centurion frown until Silanus's gaze fell on Galen. Then his mouth flipped into a smile.

"Crassus, it's good to see you and your horses again. Vitellus here has been waiting for you to bring more ever since I bought that bay colt last fall."

Silanus slapped his friend's arm. "He lost out on the bidding for the bay when I sold him. Once a tribune sets his mind on owning something, cost means nothing to him. I'm in the market again, so maybe I shouldn't have brought Vitellus today. He might outbid me for your best."

Galen's lips curved into a friendly smile. "That shouldn't be a problem." He pointed toward Otto. "Otto, son of Baldric of the Vangiones, and I brought the best from our stables. We have plenty of quality horseflesh to satisfy both of you."

Silanus glanced at Otto, gave a quick nod, and focused his attention back on Galen. Vitellus glanced but didn't even nod. Otto's jaw started to clench until he forced it to relax.

Galen swept his hand toward the horses. "Let's see what we can do to get you mounted today. All our horses are trained to be ready to ride, but never in a way that breaks their spirits." He grinned. "Rather like a good legionary. Plenty of spirit but ready to serve. Pick the one you like, and then we can talk price."

Vitellus strode to the first horse in Otto's string to begin his inspection. He ran his hands over the black horse's back, flanks, and legs. His eyes lit with appreciation, and a smile started to escape before he tightened his lips.

Otto fought a smile himself as the centurion crossed his arms and tilted his head. The Roman wanted the horse, and he should. It was an animal Otto would be proud to ride himself. He stroked the colt's nose as he waited for the Roman to ask the price that Baldric had set before he left.

Then Vitellus turned toward Galen, who was showing a bay colt to Silanus. "Crassus, does this one have the same sire as the stallion you're riding?"

Galen glanced over his shoulder. "No. That's from Otto's stable. They have two excellent studs, and Otto can tell you all about his bloodline."

Vitellus turned his gaze on Otto and raised his eyebrows.

Otto unclenched his jaw. "The sire is the same as my stallion's, and the mare had the same sire as Galen's. It takes a strong horse to carry me, and this colt should be one." The centurion's gaze swept Otto's bay. "He's a bargain at 500 *denarii*."

Vitellus rubbed his chin. "That much?"

Otto straightened to his full height. "Any true horseman can see that's cheap for a horse like him."

The centurion's eyes narrowed, then relaxed. Otto could see the sale slipping away.

Silanus rode past, trying out the bay Galen had been showing him.

Galen came over and began stroking the black colt's neck. "The things that make a horse worth that kind of money aren't always obvious at first glance. I know you don't judge a soldier only by what he looks like standing at ease. You watch him on the training ground to see if he has what it takes. Courage and stamina, strength and skill. Otto's right when he says their horses can carry big men long distances and be ready to do it again the next day after a night's rest."

Galen slapped Otto's arm. "Baldric and all his sons are big men like Otto, and his horses are bred for speed and stamina carrying heavy loads. Why don't you try him out? We can throw one of our saddles on him or you can ride bareback. Either way, once you feel his power between your legs, you'll know why Baldric's horses sell for so much."

Vitellus's brows rose as he nodded. "Saddle him, and I'll try him out."

Galen pointed toward Astrelo. "My saddle or Otto's?"

The corner of Vitellus's mouth turned up. "Otto's more my size."

Galen took the saddle from Otto's bay and tossed it on the colt. As he cinched it, he glanced over his shoulder at Vitellus. "You're in for a treat.

This one's fast for a two-year-old, and I can only imagine what he'll be when he's finished muscling up in a couple of years."

Galen stepped back, and Vitellus mounted. A huge grin covered Galen's face as he crossed his arms. "You might want to tighten your chin-strap, or I can hold your helmet if you want to run him."

Vitellus chuckled. "If he goes fast enough for my helmet to come off, there's no way I'll pass on this one." As he turned the horse's head toward the open field along the fortress wall, he grinned at Galen. "Maybe I'll want him even if it doesn't."

As Vitellus rode out, Silanus came back. He swung his leg over the bay colt's neck and slid to the ground. "This one is almost as good as the one last fall. Let's talk price."

As Galen strolled away with Silanus at his side, Otto's frown deepened. Galen had just made the sale he was about to lose. Watch and learn. That's what his father had said. He'd watched, but all he'd seen was one Roman take the word of another Roman that his horse was worth the money. How could a German ever expect the same response?

It was late afternoon. Otto lounged in his saddle as the two tribunes walked through the fortress gate leading Otto's last mare. It was his horse, but he might as well have been Galen's servant for all the notice the Romans had paid him.

Galen dropped the last of the twenty-two *aurei* into Baldric's bulging purse and handed it back. "I didn't expect to get 550 denarii for a mare, but who am I to say the price is too high when two tribunes decide to compete for her?" He shrugged. "More than I would pay, but she is a beautiful animal. I expect she'll have strong foals."

He whistled, and Astrelo sauntered over. "Selling all eight on the first day and none of them for less than 475 denarii...that's the best we've ever done." He jumped to lay his stomach on Astrelo's back, then swung his leg over the stallion's rump.

As he settled into the saddle, Otto rode up beside him. "It was a good day for making money if you're a Roman. They would never have paid so much to a German. They can't wait to buy a horse at a high price from you, but I have to sell cheap just to get them to look at my animals."

Galen's eyebrows rose. "But it isn't being Roman that lets me get the better deals. It's how I treat my customers. You catch more flies with honey than vinegar."

He leaned forward and patted Astrelo's neck. "I don't treat it as a contest where they lose if I win. You seem ready to pick a fight sometimes even when you're trying to strike a deal."

Otto shook his head. "That's not it. It's because you're all Romans, so they treat you like an equal. Me, I'm just a German to them."

Galen punched Otto's shoulder. "A German looking for a fight. Me, I'm just a friendly man who wants to make them the envy of their friends when they ride one of our horses. If they were going into battle, you're the one they'd want in armor beside them."

Otto's frown flipped into a grin. Galen was right. He was more than a foot taller than his Roman friend. Galen was much too short to serve in one of the elite cohorts of a Roman legion. He was so short they wouldn't even take him into the lowest cohort unless it was a dire emergency that suspended the recruiting rules. Otto would hate being shorter than all the other men. Even most German women were taller than Galen.

Funny how Galen didn't seem to care about being a runt among giants. His usual response was a shrug and "it's the heart, not the height, that matters."

Otto nudged his horse, and they started toward the vendor campground. "Probably, but if they watched you sparring, they'd want you just as much. After years training with your brother-in-law, we're both good enough to beat anyone."

A corner of Galen's mouth lifted. "And one of us is wise enough not to be trying to prove it to strangers."

Chapter 3

THE CHIEFTAIN'S DAUGHTER

A drunken German stumbled into the road ahead of Galen, and he reined in to let the man cross. Raucous laughter came from a canopy pitched by the roadside.

Otto's gaze focused on the tables where men were drinking and gambling. "Let's stop."

Galen's eyebrows rose as he scanned the motley collection of men under the canopy. Some were merely drinking. Others were focused on the women serving the drinks. Some at the tables seemed sober and much too attentive to the drunks casting dice with them.

"Maybe not the best idea to take the horse money into a den of thieves and scoundrels."

Otto pushed on his shoulder. "Don't be such a cautious old woman. No one knows what we're carrying." A grin split his face. "Besides, I'll protect you."

Galen returned the grin. That was often the best way to deflect Otto from an unwise course. "If we don't go in, I won't need protecting."

"But I can't win at dice if I don't play, and a few beers will wash the taste of the Romans from my mouth. I'm stopping."

Otto's jaw set, the sure sign he wouldn't listen to reason.

Galen rubbed the back of his neck. "If you want to gamble for a while, go ahead, but let the cautious old woman hold most of the horse money. Some of those are probably sneak-thieves, and it's easy to get so focused on the game they can take a purse without you feeling it."

Otto's head tilted as Galen's words struck home. He took ten denarii out of the large purse, dumped them into the smaller purse tied to his belt, and handed the horse money to Galen.

"You got the money for Father; you may as well guard it."

Galen loosened his belt and slipped Otto's purse under his shirt. He tied it to his money belt before lowering the shirt and buckling his belt over it to hold it in place. "I'll go on to the western vendor camp and find us a good spot."

As Otto prepared to dismount, Galen slapped his shoulder. "Don't stay too long, big man. I'm hungry already, and I don't want to wait too late to eat." His mouth started to open, but he shut it before his next thoughts escaped. *Don't do anything stupid. I don't want to answer to your father if I let you get into trouble. Or to Val, either.*

One corner of Otto's mouth lifted. "You're always hungry. How can you eat as much as me and not get fat?"

Galen grinned back. "Maybe I need more since I have to take more steps than a giant like you to walk the same distance." His mouth straightened. "Seriously, watch your back. You can't trust the men here, and I won't be with you to cover you."

Otto squared his massive shoulders. "You sound like Father. I've had twenty-one birthdays. I'm a man, not a boy. I can take care of myself in a fight."

"But maybe I can't. I'm carrying enough money to be a tempting target. Anyway, don't stay too long. My stomach's growling already."

Otto tossed his reins to Galen and sauntered away, giving him one backhanded wave before pushing into the crowd of men surrounding the gambling tables.

Galen nudged his horse and headed for the vendor camp, leaving Otto to carouse and gamble. His lips tightened as he shook his head. Val and Baldric were right. Otto towered over most people, but his best friend had some growing up to do before he'd truly be a man.

Otto drained his fifth tankard of beer...or maybe his sixth...and raised it to catch the attention of the serving girl. As she refilled it, he scooped up the dice and shook them.

"The dice are not your friends today, Gundahar. Too bad. I guess we quit now with all your coins in my purse." He tried to hold back the grin, but it leaked out anyway.

Gundahar rubbed his chin. "You owe me one more chance to win it back. I have something worth much more than what you've won from all of us." His mouth twitched as he turned to the man standing behind him. "Bring the girl." Turning back to Otto, his eyes narrowed as a friendly smile curved his lips. "I'm short on money, but I have just the thing to cover my bet. It's worth many times over the coins in your purse. One roll each, winner take all."

◆

Adela pulled against the lead rope tied to the leather strip that bound her wrists, but her captor was much stronger. He dragged her under a canopy and past a cluster of men who eyed her hungrily. Rough hands gripped her shoulders and shoved her up to a table.

The kidnapper called Gundahar gripped her arm. "This one is especially valuable because she used to be a chieftain's daughter. I guarantee that she was a virgin when I got her. I checked myself."

Gundahar turned his face toward her. "Isn't that so, pretty thing?"

Adela squared her shoulders as she drew herself up to her full height. "It is, and my father will find me and skin you alive for taking me. If you're wise, you'll return me without delay. Then he might spare your life."

Her stomach clenched. What did he mean about checking her himself? She couldn't remember him or anyone else touching her, but somehow she got into the slave tunic. What else did he do while she was knocked out? She shoved the thought to the back of her mind. *The daughter of a chieftain is always brave. Never show weakness.* He mustn't suspect she'd been scared half out of her wits for the last three days.

He drew a finger down her cheek, and she snapped her head sideways, teeth poised to bite him. An ugly laugh met her failure to catch his hand.

"I'm faster than you, pretty thing." His eyes narrowed. "Meaner, too, so be careful."

She forced her eyes to meet his, but the cold laughter she saw there convinced her he saw the fear she was struggling to hide.

"The pretty daughter of a chieftain should know how a slave shows respect to its owner. You'll learn to do it quick enough."

Gundahar turned back to the man sitting across the table from him. "The son of a chieftain should know what to do with the daughter of one."

Adela kept up the courageous mask as she turned her eyes on the young man.

He was brawny and much taller than most. Strikingly handsome as well. A mane of blonde hair and a trimmed beard. Piercing blue eyes that were dulled by the drink. A proud man who might just be the son of a chieftain. His eyes as he gazed at her didn't look mean, but looks could be deceiving. Still, she'd rather be with him than the kidnapper. He might be won over to let her go, or she might be able to escape. Especially if he got drunk enough. He was close to that now.

The big man shook his head. "I don't need a slave. I'd rather have a good horse...but she is very pretty, so maybe this time I'll let you use her to cover the bet."

Gundahar leaned back in his chair. "Go ahead, make your play."

The big man shook the dice and let them roll. He won. A sappy grin split his face as he looked first at Gundahar, then her. "I guess I need a pretty slave after all. What's her name?"

Gundahar shrugged. "Whatever you want to call her."

She raised her head high. "I am Adela, daughter of Adalmar, chieftain of the Hermunduri. It is now you who must return me to my father."

The big man tilted his head as he watched her without uttering a word. She saw no fire of cruel anticipation in his drink-dulled eyes. It might prove to be a very good thing that he'd won her.

Gundahar picked up the dice and shook them. "The dice haven't been kind tonight. Let's play tabula instead." He snapped his fingers and held out his hand to the man behind him. The man placed some coins in it. "Give me a chance to win some back."

The big man turned his eyes on Gundahar. "Set up the board."

Adela watched them moving the colored slices of bone on the grid carved into the plank of wood. The play went back and forth, with the big man winning more than he lost.

She'd almost figured out what seemed to be the rules when Gundahar rested his arms on the table and leaned in.

"At the gaming table, you're as good as I've played in a long time. Are you as good with a sword?"

The big man took another swig of beer. "Good? That's not the word for it. There's none better. How many do you know who can fight two at once and disarm them both in less than ten strokes?"

Gundahar's eyebrows rose. "Two at once?"

The big man took another drink. "In less than ten strokes."

"That I would like to see." Gundahar's smile started small and broadened.

The big man grinned. "Many would."

Gundahar rubbed his chin. "Want another drink before the next round?"

Big man wiped his mouth with the back of his hand. "Why not?"

Galen sat by the fire pit, waiting. The wood and kindling were laid, ready to light as soon as Otto appeared. The problem was he hadn't. It had been more than two hours. He should have come by now.

A deep sigh escaped his lips before he tightened them. Keep Otto out of trouble. That's what Val had said. That's what Val always said when they headed out with horses to trade. Did she have any idea what that took sometimes? He and Otto were the same age, best friends for fourteen of their twenty-one years. So why was Otto still more like an impetuous youth than a grown man when some temptation dangled in front of him? Whether it was gambling, fighting, or getting drunk, Otto would leap right in if Galen didn't hold him back.

Galen rose and strolled over to the hobbled horses. He squatted and removed the hobbles from his stallion. The horse bumped him hard with his head, making Galen sidestep quickly to catch his balance.

"You trying to cause me trouble, too, Astrelo?" The horse bumped him again, begging for a nose rub. Galen rewarded his persistence. "Time to break camp for a while, boy." He threw his saddle on Astrelo's back and cinched it. Then he unhobbled and resaddled Otto's horse. Anything he left behind might not be there when he returned.

He jumped to get his stomach on Astrelo's back before swinging his leg across the stallion's rump. As he settled in the saddle, he reached forward and patted the horse's neck. "Let's go pull Otto out of that gambling den while he still has some money left." One more pat. "I swear, you have more sense than he does."

As he rode past Otto's bay, he leaned and scooped up its reins. Even Otto's horse had more sense.

Galen dismounted at the hitching rail beside the canopy. He tied Otto's stallion's reins to the cross bar. Astrelo would stay with his reins simply dropped to the ground. He'd only scanned half the tables when he heard Otto call.

"Galen. Over here."

Too many eyes turned on Galen as he walked past the tables in the front to the one where Otto half-stood and waved at him.

Otto had four stacks of coins in front of him worth at least five times the ten denarii he'd started with. Galen scanned the faces of the others at the table. None looked happy, and the man with blond hair and a scraggly beard who sat across from Otto had a fake smile pasted on.

A tabula board sat between them, and a quick glance revealed Otto was winning.

Galen rested his hand on Otto's shoulder. "I thought you'd be coming before this. Almost through?"

"We're in the middle of a match. I can't leave yet." Otto grinned. "Gundahar has some coins I need to win back." Otto's speech was slurred.

Galen felt the coldness behind Gundahar's smile as the gambler's gaze swept him from head to foot and back. This man was not to be trusted, and Otto was too drunk to see it. Galen rubbed his cheek. "Looks like you've more than tripled what you started with. Maybe it's time to declare victory and come eat."

Otto chuckled. "You're always hungry, but there's plenty of beer here to fill an empty stomach." He offered Galen his tankard. "Try some."

Galen took a sip. "It's good, but I'd rather eat." He picked up the biggest stack of coins. "Better for you to come eat, too. Let's take your winnings and go."

Otto slapped his shoulder. "I'm not ready to quit. But you can take some of what I've won." He separated ten denarii from the pile and shoved the rest toward Galen.

Galen scooped up the coins and dropped them into the purse hanging from his belt. It was risky to have so many see him take that much money, but arguing with Otto would draw even more eyes.

A woman stood behind Otto with her hands bound. Otto twisted in his chair to pick up a rope. He gave it a tug, and she was forced to step closer to the table.

"This is Adela from…I forget where." A sappy grin split his face. "I won her. She's much prettier than a horse."

Galen's eyes widened as he raised his eyebrows. Much prettier than a horse? That might be the greatest understatement he'd ever heard. Enormous ice-blue eyes flashed with anger. Flaxen hair swirled around a face of perfect symmetry. Gracefully arched eyebrows, chiseled cheekbones. Full lips that Otto would describe as irresistibly kissable were set in a determined line. A threadbare slave's tunic with a tear at the neckline revealed too much of her curvaceous figure. Scarcely longer than a tall man's shirt, the tunic provided a heart-pumping view of a pair of legs with graceful curves in all the right places.

His hand covered his mouth and pulled down across his chin as he shook his head almost imperceptibly. Baldric's family had never owned slaves. Many times, he'd heard Baldric's scathing comments about the Romans who thought of their slaves as no more than work animals or living household furniture. What was he going to do when Otto brought one home? Especially a stunning beauty like this girl.

Otto offered the rope and shook it a little when Galen didn't immediately take it. Galen forced his tightened lips to relax. Otto could get his back up at the slightest thing when he was drunk.

When Galen took the rope, the sensation of those arresting blue eyes focusing on him pulled his eyes to hers. The anger had vanished, but was he looking at a mask? Those eyes weren't placid like a lake. More like the still stretch of a river just before you rounded a bend to find treacherous whitewater.

"It's getting late. I'll take her back and set up camp. Better come soon if you want me to leave any supper for you."

Otto grinned and slapped Galen's shoulder. "You thought me gambling wasn't a good idea. Just goes to show you...but I'm almost through."

Galen tapped Otto's arm with his knuckles. "Maybe it would be good to slow down the drinking if you're going to keep gambling."

A deep laugh rumbled in Otto's throat. "Getting drunk is something real men do. I can handle it, Mother."

Galen took a deep breath and slowly released it as he scanned the faces around them. Scoundrels and thieves without a doubt. Hanging out with these men when he was roaring drunk was not wise, but there was no way he'd convince Otto of that.

"See you back at camp." Galen led the girl over to the waiting horses. With two spirited horses and one gorgeous girl following behind him, too many eyes were watching. Better to head out the wrong way, then double back.

He'd have to stay up until Otto came to spell him on watch. He didn't want an unexpected visitor to relieve him of money, horses, or girl.

Otto's drunken guffaw echoed behind him. On second thought, he'd better plan on watching all night. Otto would be worthless as a guard when he finally came.

Chapter 4

Not What She Expected

Adela followed the big gambler's short friend like a docile milk cow. Freedom was getting closer. From three kidnappers to the drunken giant to this man who was shorter than anyone else around the gaming tables—each in turn less able to keep her from escaping. It should be easy to get away from this Galen.

The gambler's friend didn't impress her. He only came up to her eyebrows, and she liked tall men. The taller, the better. His deep, strong voice sounded odd from a man no taller than the boys who were starting their spurt into manhood. Maybe some would think his face handsome, but he looked too Roman. Wavy, dark brown hair with a strand that fell across his forehead, dark brown eyes, nose with a bulge near the top— he looked nothing like the blonde, blue-eyed Germanic warriors who made her pulse jump when they stood close. Well, almost nothing. He was broad-chested, and the forearms bared by his rolled-up sleeves were brawny.

She admired men who had that hard edge to them, like they were ready to go into battle, ready to fight at the slightest provocation. This short one had no sign of the warrior about him. He smiled and cajoled his big friend rather than telling him to stop gambling and drinking. But that was probably all a short man could do with a man so obviously better than him. His friend had handed over his winnings and her without any argument, but he was still drinking and gambling.

Adela sucked air between her teeth as something sharp poked into the arch of her foot. Mistake to be watching her captor instead of where she stepped. The kidnapper had stolen her shoes. Her feet weren't toughened for walking barefoot on rubbish-strewn streets, and this Galen was taking forever to get to their camp. First north, then west, then south—it was like he had no idea where he was going.

She shuffled along behind him. By the time they finally reached a campground, each step was like lifting and swinging a lead weight. Three days of riding followed by three nights of fighting sleep until she heard her captors snoring, then most of this day in the wagon cage with her hands tied to the bars so she couldn't lie down—she had never been so tired. But she needed to escape before the big one came. Even drunk, he would make it harder to get away.

She followed Galen past other campsites toward the farthest edge of the camp. Several men waved at him as they passed, but one called him over.

"Galen, I thought you went for Otto." A gap-toothed grin split the wrinkled face of the old man. "Did you trade him for this beauty? If I was a young man again, I'd be glad to bargain for this one."

Adela struggled to keep her docile look. No man, old or young, had any right to trade her as if she were a horse.

"She's not mine to trade, Bruno. Otto won her."

Bruno leered and bounced his eyebrows as he scanned her body. "The goddess Fortuna smiled upon him. He'll want to keep his prize, but you can't blame an old man for dreaming."

It was all Adela could do not to rip into him with razor-edged words, but she held back. Show no anger so the short one won't be expecting her break for freedom. Like freezing with an arrow nocked and drawn when a stag jerked up its head, waiting for that moment of inattention to return before letting the arrow fly.

Finally, he stopped by a fire pit with the tinder and logs already set for lighting.

Galen dropped the horses' reins and stepped close. He drew his dagger. "Hold out your hands."

The fool was going to cut her loose. Adela cast her eyes down. He mustn't see her excitement as she felt the vibration of the knife sawing on the leather strap between her wrists. She pulled her wrists as far apart as the strap allowed, putting tension on the strip that grew thinner with each pass of the blade.

Thin enough! She jerked her wrists apart, and the remaining thread of leather snapped. She slammed her fist into his hand, knocking his dagger into the air. She snatched it as it fell and slashed at his throat.

His head jerked back, and the blade sliced into his cheek. Not too deep, but the blood flowed freely along the length of the cut. Before he could respond, she kicked him strategically as hard as she could. He bent double.

Adela hurled herself onto the black stallion and drove her heels into his flanks. The horse leaped forward.

She was free.

A shrill whistle pierced the air. The stallion stopped and tried to turn back. She fought to keep his head directed forward. Again and again, she drove her bare heels into his flanks, but he refused to budge.

Another whistle split the air. The stallion's ears lay back flat against his skull. He fought to turn his head, but she pulled hard on the reins to prevent it. Her strength was no match for his. Snorting and dancing in place, he swung his head back toward the camp.

Adela jerked the reins to turn him forward again. With an angry snort, he arched his back as he launched himself upward. Her thighs lost their grip, and she lurched sideways as he landed on four stiff legs. Once more, he catapulted skyward, and Adela was hurled into the air. Afraid she might stab herself when she hit, she dropped the dagger. She slammed into the ground, landing flat on her back, shaken to her bones. She gasped for air as the wind was driven from her lungs. Her head smacked into the ground, and stars danced before her eyes. Her eyelids closed as she tried to clear her vision.

When she reopened them, the short man stood over her. He was reaching down to pull her up.

Fool. He was in range again. Her hands shot up to claw his eyes.

With the speed of a striking snake, he grabbed both her wrists before her nails could reach him. He straddled her before sitting on her thighs. His large hands pinned her arms to the ground. She writhed and squirmed and tried to toss him off, but he kept her pinned as if she were no stronger than a child.

His face leaned closer to hers. "I don't want to hurt you. Stop fighting."

Liar. Of course he wanted to hurt her. She'd cut him and kicked him, and now she was at his mercy. She kept struggling.

"Adela."

She froze when he spoke her name. His voice was quiet, gentle. No one had spoken her name like that since her mother died. Her eyes were drawn to his face.

Where was the anger? Where was the snarl that should be twisting his lips? They curved up in a slight smile instead. And his eyes—not a trace of anger there, even though dribbles of blood left trails on his cheek below the cut.

"That's better. If you stop fighting and promise you won't try to run, I'll release you." The smile got a little bigger. "I'm not going to hurt you, Adela."

As she looked deep into those brown eyes, she relaxed. Strange as it seemed, she believed him...almost.

"I'll take that as your promise. Don't break it."

He released her arms and rose. Again, he offered his hands to help her up. This time she took them. He pulled her to her feet, then released her.

She tossed her head as she ran her fingers through her hair to tidy it. Mistake. Her head throbbed where it had smacked into the ground. Her whole body ached from the hard landing. Still, she squared her shoulders and straightened to her full height.

Her own eyes were level with his hairline. She tilted her head to raise her eyes even higher.

"I'll leave if I want to. My father is Adalmar, chieftain of the Hermunduri. My stepsister and I were ambushed by slave traders. Their leader used me to cover his bet with your tall friend. If you take me back to Father, he will pay you handsomely for serving me. It's only three, maybe four days from here on horseback."

The short one shook his head. "I can't do that. I don't know whether what you say is true. All I know is that your clothes are those of a slave, and Otto thinks he won you from your rightful owner. Even if I could be sure you're telling the truth, Otto is the man who can make that decision, not me."

"I'm no man's slave, and you *will* release me *now* so I can return to my father." She thrust her chin out and looked down her nose at him.

He showed no sign of being impressed by her haughty attitude, and that smile remained.

"No. I can't let you go. If I did, some other man would grab you to sell again. But when Otto comes, you can tell us the whole story. I can persuade him to take you back to your home if you can convince us what you claim is true."

He kept looking straight into her eyes. Men never kept their eyes on that part of her. He was explaining instead of commanding like he would a child or servant. Or a woman. Hermunduri men didn't treat her with the kind of respect they'd show another man.

But that smile might be concealing what he was really thinking. Her eyebrows lowered as she tried to take his measure. No lust burned in his eyes before he spoke again.

"You know your best chance of getting home is to stay with us. Don't try to run away if going home is what you want." His eyes never wavered from her own. "I want you to promise me you won't."

She could see the wisdom of what he was saying, but she didn't trust him, even with those brown eyes that seemed honest. She'd give no such promise. She stared at him, not uttering a sound.

He sighed. "Since you won't give me your word you won't run, you'll have to stay tied up when I'm not watching you. When Otto comes, we'll decide what to do."

As Adela glared at him, a shiver vibrated from her head to her ankles. The tunic the kidnapper had put her in was sleeveless and short, reaching not even halfway down her thighs. The fabric was thin and so worn out in places she could almost see through it. The sun was low on the horizon, and it gave little warmth. She rubbed her arms to ward off the chill.

As he kept his eyes on hers, he whistled. The black stallion with the star-shaped blaze sauntered over to him. He reached into a sack tied at the back of the saddle and pulled out a brown shirt and pair of pants.

He held the clothes out to her. "Here. You'll be warmer in these."

She took them without a word. Why would he show her such kindness? She'd tried to kill him. Even now, a little blood oozed from the cut she'd made on his cheek.

She stepped into the pants and pulled them up, tucking the threadbare tunic in. Then she pulled the long-sleeved shirt over her head. The pant legs didn't even reach her ankles. The waist was too big, but it fit well enough at the hips. His shoulders were broad, so the shirt enveloped her like a father's shirt on a child. The sleeves hung past her fingertips, so she rolled them up to her wrists.

He retrieved his dagger, then picked up her lead rope. He cut off a short length to make a belt and tossed it to her. She tied it on top of the shirt, cinching it at her waist. When she looked at his face again, a broad grin met her gaze.

"What's so funny?" A testy edge sharpened her voice.

"My clothes don't do a pretty girl like you justice."

She scowled. "Don't think your flattery will get you something from me."

His grin mellowed into a simple smile. "I'm not asking for anything."

She made no reply. She wasn't sure how to respond. She'd never had a compliment before from a man who wasn't trying to manipulate her.

"Sit down on the log there. I'll start us a fire."

Adela strolled to the log with head held high. She wasn't going to let him think she was in any hurry to obey anything he said.

It took only a few moments before he had it lit. The flickering flames and yellow-hot coals at the base drove away the chill. It was the first time she'd been comfortable since she'd awakened strapped to the horse.

He lifted the saddles from the horses and carried them over near the fire. From the large sack that held the clothes, he extracted a smaller one. He pulled out a wooden plate, three rolls, and a chunk of cheese.

Adela's eyes locked on the food. The kidnappers had given her water, but she hadn't had a morsel of real food since she'd been taken. She forced herself not to lick her lips. She was not going to ask her captor for anything.

As he cut the cheese into smaller pieces, he paused and looked up at her. "When did you eat last, Adela?"

She raised her eyes from the food to his. She swallowed. "Before they took me."

She hadn't meant to say that, but the food was so tempting and she was so hungry...

He took one piece of cheese and handed her the plate. "Then you should have this."

She stared at the plate, then at him. "But what will you eat?"

He tossed his piece of cheese in the air and caught it with his mouth. "I've had it. I eat too much most nights anyway."

He left the fire to hobble the horses. The black one nuzzled him, and he stroked its nose and patted its shoulder before returning. He glanced at her often, and she returned his scrutiny.

A stump stood near the fire, and he settled onto it.

She stared at the plate and then at him. He'd given her all his food. What was he going to want for it?

He tipped his head toward the plate. "Go on. Eat."

Although she was tempted to gobble it down, she made herself eat slowly, savoring every bite. She sneaked a peek at him. He was staring into the fire, his face relaxed into the slight smile that seemed to be his permanent expression.

He was treating her too well. He must want something. Men always did.

Chapter 5

THIEVES AND SCOUNDRELS

The final trace of orange faded from the slice of sky visible past the edge of the canopy. Otto drained the last drops of beer from his tankard and wiped his mouth with the back of his hand. His stack of denarii had grown since Galen left. As he stared at the tabula board, Gundahar shifted a bone rondel between his left and right hands.

"The horses your short friend had...they were fine animals."

Otto shifted his gaze from the board to Gundahar's face. "Some of the finest in Germania."

"I won a beauty yesterday. A fine stallion with markings unlike any I've seen before. Nearly black but the mane and tail are pale."

Otto's eyebrows rose. "I've never seen one like that."

"I have him back at the camp. I'm through here for the night, so come with us and you can see him."

Otto scooped up his coins and dropped them into his purse. "Let's go."

He wobbled some when he first stood. "Is it far? Galen's waiting supper for me in the western vendor camp."

"We're in the southern camp, and it's close."

"Are you thinking of selling him?"

"Maybe, if the price is right. I don't raise horses myself."

Otto slapped Gundahar's shoulder. "I do."

Gundahar turned to his friend who'd brought the girl. "Let's take Otto to see the horse." His smile broadened into a grin. "He's ready for a new owner."

He summoned the man who'd lent him the coins for tabula with a flick of his fingers before turning back to Otto. "Follow me."

It was dark by the time they reached the campground. The smell of smoke and roasting meat wafted around Otto as they worked their way past the cookfires.

Gundahar looked back over his shoulder at Otto. The other two men followed close behind. "Our camp is on the far side, past the bushes. We like it quiet."

At the edge of the campground, Otto glanced at a cage mounted on wheels. His mouth turned down. "Is that yours?"

Gundahar's eyes flicked toward the cage. "That belongs to the man who owned that slave you won."

"Not very big to keep a woman in. She couldn't lie down."

Gundahar shrugged. "He tied her hands to the roof bars, so she couldn't lie down, anyway."

Otto's frown deepened. "Even a slave should get to sleep."

They walked through a narrow opening into a small clearing behind the tall bushes.

Gundahar's mouth split in a wicked grin. "And we're going to help you get some."

Otto's arms were jerked behind him. He bent double, flipping the man gripping his arms over his head. As he straightened, an explosion of pain pulsed through his head, and he collapsed to his knees. Another blow, and he crumpled to the ground.

A booted foot slammed into his jaw, and Gundahar's leering face faded to black.

Adela's shoulders slumped as she swallowed the last bite of bread. Her eyes kept drifting shut, and she blinked hard as she fought to keep them open.

Galen's gaze locked on her. He rose from the stump and approached with hand held out. "Through with the plate?"

She passed it to him without a word.

He swept the surface clean with his hand, then returned it to the sack by his saddle. He came back to the fire with a bedroll tucked under his arm.

Her spine straightened when he unrolled it beside her.

She forced a scowl to hide her accelerating heart rate. "I'll kill you if you touch me."

His brown eyes were unperturbed as his smile broadened. "I don't plan to, not that way. You need to sleep before you fall into the fire. But since you didn't promise not to run, I do have to tie you up."

He shrugged. "Sorry. Lie down and get comfortable first."

Adela's gaze shifted between the bedroll and his eyes. No threat lurked there. It had been so long since she'd allowed herself to sleep deeply. Maybe she could trust him.

"I won't try anything. I'm only going to sit by the fire." He squatted by the bedroll, with her lead rope in his hands. "The sooner you lie down, the sooner you can sleep."

Adela pulled a deep breath and took the first step toward trust.

After she lowered herself onto the bedroll, he bound her ankles, but not so tightly it was uncomfortable. She lay on her back and held her hands out, wrists together. Again, the rope was not too tight.

He flipped the top blanket over her. "Rest in peace, Adela."

She didn't answer.

With a smile slightly broader than his normal expression, he turned and strolled back to his saddle. When he untied the roll at the back, it opened to reveal a fleece-lined vest. After slipping into it, he resumed his post on the stump.

◆

As Galen sat by the fire, he faced a dilemma. What were they supposed to do with a slave, if she really was one? If she had been kidnapped, it would be an easy matter to take her home. But what if she hadn't been? Baldric didn't own slaves, and he despised the Romans who kept them. He would be furious with Otto for bringing one home to keep. What should they do with her if she didn't have a father to return to?

He glanced at her. She was the prettiest woman he'd ever seen. Otto often let his eyes instead of his head do his thinking. He might just think keeping her was a good idea, even if she had been kidnapped. It was very clear Adela didn't want any man to touch her. He couldn't let Otto use her for entertainment, even if she was a slave. He sighed. Keeping Otto out of trouble like he'd promised Val could be a lot harder than she ever imagined.

He rested his elbows on his knees and leaned his forehead against his clasped hands. *Dear God, I thank you for the many blessings of this day. Thank you for...*

The tension flowed out of him as he communed with God. It was the perfect ending of a mostly good day. Good except for Otto's choice to drink too much and gamble too long. But God could bring good from bad. At least the girl was better off with them than with her former owner. And if she really had been kidnapped, then God's hand had surely been upon her when Otto won her tonight. He'd convince Otto to do the right thing. He'd always been able to do that. No reason to think he couldn't do it again.

◆

Adela watched the short Roman as he sat with his eyes closed and a relaxed smile. She'd never seen a man close his eyes for so long when he wasn't asleep. When he finally opened them, he stared into the fire. Then he glanced at her. When he caught her watching him, a bigger smile tugged at the corners of his mouth before his eyes turned back to the fire.

Adela's brow furrowed. This Galen confused her. How could a man she'd tried to kill treat her as if they were friends? He seemed harmless, but was he? Could she risk letting her guard down to sleep without him doing anything?

In the darkness outside the circle of light cast by the fire, something moved, then stilled. Was it only an animal? Adela peered past Galen, trying to make out the moving form. Suddenly a man with a raised dagger stepped into the light behind him.

She gasped. "Behind you!"

Galen dove into a somersault and rolled away from his attacker. He rose with his *gladius* in his hand and spun around. The man lunged, but Galen caught his dagger with the sword. He stepped into the attack, sliding the sword up the dagger blade until it nicked the attacker's thumb. One sideways sweep of the sword flicked the knife from his hand and flung it fifteen feet away. The attacker's eyes widened as Galen raised the gladius and slammed the rounded pommel at the end of the handle into the man's temple. The man collapsed at Galen's feet.

He slid the gladius back into its scabbard before bending over the crumpled form to release the man's belt and pull it free. He untied the attacker's purse strings from the belt, tossed the purse down beside him, and pushed it under the man's body with his foot. Then he picked up the dagger and slid it into its sheath before strapping the belt around his own waist.

Adela's jaw dropped, but she snapped her mouth shut before the Roman could see. She had never seen anyone fight like he just did.

Galen unhobbled the horses and led them near the fire to saddle them. Adela stared at him, but he ignored her until he finished.

Then he knelt by her ankles and freed them. He began untying her wrists. "We need to leave right now, in case he has friends who come looking for him."

She stared at the unconscious man. "Why didn't you kill him?"

"Because I didn't have to."

"He's one of the men who kidnapped me. He deserves to die."

"But I don't want to kill him." His fingers froze. "And if I untie you, you're not going to kill him, either."

She glared at him. What right did he have to tell her not to take her revenge on this worm of a man?

"You're not going to kill him. If his friends find him knocked out, they probably won't look for us. If they find him dead, they'll hunt us. I might not be able to defend us if there are too many. Understand? I want your word you won't kill him."

His eyes had lost any hit of laughter. His mouth was straight, lips pressed together. There was steel inside this man that hadn't been obvious before.

"I won't."

His face relaxed, and he finished untying the knots. "I do believe you were kidnapped now."

Galen knelt by the bedding and rolled it up. "We'll find a safer place to camp and come back for Otto in the morning."

He stood and tucked the roll under his arm. "I'll talk with Otto about taking you back to your father. Otto's a good man. Once he knows you've been kidnapped, he'll be willing to take you home."

Adela's eyebrow rose. Why would any man who thought he owned her be so willing to let her go? It would even take him at least six days out of his way to take her home and return. She couldn't name any man in her village who would go to that much trouble for a woman.

Would a giant of a man like the gambler Otto be willing to give her up just because his short friend tried to talk him into it? The big one had handed over most of his money and her, but this Galen hadn't talked him out of continuing to drink and gamble. His influence over the big man had limits, and taking her home was probably past them.

But he was right. She'd be a fool to try to return on her own. She'd end up someone else's slave if she didn't stay with this skilled fighter, even if he didn't like to kill.

Chapter 6

Not a Fool

As the short Roman led the two horses through the dark streets of Argentorate, Adela shifted in the saddle. Just past his stallion's ears, she could see the back of Galen's head. He'd put her back on his horse because she had no shoes. He said he didn't want her to hurt a foot by stepping on something sharp in the dark before he could get her some.

What he did made no sense. He didn't want the kidnappers to find them, but he risked that by putting her up on a horse, where all could see, to protect her bare feet. And what kind of man would buy shoes for the woman who cut his face open? She felt a twinge of guilt each time she looked at the gash on his cheek. But how was she supposed to know he only wanted to help when she cut him? No one would blame her for trying to get away, no matter what it took. Even he didn't seem to, but that was very strange.

Galen led them deeper into the town. Her eyelids kept drifting shut. She'd been afraid to sleep while the kidnappers held her and was tied so couldn't in the cage. It might be safe with him. When would he get to the campground? After so many twists and turns, surely no one could still be following them.

They finally emerged from a narrow street into an open field. Directly ahead loomed massive walls of gray stone.

He turned to face her. "I don't know which of the regular camps your kidnappers might be staying in, and we need to find someplace they won't think to look. I know where to ask."

Her eyes saucered as he gestured toward the arched gate with its blazing torches and sentries in full battle armor. "Isn't that a legion fortress?" She tried to keep the tremor from her voice, but a trace remained. "We shouldn't be so close. My father says the legion warriors are fearsome in battle, and the men they don't kill, they haul away as slaves."

Galen turned and stepped between the horses' heads. He placed a reassuring hand on hers where it rested on her thigh. "You don't need to be afraid, Adela. Roman soldiers are safe when you're a Roman, and I'll protect you. Just stay close to me and try not to look too frightened."

Adela put on a warrior face with eyebrows scrunched and lips parted to show her teeth.

His face split in a grin. The grin became a chuckle. What did he find so funny?

"That isn't quite what I meant. I don't want you to frighten the soldiers, either."

She worked at relaxing her face until she hit something between fearful and frightening.

"That's perfect. Now just sit quietly and let me do all the talking."

She gave him two quick nods. He didn't need to worry. With Roman warriors so close, she'd do exactly what he said. Besides, she wouldn't know what to say. Even though her father had her brother learn Latin, she'd heard him say he wasn't going to pay for his daughter to waste her time trying to learn what only a man needed to know.

◆

Galen approached the sentry at the gate with his hands held up in a peaceful gesture. The sentry pulled his sword.

"Halt. State your business."

He kept his hands in plain sight and away from his sword. "I'm seeking information. Someone tried to rob me in one of the vendor camps, and I want to find a safe place for me and my woman to camp tonight."

The centurion in charge of the guards turned at the sound of Galen's voice. "Crassus?"

Silanus strode over and flicked his fingers first to tell the sentry to lower his sword and again to summon Galen closer. "Tell me what happened."

He glanced at Adela, then turned his eyes back on her for a longer look. An appreciative smile curved his lips. "I'd want a peaceful resting place if I had such a companion. Much prettier than your big friend."

Galen chuckled. "And more exciting company. It's good to see you again, Silanus. Otto is somewhere drinking and gambling. Someone tried to knife me as I sat by the fire waiting for him."

The centurion drew his finger across his own cheek. "Looks like he got close."

Galen shook his head. "No. I already had that."

Silanus's eyebrows rose. "How?"

Galen shrugged and grinned. "Let's just say it's not wise to sneeze when you're shaving with a dagger and no mirror."

The centurion chuckled. "I'll remember that. Which camp and what happened?"

"The western vendor camp. I was sitting by the fire, and he came at me from behind."

"And you killed him?"

"No. I only knocked him out. He might still be there. I was concerned he might have friends coming after him, so we left right away. The horses brought good money today, and I saw him where Otto was gambling. Otto might have said too much where he and others could hear." He turned and looked at Adela. "I think he and his friends are kidnappers as well as thieves. Otto won her, and she's under my protection now."

The centurion's eyes scanned her again. "A job I'd gladly take myself, Crassus."

Galen's smile was noncommittal. "What I need is a safe place to spend the night away from the regular camps. Where do you suggest?"

The centurion's eyes returned to Galen. "Just west of the fortress, there's a camp for the waggoneers who deliver the legion supplies. I would expect no trouble there."

"Then that's where we'll stay." Galen's smile broadened. "Thank you, Silanus."

Silanus slapped Galen's shoulder. "Glad to help my favorite horse trader. That colt you sold me today—I've already been offered more than I paid for him. Tribune Aemilius Lepidus would pay me double. It's certain he'll want to see what you bring to trade in the fall."

Galen returned the slap. "I may have exactly the colt he'll want. We'll bring him."

He glanced at Adela. Each blink lasted too long, and she was swaying a little. "Time to make camp before she falls off my horse. I'll see you come fall, Silanus."

The centurion folded his arms and watched as Galen turned his horses and walked toward the west. He called out, "If you want to sell that black stallion of yours then, give me first chance."

Galen raised his hand in response but kept walking. Astrelo wasn't a horse he'd put up for sale.

◆

Adela's heart had beaten faster as they got closer to the fortress gate. When the sentry barked something at them and drew his sword, she could feel it thumping against her ribs. When the man with the fancy red crest on his steel helmet spun and walked toward them, it was all she could do to keep the fear off her face. The way he looked at her, like a hungry wolf, made it even harder.

If only she could understand what Galen was saying to the man who must be at least the son of a chieftain, but it was all Latin. Not a word made sense. Galen was so brave the way he stood there, so relaxed as he talked to the warrior. Maybe it was because he was such a good fighter himself, but that wouldn't help much with so many of them.

Suddenly the man with the crest was laughing with Galen about something, and it seemed like they were friends. She relaxed in the saddle. He was right about Roman warriors being safe for Romans. Even the chieftain's son didn't seem so scary when she watched how friendly he was with her protector. She didn't like how the Roman looked at her, but with Galen there, she didn't feel threatened by it. As the fear drained out of her, the fatigue came back with a vengeance. It was getting harder to keep her eyes open.

She awoke with a jerk when the warrior slapped Galen. A few more friendly words, and Galen slapped him back. Maybe they actually were friends. Still, she was glad when Galen began leading the horses away from the gate. Everything would be fine, at least for the night, as long as she was with him.

As Galen led the horses past the cluster of wagons to an empty space toward the center of the camp, Adela's eyelids kept drifting shut. She shook her head, fighting to stay alert.

"Adela." He said it gently, like he had when he had her pinned after she cut him. He reached up to help her down. She pushed his hand away; she could ride with the best of the men. She didn't need any help. He stepped away as she swung her leg across the horse's neck and slid from its back.

"We'll stop here." He stepped past her and untied his bedroll from his saddle. He flipped it to make it roll out on a smooth place near a fire pit where the last camper had left tinder and wood. "Time for you to get some sleep before you drop."

"Are you going to tie me up again?"

His mouth was twisting up into a grin before he stopped it. "No. You don't strike me as a fool. You've seen enough tonight to know you're safest staying close to me. Just lie down and rest."

He turned from her to tend the horses. After lifting off the saddles and placing them near the fire pit, he hobbled the two stallions and released them to graze beside their camp.

As he squatted to start the fire, she slipped into his bedroll, turned on her side, and pulled the top blanket up around her chin. Her eyelids were so heavy, but she wanted to watch him for a while. When he had the fire going, he settled on one of three upended sections of tree trunk that had been left there as stools. He didn't look like he planned to sleep.

The short Roman must be as tired as she was, but he was going to watch over her. Well, maybe he was really watching over the horses. They were beautiful animals, worth a lot of money. She couldn't be that important to him. Except whenever she opened her eyes to check on him, he seemed to glance at her. The smile that hovered on his lips got a little bigger then and relaxed when he turned his eyes back on the fire.

He held a short stick, and he occasionally poked at the coals with it. He looked alert but also peaceful. He was a strange one, this man who hadn't tried to take advantage of her and was making sure no one else did.

As Adela let down her guard for the first time in days, sleep overpowered her in seconds.

Otto awoke with a head that felt like he'd been kicked by a horse. He was draped across a horse's back with his hands and feet tied together. He bounced a little with each stride of the trotting animal. A gag pulled the corners of his mouth tight enough that his lips pressed against his teeth.

He raised his head, trying to see where he was. As he began to thrash, struggling against his bonds, a mounted Gundahar slipped into his field of view.

A hand grabbed his hair and tipped his head back until their eyes met. "Stop struggling. It's hard on the horse."

Otto's eyes threw daggers, and Gundahar chuckled.

"That's the look I like to see. If the trainers think you've got fighting spirit, that's more denarii in my purse. You said you could fight two at once and many would love to see it. You'll get your chance to entertain a few...at least once. Maybe more, if you don't die in the first match." He dropped Otto's head. "There's always a market for big Germans. Most don't last long, but maybe you'll beat the odds."

His chuckle turned into a wicked laugh. "You thought you were a good gambler, but everything you won is mine again. Gerlach took care of your short friend, and I'll have the girl and those fine horses to sell when I sell you."

Otto's heart shriveled within him. Galen...the best friend a man ever had...dead because of his own stupid choices.

The galloping hoofbeats approaching from the rear drew both their gazes.

The man who'd brought the girl to the table rode up beside Gundahar.

Gundahar's brows scrunched. "Where's the girl?"

"There was a problem. The girl saw me and warned the runt. He knocked me out when I tried to knife him. When I came to, he and the girl were gone. Why he didn't just kill me..." He shrugged. "I left right away in case they came back with soldiers."

A string of curses spewed from Gundahar's mouth, and he cuffed the man's ear. "You worthless son of a donkey! How could you lose all that money and the girl? Especially the girl. I'd planned on some fun with her after we got some distance between us and Argentorate. The first time wasn't much sport. I like it when they put up a fight before I have my way, and she had enough fight in her to satisfy any man."

Otto closed his eyes and drew a deep breath. A seed of hope sprouted within him as he released it. His friend was alive. Galen would search for him, and he wouldn't stop until he found him. If anyone in the Empire could rescue him from the stupid mess he'd gotten himself into, it was Galen.

A couple of hours before dawn, Adela jerked awake.

Galen turned his gaze on her. "Anything wrong?"

She sat up. "No." She rose and walked to his side. "Let me watch so you can get some sleep."

He tilted his head and cocked an eyebrow at her. "Will you give me your word you won't run away?"

She tightened her lips. "Of course. I'm no more of a fool than you think I am."

He stared into her eyes before he nodded once. "I could use some sleep."

He rose and held his hand out to offer her the stump. She settled onto it and sat watching him as he added more wood to the coals in the fire pit. He strolled over to the bedroll and picked up the top blanket.

When he walked back to her and wrapped it around her shoulders, she almost fell off the stump as she leaned back to look at his calm eyes and that trace of a smile.

He unbuckled the belt holding the kidnapper's dagger and offered it to her. "Here. In case there's trouble I can't handle alone. Wake me right away if anything makes you nervous."

Her jaw started to drop, but she snapped it shut. She sat frozen as she stared up at him. "You're giving me a dagger? But I cut you. Aren't you afraid I might again?"

Galen lifted her right hand away from where it clutched the blanket at her throat. He placed the sheathed dagger in her palm and wrapped her fingers around it. "Like you said, you're no more of a fool than I think you are."

He returned to what remained of the bedroll and moved it a little closer to the fire. Then he lay down on his side with his face toward her and closed his eyes. His deep, slow breathing told her he'd gone to sleep almost instantly.

After strapping on the belt, she drew the blanket around her shoulders. The night was cool. It would feel cold without the blanket.

Was he warm enough in what was left of the bedroll after he gave it to her? Maybe he was just a man who didn't feel the chill.

The rustling as he shifted in his sleep drew her gaze from the fire. He had drawn his legs up like she did herself when she was cold.

She picked up his stick to poke at the coals, but she couldn't keep her eyes from drifting to his face. So peaceful, like a sleeping child. Handsome, too, for a Roman, even with the gash. It was probably going to scar, but he would still be handsome...to a Roman woman, anyway.

Chapter 7

Not Where He Should Be

The fortress walls wrapped Adela in chilled shadow as the eastern sky brightened from gray through violet toward blue. Her short protector was curled up in a ball by the dying embers.

She flexed her shoulders and drew the blanket a little closer. She'd put the last of the wood on the coals as the black of night began to lighten toward the gray of dawn. The corners of her mouth turned down as her gaze drifted to the Roman...again. He'd spent a cold night so she could be warm enough.

He stirred, sat up, and stretched. When his gaze settled on her, that perpetual smile appeared. "Good morning, Adela." He rotated his shoulders. "A good night, too. I'm glad you wanted a turn on watch."

Adela walked around the firepit to give him the blanket.

He shook his head. "Keep it until after we eat." He rose to fetch the sack that held his food. "Cheese and bread again, but we'll get something better after we get Otto." A smile tugged at the corner of his mouth. "He should be ready for some food other than beer when we find him." The smile morphed into a grin. "But after all the beer he drank, maybe his stomach won't be ready for it."

He settled onto one of the stools, and she sat on the one farthest from him. He divided the chunk of cheese in two before handing half of it and one of two rolls to her. Before the first bite, his eyes closed for a very long blink.

They ate in silence, watching the men at the nearby campsites eating their own breakfasts and harnessing their teams. Most were blonde, fair-skinned Germans, but a few had dark hair and browner skin, like her Roman protector.

Galen took a swig from the water skin and rose to pass it to her. "Time for us to get moving, too."

He spread the last glowing embers with his stick and strolled toward his hobbled horses.

Adela spread the blanket over the one he'd slept on, folded them, and rolled them up. As she tied the second short rope around the bundle, Galen returned, leading his big friend's horse while his own followed him like a puppy.

"Otto should be waiting for us in the western camp. We'll get him first, then pick up a few things for you. You'll ride behind me." One corner of his mouth pulled up. "Astrelo should be glad he has a short master. The two of us together won't be too heavy for him."

He turned his back on her to saddle the bay. She tossed his saddle on the black and cinched it.

"You're handy to have along." His voice at her shoulder made her jump. He stepped beside her and tied the bedroll in place. Then he led the horse over to one of the stumps, climbed up on it, and swung his leg over. He held his hand out to invite her to do the same.

He slid forward to make room, and she mounted behind him. He patted his stomach. "Wrap your arm here."

She tensed. That was closer than she wanted to be to him.

He glanced over his shoulder. "Or not, if you don't need to."

Her spine straightened. "You've seen me ride."

The upward twitch of the corner of his mouth accompanied a shrug. "I've seen you fly, too." The twitch turned into a full-blown smile. "But suit yourself."

The slightest nudge started his stallion forward. As they passed the bay, Galen leaned over and scooped up its reins.

"We'll be sharing Astrelo for three days, so figure out what's comfortable for you." He nudged the horse into a trot.

She kept her hands resting on her thighs. No short Roman could teach her anything about how to ride.

It took almost no time to reach the western camp. As they rode among the remaining campers, Adela scanned the area for Galen's handsome friend. No sign of him, but she recognized the gap-toothed old man who'd wanted to buy her. Galen turned his stallion toward his campsite.

The old man grinned up at them as Galen reigned in. "I see you got the pleasure of being with Otto's beauty last night instead of him. When I didn't see you this morning, I thought you'd all left."

Galen rubbed the back of his neck. "Someone tried to take her last night before Otto came, so I found another campsite. I thought I'd find Otto here this morning. Do you know where he is?"

The old man stroked his beard. "I didn't see him come before I slept, and he was gone before I woke. Maybe he went back to see if he could win another one like her."

"Maybe. If you see him, tell him I'm looking for him. We're heading home as soon as I find him, but I hope to see you in the fall. Good trading, Bruno."

"Good trading to you as well, Galen."

Adela felt Galen sigh as they headed toward the gambling tent.

"I'd hoped to find him at the camp so we could start home. If he's still drinking..." Another sigh expanded his chest before he released it.

Another short ride brought them to the canopy. Adela glanced down at her bare feet. It had seemed so much farther when Galen lead her between the gambling den and the campground in the dark...and much less straight. Her brow furrowed. Perhaps the short one hadn't been confused at all last night when he took the longer route.

The tables under the canopy were deserted. Galen rode close to a sign covered with writing, but she couldn't read it.

He looked across his shoulder. "They won't be open for five hours. Otto will probably be back then. There's time for us to get a few things before he comes."

When Galen rode straight to a shop-lined street, the corner of Adela's mouth lifted. The smiling Roman had more warrior in him than she'd thought. Laying a false trail and doubling back...

He handed her the reins of Otto's horse before he swung his leg over his horse's neck and slid off. "Stay here with the horses. I need to get a few things in this shop."

He rested his hand on the side of her foot. She put her foot on his chest and shoved him away.

"It's not what you're thinking. I just want to measure the length of your foot for the shoes."

Her brow furrowed, but she held her foot out to him. He measured it with the span of his hand.

"Shouldn't take me long to get them."

As he took the first step away from her, she moved forward on his saddle and picked up the reins.

He was leaving her with two expensive horses and expecting her to be there when he returned. Her eyebrows rose.

He glanced back at her and that half-smile that revealed his amusement appeared. "We both know you're not fool enough to try to get home without me. I trust you'll be here when I come back."

She squared her shoulders. "Of course."

In less than a quarter hour, he returned with a pair of leather shoes, some bread, and two small sacks. He handed her the sacks and bread. She looked inside as he was putting the first shoe on her left foot. The first held cheese and dried apples. In the second, she found a comb, some hair ties, some underclothes, and other things a woman needed.

He'd moved around to the right side. As he slipped the second shoe on her right foot, she stared at him.

"How did you know what to get?"

That crooked smile appeared. "Even an unmarried man can't have two grown sisters without learning something about women." The smile faded with his shrug. "Slide back and make room for me."

She complied, and he jumped to lay his stomach across the stallion's back. Then he twisted to swing his leg over the neck and settled in.

"We'll eat and wait in the campground until the tavern opens. Maybe Otto will come before then, and if not...at least the horses can enjoy the wait there."

As they headed back to the western campground, Adela relaxed behind him. Unexpected problems didn't seem to affect Galen's good humor at all. Not what she'd expect from the warriors she admired, but certainly easier to be around when something did go wrong.

The laughter of the drinkers reached Galen's ears when he was still half a block from the gaming tables. He reined in under a tree just west of the canopy and scanned the tables from the vantage point of his horse. No Otto.

"Stay with the horses." He slipped off Astrelo. "I'm going to see if anyone knows where Otto went last night."

Galen strolled to the post near the table where Otto had been gambling and leaned against it. From that point, he could watch how the servant girls divided up their service among the tables. It took only a short time to identify which girl worked that corner of the canopy.

He approached her. "Did you serve this part of the canopy last night?"

The girl's eyes narrowed. "I did."

"Good. I'm looking for my friend. He's a big German, red shirt, trimmed beard, blond hair to here." He indicated shoulder length. "He was at that table. He was pretty drunk when I left him about sundown."

Her face relaxed. "The handsome one who kept bragging about how great he is with a sword? The one who claimed he can fight two at once?" She squeezed her lips to suppress a smile.

Galen's mouth tipped up at one corner. "That would be him."

She cast a glance toward Adela, then pointed. "He won that one."

Galen's smile leveled. "Yes. That's him."

"The man he won her from, he told your friend he had a special horse in the southern campground. They went to look at it." The side of her mouth pulled up. "Your friend and two others went with him."

"Did my friend come back?"

"None of them did."

Galen took a *dupondius* from his purse and pressed it into the girl's hand. "My thanks for your help."

Her subdued smile morphed into a grin when she saw the coin. "Any time."

Galen returned to Adela and mounted. "He went to the southern vendor camp with the man who kidnapped you. We'll look there."

His mouth squeezed into a thin line. Otto, probably drunker than when Galen had taken Adela, had gone off with her kidnapper. Tendrils of unease wrapped around him as he kicked Astrelo into a trot and headed south.

When they reached the campground, Galen turned to Adela. "Where did you camp?"

Adela peered over his shoulder, then pointed to the far edge of the camp. "Over there by the bushes." She tensed, and that made him glance back at her. "That cage. It's where they held me yesterday. Gundahar had two other women in it, but he sold them in the morning to a Roman who already had two girls with their hands tied."

"Did he try to buy you?"

"Maybe. They stood over there, and I couldn't make out their words."

Galen drew a deep breath and forced it out through puckered lips. "Maybe someone saw something."

A woman with a baby on her hip stood chatting with an older woman who was stirring a stew pot. Galen reined Astrelo toward them and dismounted when he reached them.

"I'm looking for my friend. A big German. He came to see a horse with the men who were camped near the wagon cage. Did you see him?"

The younger one glanced at the older, a question in her eyes, before focusing on the stew. Her nervous silence answered his question.

"Do you know where they went?"

The older woman scanned Adela on the horse, then Galen, and a frown pulled her mouth down.

"They were gone when I got up this morning." Her gaze fixed on Adela. "You're one of the slaves they had in their cage."

Adela squared her shoulders. "I'm no one's slave. They kidnapped me."

The older woman shook her head. "Then your friend is in deep trouble."

The baby reached for his mother's nose, and she kissed him. "I saw them. Herman woke, and I was feeding him. I saw two men ride out. They had a large blond man draped across the third horse. They headed that way."

She pointed toward the road to Augusta Raurica. A cold hand seized Galen's heart and began to squeeze. He rolled his eyes and stared at the sky. He struck his thigh twice with his fist. Then he strode to a stump by the cold firepit in the next campsite and sat. He rested his elbows on his knees and buried his face in his hands.

Oh, God! Why did you let this happen? I can't go home without Otto. I've got to find him and free him. But how? He took three deep breaths, and his pounding heartrate slowed. *All things are possible with you, Lord. Help me find him...alive.*

◆

Adela stared at Galen. His friend had been kidnapped, and he was sitting like a helpless child, like he had no idea what to do. Not what she expected from a real man. Especially not from a man who could fight like he did.

She startled when he suddenly stood. The man before her had been transformed. His eyes were intense, his lips straight and pressed together. Before her stood a warrior ready for battle.

He took a deep breath, then released it. "Change of plan." He fixed his eyes on hers. "Otto's been kidnapped by the men who took you. He's being taken south to be sold as a gladiator. I intend to get him back, but I've got to go after him right away to have any chance of that. That means I can't take you home right now. Your best hope of getting home is to stay with me until I rescue Otto, so I'm going to take you with me. Then Otto and I will take you home."

"I understand, and I want to go with you."

Of course she wanted to go. She didn't care about his drunken friend, but no warrior would abandon a friend to slavery. Galen confused her with his kindness, but he was still a warrior. Besides, she had no idea how to get home without his help. That alone would have been enough reason to go with him, but she had another.

She wanted to see the kidnappers punished for what they'd done to her. She wanted that so much she could taste it. To have any chance of saving Otto for Galen and making the kidnappers pay for killing Gunda and taking her, they must move fast. Revenge was a meal best eaten hot, and she was hungry for it.

◆

Galen's head tilted as Adela stood before him, fists on her hips, fire in her eyes. A warrior woman.

Even going after the kidnappers, it was safer for her if he took her with him than if he left her in Argentorate alone. It was good she wanted to go. He would have to force it otherwise, and a contest of wills with her would make the hunt even harder.

"First we need to go to legion headquarters and report Otto's kidnapping. Then we'll start tracking them down."

He eyed the two horses. Which would be the easier mount for a woman? "Can you handle a stallion?"

Her lips tightened. "I'm a chieftain's daughter. I can ride anything you can."

He moved to the left side of Otto's bay. "Then come here in front of me."

She marched to his side and grasped both reins and the horse's mane. He gripped her waist and lifted her up so she could swing her right leg across the rump of the tall horse. She settled into the saddle, back straight, chin high as she looked down at him.

Galen mounted Astrelo. "Follow me."

Chapter 8

BEGINNING THE HUNT

Once more the fortress walls loomed before them. Galen dismounted about ten feet from the sentry.

The soldier drew his sword. "State your business."

"I want to speak with Centurion Silanus. Tell him Gaius Crassus has a kidnapping to report."

The sentry summoned another soldier and sent him to fetch Silanus.

"Enter and wait inside." The sentry motioned for them to proceed through the gate.

Galen remounted. His glance at Adela caught her with lowered eyebrows and an upraised chin. No sign of her fear of the Romans on the warrior-woman today.

Together they rode past the arches of the passageway through the stone gate house. Silanus strode toward them, his mouth curved down and his eyes stormy.

"You say there's been a kidnapping, Crassus?"

Galen swung his leg over Astrelo's neck and slid off. "Yes. Two, in fact. My partner Otto was kidnapped last night in the southern traveler's camp and this woman four days ago from the Hermunduri."

Silanus glanced at Adela. His eyes lingered, but not for long. "The Hermunduri live across the frontier, so her kidnapping is outside Roman jurisdiction. The kidnapping of your friend—that's a different matter. Is he a Roman citizen?"

Galen shook his head. "No. His father's a chieftain of the Vangiones."

48

Silanus shrugged. "Too bad. I would send out a patrol to try to catch them if he was. I will send notice of the kidnapping to the forts and garrisons, and the patrols will watch for him. That's all I can do until someone reports where he and his kidnappers are. There are enough German slaves who fight in the arenas that finding your friend could be hard. He looks like too many young Germans, but perhaps his great size will stand out." Silanus shrugged again.

Galen's lips started to tighten, but he stopped them. Otto was right that Roman officers cared less about a German. "There's something else that might help. Otto's an extraordinary swordsman, especially when fighting two at once. Anyone who's watched him fight would remember him."

Silanus frowned as he nodded. "That might help. If he's so good, maybe he would have been safer serving as a Roman auxiliary instead of selling horses and getting drunk with kidnappers."

"Perhaps. A woman in the camp saw them heading south. I'm going to try to catch up with them and free him."

Silanus's eyebrow popped up. "If you find him, it might be wiser to get some soldiers to free him."

Galen's mouth relaxed into a smile. "It's the heart, not the height that matters. And the training. I may not look like it, but I'm good in a fight. I've trained for years with the same swordmaster as Otto."

Silanus rubbed the back of his neck. "No offense intended, Crassus. I just want to make sure my favorite horse trader keeps bringing horses."

"None taken. It can be an advantage when an enemy doesn't take you seriously until it's too late."

"I can't send my men out to hunt for him, but I can write a warrant instructing any local commander to help you capture the kidnappers. To take a man in a legion town—such contempt for Roman law cannot be tolerated. Catching a kidnapper to make an example should make travel safer around here. Our patrols can't be everywhere."

"Thank you, Silanus. That should help. We were about to head home. I need to send a message downriver to an innkeeper in Borbetomagus. He'll get the message about what's happened to my family so they'll know why I'm delayed. Where can I buy papyrus and find a courier?"

"No need for that. I'll provide what you need. Write your letter while I'm preparing the warrant. I'll get it to Borbetomagus for you. A courier leaves for Mogontiacum tomorrow morning."

Silanus slapped Galen's shoulder before he spun and strode into the gatehouse office.

◆

When the Roman with the red crest disappeared through the door in the stone wall, Adela nudged her horse forward. She reined in next to Galen where he could hear soft words. It might be dangerous to speak too loudly with Romans around.

"Is he going to help?"

Galen tipped his head to look up at her, and his brow furrowed. "Can you speak any Latin?"

"No."

His eyes turned thoughtful. "We're going to work on that. You need to be able to understand what's going on around us when people aren't speaking Germanic. We might have to leave Germania before we catch up with the kidnappers and rescue Otto."

Adela shrugged. "My father says a woman doesn't need more than one language, but I wouldn't mind learning. He hired a man to teach my brother Latin, but Father says a girl doesn't need to learn anything except how to run a household and handle a weapon." She glanced at the ground before returning her gaze to his face. "The teacher told me to go away when I tried to listen."

Galen's mouth pulled sideways. "That's not right. A woman needs more than household skills. My sisters speak Latin, Greek, and Germanic, and they read both Greek and Latin." He rubbed his chin. "Latin is more common than Greek on this side of the Empire, so that's what I'll teach you first. We can work on speaking while we ride. I can start teaching you to write and maybe read some at night."

Adela's eyes narrowed. "It took my brother years to learn."

A smiled tugged at the corner of his mouth. "But maybe he's not as smart as you." The smile broadened. "Or maybe he didn't want to learn enough to try hard. You do want to learn, don't you?"

She raised her chin. "Of course." She tightened her lips, but a smile still crept out. "He did try to find excuses to do something else...anything else."

"There's a lot of riding ahead of us, but we won't get bored with this to keep our minds busy."

A warrior emerged from the door Galen's friend had entered. He carried a shallow wooden box to Galen and went back inside.

Galen handed her the box. After he mounted, he raised one leg up to lay his calf across his horse's withers. When he took the box back, he balanced it on his leg and lifted the lid. Inside were thin sheets that looked like flattened bark, a small bottle, and a pointed stick. Galen lifted out one sheet and put the bottle in a well in the top of the box. He removed the plug and dipped the stick into it. Then he began forming different shapes on the sheet.

◆

Galen glanced at Adela when he finished the first two lines.

Her gaze was locked on his hand but shifted to his eyes when he paused. "You do that so fast."

"You will, too, after I teach you." He dipped the pen in the ink again. "I'm sending word to my sister that Otto's been kidnapped and I'm going to get him back." The corner of his mouth twitched up. "She told me to be careful on this trip and to keep Otto out of trouble. I haven't done too well with that so far."

Adela's brow furrowed. "Because of his mistakes, not yours. He shouldn't have gone with them when he was drunk."

"No, but two good things came from him gambling. You're free again, and I have a warrior woman to help me get him back." He bounced his eyebrows at her.

At those words, she raised her chin, but her smile softened the warrior look.

He finished his letter and flipped the papyrus. On the back, he wrote two addresses. The first was to the owner of the inn in Borbetomagus. The second was to Valeria, with a request for the first trustworthy person heading west to deliver it to the innkeeper in their market town where the road south from Mogontiacum met the road west from Borbetomagus.

As he finished, Silanus approached, papyrus in hand. He handed Galen the warrant and took the writing desk. Galen folded the warrant and slipped it into his purse.

"Good fortune on your hunt, Crassus. I hope I see you back with your giant friend come fall."

"I hope you do, too. I'll do my best to make it so."

Silanus raised a hand in farewell and headed toward the headquarters building at the center of the camp.

Galen shifted his gaze from Silanus to Adela. "Let's go. It's two and a half days to Augusta Raurica. There's an arena there, so it's the first place they're likely to sell him. We want to get there before his first fight."

He nudged Astrelo, and they rode toward the stone arches of the gate. His gaze swept the gray walls that stood as a monument to Roman power.

God, the next time I see this fortress, let it be with a string of horses and Otto beside me.

◆

Adela glanced at Galen often as they rode through the town. The grim set to his face looked out of place. When they finally reached the edge of town, he nudged his stallion into a trot.

She rode up beside him. "I can ride as fast and as far as you want."

He nodded, then kicked his horse into a canter. He didn't keep that speed for long; it would tire the horses too fast. He settled into a trot at a pace the horses could sustain for long distances.

She rode beside him but a little back so she could watch his face without him knowing. He looked serious and focused, more like a German warrior than she'd seen before. Odd, but he looked better when that hint of a smile was on his lips.

This short Roman had strange ideas, but she liked some of them. He saw her as more than someone to keep a man's house and bear his children. He was so different from any man she'd met before. It felt good to be treated with respect, like she mattered for herself and not just as her father's daughter.

He'd be no match for the tall, proud German warrior she wanted as her husband someday, but he was proof that an impressive man could come with a short body and lips that mostly smile.

Chapter 9

Reason to Hope

Two days later

Even for a horseman like Otto, riding for two days with his hands tied behind his back had proven exhausting. His ankles were tied together by a rope under the horse's belly while Gerlach led it, leaving no chance for escape. As hard as it was to imagine things getting worse, his heart sank when the amphitheater of Augusta Raurica came into view.

Gundahar dropped back to ride beside him. "Time to make some money from you. Maybe you'll sell for more than the girl you cost me."

He slapped the back of Otto's head before kicking his horse into a trot.

Gundahar rode up to a man lounging against a tree by the public entrance. "Where will I find a trainer who needs a new gladiator?"

"You want the senior *lanista*, Scaurus." The man pointed toward a low stone building across the street. "That's his *ludus*."

Gundahar nodded his thanks and reined his horse toward it. He turned in his saddle to face Gerlach. "Stay mounted. Our fighter looks bigger that way."

He swung his leg over his horse's neck and slid off. He slapped Otto's thigh. "You should bring at least a thousand. Try to look mean when I bring the lanista out."

Otto's glare pulled a chuckle from Gundahar. "Angry is almost as good as mean."

As Gundahar disappeared through the doorway, Otto's heartrate rose. This might be his chance to escape. If he could only convince the lanista that he was really a free man...

The door swung open, and a man of about forty emerged with Gundahar. His gut suggested he had a good cook, but his arms were brawny and bore many scars. Another scar ran from the outer edge of his eyebrow to his chin.

Gundahar pointed at Otto. "As you can see, he's a big one. Handsome, too, and the women like that."

Scaurus crossed his arms as he contemplated Otto. Otto's pulse raced. It was time.

"I'm not a gladiator. I was kidnapped in Argentorate by these men. I'm a freeborn German and—"

Gerlach wrapped an arm around Otto's neck and shoved a rag into his mouth until he started to gag.

Scaurus's eyes narrowed as he focused them on Gundahar. "A freeborn German?" A frown dragged his mouth down.

◆

Gundahar conjured up a confident smile as his hand swept Otto's words away. "He's freeborn, all right, but he wasn't freeborn inside the Empire. Bjorn was captured when his Langobardi clan failed with their raid into northern Hermunduri country. I bought him from a Hermunduri trader in Argentorate. His great size shows where he came from and reveals his lies."

The lanista's brow furrowed. "Do you have a bill of sale?"

"I do." Gundahar reached into his purse and pulled out a folded sheet of papyrus.

Scaurus scanned it. "Where's the mark of the questor that certifies the sale?"

Gundahar took the sheet back and peered first at the front, then the back. "But it should be here. We went to the desk in the market to get it."

The lanista crossed his arms again. "I only buy from men I know or when the questor's seal tells me everything is in order."

Gundahar rubbed the back of his neck. "I understand. I'm usually careful myself." He squeezed his lips together and shook his head. "Five days to Argentorate and back, but I guess there's no choice if I'm going to get the missing seal for you. I should have watched more carefully at the questor's station."

Scaurus's arms dropped to his sides. "Get the seal that verifies the sale, and then I might be interested. This one looks promising." He turned and took a step away before he glanced back over his shoulder. "I know what that questor's seal looks like. Wrong seal, no sale."

As the lanista walked away, Gundahar turned to Gerlach. "I'd hoped to sell him here, but there's an arena a day's ride east. It's near the old legion fortress of the XXI Rapax in Vindonissa."

Gerlach's mouth twitched. "Won't there be the same problem with the bill of sale there?"

Gundahar opened his mouth, but no words came out before his ears caught the braying of a mule. Two shackled men shuffled out the side door of the ludus. One man stood by the cart, watching with his fists on his hips, as the first prisoner crawled in. Another man, who was built like an ox, prodded the second chained men with a staff.

A crooked smile tugged at Gundahar's mouth. "The goddess Fortuna may have just smiled on us. Maybe we won't have to go to Vindonissa after all. Bring Bjorn."

The man in charge glanced at them as they approached.

With a fake-friendly smile, Gundahar stepped close to him. "Are you looking for gladiators? I have a superb Langobardi fighter from the North country." He waved his hand toward Otto. "Bjorn, famous for his skill in battle, fighting two at once with only a sword."

The man's gaze swept Otto from head to foot and back. "He doesn't look like a fighter to me." His eyes narrowed. "If he's so good, why didn't the lanista want him?"

Gundahar shrugged. "He said he didn't want one who might not be willing to stop short of the kill in the arena."

The slave trader tilted his head as a crooked smile appeared. "I don't want one of those, either, but I do need another one as arena fodder for the three-on-three fights in Octodurus. He looks good enough for the procession, even if he doesn't last long in the fight." He stroked his beard. "I'll give you 100 denarii for him."

Gundahar's lips started to tighten. He'd expected at least five, maybe eight times that for the Hermunduri beauty.

"That's not enough for a fighter like Bjorn."

"It's too much, but I'm being generous because he's so big and handsome. Group fighters are cheap. Even the best *gregarii* only bring 250 denarii to the owner of a ludus when they're killed."

A crooked smile curved the trader's lips. "If there's any problem with the bill of sale...I can take care of that."

Gundahar drew a deep breath. Something was better than nothing. "One hundred...I'll accept that."

The slave trader signaled his ox-like servant, who reached into the cart and pulled out one set of iron wrist shackles and another of ankle shackles. "Get the big one ready to load. It's four days to Octodurus, and I want to get there in time for the games this week."

◆

Otto tensed as Gerlach slipped from his horse. Gundahar and the man with the shackles approached. They'd have to untie him to get him off the horse. Finally, a chance for freedom. If he could break loose and run to the local garrison...Three against one was bad odds, but they were better than no odds at all.

A sack slipped over his head from behind, and a rope jerked tight around his neck.

His third captor's voice growled near his ear. "Don't try anything, Bjorn, unless you want your neck broken." The rope tightened, and Otto fought for each breath.

The rope binding his ankles loosened, and he was dragged from the horse. Iron bands clamped around his ankles and locked. His hands were untied and shackled in front of him. Hands on his shoulders shoved him forward and into the cart before the rope around his neck went slack and the hood was yanked off.

Gundahar pulled the rag from Otto's mouth, and a sneering grin accompanied Gundahar's slap on his shoulder. "Give them a good show in Octodurus, Bjorn. They've probably never seen someone disarm two men with less than ten strokes."

A snap of the reins started the mules forward. The cart jerked, and Otto jostled against the other chained man on his side of the cart. His fellow prisoner shouldered him away.

As the cart pulled away from the amphitheater, Otto closed his eyes and took several deep breaths. Ropes replaced by iron chains. A horse replaced by a cart. Things kept going from bad to worse.

But Galen was alive, and his friend would be hunting for him. Until a sword took him down in the arena, there was still reason to hope.

Day 2 of the Hunt

At the end of the second full day of riding, Adela was ready for a few hours of not sitting on Otto's horse. He was a spirited animal, but she enjoyed that. He seemed tireless as Galen alternated between walking and trotting. But he was a giant beast, and his back was broader than any of the horses she usually rode. That kept her legs at a different angle than she was used to. Her muscles were ready for a rest.

They had just waded a shallow stream when Galen turned his stallion off the road.

He glanced back at her. "I'm not sure how far it is to the next town. I've been down this way once with Otto's father, but it's been a few years. We'll camp a short distance up this stream."

An approving smile tugged at the corner of her mouth. Galen was cautious. Camping off the road where thieves wouldn't stumble across them was wise. The smile broadened. Just like he'd taken the crooked routes to the campgrounds in Argentorate. The kidnapper had found their first campsite, but he probably had the careless talk of Galen's drunken friend to guide him.

In a grassy clearing by the stream, Galen dismounted. "This should do for the horses. Plenty of wood for our fire, too."

After unsaddling, they gathered twigs and small branches. Galen took a hand ax from the roll at the back of his saddle and chopped some larger pieces of wood from the limbs of a fallen tree. Then he cleared an area for the firepit. He finished by rinsing off his hands in the stream.

His hand swept toward the downed tree. "Sit, and we'll dine. What shall we have tonight?" He rubbed his bristled cheek. "Would you like cheese, dried apples, and bread? Or maybe dried apples, bread, and cheese?"

His playful eyes made her smile. "I'd prefer bread, cheese, and dried apples."

He tightened his lips, but a grin still leaked out. "That does sound better. When we get to Augusta Raurica, I'll get something different for us. I'll eat anything, but I do like some variety."

When they finished eating, Galen knelt next to her. Her spine straightened as her eyes locked on his face. His own eyes seemed focused near her feet.

He took a stick and loosened the dirt. Then he smoothed it before turning the stick to point the smaller end toward the ground.

"Time for your first writing lesson. Father always said it was speaking Latin well that made my sister Val a well-educated lady, but I think writing is more important. We'll work on both."

He settled in next to her on the log. "Letters come first. I'll draw one in the dirt, then you'll copy it to learn the shape." He rubbed his mouth. "There are twenty-three of them. Well, actually forty-six when you consider there's the cursive form you saw in the letter to Val plus the capitals that are used on the inscriptions." He rubbed his mouth again. "It's more likely you'll be reading inscriptions like road markers, so we'll start with that."

Adela's eyes widened. Forty-six?

That slight smile of his grew deeper. "Don't let the number scare you. They're not that hard, and once you learn them and their sounds, they just go together to make the sounds of the words." He rested his hand on hers and gave it a pat. "Let's start, and you'll see."

She took a deep breath and turned her gaze from his face to the dirt patch at their feet.

"The first letter is A." He drew two lines that met at the top, spread apart at the base, and had a short line connecting them in the middle.

"You try now." He handed her the stick.

She drew an exact copy of his.

"Very nice. Four more, and I'll have a surprise for you." He drew a straight line then connected the top and bottom with a half circle next to his A.

She copied it beside her own A.

Then he drew a top-to-bottom line next to the half circle and added three short lines at the top, middle, and bottom of the long one. She did the same. Next, he drew a top-to-bottom line with a short line at the bottom, followed by another A.

When she finished copying those, he grinned at her.

"Do you know what you've done?"

She shook her head.

"You've written your name. A-D-E-L-A. Adela."

A smile broke free that grew into a huge grin as she stared at the marks in the dirt. "I have? But that wasn't hard."

His grin was as big as her own. "No, it isn't. That was only four letters, but you can see it will take no time to learn twenty-three."

She traced the letters of her name before turning her gaze back on his smiling eyes. "How do I write your name?"

"You'd need twenty letters to write my full name with eight of them being different. Let's start with just Galen. You only need two more for that. G-A-L-E-N." He drew them as he spoke them.

Adela drew his name beneath her own. It had a nice shape.

He stood and arched his back. "That's enough for tonight. Time for some sleep. Pick your side of the fire, and I'll take the other."

As he hobbled the horses for the night, she rolled out the bedroll that had been Otto's. It was very long. She'd only seen Otto seated, so his great height wasn't that obvious. But maybe being so tall was why he was so stupid about putting himself in harm's way. Her gaze settled on Galen as he rubbed his stallion's blaze. Too short to ever think his size would protect him. Too smart to think it would, even if he were tall.

◆

Galen settled onto the fallen tree. He rested his elbows on his knees and his forehead against his clasped hands.

Thank you, God, for safe travel today. Let tomorrow be the same, and let us find Otto in Augusta Raurica. Keep him safe until we catch up and rescue him. I thank you that Otto gambled and won Adela from the kidnapper, even if he did stay too long after that and got kidnapped himself. I thank you that she came with me so willingly. This would be so much worse if I were chasing Otto alone. Thank you for...

As always, the day's tension drained away as he prayed, and he felt God's peace when he finally opened his eyes.

He banked the fire before he lay down and pulled the blankets up around his neck.

"Good night, Adela. Rest in peace."

◆

Adela watched his eyes close. His breathing slowed and deepened. A smile curved her lips as her own eyes closed. Resting in peace wasn't hard when Galen was resting nearby.

Chapter 10

A New Direction

Augusta Raurica, Day 3

Anticipation surged as Galen rode into Augusta Raurica early the next morning. He twisted in his saddle to face Adela. "If Gunda-har tried to sell Otto here, he'd head for the amphitheater first. The gladiator schools are usually close to the arena."

Adela's head tipped. "Schools? What do they teach?"

"Different ways to fight, and how to give a good show without killing your opponent too quickly. The *secutor* uses a sword and shield, the *retiarius* uses a net and a trident. Sometimes it's two swordsmen fighting, sometimes a swordsman and a net man. The fighters are mostly slaves who belong to the ludus that trains them."

"Your friend is already a master swordsman, isn't he?"

"Yes, but he's never had to fight where he only has the choice of kill or die."

"Isn't that always what a warrior faces?"

Galen ran his hand through his hair. "Probably, but Otto and I aren't warriors. Knowing how to use a sword well when we're sparring isn't the same as having to bury it in a man's heart to stay alive. If Otto hesitates, he'll die."

"Would you hesitate?"

Would he? Only God knew.

Galen's brow furrowed. "A man can't be sure until he faces that choice. And what comes after his choice stays with him until he dies. God says not to murder. That's different from killing to save a life, especially someone else's. But I still don't want to...ever." His mouth pulled sideways into a slight smile. "I'm hoping we'll get Otto freed before he has to face that choice."

Adela's eyebrow lifted. "So that's why you didn't kill in the campground?"

"Yes. There's the amphitheater. The *ludi* shouldn't be far." His smile broadened. "If I have your kidnapper pegged right, he'll sell Otto as soon as possible to avoid getting caught with him. I'm hoping the trainer who bought him will be willing to turn a quick profit by selling him to me. He shouldn't have discovered yet how spectacular Otto can be when he's sparring, but even if he has, Otto should cost less than eight good horses. He shouldn't even cost as much as two. I'll have enough to buy him."

A faded sign hung above the door of a building across the street from the amphitheater: Ludus Scauri.

Galen slipped off Astrelo. "This looks like a good place to start." He ran his fingers through his hair. "If God's hand is upon us today, I'll be coming back with Otto. Or at least with some information about where we can find him."

He handed his reins to Adela and strode through the door.

Galen followed the sound of wood striking wood to a low wall overlooking a small arena. Several gladiators were striking man-high stakes with wooden swords, and some were sparring with each other.

He leaned over the edge and called out. "Is lanista Scaurus here? I'd like to speak with him."

The man overseeing the sparring turned and looked up. "I'm Scaurus."

"I'm looking for a tall German that some men are trying to sell as a gladiator. Have you seen him?"

With a flick of his fingers, Scaurus summoned his assistant to watch the sparring men. "I'll be right up."

Galen's pulse pounded as he waited for Scaurus to appear at the head of the stairs leading down to the arena.

The lanista strode to where Galen stood and crossed his arms. "Tell me about the man you're seeking."

"He's Otto of the Vangiones tribe. He's more than a foot taller than me. Blond, trimmed beard and hair to here." His fingers brushed his shoulders. "We were selling horses in Argentorate three days ago. He got himself kidnapped, and I'm trying to track him down."

Scaurus's mouth pulled sideways. "Some men tried to sell me such a man yesterday. They claimed he was a Langobardi called Bjorn, but the bill of sale had no questor's seal. I didn't buy him, and I don't think the owners of the other ludi in this town would, either."

Galen sucked air between his teeth as his hope for an end to the chase withered. "Do you have any idea where they went from here?"

"After I turned down his offer, I heard the leader mention Vindonissa to his friend. That's a day's ride east toward Brigantium. There's an arena there that was used regularly when it was headquarters for the XXI Rapax. Since the legion left, I don't think it's used very often. There are games in Brigantium sometimes. That's two days farther east. It's the headquarters of the provincial fleet on Lacus Brigantinus. The prefect of the fleet likes the games, and there's a large garrison, too."

"So, you think they went that way?"

The lanista tightened his lips as he shrugged. "It's where I'd look if it was my friend."

Galen heaved a sigh. "Thank you, Scaurus. I guess that's where we go next."

Scaurus slapped Galen's shoulder. "Your friend is lucky to have you searching for him. May the goddess Fortuna give you success in your hunt...before your friend gets his first taste of the games on the arena sand." He headed back down the stairs to the training arena.

Galen's shoulders drooped as he returned to Adela and the horses. Time to tell her they'd be riding east instead of north to take her home.

Her mouth curved down. "You didn't find him."

"No, but I know which way they took him." She handed him Astrelo's reins, and he mounted. "Vindonissa or on to Brigantium. They're a day ahead of us on horseback, so we should catch up in time to keep Otto from fighting."

He pushed back the lock of hair that had fallen onto his forehead. "I'm sorry I can't take you home yet."

Her hand flicked his apology away. "That's not your fault. We need to get him back, and I want to see them punished. I'll gladly ride as far as it takes for that."

The fire in her eyes proclaimed the truth of her words.

"Then we stay on the hunt." He reined his horse toward the town market. "Time to stock up on supplies. We may have three days ahead of us before we find him." His elbow brushed the lump that was the purse holding Otto's horse money. That would be replaced by another money belt before it tempted a thief. "Good thing you can ride horses with the best, and good thing we have two of the best horses." He squared his shoulders. "We'll find him. Otto will be riding his bay after we get him back. I'll get you a horse that's more your size for the ride home."

Adela's face was grim, and he smiled to lighten her mood, even though he didn't feel like it. "Don't assume the worst, Adela. God will help us find him. As long as we're still hunting, there's hope."

South of Augusta Raurica, Day 4

The bed of the mule cart sat on the axle so every rock and rut jostled Otto into the sidewall. Being on Gundahar's horse again would be almost luxurious, even with his hands tied behind his back. The prospect of four or five more days in the cart, shackled hand and foot, gnawed at him. Ropes he might loosen enough to escape. Iron bands connected by chains: there was no hope of freedom without the key.

He eyed the man who'd bought him, who rode some distance ahead of the cart. The key hung on a chain around his neck. But how to get it from him when he kept his distance?

It didn't help that Otto shared the misery with two other men. One was older, maybe as old as his father. The other looked close to his own age. While the older man's glowering eyes warned him to keep his distance, the younger mostly stared at the floor of the cart.

Otto leaned in to catch the younger man's attention. "What's your name?"

The slender youth raised his head. Eyes shadowed with despair stared at him. "Baldwin."

"How did you get here?"

"My clan and another of my tribe fought." He raised his head, and pride washed the despair from his eyes. "I made my first kill in battle." His eyes dulled. "But I was hit from behind, and when I awoke, I was in these chains. They should have killed me, not sold me." He shook his wrists, making the chains rattle. His head tipped toward the older man. "Lothar and I deserve an honorable death as warriors, not slaves."

The rider reined in and let the cart pull up beside him. He leaned in and slapped Otto on the side of his head. Otto's eyes threw daggers, and that drew a twisted grin from the rider.

"Stop talking. You don't want to know too much about the men you'll fight to kill."

Baldwin squared his shoulders. "Killing and dying don't bother me. I'm a warrior of the Bear Clan of the Suebi, and I welcome battle."

Otto said nothing. He was no warrior. Battle meant either killing or dying, and he didn't want to do either.

Chapter 11

Catching Up

Vindonissa, Day 4

The sun was low in the sky when Galen and Adela rode into Vindonissa. He'd balanced trotting and walking to cover the distance without overtiring the horses. The gray walls of the old legion fortress rose in the over-grown training field to their left as they approached the amphitheater. Shrubs grew in the arched entryways that once welcomed soldiers wanting to relax watching bloodshed from a distance instead of shedding blood with a sword in their own hands.

But hope deferred was not hope defeated. One day until they found Otto would have been good, but three days was not too long.

Galen shrugged. "It looks like Scaurus was right that the games ended here when the legion moved out."

He swung Astrelo back toward the street of shops they'd passed. "But at least we can get a hot meal before we head for Brigantium. A *taberna* should still be open. Then we'll spend the night here."

The tantalizing aroma of a savory stew hovered around the second shop on the left. Galen turned aside. Several tables inside were surrounded by patrons, but two stools stood vacant at the counter fronting the street.

He slipped off Astrelo. "Hand me your reins." Adela slid off Otto's bay and gave them to him. He tied them to a loop at the front of Astrelo's saddle. Astrelo was as good as any hitching rail once his reins were dropped.

He sat and patted the second stool. As Adela seated herself, the proprietor sauntered over. "*Salve.* What can I get you?"

Galen leaned on the counter. Time to gather information. "Two bowls of that stew that smells so good and some bread. And maybe some advice. We're looking for someone who would have come through here yesterday."

The proprietor's mouth pulled up at the corner. "My stew is famous for many miles. Many stop to taste it."

Galen closed his eyes and inhaled. "Just the smell of it tells me why that would be. Even someone passing in a hurry would be tempted to stop. And these might have been in a hurry."

"What do they look like?"

"Three, maybe four men. One about this tall." He reached up to show where Otto's head would have been. "The others are..." He raised his eyebrows at Adela with the question.

She held out her hand at Gundahar's height. "Their leader is this tall. Dirty. Stinky breath. Scraggly beard. Cheating eyes."

The proprietor's eyebrows rose. "Cheating eyes?"

Adela squared her shoulders. "Yes." Her mouth turned down.

Galen placed his hand on her arm to quiet her. "Deceiving eyes might be a better description. The tall one is my friend, and the scraggly one kidnapped him in Argentorate. We're trying to catch up and get him back."

The proprietor's mouth turned down. "I haven't seen the giant, but the scraggly one...maybe. But there were only two, not four."

Galen rubbed his chin. "That might still be them if they were keeping my friend out of sight."

"The scraggly one asked when the arena closed, so maybe. They ate, then rode out toward Brigantium."

Galen didn't even try to stop the smile those words spawned. They'd found Otto, and they were still only a day behind. "So will we tomorrow. Now it's time for some of the best stew for miles."

The proprietor's frown flipped into a smile before he left to fetch their food.

Galen grinned at Adela. "Tonight, a good dinner and a peaceful night's sleep. There will still be a garrison stationed in the fortress, so there should be a safe campground there."

A boy placed two steaming bowls in front of them. Galen dipped his spoon in and raised it in a salute. "Two more days, and we rescue Otto in Brigantium."

Day 6

A few miles west of Brigantium, the road dropped out of the hills to the shore of Lacus Brigantinus. Fifty feet from the shore, a bireme cut through the water. The perfectly synchronized oars dipped and rose as they propelled the ship forward. Water drops fell from the oar tips, sparkling in the sun.

Galen glanced over his shoulder at Adela's gasp.

Her face lit up like a child opening a present. "I've never seen such a thing! It's so beautiful!"

The corner of his mouth lifted. "I've never seen one before myself. As to beautiful...I'd say so, but that's a Roman warship. Not everyone on the lake wants to see one of those."

Adela turned a dazzling smile on him. "At least the Romans should like it. You said Roman warriors weren't dangerous for Romans."

Galen rubbed his lower lip. "They aren't, as long as Rome doesn't decide you're breaking Roman law. If it does..." He shrugged. For as long as he could remember, his faith made him guilty of a capital crime in the eyes of Rome.

Brigantium

Astrelo danced as they entered Brigantium, as if he sensed Galen's excitement. Somewhere in that town, Otto was waiting to be rescued. Galen guided his stallion past the harbor, where merchant and navy ships shared the piers. A stone building sat just above the lakeshore and at the end of the market street. The sentry standing by the door in battle dress marked it as the garrison. The inscription marked it as the headquarters of the fleet.

Another stone structure housed the bath. Scraping away three days of grime, a slow soak in hot water, a good swim in the cold pool—it would be the perfect interlude before starting home.

But first, he needed to find Otto, and the best place to start was a taberna.

Galen and Adela rode down the market street with Galen scanning the storefronts. When he passed one filled with the sound of men laughing, he reined in.

"This one's lively, just the place where a man might find someone drunk and eager to gamble. And we know Gundahar likes a drunken opponent at tabula." His mouth curved as his gaze settled on Adela. "It's a good thing Otto plays it better, even when he's full of beer."

Adela didn't return his smile. "He won me playing dice. No skill needed there. It's all chance if the dice are honest."

"It might not have been Otto's skill that won you, but it wasn't chance." *Not chance at all. God wanted us to rescue you.* "And it won't be chance that frees Otto, either."

They dismounted, and Galen tied Otto's bay to Astrelo's saddle. His brow furrowed as he glanced at Adela. Even wearing his clothes with her flaxen hair drawn back in a long braid, she was much too pretty to pass unnoticed in a room full of men. And what drunken men looked at, they often wanted to touch.

"Stay close behind me, and don't be too quick to draw your dagger."

She rolled her eyes. "I know how to handle drunken warriors without stabbing them."

Galen fought the grin as he touched the scabbed-over cut on his cheek. "I'll have to take your word for that."

Adela's cheeks flamed, and she turned her gaze away. "You weren't drunk."

"And I don't intend to be." He rubbed his hands together. "I have a good feeling about this place. Let's see what we can learn."

Adela almost pressed against his back as Galen wove his way between two groups of men talking in the entryway. The proprietor was topping off an old man's beer when Galen moved into place beside them.

The tavern keeper turned an oily smile on Galen. "What can I give you?"

"The answer to a question. Where would someone sell a gladiator?"

"I'd say Mediolanum. Take the road south over the Alpes." The old man's words were slurred.

The proprietor rolled his eyes. "That's not his question, Herman. He means where here in Brigantium." His gaze swept Galen. "There's no ludus here, but the prefect of the fleet might buy. He sponsors games sometimes." The corner of his mouth lifted. "But he usually puts on a show with big men. Haven't seen him use runts yet." His eyes shifted to Adela and lit with appreciation. "Or pretty girls."

Galen offered a relaxed smile. "Not a problem. I'm not selling runts or girls."

Before Galen could say another word, Adela poked him in the back. He reached behind his back to pat her arm. That provoked three more hard jabs into his ribs. He glanced over his shoulder to find her pointing at a table tucked into an alcove at the rear of the shop.

A serving girl set two bowls of stew down in front of the gambler who lost Adela and the man who tried to knife him.

Galen turned back to the proprietor. "Thank you."

He took Adela's hand and led her out of the shop.

◆

Once outside, Adela set her feet and tugged on Galen's hand to pull him back inside. "Why are we leaving? That was Gundahar and Gerlach."

"I know. Time to get the soldiers to arrest them. Otto and the third kidnapper weren't there. The garrison commander will get to the truth about where they're holding Otto."

Her eyes narrowed. He was right. Three men had taken her, and none should escape paying for that.

They mounted and rode to the garrison. Galen slid off his horse and approached the sentry. Words were exchanged in Latin before the sentry nodded and stepped aside for him to enter.

When Galen reappeared, a warrior with a red crest like Galen's friend in Argentorate and eight other warriors came with him.

Galen glanced at her as he passed. "Stay here with the horses."

She twisted in the saddle to keep the band of men in view. What started as a tug at the corner of her mouth blossomed into an angry grin. Her hunger for vengeance was about to be satisfied.

Chapter 12

Roman Justice

The hum in the room silenced when the soldiers entered. Galen walked at their head beside the centurion. The kidnappers were lingering at the table over their beers. Galen pointed, then stepped back to let Roman power take over.

The centurion strode to the table with his hand gripping his gladius. "I have a warrant from Centurion Silanus of the VIII Augusta for your arrest. The charge is kidnapping. You will come with me."

Gerlach's eyes bulged as his face turned fish-belly white.

Gundahar set his tankard down. "There must be some mistake. We haven't been in Argentorate. We're only travelling through Brigantium from Augusta Raurica on our way to Augusta Vindelicum. I got word my cousin broke his leg, and we're going there to help his wife and four children with their farm."

The centurion's gaze flipped from Gundahar to Gerlach and back. His standard centurion's frown deepened. "You will come with me to the garrison, and we will sort out the truth of this."

Gundahar rose and placed a coin on the table to pay for the beer. "Of course." Gerlach rose as well, but his color was still closer to a dead man than a live one.

The centurion stepped back to let them pass. His men surrounded them front, sides, and back as they left the taberna. As he passed Galen, his eyebrow arched. "Kidnappers, you say." His mouth turned down again. "We shall see."

Galen followed him through the door. His gut twisted. What would happen to Otto if he couldn't convince the centurion and get him to force a confession of where his friend was?

He began to pray.

When they reached the garrison gateway, the centurion fixed his gaze on Adela. "You. Come with us." His gaze shifted to the men ahead of him. "Rufus. Stable their horses." The last legionary peeled off and waited to take their reins.

Galen summoned her with a flick of his fingers. Adela slid off Otto's bay and moved close to him. He smiled to reassure her, but the look she'd worn when they first approached the fortress in Argentorate had returned. He wrapped his hand around hers and squeezed. She took a deep breath, and her face relaxed.

Galen forced a broader smile he didn't feel. *God, help us find Otto and bring justice out of this.* His lips straightened. *Don't let evil win.*

The centurion turned left when they entered the inner courtyard and strode past the kidnappers. He stopped in a doorway and turned.

"You and you." He pointed at Galen and Adela. "Come inside." His gaze flipped between Gerlach and Gundahar. "And you." His finger pointed at Gerlach. As he turned, he glanced over his shoulder. "Hold the other one here until I send for him."

The room smelled like damp stone and was dimly lit through a small rectangular opening near the ceiling. One of the legionaries moved around the room to light four lamps. They cast a warm yellow light, but they did nothing to cut the chill permeating the room.

Adela wrapped her arms around herself as her nervous eyes flipped between centurion and kidnapper.

The centurion spread his feet and placed his fists on his hips. "You, Gerlach, are charged with kidnapping. This man..." His hand swept toward Galen. "He claims you got his friend drunk in Argentorate and kidnapped him to sell as a gladiator. He claims you also kidnapped this woman across the frontier, and his friend won her gambling with your travelling partner. He claims you tried to kill him to get her back, but he knocked you out and moved to a different campsite. When his friend didn't show up the next morning, he looked for him and was told that you had left in the night with his friend draped across a horse. He and the woman have been trying to catch up and free his friend for the last six days."

The centurion crossed his arms. "What do you say against these charges?"

Gerlach swallowed hard. "That's not what happened. I had nothing to do with any kidnapping of anyone. I came back from an errand to find Gundahar had won a gladiator slave in Augusta Raurica. But we're not slave traders, so we sold him before heading east."

The centurion turned his eyes on Galen and raised one eyebrow.

Galen straightened. "The errand he was on was trying to kill me in the western vendor camp in Argentorate and kidnap Adela a second time. You can still see the bruise on his temple where I hit him with the pommel of my sword and knocked him out."

Gerlach's head shook violently. "That's not what happened. The bruise is from my horse kicking me." He wrinkled his nose. "Look at him. Do you really think a runt like him could knock me out in a fight?"

Galen's eyes narrowed. "Adela can tell how you and Gundahar kidnapped her in Hermunduri country north of the frontier and brought her to Argentorate to sell. Your plans changed to kidnapping Otto after he won her and I took his winnings back to our camp. You attacked me with a dagger to get her back."

Gerlach shook his head again. "That's not true. If someone attacked you, it wasn't me. Maybe it was someone who looked like me, but it wasn't me." His eyes focused back on the centurion. "There's no reason to take his word over mine."

The centurion rubbed his mouth as his eyes flipped between Gerlach and Galen.

"Sit back there in the corner, and don't make a sound while I ask your friend a few questions."

Color came back to Gerlach's face, and a hint of a smile lifted the corners of his mouth. "Of course. Not a sound."

The centurion flicked his fingers, and the legionary who'd been standing by the door left. He returned with Gundahar and a second soldier.

Again, the centurion stood with feet spread and fists on his hips. "You, Gundahar, are charged with kidnapping," His head tipped toward Galen, and his mouth turned down. "This man claims you got his friend drunk in Argentorate and kidnapped him to sell as a gladiator. He claims you also kidnapped this woman across the frontier, and you lost her gambling with his friend. When his friend didn't show up the next morning, he looked for him and was told that you had left in the night with his friend draped across a horse. He and the woman have been trying to catch up and free his friend for the last six days."

The centurion lifted his chin as he crossed his arms. "What do you say against these charges?"

Gundahar glared at Galen. "The short Roman is confused, and the girl is lying. I never kidnapped anyone. There's no proof I've ever seen either of them before. No proof I was even in Argentorate when he claims."

Adela couldn't understand a single word of the Latin, but she could read what the warrior's body said. Galen hadn't convinced him these were the men who'd taken Otto. The warrior was going to let them go. Galen would never find and free his friend, and the evil ones would never pay for killing Gunda and taking her.

Then Gundahar rubbed his neck. When the neckline of his shirt pulled sideways, she saw the thin, braided string of red, blue, and green threads. Her mother had made that to hold the amber amulet Father had given her at their wedding. Adela had worn the smooth, yellow treasure since her mother died, but it vanished with the rest of her clothing after she was dragged from the horse.

She stepped forward and tugged on Galen's sleeve. He glanced over his shoulder with a question in his eyes.

"He's wearing my mother's amulet."

"Are you sure?"

She nodded.

"What does it look like?"

"It's amber, and it's like three waterdrops joined at the top. It's hanging on a blue, red, and green braided string."

Galen's mouth, which had been straight, curved into a slight smile

"The proof that he's lying is hanging around his neck. He took an amulet from Adela. It's amber, shaped like three waterdrops joined at the top, and hangs on a three-color braided string."

Gundahar's eyes saucered. Then he made a break for the door, but a legionary blocked his way. Another grabbed his arms and jerked them behind him, When the first pressed his gladius against Gundahar's side, he stopped struggling.

The centurion reached inside his shirt and pulled out the amulet. He lifted the string over Gundahar's head and closed his fist around the amber pendant.

Gerlach shot to his feet. "I had no idea he kidnapped anyone! I had nothing to do with any of that. I didn't even help him sell the big German in Augusta Raurica. The buyer had two more gladiators in his cart. He said he was heading to Octodurus for the games next week."

The centurion's mouth twitched as he looked down his nose at Gerlach. "Which ludus was he supplying?"

"I don't know! But I never knew Bjorn was kidnapped. I thought Gundahar won him, like he said. If I wasn't innocent, would I have told you about the buyer?" The pitch of Gerlach's voice spiraled upward. "Find Bjorn, and he can tell you I'm innocent. You have to believe me!"

The centurion handed the amulet to Adela before turning frowning eyes back on Gerlach. "I'm convinced you both kidnapped the German called Otto in Argentorate and this woman across the frontier. I'm convinced you tried to kill this man while trying to steal the woman from his friend, who is her legal owner after he won her from you. Kidnapping and attempted murder during a robbery both carry a death sentence in the province of Raetia, and it will be carried out tomorrow morning."

Gerlach would have collapsed if two legionaries hadn't seized his arms. Vile curses rolled from Gundahar's tongue as his gaze raked Galen. Then his eyes spit fire as he turned on Adela.

"You think you won, chieftain's daughter, but you lost everything the day I took you. You might think you can go home, but your father won't want you. You're worthless now. I took you in more ways than you know, and you have less value to a chieftain now as a daughter than you do as a slave."

He spat at her feet as the soldiers dragged him away.

◆

A war cry burst from Adela's throat as she drew her dagger and lunged toward Gundahar. Before she could drive the blade into his back, Galen's arms pinned her like iron bands. She arched her back and writhed against him until the warriors dragged Gundahar and Gerlach through an iron door and the door closed behind them.

Galen released her and took the dagger from her hand.

She spun to glare at him. "Why did you stop me? Among my people, it's my right to kill that man for what he did to me."

He slipped her dagger back into its sheath and placed his hands on her upper arms. "Maybe so, but I won't let you. Roman justice will take care of him."

She tossed her head. "Then I want to watch him die."

A sad smile curved his mouth as he shook his head. "I'm not going to let you do that, either. They're not Roman citizens, so it will be a cross, not a sword, for both of them. That's not a quick, clean kill. It's a slow death by torture. It can take days. I won't let you watch that. What you saw would haunt you for the rest of your life."

"But it's my right..." Her voice faltered. The daughter of a Hermunduri chieftain was supposed to be a warrior's woman, eager to kill her enemies, unmoved by emotion, never showing weakness. But the concern in the depths of those honest brown eyes punched huge holes in her hard shell.

That breached the dam that held back her tears, and the flood broke loose.

Galen drew her into his arms. She slipped her arms around his chest and rested her cheek on his shoulder. She managed to stop the sound of the sobs ripping through her, but she couldn't stop the jerks and shaking.

His arms tightened around her, and he rocked them until her tears subsided. Then he stepped back and placed his palms on her cheeks. He swept away the teardrops with his thumbs.

"Forget what he said. It's not true. Nothing he could have done would make you any less a treasured daughter than you were before he took you. A father's love won't change because of what's happened. As soon as we rescue Otto, I'll take you home to him. You'll see how glad he'll be to get you back."

"You don't know the Hermunduri. We're not like you Romans." Another tear dribbled down her cheek.

"I'm a Roman citizen, but I'm more German than Roman. The Hermunduri can't be that different from the Vangiones I live with. Otto comes from a chieftain family. No man could do anything that would make his father cast off his daughters. A man would have to be crazy not to be proud to have a daughter like you, and any son of his friends would be a fool not to think himself fortunate to have you as his wife."

With his fingertips, he swept the final trace of tears away. He took the amulet from her hand and hung it around her neck. "Now, it's time for us to head back to Augusta Raurica and take the other road south. Otto is counting on me...on us. We won't let him down."

Chapter 13

BACKTRACKING

Galen had been looking forward to a long soak at the baths that afternoon, followed by a good dinner with Otto at his side, but that was not to be. At least not yet.

When the soldier brought their horses from the garrison stable, Galen moved behind Adela. With his hands on her waist, he gave her the lift that made it easy to swing her leg over the tall bay's rump. Then he mounted Astrelo.

Adela's eyes were puffy from the attack of tears, but her back was straight and her head held high. It was a relief to see the warrior woman back.

Her cool gaze fixed on him. "Now what?"

He rubbed his chin. He needed to get her out of Brigantium before morning. The execution field would be at the side of a major road. The main one would most likely be on the road south to Mediolanum, but they'd passed a field just west of town with tall, heavy posts that could be used for executions. Two condemned men, one for each road...double the impact for discouraging a repeat of their crime by another.

"The horses had a rest and some food in the stable here, so we can ride a few miles west to get a good start on our return to Augusta Raurica. We're seven days behind Otto now. Gerlach said the games were next week, so we should get there in time as long as we keep moving. We'll buy a few days' worth of food, then head out."

"Let's go."

He reined Astrelo toward the garrison gate. Adela fell in beside him. An hour or so up the road, then he'd make camp. That would leave time for a Latin lesson. Octodurus was south of Germania Superior in the province of Alpes Poeninae. The locals would speak Gallic, not Germanic. Good thing she wanted to learn the Imperial tongue. If Otto wasn't in the ludus there, she might need it before they were through.

He glanced at the lovely profile of the strong woman beside him. It was good to have her as company on the hunt. She'd be good company, no matter what they were doing. She shouldn't worry about what would happen when he took her home. Any man who didn't follow Jesus would be a fool if he didn't want her as his wife.

Galen had taken them ten miles down the road back to Augusta Raurica before he turned aside at a small stream and led Adela up it.

"We're in luck." He pointed at a beaver dam. The pond behind it was surrounded by a meadow with scattered splashes of yellow and blue from wildflowers. "Grass for the horses, and enough water for a swim. That's almost as good as going to the baths. Not as warm as the *caldarium*, but it should be warm enough."

He swung his leg over Astrelo's neck and slid off. "Time for a break, boy...for you and me." He released the cinch and lifted the saddle from Astrelo's back. The stallion swished his luxuriant tail and ambled away to graze.

Galen arched his back and found himself looking up at Adela's uneasy face. He rested his hand on her horse's neck. "Do you know how to swim?"

"Some..." She bit her lip. "But I don't think I will."

"I'll stay away while you do, if that's the problem."

"It's not." The hint of pink on her cheeks told him the opposite.

She cleared her throat. "I think I'll set some snares to catch a rabbit or something while you swim. That was why you bought the twine, wasn't it?"

"It was." He grinned at her. "You catch it, and I'll skin it and cook it. As much as I like cheese and dried fruit, roast rabbit sounds better."

Adela slipped off her horse, and Galen unsaddled it.

"The twine's in the sack I tied on your horse." He reached into the sack, rummaged a little, and pulled out the ball of twine.

Galen watched Adela walk to the woods at the edge of the meadow and begin looking for a game trail. Then he strolled to the edge of the pond. He pulled his shirt over his head. As it cleared his eyes, she came back into view. She was bent over, setting a branch that would trigger the snare. The corner of his mouth rose.

Hunting for Otto was the last thing he'd ever wanted to do, but he couldn't have a better companion in the hunt.

Adela nibbled the last bit of flesh from the leg bone of the rabbit. Galen had cooked it exactly how she liked it—no pink near the bones but not cooked until it was tough. It had been the best meal since they started the hunt for his friend.

Galen had moved two rocks that were big enough to sit on near the campfire, and he stretched his legs out in front of him. The slight smile that always played on his lips accompanied his contented sigh. He laced his fingers together and rested them on top of his head.

"That was a good dinner. Good thing you know how to read the trails and set a trap a rabbit won't see. I didn't expect a catch that fast."

Adela felt her smile grow. "To hunt and fight are two things all Hermunduri women must learn."

Galen unlaced his fingers and pointed at her. "There's something else this Hermunduri woman needs to learn, so let's get started. I thought we'd practice a few words before we work on writing again."

He rubbed his freshly shaved cheek. He'd used his dagger, and there had been something fascinating about him scraping away the short hairs. But with the beard gone, she could see the cut clearly.

A twinge of guilt niggled at her as she looked at what would soon be a scar.

"What words?"

"Some that you'll likely hear me speak in the towns we pass through. Others might speak them, too."

"I'm ready for that."

Galen ran his fingers through his hair. "I'll be asking some directions when we get back to Augusta Raurica, so let's work on those. Where is the garrison? *Ubi praesidium?*"

Adela perked up. "Where is the garrison? Ubi prae...How did it end?"

"*Praesidium.* That means garrison. *Ubi* is the "where is" part.

"Ubi praesidium?" Adela arched her eyebrows as she asked.

"Very good. *Quod via Romam?*"

"Quod via Romam?" Her head tipped "What did I just say?"

"Which road to Rome?" He chuckled. "Not that we'll have to go that far. Otto will be in Octodurus, and I know the way there. *Quod* is which and *via* is road or way."

He rubbed his uncut cheek "Of course, I could also ask *Romae via qua?* Which road goes to Rome?"

Adela's brow furrowed. "But that's the same question, and you said two different things for it."

"I did. You can ask either way, but maybe we should stick to one for now. Which do you like better?"

"Quod via Romam."

He nodded. "For different towns, you just use the town name instead of *Romam.* The end on the name of the town changes, but people will know what you mean even if you don't change it."

Adela rolled her eyes. It was not going to be as easy to learn this as Galen claimed. Maybe there was a good reason her brother took years to learn Latin.

Her eye-roll pulled a smile from Galen. "You can practice those two for a while. Ubi praesidium? Quod via Romam?"

She picked up a stick. "You taught me letters faster." She traced out A-D-E-L-A, then G-A-L-E-N. The words made a good pair together in the dirt.

She glanced at Galen in time to see his broad grin. When it came to hunting a missing man, she and Galen made a good pair, too.

Octodurus, Day 6

Sunset painted the massive snow-capped mountains rising east of Octodurus with changing shades of pink, but Otto's gaze focused on the gray stone walls of the amphitheater. They weren't even two stories high. No graceful arches invited the spectators in. No carved figures of fighting men adorned its walls to create the illusion that fame and glory awaited the fighters who would bleed and die on the sand inside.

It was smaller than the one in Mogontiacum. But Germania Superior was an important frontier province, and its location on the Rhenus made it much more than a legion fortress town. Even with so many of the six thousand legionaries of the XXII Primigenia stationed in remote garrisons, it needed more space for its spectacles of death. Octodurus was the capital of a small senatorial province. The days when legions fought there for the future glory of the Empire were long past.

Otto swallowed hard. He'd never dreamed of a glorious future in battle. What awaited him inside those walls was not glory. It might not even be a future.

The mule driver skirted the amphitheater and reined in by the building next door. The gate at the back of the cart dropped, and the ox-like man poked Otto with his stick. "Get out, and don't speak unless you're spoken to."

When his fellow prisoners had joined him, they were prodded toward the door under a sign made of two short wooden planks: Ludus Octoduri.

The man who'd bought him from Gundahar met them inside and led them down a ramp to an inner courtyard covered with sand. Around its edge were heavy wooden stakes the height of a short man.

A burly man with a long scar on his cheek stood with arms crossed and a slight frown.

Otto's captor waved his hand at the three shackled men. "You couldn't find better than these for three-on-three." He strode over to Otto and slapped his shoulder. "Bjorn here is the son of a Langobardi chieftain, lethal with the weapons of the north country, and handsome enough to please the ladies during the procession."

Otto opened his mouth to declare that a lie. Before he could speak, the stick of the ox-man struck the side of his head. His captor glowered. "Silence."

The trainer rubbed his scar. "I'll give you 400 denarii for the whole lot."

Their captor frowned as he shook his head. "They're worth at least 200 each."

"Not to me, and probably not to anyone else. But you can keep driving south to find out."

"You know I can't do that." He heaved a sigh. "I'll take the 400."

Otto's new owner summoned his assistant with a flick of his hand. "Put them in the cell and feed them."

As Otto left the arena, he heard his captor's voice. "The big one is hard to handle. You'll want two men to take his shackles off."

He was herded with the others into a cell with two sets of bunk beds. Lothar and Baldwin were unshackled and took the longer set, leaving him with the bed too short for a man his height to stretch out on. Another gladiator joined them and pinned his arms while his shackles were removed.

Otto offered no resistance. There was no point in fighting when there was no chance of escape, and guards get careless when a prisoner submits without complaint.

A boy of about ten brought a tray with three bowls of porridge and handed one to Otto as he stood by the bars. He filled the spoon and took his first bite.

The gruel was disgustingly bland. There was no seasoning to give it a tantalizing flavor, like when Galen's sister made it. Not what he'd choose to eat, but he was hungry enough to eat anything. Galen would tell him it was tasty enough to be thankful for and ask for the rest of Otto's bowl when he'd eaten all he wanted.

He drew a deep breath and shoveled another spoonful into his mouth. Galen was right. For a man who was hungry enough, even unseasoned barley gruel was worth being thankful for.

Galen put another small log on the fire as Adela lay down on the bedroll and pulled the blankets up to her chin. She wiggled under the covers to get comfortable and let her gaze settled upon him.

He settled onto his rock, rested his elbows on his knees, and lowered his forehead onto his clasped hands. His eyes closed. His breathing slowed, and the trace of a smile that always lingered on his lips broadened. Then all the tension seemed to drain out of him. When he finally opened his eyes, his gaze settled on her, and the smile grew.

"Good night, Adela. Rest in peace."

He settled under his blankets, closed his eyes, and was asleep before Adela decided whether she should answer.

A shiver ran up her spine. Rest in peace. She'd done that before Gundahar's final words; it wasn't so easy now. But Galen was probably right that Gundahar had never done what he said. Her kidnapper was so good at lying that he'd almost convinced the warrior with the crest that Galen was lying instead of him. Only her amulet had proven to the Roman that Galen spoke the truth.

Besides, surely she would have known if Gundahar had done something when she awoke, bound and draped on the horse. Even if she was dressed in the slave tunic.

It's only a lie. It's not true, like Galen said. She forced her breathing to slow as she repeated Galen's words, and sleep finally came.

Chapter 14

No Better Teacher

Day 7

Adela and Galen set out early the next morning. It was still a two-day ride back to Augusta Raurica.

She was mostly satisfied with what happened to Gundahar and Gerlach, even though Galen hadn't let her watch them die. But the third kidnapper had escaped justice, and Galen's friend was still a slave.

And what had they done with Gunda? Adela's lips tightened. She was gone when Adela awoke, bound and draped over the horse. They must have killed her. Had Father found her body to give her proper burial?

Her brow furrowed. But maybe Gunda got away, and Gundahar just hadn't wanted to admit that. He never did answer her questions; he only laughed. She'd taken the third kidnapper's horse, and Gerlach and Gundahar both chased her. If Gunda ran fast enough or hid well enough...

If Gunda told Father they took her, he would have hunted for her. After ten days, had he given her up as dead, or was he still looking? Even if he was, he would never look so far from home and inside the Empire.

Adela bit her lip. She'd already been missing ten days. It would be at least another ten before Galen could get her home. After so long, would Father think she'd been spoiled for marriage to a chieftain's son? Gundahar hadn't done anything, but would Father believe that? And even if he did, would any chieftain want his son to marry a woman who'd been gone for so long from her father's household and couldn't prove she hadn't been with a man? Was Gundahar right? Was she less valuable to her father than a slave?

She focused on Galen as he rode just ahead of her. Maybe she was worrying over nothing. Galen was wise in the ways of the world, and he thought what Gundahar said must be lies. At the gaming table, Gundahar told Otto she was worth a lot of money because she was a virgin, so he didn't do anything when she was knocked out.

Galen was right that she shouldn't believe anything Gundahar said in Brigantium. Galen would swear she'd been under his protection and that he'd made sure nothing happened from the moment Otto won her.

And Galen was so sure a German chieftain would be glad to get his daughter back. Father hadn't always listened to her, but he did trust her. She'd be able to convince him that Galen had protected her during their journey, and there was no reason he couldn't arrange her marriage to a chieftain's son.

She studied Galen's dark hair and the skin of his neck that was so brown compared to hers. He was so obviously Roman. Father hated the Roman warriors, but he admired them, too, for their bravery and loyalty. Galen had both.

Father was an honest man. Surely he'd be able to tell that Galen's word could be trusted. Who could look into those honest brown eyes and not see Galen spoke the truth?

Galen had been leading them at a trot, but he reined in and dropped back beside Adela.

"Ready for your next Latin lesson?"

"Of course." Anything to get her mind off her kidnapping was welcome.

"You'll need to know some words that name things. The ends of the naming words change, depending on how you use them. There are six endings, but if you use the wrong one, it's not a problem. People will figure out what you mean."

He reached to rub his cut cheek, then dropped his hand before touching it.

Adela glanced away, then back at him. "It won't look bad, you know. Some women think a scar makes a man look...strong."

A chuckle escaped him. "Looking strong is good. Being strong is better, and that has nothing to do with how a man looks...or how big he is. It's the heart, not the height that matters." His lips settled into a crooked smile. "I don't care what it looks like. Don't worry about it."

His eyes said he meant that, but her regret remained.

"You'll also need to know some of the words that tell what you're doing or what you want to do. That's a little harder. There are..." He ticked something off on his fingers. "I'm sorry to say there are fourteen different sets of endings, and two to six endings in each set."

Adela's hand flew to her mouth.

"Don't panic, Adela. I can make it a lot simpler than it sounds and still teach you enough for you to talk with someone."

"Maybe it's too hard for me."

The crooked smile appeared again. "Nothing is too hard for a chieftain's daughter like you. We have plenty of time to work on it as we ride." The smile turned into a full-blown grin. "After all, even a three-year-old Roman can speak enough Latin to be understood, and you're much smarter than that."

Galen's head tipped. "Let's start simple so you can hear how endings change from me to you to him. Or her. The ending is the same for those. For I am, you are, he is, we are, you are, they are, the Latin is *sum, es, est, sumus, estis, sunt.*"

Galen raised one hand and waved it in time with the Latin words as he said them again. "I think reciting to a rhythm helps me remember. Try it."

She sucked air through her teeth. "*Sum, es, est, sumus, estis, sunt.*"

He flashed a grin at her. "Yes! See how easy that is?"

She shrugged. "I guess."

"It's even better to sing it." His deep voice broke into song as he waved his arm.

Adela couldn't stop the giggle.

His hand paused mid-air. "Join me in the song."

As his hand kept the rhythm, her voice blended with his. The fourteen sets of six endings might be more than she'd ever master, but no one could have a better teacher.

Otto stirred the third bowl of steaming *polenta* the kitchen boy had placed before him. He was glad to have it, even if the barley porridge was bland and boring. Barley porridge, barley bread, barley in the vegetable stew—no wonder a gladiator was sometimes called a *hordearius.* "Barley man" summed up his diet perfectly.

At least he was out of the shackles, and he'd been served as many bowls as he asked for. As he licked the last morsels from the spoon, the lanista strode into the dining area.

"You three." He pointed at Otto and the other two men who'd come from Augusta Raurica with him. "You'll be with Magnus today."

One of the gladiators stood and summoned them with a flick of his hand. Otto rose and followed him down a short hall and out into a small, sandy arena. Around the edge, heavy stakes about the height of a man were set upright in the ground.

He scanned the arena wall. Only one entrance, and no way to go through it without being seen by a trainer.

The gladiator led the three to a rack of long wooden swords, each with metal embedded in the handle to increase the weight. "You'll be using these on the *palus*, and I'll be telling you how to use them." He swung the sword through the air at waist level, lifted it high to twirl it over his head, and finished with a lunging stab.

"You'll get your chance before the crowd in three days. My job is to make sure you make this ludus proud when you fight. Do what I say and train hard, and you have a chance of walking back here after the games. If you don't...you'll at least have your moment of glory on the sand."

He tossed a sword to each of them. "Pick a palus, and let's get started."

Otto swung the sword, testing the weight and balance. It handled nothing like the gladius Gundahar had stolen from him. Then he focused his full attention on the gladiator. Any man who had survived the arena long enough to be the teacher of others must know something that could keep him from dying.

Galen was hunting for him, but where? Why hadn't he caught up yet? Horses traveled much faster than the mule cart. But there were three major roads out of Argentorate, and two out of Augusta Raurica. Had Galen taken the wrong one? Even if Galen had traced him to Augusta Raurica, did he know Gundahar had sold him before riding east?

Otto shook his head to banish those thoughts about Galen and focused once more on the words and movements of the gladiator. He had only three days to learn enough from the expert to stay alive.

Chapter 15

First Fight

Day 10

Moonlight streamed through the small, barred window near the ceiling of Otto's cell. He'd been staring for hours at the shadows of the bars as they moved across the wall. For three days, he'd been whacking at a man-sized wooden stake with a weighted wooden sword. Three days with a sword longer and heavier than the gladius he could wield second to none, except maybe Galen and Decimus, who'd trained them both.

Today the weapons would be steel. It would be human flesh, not wood, that he'd have to strike. And it would be experienced warriors like Lothar and Baldwin, not a wooden post, that faced him. Warriors as eager to stay alive as he was.

He was trained for fighting legion-style, deflecting thrusting and slashing attacks by a *gladius* and stabbing back in close quarters. But was that good enough for him to survive the arena?

What if his opponent stayed too far away for a thrust to strike home? What if he had to use a sword like he'd been given in practice, too long for the moves he'd mastered years ago? What if he had to use a battle ax instead of a sword?

It had been ten days since Gundahar abducted him. Nine days since Galen would have discovered he'd been taken. But it should have taken only five, maybe six days to ride to Octodurus from Argentorate. What could have delayed Galen? Was he even coming?

Would Galen arrive at the last minute to buy him out of the ludus? Even if he did, would the lanista sell him when he was already scheduled for a match tomorrow?

Otto willed himself to relax. Worrying over it wasn't going to change anything that happened. If he had a choice, he'd get a gladius. If no choice, he'd just have to hope something Decimus taught him would prove useful in the first fight for his life.

He closed his eyes. Worry did nothing. Sleep would help more. He forced his breathing to slow.

If he could just make it through the first fight, Galen would come. Nothing would stop his friend until Galen rescued him...if he was alive when Galen came.

Otto stood in the dark tunnel with the other gladiators, waiting for his turn to march onto the sunlit sand. The lanista had lined them up for a procession to whet the appetite of the 5,000 spectators. Bare-chested and decked out in loincloths and armor that protected sword arms and legs but not vital organs, they would parade around the arena before standing in front of the sponsor of the games. They'd been drilled in what to say.

We who are about to die salute you. He'd speak the words, but he didn't plan to die.

He'd been ordered to wear the helmet that blocked too much of his vision and a sleeve made of thick strips of leather to protect his sword arm, but he'd been allowed to pick his weapon. His knuckles whitened as he tightened his grip on the gladius he'd chosen. It wasn't as well balanced as his own, but it was close enough.

After their march in front of the cheering crowd, he was sent back into the tunnel to wait with Baldwin, Lothar, and three other men who would be in his three-on-three match. They were the first event.

A trumpet blast called them out, and the arena master split them up into pairs. Baldwin was his first opponent. A battle-hardened warrior, even if it was only a single battle. Otto was half a head taller, but it was speed, not size, that mattered in a swordfight. Galen had bested him many times in a friendly match. It was speed and seeing the opponent's move before he made it.

But this wasn't sparring, and Baldwin's eyes filled with fire. The Suebian warrior was hungry for the kill, like Otto felt when he rode up on a wild boar with a spear.

The next blast would start the combat.

Otto drew a deep breath, blew it out, and steeled himself for the first time he'd have to kill another man to stay alive.

The trumpet sounded. He pulled the helmet off and tossed it aside. Seeing the enemy was more important than any protection it might afford. As Baldwin swung the sword that was twice the length of his toward his ribs, Otto caught it with the gladius. With a twist and a shove, he flipped it out of the way before grabbing Baldwin's sword arm. One step forward, and he drove his blade into the youth's chest, slipping the blade between his ribs and into his heart.

Baldwin's eyes saucered. The sword fell from his right hand, and his left hand grasped Otto's shoulder in a vise-like grip. His mouth opened as if to speak, but no sound came. Then his eyes lost focus, and his grip relaxed. The weight of his body settled on the gladius.

Otto swallowed hard to keep the vomit from getting into his mouth. Killing a man was nothing like spearing a boar or dropping a stag with a well-placed arrow.

As a gasp rippled through the crowd, Otto pushed the body off his sword. He kept his eyes off Baldwin's face. He couldn't let the surging regret over what he had to do keep him from doing it two more times.

The other two pairs kept fighting, and Otto watched them closely, gauging how each of them fought. A man with a long sword made for slashing dropped Lothar, who had an ax. Lothar raised his arm, asking for mercy, but the crowd shouted for the kill. The swordsman gave it to them, but he made no attempt to attack Otto.

The second pair both had gladii, and they fought longer. They were well matched, but one finally fell. This time, the raised arm received mercy. Two men loaded the wounded man on a stretcher and carried him into the tunnel.

The two victors moved close enough to each other to speak in voices Otto couldn't hear over the yells of the crowd, but he didn't need to hear their words. A two-on-one was coming.

They fanned out as they approached. Otto kept backing up so they couldn't flank him. Then the one who killed Lothar came at him with his long sword, swinging at Otto's unprotected neck. Otto caught the sword with his gladius and deflected the blow. As the man drew back his arm for another stroke, Otto lunged at him and made the lethal thrust to his heart.

Before he could pull the gladius out, his third opponent came at him from the side. Otto twisted to put the dead man between them and shoved him onto the attacker's sword. He yanked his own sword free and finished off the third man with a thrust to the throat.

As the body crumpled, Otto looked away. His gaze fell on narrow steps built into the arena wall. Still clutching the gladius, he sprinted toward them. Three leaps up the stairs took him from the sand to the stands. As the spectators scrambled away from him, he ran along the edge of the walkway, heading for an exit ramp.

Then a net dropped over him. The net man who was to fight a secutor in the next match had thrown it from the sand below before charging up another set of steps.

Otto struggled free of the net, only to have one more tossed on him from behind.

The two net men pinned him as the lanista clamped shackles on his legs, then his wrists. A roar rose from the crowd as two brawny *secutores* stretched him out, one gripping his wrists, the other his ankles, and carried him back into the tunnel.

The crowd was still shouting when they tossed him, still in shackles, on a bunk in his cell. The cell door closed, and he was left alone.

He stared at the blood on his sword hand, and it started to tremble. Three sharp shakes of his wrist, and the quiver stopped. He closed his eyes.

He'd killed three men. Something he'd never wanted to do. Something he hoped he'd never have to do again. But what choice did he have as a slave chained to the arena? It was kill or die...and he wanted to live.

The games were over...for now. Otto's shoulders drooped as the lanista stood outside the cell, frowning. "You fought well today, Bjorn...for a man in battle, but that's not what this is. We put on a show for the people. Blood and sometimes death are what they want, but not too quickly."

"I don't care what the people want. I'm not a gladiator. I was kidnapped in Argentorate, and I shouldn't be in the arena anyway. I'll fight however I must to stay alive. Killing isn't some game, like you Romans seem to think."

As the lanista watched Otto, shaking his head, a man who was obviously Roman approached. "This one is a wild man. Perhaps not what you want in your ludus. It's too hard for most to tame and train Northland Germans. They stir up the others to rebellion as well."

The Octodurus lanista shrugged. "I only bought him a few days ago. He acted tame enough before today on the sand."

"He won't be tame after that fight. He's likely to kill or get killed in practice, and that takes money from your purse. Anyone going up against him in the arena will go for the kill as fast as possible to stay alive themselves. The crowd wants a drawn-out deathmatch for its money, and no one will want to book a fight with him. Let me take him off your hands."

Otto's owner rubbed his mouth. "You could be right. This is a small arena, but properly trained for the big show before 50,000 in Rome, he'll earn you a fortune. Maybe I will sell him." He rubbed the back of his neck. "He's worth at least 1400 denarii."

That figure drew a snort. "Too high. A dead Class 6 isn't worth that much, and this one's too new to be more than Class 8."

The lanista's mouth lifted in a wry smile. "But this one will be at least Class 5 after his first bout. He's a bargain at 1400."

The Roman buyer tightened his lips. "You want the prices of Roma in Octodurus. You won't get that from me. But..." The Roman buyer stroked his cheek. "I can offer 1200. A fair price for a man you've spent no money training. That's more than he'll bring if he dies in his next fight." A wry smile tugged at the corner of his mouth. "Which is likely without months of training."

Otto's lanista opened his mouth, then hesitated.

"That's probably four times what you paid for him. A good profit with no risk."

The Roman buyer's point struck home. The lanista offered his arm. "Sold. I'll draw up the bill of sale."

As the two men moved off, Otto sat on the long bunk that had been Lothar's and hung his head. He rested his elbows on his knees and buried his face in his hands. Galen's Roman-to-Roman bargaining always brought top prices for horses. But even in his worst nightmares, he'd never dreamed he'd hear two Romans agree to a price for him.

Chapter 16

OCTODURUS

Day 11

The sky was still mostly gray when Otto followed his new owner, Marcus Antonius Brutus, into the street, but the hint of pink washing the broken clouds over the mountains spawned a glimmer of hope as he left the cell and sand of the ludus behind.

The smile he was fighting as he considered the possibility of escape died on his lips when he saw the two gladiator bodyguards traveling with Brutus.

Brutus stepped aside as the larger guard shackled Otto's wrists. "It's two days on horseback over the pass to Augusta Praetoria. A long ride for some, but you'll manage. Mount up."

Otto fought the smile again as he settled into the saddle. The old, swayback mare was nothing like the fiery stallions he liked to ride, but a horse was a horse. The dark-skinned guard with curly black hair still held the mare's halter, but as soon as Otto had control, he could plan his break for freedom.

Brutus snapped his fingers. The red-haired guard clamped the first iron band around Otto's right ankle and flipped the long chain under the horse's belly.

Otto's shoulders drooped as the redhead walked past his horse's rump and fastened the second ring above his free foot. The heavy chain dragged his legs down until he bent his knees and gripped the mare's sides. The jangle of the links under her belly made the old girl dance, even with the guard stroking her nose.

Brutus stepped closer and patted her neck. "Settle down, girl. You'll get used to it." He glanced at Otto and the corner of his mouth pulled up. "So will your rider."

As the long lead rope was clipped to the halter, Otto squared his shoulders and pulled a deep breath. He raised his eyes and scanned the snow-capped mountains that towered over the town.

No matter how hopeless it might seem, there was still hope. Somehow, Galen would find him.

Vivisco, Day 11

Adela's eyes were drawn to the naked crags of the rugged mountains rising to the east. What had seemed like a line of distant hills when they first headed south from Augusta Raurica had grown closer and taller with each passing day.

They were five days into their six-day ride to Octodurus, Tomorrow, they should reach the town where Galen expected to find his friend, but she was in no hurry. So many things along their route had intrigued her, from the sun sparkling on the lake just north of Aventicum to the eight towering columns with leaves and curls cut into the white stone where it held the roof of the Roman temple.

Galen said it was dedicated to the emperor. When she asked him if he worshiped in a temple like that, his lips curved into a smile as his eyes crinkled. He'd simply answered, "No," but what was so funny about her question?

At the top of a hill overlooking a lake at least as big as the one at Brigantium, Galen reined in. "That's Vivisco down there. Last stop before we reach Octodurus."

He wove his fingers together and rested them atop his head as he arched his back. "We'll ask at the garrison about a safe place to camp." He turned his smile on her. "Are you starting to understand some of what I ask now?"

Adela's smile mirrored his. "Some. You're a good teacher."

"I have a good student."

"But I still don't understand much of what they answer."

"That will come." He dropped his arms and picked up the reins. "You can tell me what you caught after I get directions to the camp." His eyes crinkled again. "I bet it will be more than you think."

He nudged his horse into a walk and started down the slope. She settled in beside him where she could watch his profile. There was that hint of a smile.

One more day to catch up with his friend, then ten, maybe eleven days to take her back home. Her lips tightened. Why was it time sometimes crawled, but it raced when you didn't want it to?

Octodurus, Day 12

Adela twisted in her saddle for a final look back down the river valley. Tall hills that would have been called mountains in Hermunduri country rose almost at the river's edge. It was half a day back to Vivisco and the blue waters of the lake. Now the tallest buildings in Octodurus rose ahead of them.

She expected Galen to kick his horse into a trot to reach his friend sooner. The closer they got to the town, the bigger his smile had been when she glanced at him.

Instead, he reined in. "Adela."

The tension in his voice jerked her gaze from the river to his face.

His smile had vanished. "I want you to keep your eyes on me or on the ground. This is the provincial capital. We're riding past the execution field, and someone is on a cross. I don't want you to see that."

She perked up and leaned in the saddle to look past him. "That's what they did to Gundahar?"

Galen shifted to block her view. "Yes. But don't look. You don't want to see it."

She wasn't so sure of that, even though she nodded. Gundahar deserved whatever the Romans had done to him.

Galen nudged his horse and crossed in front of her to put himself on the side away from the cross. "Keep your eyes on me."

He watched her, so she did as he said...until they were beside the man. Then she turned her head to see.

A wave of nausea swept through her as she stared at the naked, bloody body hanging from the nails through his wrists. Another nail impaled his feet.

Then Galen took her chin in his hand and turned her face back toward him. "I said don't look."

She swallowed several times to keep the cheese she'd had for lunch down. "How can they do that, even to someone who deserves to die?"

"It's the Roman way. It's meant to keep anyone else who's not a citizen from breaking Roman law."

"I would have killed him quick. You should have let me."

"Then you might have been the one up there."

Adela fought against it, but her lip still quivered. Galen blurred as tears filled her eyes. "The Roman way is wrong."

Galen released her chin. "Yes, it is. Mercy is not considered a virtue in Rome. May you never be in a place where you need it."

She squeezed her eyelids shut, but the image of the man wouldn't fade. She squeezed them tighter, and the tears that had pooled in her eyes dribbled down her cheeks.

Galen's hand wrapped around hers and squeezed. "Let's go find Otto."

She kicked her horse into a trot, and he followed suit. The sooner she got away from Roman "justice," the better.

◆

Galen's pulse rate rose as he rode past the main entrance to the amphitheater. The sign on the building next door drew a smile.

He pointed at the red letters painted on short wooden planks. "Can you read that to me?"

Adela tipped her head. "L-V-D-V-S. Ludus. I know that word."

"That's where Otto should be." His smile broadened. "Time to set him free."

He slipped off Astrelo and handed Adela his reins. Then he entered the door under the sign.

The sound of wood striking wood drew him to a railing that overlooked an inner courtyard covered with sand. Several men were striking vertical wooden posts with wooden swords while two sparred under the watchful eye of a burly man in his late thirties.

Galen leaned over the edge. "I'd like to speak with the man in charge."

The burly man tipped his face up. A frown grew as he scanned Galen. "What do you want?"

"To buy one of your gladiators."

The frown flipped. "I'll be right up."

Galen rubbed his hands together as the man disappeared through a door directly below him, only to appear again in a doorway to his left.

The lanista towered over Galen as he rested his fists on his hips. "I have a fine stable of fighters, trained in several fighting styles. What are you looking for?"

"I heard you were going to buy an unusually tall German just brought down from Augusta Raurica. I'm looking for him."

"The Langobardi, Bjorn. I fought him in the games two days ago. He's gone."

Galen's heart dropped into his stomach, and his jaw clenched. Too late. So many hard days riding so many miles, and still too late. "Where is he buried?"

The lanista's hand swept his words away. "He's gone, not dead. I sold him. He fought in a three-on-three. He killed three with less than three stokes each. The *ludi* in Rome scout here for talent. One of them bought him. They left to go over the pass yesterday."

Relief flooded through Galen, and his whole body relaxed. "His real name is Otto of the Vangiones. He was kidnapped in Argentorate, and I'm trying to get him back. So, he's headed for Rome?"

"Eventually. I sold him to Marcus Antonius Brutus. He has three schools. I think the smaller ones are in Luna, or maybe Luca, and Florentia. He also fights men in Rome. Your friend is a superb swordsman, but he fights like a legionary. Too quick to the kill. He'll be trained to fight for the show before he goes into the arena again. You should have time to find him and buy him." He rubbed his cheek. "But he won't be cheap. Brutus is expecting him to be at least Class 3 by the end of his training."

Galen's brow furrowed. "Class 3?"

"There's a ranking that sets how much the sponsor of a fight pays if a man dies. Class 3 costs 2500 denarii. They won't sell him for less than that."

Galen pulled a deep breath, held it, then blew it out. "Whatever he costs, I'll free him."

"They left in the gray dawn yesterday. It's a two-day ride over the pass, with a *mansio* and some other lodging at the summit. Don't start out before dawn tomorrow. It's still freezing up there at night."

Galen tightened his lips as he nodded. "That's good to know. I'll need to get something heavier to wear for that."

"You'll find what you need in the shops. Many come through here unprepared for the climb." The corners of the lanista's mouth curved. "It's a good thing for Bjorn...Otto that you found him. He's not cut out for the arena. Too fast to kill, maybe too stubborn to change that with training. May Fortuna smile on you as you try to find him."

Galen returned the smile. "I won't stop looking until I do."

◆

Adela nibbled her lip as she waited for Galen to return. Would his giant friend think he still owned her, even with Galen telling him she'd been kidnapped? Gundahar never had the right to use her to cover a bet.

She stiffened when Galen came out the door...alone. "Where's your friend?"

Galen's shrug accompanied the roll of his eyes. "Sold to a man from Rome. By now, he's on the other side of that." He pointed to the massive peaks that blocked almost half the sky. "I'm sorry, but I can't take you home yet. I must follow him over the pass. Maybe all the way to Rome."

Adela's eyebrows shot up. "How many days will that take?"

He ran his fingers through his hair. "It depends on whether the man who bought him leaves him in one of his smaller ludi that are closer than the big one in Rome. It's two days to cross the mountains, and then maybe two weeks to Rome. My sister's husband has made the trip, and he said it's three weeks from Argentorate to Rome if you take this road over the Summus Poeninus." He rubbed the back of his neck. "That makes it more than eight weeks since you were taken before I can get you home."

Adela shrugged. "Like you say, we must follow him now if we're going to rescue him. However long that takes, it makes no difference to me." A teasing smile tugged at the corner of her mouth. "That just gives me more time to learn Latin."

The broad smile her words brought to Galen's lips gave her more pleasure than he could know. Perhaps he liked her company as much as she liked his.

"We'll head out tomorrow morning. It's still like winter at the top, so we'll want to spend the night in one of the inns for travelers at the summit. That's the half-way point. But first we need to get a few things."

Galen mounted Astrelo and led Adela to a street lined with buildings with one or two rows of windows above small shops. There, he dismounted, and signaled Adela to do the same.

"First we find a vendor with some warmer clothes." His smile started slow, then grew. "And then I'll have a surprise for you."

"What?"

"I can't tell you. Then it wouldn't be a surprise."

Adela held the horses while Galen entered the first shop. When he emerged, he pointed up the street. "Second shop past the next street has what we'll need."

They led the horses along the street, weaving through the shoppers. They stopped by the second shop, and the shopkeeper left the loom where she was weaving what looked like a cape. Adela tried to catch what Galen and the woman said, but they spoke so fast, and almost none of the words were anything she'd heard before. The woman piled two scarves, four tube socks of sprang-work fabric, four small rectangles of cloth with ties on each end, two woolen tunics with long sleeves, and two heavy woolen capes with hoods. Then Galen bent and measured the length of her foot with the span of his hand. When he showed the shopkeeper, she shook her head and pointed back down the street.

Galen took many coins from his purse and paid the woman. Then they talked some more, with the woman waving her arm first left, then right, then right again.

He scooped up the smaller items. "*Gratias tibi tam.*" He took the smaller things and tucked them into the sack tied behind his saddle. Then he handed Adela a tunic and a cloak before picking up his.

After draping his own tunic and cloak across his saddle, he led Adela down the street to a shoemaker. Felt boots with leather soles for each of them were added to his sack.

As he led Adela out of the market street, he glanced over his shoulder. "What did you understand back there?"

"Thank you so much." Adela's smile was sheepish. "And "where is" before she started waving her arms at you. Why did she do that?"

"That's part of the surprise." He bounced an eyebrow at her. "The cloak is a *paenula.* It will drape your horse as well, and that makes it almost like sitting on a brazier...except you can't get burned. It will work as an extra blanket, too. The long-sleeved tunics can go under our shirts... for extra warmth."

Adela fingered the tunic. "I'll still look like a boy in this."

Galen's mouth pulled sideways, then curved. "There's nothing you could wear that would make you look like a boy. What the shop had for men was much warmer than the women's clothes."

Adela shrugged. "It doesn't really matter. I'm used to wearing your clothes. Riding is easier in them than in what I wore at home."

"You're lucky I'm a short man, or you'd have to roll up the pants like you were ready to wade in a stream." His mouth twitched sideways. "Any shorter and they'd be too short, but they fit you well enough. Even if my shirt does hang on you, it looks much better on you than on me."

He rubbed the back of his neck. "You don't have to worry about wearing men's clothes. Any man with even one good eye would know you were no boy and find looking at you a pleasure, no matter what you wear. The Latin word for you is *pulchra*...beautiful."

The heat spread to the tips of her ears.

Chapter 17

Surprises

Galen followed the shopkeeper's directions to the inn she claimed was run by an honest couple. It had a stable for their horses and served food so delicious that even the locals liked to eat there for special occasions. Best of all, it was on the same street as the small private bath where the shopkeeper liked to take her own daughters. Unlike the public baths, it separated men and women.

He glanced at Adela as they entered the stable yard. He didn't like the temptations in the mixed baths, and he wouldn't subject her to the reaction of many men to a beauty like her. Especially since she wouldn't understand a word of what most of them were saying. His mouth twitched as he suppressed the grin. The cut on his cheek was proof of how risky it could be to touch her for any reason without her permission first.

A well-fed man of about forty came from a stall to greet him. Galen dropped his voice as he arranged for the horses' rubdowns and feed and for the saddles to be moved into a private room. He glanced at Adela. She was wandering around the stable yard, her curiosity as active as always. He took the clean tunics and the bags of personal items from each horse.

Adela was looking at a stallion in one of the stalls when he stepped beside her. "Ready for the surprise?"

"This trip has been nothing but surprises." She flashed him a smile. "But I'd like one more...if it's a good one."

Her smiles were ample payment for anything he did for her, and he expected a purse-full before the evening was over. "Oh, it is. Follow me."

❖

Adela followed Galen up the street until he stopped in front of an arched gateway.

"What does that say?" He pointed to the sign next to the entrance.

"T-H-E-R-M-A-E. *Thermae.*" Her head tipped. "I don't know that word."

"*Therma* means warm, and this is a place where we can get warm baths. We've been travelling for almost two weeks, and I, for one, am ready to get clean and soak for a while in hot water before we head over the mountain."

Adela's eyes widened. "I've never been to one." She bit her lip. "I don't know what to do here."

Galen handed her a tunic and her bag of private things. "I'll get someone to help you."

She would have rather returned to the inn, but Galen had already gone in.

Inside was a narrow courtyard with a woman sitting at a table. On the walls to her left and right, closed doors hid something.

Galen spoke some Latin, and the woman handed him two large sacks. He pointed at Adela and spoke some more before the woman nodded. The young girl sitting behind her rose and went through the door to the left. Another girl came out and summoned her with a wave of her hand.

His eyes laughed as he turned back to Adela. "I told her you hadn't been to the baths before, and one of the slaves will show you what to do and stay with you."

He pointed at the door on the right wall. "I'll be bathing there. I'll be waiting here when you finish. Take your time and enjoy the warm water."

As the slave led her through the door to the women's side, Adela looked back over her shoulder. Galen stood watching her with his arms crossed and a grin on his face.

"I'll see you in about an hour." He lifted one hand to wave before he turned and headed toward the other door.

Adela took a deep breath and braced herself for whatever awaited as Galen's surprise.

Galen had thoroughly enjoyed applying the warm oil and scraping it off before taking a leisurely soak in the caldarium. He'd hired a slave to follow him around with his sword and the sack that held the clean tunic, horse money, and dagger belts. He didn't get a haircut or shave. It would be cold going over the mountain, and he wanted the extra warmth around his ears and on his face. Plus, he wanted to be waiting when Adela came through the door.

When Adela came out wearing the blue tunic he'd picked to match her eyes, he couldn't stop the grin. Her long, flaxen hair hung down her back and over her shoulders. It was good she normally wore it braided. The thought of how it would feel to run his fingers through it was tempting.

"Did you enjoy your bath?"

"Yes, but the woman helping me tried to take my comb when I started to untangle my hair." She ran her fingers through her still-damp hair. "I didn't want to make you wait while I braided it."

"Most women expect her to comb out their hair. She would have braided it again for you as well. My sister Val always tells Dec how relaxing it is when he combs and plays with her hair. Next time, you might want to see if you like it, too."

A crooked grin escaped. "I wouldn't mind waiting, but I'm glad you left it down. It's lovely, just like Val's except for the color. Yours is more like ripened wheat shimmering in a light breeze."

Her eyes widened as pink washed over her cheeks. "The woman looked at me strange when I was dressing. Do I look funny in this man's tunic?" She ran her hands down the front.

Galen chuckled. "Not at all. You're probably the prettiest girl in Octodurus. Every man who sees you is going to envy me when I take you to eat."

He led her back to the inn. Before entering the dining room, he handed their dirty clothes to a slave to wash right away so they would be dry before morning.

Galen settled them at a table by the back wall. After ordering a loaf of fresh, hot bread and two bowls of the savory stew that filled the whole room with its scrumptious aroma, he leaned back in his chair. With his legs stretched out and his fingers interlaced and resting atop his head, he released a deep sigh.

"It's been a good day, even if we didn't catch up with Otto yet. I know where he's going, and we'll get him freed before anything bad happens."

He closed his eyes. *Thank you, God, for getting us to this point.* When he opened his eyes, his gaze fell on Adela's smile. *And thank you for giving me Adela as a companion in the hunt.*

Adela leaned her elbows on the table and rested her chin in her hands. "A good day, but it's getting late. We should find a place to camp now."

"That's the other part of the surprise. I've rented a room here. No hard ground for you this evening. Tonight, it's a soft, warm bed."

Adela's eyes saucered as her breath caught.

Galen lifted his hands from the table top and spread his fingers. "It's not what you're thinking. The bed will be yours alone. I'll be sleeping on the floor."

Adela stood. "I trust you."

Her words triggered his smile. "Good. Let's get some sleep."

Galen led Adela upstairs to the room where their saddles had been taken. Then he left her to get ready alone. As he leaned against the wall outside the door, he closed his eyes. His mouth curved into a relaxed smile.

God, I thank you for this day. I thank you that Otto survived his first fight. I thank you that he won't have to fight again before I can rescue him. I thank you that Adela is so willing to stay with me until I do. His mouth straightened. *Please let her return be as welcomed as I've told her it will, even with it taking so long.*

As he continued his prayers, the tension and tiredness drained away.

◆

Adela was tucked under the blankets when Galen came back in. He rolled out his bedroll in front of the door and laid his sword beside it.

"Do you need anything before I blow out the lamp?"

"No."

The flame flickered as he blew, then vanished. His voice wrapped around her in the dark. "Good night, Adela. Rest in peace."

Adela lay in the warm, soft bed, listening to Galen's slow, steady breathing. He was already sleeping. That drew a smile.

He'd spent extra money and treated her to some things she'd never experienced before. He probably didn't mean anything by it. He was a man who looked after people, like he'd tried to look after his friend by getting him to stop drinking and gambling before there was trouble.

But the things he did certainly made her feel special, as if he found pleasure in her company and wanted her to find pleasure in his.

And she did, more than she'd ever expected to find with a man. He was more than a protector who would take her home. He was a friend, and going home didn't seem so attractive anymore if it meant she would never see him again.

Chapter 18

OVER THE PASS

Day 12

The deep, distant voice slowly penetrated Adela's comfortable darkness. "Ready for a hot breakfast before we start the climb?"

Her eyes drifted open. Galen stood at her bedside, that hint of a smile curving his lips.

Adela sat up and stretched. "That sounds good."

Galen's bedding was already rolled and tied to his saddle. Everything looked packed and ready to go.

Palm up, his hand swept toward the door. "I'll be right outside."

Adela slipped into the trousers and put the new blue tunic on. She reached up to braid her hair, then hesitated.

Shimmering fields of ripened wheat. That was how Galen described it, and his smile that accompanied those words danced in her memory. Perhaps she'd braid it after breakfast.

When she opened the door, he was leaning against the wall, his eyes closed. They opened, and she was glad she'd left her hair down as his eyes warmed at the sight of her.

"I restocked our food sack for the trip across the pass. There should be a hot dinner waiting for us at the top." He grinned over his shoulder as he started down the stairs. "Sleeping with a roof over my head, two hot meals in one day—it's almost like being at home."

He sat once more at the table by the back wall, and a girl brought two steaming bowls of porridge. Galen gave her a smile and a nod.

Adela blew on the spoon before she slipped it between her lips. A taste like this was definitely worth getting up early for.

Galen stood as she licked the back of the spoon after the last bite. "The innkeeper said it's about twenty-five miles to the top of the pass. A hard day for the horses with as high as we're going to climb. Time to head out."

Galen bounded up the stairs and stood at the top, grinning as Adela walked up behind him.

Twenty-five miles is a long distance, but it didn't seem so to Adela. Galen rode beside her, teaching her the Latin names for the things they passed, and so many were things she'd never seen before. Hermunduri forests were filled with leafy trees and thick undergrowth. As they climbed, the forest around them changed from beech trees with their many-branched trunks and canopy of leaves to beech mixed with spruce, then spruce and fir and larch. The trees grew so tall and pointed, and they had needles like tiny daggers instead of leaves.

But even though the sun rose higher in the sky, the air grew cooler as the horses carried them farther up the mountain slope.

Galen called a halt long enough for them to eat a lunch of cheese and dried apples and add a layer of clothing. Adela pulled his brown shirt over her light blue, long-sleeved tunic. She didn't roll up the sleeves because the extra length of the long arms covered her hands, providing welcome warmth.

What to do with the rectangular fabric with the ties on each end baffled her. Then Galen showed her how he wrapped his around his calf and tied it to make leg warmers underneath his trouser legs. He untied his fleece vest from the back of his saddle and handed that to her as well.

She wiggled her toes inside the felt boots. With the tube socks, her feet stayed warm. Warm feet usually made for warm hands, but her hands were cool, even with the sleeves hanging past her fingertips.

The road grew rockier as the tall trees changed to stunted shrubs, but the view back down the mountain toward Octodurus drew more than one gasp from her. A hawk circled overhead, screeching. For the first time, Adela understood what it meant to have a hawk's-eye view of the world stretching out below her, with giant trees looking no taller than grass, and the rivers they'd followed seeming no more than trickles.

But the sparse growth of stunted trees and low shrubs provided little protection against the wind as they got closer to the summit. Adela tucked the edge of her cape under her knees to keep it from flapping in the breeze and flipped the hood over her head.

Stunted trees gave way to heath and grasses and blankets of wildflowers. Splashes of blue, yellow, and white dotted the rocky soil around them. Yellow and orange patches of lichen softened the harsh gray of the rocks.

The wind nipped at her face, even with the hood up, so she wrapped the scarf over her ears and across her mouth. But her cape, which draped her horse as well as her, trapped the horse's warmth. Almost like a brazier, Galen had said, and he was right.

The sun was low on the horizon when the stone buildings at the top of the pass came into view. Despite the beauty surrounding her, Adela was more than ready to get inside.

Galen reined in, and she stopped beside him.

He pointed at a sprawling stone building. "That's the mansio. My sister's husband Dec would have stayed there when he was tribune of the legion in Mogontiacum. I've heard some *mansiones* even have baths. Soaking in some hot water would feel good right now, but you have to be on official Roman business to stay there." His hand moved toward a cluster of smaller buildings. "That's probably the inn for regular travelers the lanista mentioned."

He turned Astrelo's head toward the inn and nudged him into a walk. They passed a stone corral holding a dozen or so horses. The stable beside it had an attached stone-wall corral on the end opposite the main door. Raucous laughter could be heard through the closed door of the inn just past it.

Galen's forehead furrowed. "Stay here while I go see if there's a room available."

Adela watched him push open the heavy door and go inside. It was only a few moments before he came out, and his mouth curved down.

"The private rooms are all taken. There's only the common room where we could spread our bedrolls, but..." He shook his head. "There's a lot of drunken men already, and the women are all...for rent. I don't want to take you in there."

He rubbed his chin. "Back to the stable." He took Astrelo's reins from her and started walking.

Adela shivered, even though she wasn't especially cold.

Galen left her with the horses and entered the stable. She heard his voice in conversation with another man, then he returned wearing a smile.

"I've rented a stall for the horses and a place in the loft for us. It won't be as warm as the inn, but it's out of the wind and better than nothing. The stable boy will bring us some hot stew as well."

As she followed Astrelo into the stable, Adela glanced back at the inn. A drunk stumbled out the door and threw up by the wall before going back in.

It was much better to be cold in a stable with Galen than warm in an inn with that.

The hot stew had been tasty, but now it was time to sleep. Adela shivered as she knelt and spread her blankets on the straw. A chill wind blew into the loft through the broken shutter that only half-closed the opening through which hay was tossed. A few snowflakes floated on the wind.

Better than sleeping in the open, but still much too cold. She fixed her gaze on the smoke drifting out of the chimney of the inn before the wind blew it sideways, and she sighed.

Galen took the top blanket from his bedroll and spread it on top of hers.

She looked up at his face. "Take it back. You'll be too cold without it."

"I'll sleep better knowing you're warm enough. I don't need it."

"And I won't take it and leave you cold. But..." Her head tipped. "If we put yours on the bottom and mine on the top and spread the cloaks on top of that, we can both be warm enough."

His eyebrow shot up.

"I trust you, Galen. We can share and both be warm."

He rubbed his mouth and glanced at the opening. A plume of snow blew in and settled on his bedroll.

"If you're certain...I won't argue."

"I am." She scooped up his blankets and shook the snow off. Then she spread them to be wide enough for two and added hers on top.

Galen picked up her cloak. "Lie down."

She slipped between the blankets, and he spread her cloak over her. Then he slid into the blankets and spread his over both of them.

He stretched out with his back toward her. "Good night, Adela. Rest in peace."

She rolled on her side, facing away from him, but she felt his every breath as the blankets moved with each expansion of his chest. She pulled the blankets up over her nose and relaxed in the warmth they shared. Her own breathing slowed, and she drifted off.

◆

Adela wasn't sure how long she'd slept, but when she awoke, she felt Galen's warm breath on her neck. His arm was draped across her as he held her against his chest. Her heart started to race. But he was breathing so slow and steady; it was clear he was asleep.

She lay still as a stone. If she moved and awakened him, he'd take his arm away, and that was the last thing she wanted. That arm made her feel wanted and protected.

What would it be like to lie with Galen as her husband? No man had ever treated her like he did: respected as a person, valued as a friend, admired for herself and not for whose daughter she was.

That thought drew a broad smile. Then it faded. She was expected to marry the man selected by her father, the warrior son of another chieftain. Would her husband be rough and demanding? Would he be like her own father, drinking too much before coming to her, then only caring about his own pleasure?

Galen would never come to her drunk. He'd never hurt her or make her do anything that wouldn't give pleasure to both of them.

He rolled over, pulling his arm across her arm as he turned.

Adela fought the sigh. That was much too soon. Then his breathing slowed. He was sound asleep again, not likely to wake easily.

She rolled over and snuggled against his back, draping her arm over him ever so slowly so she wouldn't awaken him.

In his sleep, his arm moved to hold hers against his chest. His hand settled over her own. Her smile returned. What would it be like if it was warm and her arm could rest against his bare chest instead of a shirt and tunic? But if it was warm, he would never have let himself sleep next to her like this.

Her breathing synchronized with his, and her smile broadened.

Being with him on this quest to rescue his friend had turned into the best time of her life, despite the horrible beginning. Despite the long days in the saddle, poor food, hard ground, and cold nights.

For Galen's sake, she wanted to find his friend safe and rescue him... but not too soon.

Chapter 19

Day 13

When Adela opened her eyes, white clouds of frozen breath greeted her.

Galen was gone. She lifted herself on one elbow and pulled her cloak up around her shoulders. Somewhere below her, she could hear him humming. She rose to her knees and peered over the edge of the loft.

Galen was in the stall below, brushing Astrelo. The rustling of the straw as she stood drew his gaze. Then it drew his smile.

"Good morning. I hope you slept as well as I did."

"I did." The thought of his arm around her drifted through her mind. "Maybe even better."

Astrelo bumped him to demand more brushing. Galen obeyed, but he turned his eyes back on her after each stroke.

"Thank you for trusting me enough to share the blankets. It would have been too cold sleeping alone."

"I trust you as much as any man could deserve."

That drew his chuckle. "Given some of the men you've met lately, that's not saying much."

If only he knew how much she meant those words.

◆

The stable boy entered, bearing two steaming bowls of porridge on a tray. Galen took it and paid him as Adela leaned over the edge of the loft. A gust of wind came through the broken shutter, and her hair swirled against her cheeks. Then she pulled it back and tied it with the blue ribbon that matched her eyes.

Galen turned his eyes away, and she climbed down the ladder.

He raised a bowl closer to his nose and inhaled. "Not as good as my sister's, but much better than what's in the food sack. Tonight, we'll stay in Augusta Praetoria and get a hot meal at an inn." He bounced his eyebrows. "I do like roast rabbit, but there won't be time for my Hermunduri hunter to snare us one. Plus, we won't have the wildland like we've been riding through north of the pass. Much of Italia is under the plow or covered with orchards and vineyards."

After they'd eaten, they saddled up and headed south. As they passed a stone marker, Galen pointed down at it.

"What's the number there?"

Adela glanced at it. "XXIII. That's twenty-three."

"That tells us how far it is to Augusta Praetoria. Going down should be easier than coming up, but I still want a good rest for the horses today and another hot bath for us."

Adela pointed at the stone building rising a short distance from the *mansio*. "What's that?"

"Someone built a temple to honor Jupiter Poeninus." Her head tipped, a question in her eyes. "That's a combination of the main Roman god and a Celtic god worshipped here before Rome claimed the pass."

"What are those people doing?" A small group waited on horseback as the oldest of their party came from the temple.

"Probably leaving an offering to ensure a safe trip over the pass."

"Do we need to do that? We're only halfway."

A crooked grin punctuated his chuckle. "No. A Roman god can't guarantee our safety on the pass...or anywhere else."

As he opened his mouth to tell her which God could, a troop of Roman cavalry rode up beside him. The officer's stallion was draped with the Roman military harness of leather strips with bronze medallions at their crossings; it would have been a proud addition to Val's herd. The officer himself, with his metal body armor and red horsehair crest atop a gleaming brass helmet, was almost as magnificent.

The tribune reined in beside Galen. His gaze raked Galen from head to foot. Disdain twisted his mouth into a smiling frown. That vanished when his calculating eyes took Astrelo's measure before shifting to Otto's stallion.

Galen's shoulders tensed. He couldn't afford to have either horse taken by military seizure. "*Salve.* I see you appreciate good horses. That's a fine animal you're riding, but we citizens of Rome deserve the best. Where did you buy him?"

The tribune's eyes lost their predatory gleam when Galen said 'citizen.' "From the best stable in Rome."

"I breed horses. I'm always looking for good brood stock. The name of the stable?"

"It belongs to Tiberius Cornelius Lentulus."

"I'll have to visit it this trip." Galen suppressed a wry smile. Visit the former governor of Germania Superior who made it a capital crime to follow Jesus? Not likely.

The tribune nodded once and nudged his horse into a fast walk. The two younger officers and sixteen cavalrymen followed suit.

Astrelo snorted, and Galen reined to the side of the road to give them more room to pass.

As he considered whether it was wise to talk about the only God with real power while a cavalry troop rode so close to them, Adela's arm shot out, her finger pointing.

"That lake is still frozen. Look at how the ice sparkles." She urged her horse off the road for a closer view.

Galen blew out the breath he was half-holding. It would be unwise to tell her about God with soldiers so close. But their presence did mean he wouldn't have to worry about bandits. His God could protect him from hazards on any trip...and it looked like He just did.

Augusta Praetoria, Day 14

The sweeping vistas of distant peaks near the top of the pass gave Adela the hawk-like feeling again, but she was glad to trade it for the warmth of the sheltering forest at lower elevation. It was the middle of the afternoon when they finally rode toward the stone wall surrounding Augusta Praetoria. It stood more than three times the height of the legionaries standing guard by the arched gate.

Adela's eyes widened. "The whole town looks like a legion fortress." She turned a smile on Galen. "But Roman warriors are safe for Romans... and the one a Roman is protecting."

"And they're good to ask questions when you want honest answers. Listen and remember what I ask next."

He rode past the man standing outside the gate and reined in by the men standing at ease inside. "*Ubi honestum diversorium?*"

A flow of words and some gesturing by a legionary earned a thank you from Galen. Then he led her into the city.

"The most important word was *honestum*. It means respectable. When you ask for a place to stay or eat, be sure to use it. Most use *caupona* for an inn, but that might get you sent to a place like the one at the top of the pass." His forehead furrowed. "That's not a problem for a man but for you...not a good choice."

Adela followed Galen as he wove through the streets. She scanned the signs on the shops. Here and there, she saw a word she knew.

He was about to enter the stable yard of an inn when he turned in his saddle and pointed across the street. Above an arched entryway hung a sign that said "Thermae." His eyebrows bounced as the corner of his mouth pulled up into a smile. His smile broadened when she nodded.

A stable for the horses and a respectable inn for them. Add to that a visit to the bath and a tasty hot meal, and it would be a good evening.

But she would rather be cold at the top of the pass with his arm wrapped over her than warm in a soft bed without it.

Day 15

It was a four-day ride from Augusta Praetoria to Ticinum. The route through the foothills along the Duria Major river had been pretty and an easy ride. But after two days, they'd left the hills behind, and now they rode across a plain covered with farms and large estates.

After the wild beauty of the Alps, Adela would have been bored to tears if it weren't for Galen. He pronounced the Latin name of each new thing that came into view in a solemn voice, with a grand sweep of his hand toward it for good measure. More than once, he'd pulled a giggle out of her when he announced something as unimportant as a fence post as if it were a temple column.

They stopped by a stream to water the horses, and Galen placed his hand on his chest as if he were about to make a speech to the tribal leaders.

"Adela of the Hermunduri, I proclaim you the best student of Latin I have ever taught, and I declare you ready to learn the mysteries of the many forms of the words that describe what we do."

"All fourteen of them?" She fought the giggle again. "With six versions each?"

Galen relaxed in the saddle. "Not all fourteen. Not yet, but we can get started on the most useful ones. There are five main patterns, but they aren't all that different."

He rubbed his cheek without the cut. "I'll take an example of each, and we'll add their endings. *Amo, amare*...no, that's not a good one for you."

Her eyebrow rose at his chuckle. "Why isn't that one for me?"

"*Amo, amas, amat.* It means I like, you like, she likes something. But you'd never be saying *amo* to a Roman sentry when you ask directions. You probably shouldn't say that to anyone. They might get the wrong idea about you."

His brow furrowed. "I know what you might find useful from the first pattern. The word asking for help. *Iuva me* means 'help me.' You can put *ad* at the front to make *adiuva me*, and it still means the same thing."

Adela clasped her hands and made her voice quaver. "*Iuva me.*"

His laugh startled Astrelo, and the stallion swung his head to look back at his master.

Galen patted his neck. "Who could resist that plea? But you still need to learn the rest of the first pattern." His hand settled on his chest as he raised his chin. "*Iuvo, iuvas, iuvat, iuvamus, iuvatis, iuvant.*"

His eyes warmed as Adela repeated it several times. Then he nudged Astrelo into a walk.

As the horses began to trot, Galen's lips curved into that slight smile Adela found so appealing.

Any woman could say *amo* to Galen and mean exactly what she said.

Chapter 20

Nothing to Worry About

Ticinum, Day 17

After hours in the saddle, Adela and Galen finally crossed the bridge over the Flumen Ticinum. The sun was low on the horizon, and it painted the white buildings of the town ahead with a soft pink.

It was pretty, but Adela preferred the sunset pink on the snow-capped peaks of the Alpes. The rivers of the high mountains had been rushing cascades that made it hard to hear anything but their swirling waters. The Ticinum was the same as the other two rivers they'd crossed since reaching the plain: quiet, with a placid surface more like a lake than a river.

Galen flexed his shoulders. "It's been a long ride from Augusta Praetoria, but we're two thirds of the way to Parma now. At least the flat is easy on the horses."

"And boring for the people. I like the mountains better."

Galen pointed toward the mountains rising to the south. "We have some more to cross before we get to Otto."

The buildings grew taller in the distance.

He pushed back the strand of hair that was always falling onto his forehead. "It's hard to believe it was eighteen days ago I met you. It seems like forever...and yesterday. Funny how time does that." The corner of his mouth turned up. "I should have been home two weeks ago. When I left, I never expected I'd be taking my first trip to Italia since I was six."

"You weren't born in Germania?"

"No. We had an estate north of Rome. But Germania is my real home. I'll be glad to get back to my family."

Adela said nothing. She'd been so eager to return home to Father when Gundahar first took her. Since Brigantium, doubt about what had happened nibbled at that desire. And the mouse that nibbled had grown into a rat that gnawed the last two days. It should be the time for her days of a woman, but nothing was happening yet. With each day that passed, the words of Gundahar as the soldiers dragged him away rang louder at the back of her head.

She dragged her thoughts back to what Galen was saying.

"Too late for the baths, but a good night's sleep will be enough for tonight."

"Tonight, I should take the floor and you take the bed. It's only fair."

"I've dragged you halfway across the Empire, and you never complain. For that you deserve the bed. Besides, I'd keep hearing my sister's voice if I traded."

He rested one fist on his hip and shook his finger at Adela as he raised the pitch of his voice. "Galen, what were you thinking?"

Adela nearly choked, trying not to laugh.

His deep voice returned to normal. "She's mothered me since I was ten, and she prides herself on training me to know how to treat a woman."

They'd reached the city gate. No sentry stood guard, so Galen turned Astrelo toward the line of shops. At a *taberna*, he slid off the horse.

Adela kept her gaze fixed on him as he talked with the owner to learn where they might spend the night. A smile played at the corners of her mouth. His sister had every right to be proud of the man Galen had become.

Adela wrapped her arms around her head to protect it from the stones. Hildegard stood by her father, her face twisted with a mixture of anger and pleasure as Father threw another stone. "Take that man's child and leave this village."

She fell to her knees when the next stone hit. Her lips quivered as she reached out to Father. "I didn't choose this. I couldn't stop him. Father, please!"

He picked up a larger stone. "Never call me that. I have no daughter now."

As he hurled it at her head, Adela screamed...and jerked awake.

When her eyes opened, Galen stood beside her. She swung her feet off the bed before burying her face in her hands.

His voice was gentle. "Are you all right?"

Shivers rippled through her body. He left her side and returned with her cloak. He draped it around her shoulders. Then he sat beside her and wrapped his arm around her.

"It's only a dream. You're safe here with me."

Dim moonlight came through the small window near the ceiling. The pale rays lit his face. No trace of a smile there, and concern clouded his eyes. She was safe with him now, but what about when she returned home? What if she was carrying Gundahar's child?

His free hand pushed a loose strand of hair behind her ear. "Don't be afraid. I'm here."

She turned and slipped both arms around his chest. He wrapped his second arm around her and drew her close.

"Dreams aren't real. You don't have to be scared. I'll keep you safe."

His arms around her did make her feel safe. But what if the dream really was a vision of her future? She fought the tears...and lost.

As her chest jerked and the tears rolled down her cheeks, he kept her wrapped in his arms and started rocking.

"Shhh. There's nothing to worry about. Dreams aren't real, and this one is over."

She took a deep breath and held it. When she finally released it, she had the tears under control...almost.

As her cheek rested on his shoulder, he lifted his hand to rest it on the back of her head.

"What did you dream?"

She shook her head. It hurt too much to think about, let alone speak it.

Galen kept rocking. "Whenever you want to tell me, I'll listen. It can help just to speak the pain and fear."

The tears had stopped, and the silent sobs had quieted, but she kept her arms around him so his would stay around her. It was almost like being in Mother's arms again, except his were so much stronger and resting her cheek on his shoulder made her heart beat faster.

Galen was such a kind man. He would be a wonderful husband, so much better than the aggressive warrior she always thought she wanted. But if she was carrying Gundahar's child, not even a kind man like Galen would want her.

But maybe she wasn't with child. Sometimes the days of a woman were late for no particular reason. When her mother grew sick, her days were often two or three weeks late. It wasn't even a week. Maybe there really was nothing to worry about.

Chapter 21

Perhaps a Future

North of Futa Pass, Day 19

The old mare Brutus had purchased for Otto to ride was wearing out after crossing the Alpes and carrying a big man like him for ten days. Brutus called another stop to rest the horses.

Florentia was only two days away, just across the mountains they were now crossing. Otto had watched for any opportunity to break free, but none had presented itself. Each time his legs were unshackled for him to dismount, Brutus ordered them chained again when his feet hit the ground.

As the horses grazed in the long grass by a stream, Otto's eyes scanned the road they'd just travelled.

His back straightened. On the hill opposite them, a distant rider appeared. The short man on a tall, dark horse disappeared behind a clump of trees. Otto's heart pumped faster as he waited for the man to reappear.

And when he did…it wasn't Galen. It was only a youth mounted on a dark brown horse.

Despair gnawed at the edges of his mind. Then he lifted his chin. Galen would never abandon him to slavery and certain death. Galen must be alive; he was too smart to let himself get into a situation where he'd get killed easily. And Galen would find him and set him free.

Otto closed his eyes. No matter how impossible it seemed for Galen to come, he would hang on to that hope. Without hope, a man trapped in slavery might as well die.

Florentia, Day 21

It was late afternoon when Florentia came into view. Otto's gaze focused on the wooden amphitheater. It was at least twice as large as the one in Octodurus. Brutus reined in and dropped back to ride beside him. He pointed at a large brick building next to it.

"There's your new home, Bjorn. Ludus Florentiae." His hand swept toward the amphitheater. "And in there lies your chance to show the men of Florentia how a true master of the gladius fights."

Otto snorted. "It's wood. I expected more so close to Rome. Even the arena in Octodurus was stone."

"Wood, stone, it doesn't matter when you're on the sand. There's talk of a new stone amphitheater that will be built east of the city in a couple of years. If the goddess Fortuna smiles on you, you'll live long enough to fight in it."

A crooked smile punctuated his words before Brutus kicked his horse and trotted ahead.

Otto didn't believe in the Roman gods. Fortuna had no control over his future, but if he was lucky, Galen would be there to free him long before he saw the first stone laid.

North of Cisa Pass, Day 21

Galen turned in his saddle to face Adela. "One more night sleeping under the stars this side of Cisa Pass didn't sound bad to me when we left Forum Novum." He scanned the ominous bank of clouds hovering over the mountains ahead. "Now I'm not so sure. I'd like it better if we ended the day with flaming orange clouds and the promise of a clear night instead of that."

Adela eyed the rain clouds, and they almost brought a smile. It wouldn't be a night of sleeping on opposite sides of a firepit if she could help it.

"At least we have trees, and it isn't snowing. Much better than the pass in the Alpes. We can use the lead ropes you still have. The trees are thick enough here. If we stretch them between two pairs of trees, we can drape one set of blankets over them to make a canopy. That should keep us dry if it rains in the night."

She pointed to a rock outcrop a short distance off the road. "And if we do it over there, the rocks will block most of the wind."

Galen rubbed his mouth. "We'd have to split the second bedroll, but with the cloaks, it might work."

Proposing a logical solution to Galen was like baiting a snare on a game trail. How could he resist?

"I have a better plan. My cloak is too short to cover me. But if we share the bedroll like we did at Summus Poeninus, we can cover our feet and legs with one cloak and the rest of us with the other."

Galen's eyebrow shot up.

Before he could object, Adela pressed her point home. "It would be silly for us to sleep apart and be cold when we can share and be warm."

His mouth twitched. Was he fighting a smile himself? "You trusted me once. You can trust me again. Let's set up the canopy before those clouds get here."

Adela reined her horse toward the rocks. Her smile grew broader as she contemplated another night snuggled next to Galen, basking in his warmth and under the comforting weight of his arm.

An owl hooted in the tree above him, and Galen's eyes popped open. He held his breath as he listened to the sounds of darkness. Nothing was moving in the woods nearby, but something much closer made him freeze.

Adela's arm was wrapped across his chest. She was snuggled up against his back, and he felt the heat rise as she drew the slow breaths of deep sleep.

He wouldn't try to move her arm. That would awaken her, and after so long in the saddle yesterday, he didn't want to disturb the rest they both needed. Part of the time, she'd been too quiet, like her mind was a thousand *stadia* away. Each time he said something to her, she perked up, but maybe that was only an act.

Moving at a caterpillar's pace, he placed his hand over hers. She stirred, but only to snuggle in closer. Her breathing paused, then resumed at a slow, measured pace.

Galen willed his own breathing to slow. That he could control. His heart rate...not so easy, but with many deep breaths, he finally managed.

Adela was a truly beautiful woman. Strong and smart with a sense of humor that appreciated the quirks of his own. The kind of woman any man would be proud to make his wife.

Almost any man. She was also a pagan. Like his sister Val before him, he would never marry someone who didn't follow the Way.

God, you know how much Adela attracts me. It's you above all others, but is she the one you intend for me? Did you have me rescue her because she's meant to be your follower, too? If she is your will for me, please give me a sign.

Her hand slid farther across his chest, pulling her body snug against his own and ramping up his heart rate again.

He closed his eyes, and a smile grew as he contemplated the possibilities. She'd be the perfect wife, if only she followed the Way. The right time to tell her about Jesus would come. If she was willing to listen, perhaps God had a future for them that Galen had never planned.

Chapter 22

A CAREER OPPORTUNITY

Florentia, Day 22

Brutus sat near the top of the wooden benches overlooking the small arena at the Ludus Florentiae, watching his latest purchase spar. His opponent was one of the veterans whose skill with a gladius had earned him the position of *doctor*, a trainer of less-skilled fighters. For half an hour, he'd been watching Bjorn the Langobardi parry every slash and thrust and slip past the doctor's guard to touch him with the wooden practice sword.

In real combat with a steel sword, the doctor would be dead twenty times over.

Brutus rubbed his fresh-shaven cheek, and his eyes narrowed. In Octodurus, Bjorn had killed three men with only twice as many strokes. With no obvious effort, he was besting a man who'd survived eight years on the sand. What was the most profitable way to use such skill?

His lanista, Ursus, climbed the rows of benches and settled next to him with a grunt.

Brutus tipped his head toward the tall German. "Impressive."

Ursus pushed his cheek out with his tongue as he ran a hand through his red hair. "Yes, but there is a problem."

Brutus's brow furrowed as his gaze shifted from Bjorn to Ursus. "And that would be?"

Ursus's lips tightened. "He is good with a gladius, but that is all he knows. He has never been in battle. He has never fought with a shield or a longer sword. He is big and strong and, as far as I can tell, smart. But

123

he has told me more than once he was kidnapped and he should not be a gladiator. I think there is a stubbornness there that might make him hard to train. Any stallion can be broken, but a man…what it takes to break some makes them useless when you are done. He might be one of those."

Brutus rested one arm across his stomach to make a resting place for his other elbow. Then he tapped his lips with a closed fist. "But with that much talent, even with only a gladius, there's money to be made from him. But perhaps not here and perhaps not in the ordinary way."

Three more taps of his fist on his lips. "Send him up here."

◆

Otto flexed his shoulders as the trainer walked away. It had been easy to parry every strike and get through with his own fake sword, but each time he did, the trainer's eyes grew angrier. But what did the man expect? He wasn't going to pretend he couldn't fight as well as he could.

A bucket of water sat on a stool by the wall. Otto strolled over and picked up the dipper hanging on its side. As he swallowed the tepid water that tasted like pond scum, footsteps approached from behind.

"Bjorn."

Otto turned to face Ursus. "My name is Otto, son of Baldric of the Vangiones."

That drew the lanista's scowl. "Your name is whatever I call you, and in my ludus, you are Bjorn."

Otto's reply froze on his lips as the lanista fingered a three-corded whip that hung from his belt. The name Ursus called him wasn't worth a lashing.

The lanista directed his thumb toward the benches, where Brutus lounged on one while his arms spread out to rest on the bench above. "Your owner wants to talk with you."

Otto's eyes raked Ursus before he lifted them to focus on Brutus. The only owner he had was himself. But speaking that truth wasn't worth a lashing either.

Otto climbed the tiers of benches until he stood below Brutus on a bench that put his eyes above Brutus's. Otto was used to looking down at other men, and Brutus was no exception, even if he did think he owned Otto.

Brutus patted the bench beside him. "Sit. We need to talk."

Otto moved up to Brutus's level and settled onto the bench. For a man who thought he owned him to speak like he would to an equal…that triggered a wave of suspicion.

Brutus shifted to face him, and Otto did the same.

"Where did you get your training with the gladius?"

"Germania Superior."

"Who taught you?"

"The husband of my trading partner's sister. He fought with a legion there. I've told you I'm Otto, son of Baldric of the Vangiones. My partner and I were selling horses in Argentorate when I was kidnapped. I shouldn't be in this arena at all. I'm a free man, and you should let me return home."

The corner of Brutus's mouth pulled up as he swept away Otto's words with a flick of his hand. "I paid 1200 denarii for you. I have a certified bill of sale from the questor in Octodurus. You may not think you're Bjorn of the Langobardi, but you're anything I want to call you until you fight so well in the arena that some sponsor of the games decides to free you and pays the price I set on you."

Otto's jaw clenched as he bit back the words he wanted to spit at the arrogant Roman who thought he owned him.

Brutus's mouth curved into a crooked smile. "I've been watching you, and you present an... opportunity. And I'm not one to waste an unusual opportunity."

Otto's brow furrowed.

Brutus rubbed his palms together. "You killed too quickly in Octodurus, but your skill at sparring without going for the kill is unusual, to say the least. I can use that to both our advantages. A new gladiator trains for the first year so he can fight well enough to please the crowd in his first bout. I get paid if you die, although I prefer to earn money from the organizers of the games with wins instead of deaths."

He shrugged. "But there are ways to make money long before your first real fight in the arena, if you're smart enough to do what you're told and don't cause any trouble."

Otto's head popped back. "I've had my first real fight."

Brutus shook his head. "That was only a three-on-three with arena fodder. The real fights are one-on-ones between professionals. If you fought today, you'd die. Your skill with the gladius is impressive, but Ursus tells me you know nothing about using a shield as a weapon or how to fight a man who knows how to keep you too far away to kill with a gladius."

Otto rubbed his lips. "He's right."

"If I leave you here in Florentia, Ursus will train you until you use a shield well enough to have a chance of surviving a bout with a seasoned gladiator. Then he'll book you into the games, just like all the other gladiators trying not to die in one-on-one combat."

Otto drew a deep breath and held it before releasing it slowly.

Brutus crossed his arms. "But I have a better use for you if I take you to the ludus in Roma."

Otto's eyebrow rose. "And that would be…?"

"Roma is gladiator-mad. All the young men of the senatorial and equestrian orders want to fight like one. And that means many want to spar with one. Some want to impress their friends. Others, it's their fathers who want them trained before they join the legion and might need the skill to stay alive."

Brutus shrugged. "Why doesn't matter to me. But with a man like you, who can spar legion-style without hurting them, who speaks good enough Latin to give instructions as their personal trainer, I can charge high rates for the privilege of joining you in the practice arena at the ludus."

Otto's mouth turned down. "But it wouldn't be my money. Why should I want to risk dying if some young Roman nobleman happens to get a lucky thrust in? You'd kill me if I hurt him to stop it."

Brutus's eyes turned icy. "Death is certain if you don't cooperate." They thawed, and he shrugged again. "If you do, and the customers are satisfied enough to bring their friends to us, you might get a small share of the earnings."

This Roman reeked of the arrogance Otto hated when selling horses, but he was in no position to bargain. "Sounds reasonable. What you propose interests me."

Brutus's eyes warmed. "I thought you might be smart enough to appreciate this opportunity."

Otto allowed his face to mirror Brutus's. "My father raised no fools."

The corner of Brutus's mouth lifted. "Another advantage of being in the ludus in Roma is the visits from the noblewomen who like to watch gladiators train. Nothing pleases them more than a big, handsome German like you. Your Latin will make it more pleasant for those who want personal time with you as well. We charge fees for the entertainment.

"And there are some women who like to spar like the men do." Brutus's mouth pulled sideways. "I don't understand why any woman would want to fight like a man, but some do."

Otto choked down a laugh. It took no imagination to see why a Roman woman might want to kill a Roman man, with a sword or otherwise. "German women are fighters, just like their men. I see nothing wrong with Roman women wanting the skill." A grin tried to escape. "Maybe some have husbands they'd rather keep away at sword point. Maybe some would like to use a sword to stop any future visits. But I have heard that poison is more in fashion among Roman women when it comes to getting rid of a man."

Brutus chuckled. "I think the women will like your sense of humor, too." He slapped his knees and stood. "So, we'll ride on to Roma tomorrow."

Otto tried to keep his face straight. Each time on the road presented a fresh opportunity for escape. "It will feel good to ride without shackles again."

Brutus snorted. "I'm not stupid enough to let a slave who tried so hard to escape in Octodurus and who claims to be free ride without shackles and a lead rope on his horse. But in time, if you prove you're trustworthy, you can earn the privilege of a few freedoms in Roma."

Otto shrugged. "I think going to Rome is a good plan, and I'll gladly be the sparring partner of any Roman willing to pay you for it. I won't waste this opportunity."

"Good." Brutus flicked his hand. "Go back to your practice. We leave for Roma first thing in the morning."

As Otto stepped from bench to bench on his way back to the sand, his lips tightened. He was only a slave in Brutus's eyes, but he would never be one in his own. And even this Roman would see him as a free man again, if only Galen would come.

Chapter 23

IT'S MY PLEASURE

South of Cisa Pass, Day 22

Adela stretched as she gazed across the open meadow surrounded by forest that flanked the road. She gave Galen her brightest smile as he rode beside her.

"The Alpes take my breath, but I like these mountains better. It's no colder than at home and prettier with the trees."

Galen craned his neck to look ahead. "I keep expecting a break in the trees so we can see something."

Her brow furrowed. "See something?"

"Yes." He pointed down the road to where blue sky touched the ground. "And I think it might be right up there."

Galen kicked Astrelo into a trot, and Adela followed. As they topped the small rise, she gasped.

"What is that?" A blue expanse stretched out before them. "It takes up half the earth and stretches as far as I can see."

Galen beamed. "That, my dear Adela, is the sea."

Her hand shot up to cover her mouth. "I thought Lacus Brigantinus was big, but this is...huge, and it's so blue."

"It is, and Luna is on its shore. We'll be there sometime tomorrow."

Adela pulled her gaze from the blue water and focused on Galen. "How did you know this was here? How do you know so much about so many things?"

"One of the scrolls I have at home describes the western coast of Italia. I knew we must be getting close enough to see it. That's one good thing about being able to read. It can seem like you've been places you've never gone."

The corner of his mouth pulled up, like it always did when he was about to make a joke. "And when we get there, a surprise awaits you."

"What?"

He chuckled. "You always ask, but I can't tell you. Then it wouldn't be a surprise."

They sat for a long moment, gazing at the expanse of blue.

Galen turned contented eyes on her. "Seen enough for now?"

She nodded. He nudged his horse, and they started down the slope. She kept her eyes on the blue water until they entered the woods again.

Adela glanced at Galen's profile as he rode close beside her. The trace of a smile that she'd come to love curved his lips. It was almost impossible not to smile herself.

So many things with him were surprises, and almost every one delighted her.

If she could freeze time, she would. Nothing could be better than riding cross country with him, seeing things she never dreamed existed, learning so much, laughing at his antics and jokes.

Nothing could be better, except lying with him every night as his wife.

Luna, Day 23

As Galen and Adela rode into Luna, they passed a Roman temple. Adela turned in her saddle to keep her eyes on it as they rode past.

"We've seen so many of these temples for the Roman gods. My mother was from a chieftain family of the Suebi. She taught me to worship Nerthus, the goddess of her people. Nerthus doesn't need men to build her a temple. A sacred grove is where she wants her followers to worship."

"My God doesn't need temples made by men, either."

Adela nodded, then pointed at the amphitheater. "The Romans build almost as many of those. Are the ones who die there offered to the Roman gods?"

"There is a sacrifice at the start, but the games are mostly to entertain the crowds. They sometimes kill the followers of Jesus as punishment for refusing to worship the Roman gods. They think their gods will be offended by the refusal."

A deep frown curved Adela's mouth down. "I can't forget that man on the cross in Octodurus." She rubbed the back of her neck. "The Romans are too much like their gods, cruel with a lust for human blood." She turned her head away from him and spat.

Galen's pulse ramped up. A door was opening. "My God isn't like that."

Before he could say more, Adela shook her head. "Enough talk about gods. I don't want to think about them." She nudged her horse into a trot.

Galen drew a deep breath and released it as a sigh. *God, please open her mind to hear. Give me a chance to tell her about You before I take her home. Then help her decide to follow the Way...like me.*

He relaxed in the saddle as he urged Astrelo to follow. Even if they found Otto in Luna, it would be almost four weeks before they could reach her village in Hermunduri country. Surely four weeks would be enough for God to claim her heart.

They reined in at the ludus just east of the amphitheater.

Galen grinned as he swung his leg over Astrelo's neck and slid off. "If Otto's here, we'll be celebrating tonight."

As he passed through the entrance, the sound of wood striking wood led him toward the practice arena. The lanista stood, arms crossed, watching several men practicing at the vertical posts around the edge.

The man turned when Galen cleared his throat. "*Salve.* I'm looking for the ludus of Marcus Antonius Brutus. Is this it?"

"No, but I know him. He comes here to look for new men for his ludi in Florentia and Roma."

Galen rubbed the fresh scar on his cheek. "So, if I'm looking for one of his gladiators, I go to Florentia? How long to get there?"

"About two and a half days up the Via Aemiliana Scauri, but he has a ludus in Luca, too. That's only a day on the same road."

Galen's shoulders drooped. Another two and a half days. Then he squared them. But maybe it was only one, and even if it was two and a half, Otto wouldn't be fighting before he could get to him.

"*Gratias tibi.*"

The lanista nodded a reply before turning back to watch his men.

◆

As Galen disappeared into the ludus, Adela drew a deep breath and held it. If his friend was here, Galen would be happy, but it would be the start of the end of their time together. Four weeks, and she would never see him again. She would be back with her father, and soon he would find her a husband.

No one Father would choose could be as kind and smart and funny as Galen. That thought tugged hard on her heart.

And the niggling fear wormed its way into her thoughts again. It was now a week since her days of a woman should have come. Mother's had been later when she was sick, but Adela couldn't remember ever feeling better.

She closed her eyes and buried her face in her hands.

She jumped when she felt the hand on her foot. Her eyelids popped open. Galen stood beside her, his brow furrowed.

"Is something wrong?"

She forced a smile. "No. Is he here?

Galen's mouth turned down as his gaze locked onto her eyes.

She looked away. He'd be asking again if he saw the worry there.

He patted her foot. "No, but the lanista knows the man who bought him. Otto should be in one of his three ludi. So, I guess our tour of Italia isn't over yet. We'll start with Luna, then Florentia." His shoulders and eyebrows rose together, then dropped. "And if we have to, on to Rome."

Adela tried to keep her smile small. Galen must be disappointed, and he wouldn't understand why his failure here could make her happy.

He'd left his hand on her foot, and he gave it a gentle squeeze. "We've been traveling without a break for too long. The horses need a day of rest, and I think we could use one, too. This is as good a place as any for that."

Adela fought the smile that kept trying to grow. "Whatever you think is best."

"Let's go find a…" He held his hand out and flicked his fingers to draw out her answer.

"Honestum diversorium."

"For our horses and us, and then we'll go to the…" His fingers asked for the next word.

"Thermae."

"To get cleaned up before a good, hot dinner."

He walked around her horse and mounted his. "Then tomorrow, while the horses spend a restful day in their stalls, we'll explore Luna."

As Galen led the way to the market area to ask directions, Adela let her smile break free. A day exploring with Galen…nothing could be better than that.

He dismounted first by a woman working a loom. Adela caught a word here and there, but most were new to her.

"Adela, come over here."

She slid from her horse and tied him to Astrelo's saddle.

As she stood beside Galen, the weaver chattered away about something, and he nodded. The weaver stepped into the room behind the shop and returned with some folded blue cloth.

When she shook it open and held it up to Adela, Adela's breath caught. It was a long-sleeved tunic that reached almost to her ankles. The neck was shaped like a V, and a garland of blue and white flowers was stitched around the V.

"It's beautiful, but it must cost too much."

Galen's usual smile widened into a grin. "I can't be leading you around Luna dressed like me. Now that we're back in the civilized world, I thought you'd enjoy dressing like a pretty woman again." He drew a breath between his teeth. "Not that you aren't pretty even in my clothes... but I thought you'd like this better."

Adela stroked the crisp fabric. "What is this made from?"

"Linen. It can get hot in Italia, and linen is cooler than wool."

He spoke some more Latin, and the weaver handed Adela a sash of darker blue.

Adela's eyes widened. "This is too much."

Galen's eyes crinkled. "A piece of rope won't do for a belt on a lady's tunic."

Adela's smile turned into a grin. "*Gratias tibi tam.*"

"*Voluptas meus est.* That means it's my pleasure...or delight."

He turned to pay the weaver as Adela's finger traced the dark blue flowers. That was a phrase she would remember. For every moment she spent with this kind man with laughing eyes, she could shout it to the sky. *Voluptas meus est.*

Chapter 24

A Day of Rest

Florentia, Day 23

Brutus leaned against the wall with his arms crossed as he watched Ursus shackle Otto's wrists. "It will be a month, maybe two before I come to Florentia again. The Dacian might be ready to transfer to Roma by then. I'll be needing some that are expendable to fight in the games at Saturnalia."

Otto kept his jaw from clenching, but it was hard to stomach a Roman talking about a man as if he were an animal fattening for slaughter.

Brutus stepped away from the wall and summoned Otto to follow him with a snap and a flick of his fingers. Again, Otto forced his jaw muscles to relax. No Roman had the right to command him to heel as if he were a dog.

When they stepped through the ludus door into the sunshine, the same two bodyguards awaited them with four horses.

Otto's head snapped back. Three were the horses Brutus and his bodyguards had ridden from Octodurus, but in place of the sway-backed mare stood a prime stallion.

Otto turned to Brutus, who walked beside him. "I breed horses. That's a fine stallion, one I wouldn't be ashamed to take to the Roman garrisons to sell."

Brutus glanced at him. "I want to get to Roma quickly, and that mare would slow me down. With good horses, it's a ride of four and a half days. I'll make a profit when I sell him in Roma." He rubbed his freshly shaven cheek. "I want to get you cleaned up before we go to the ludus.

We should be at the Baths of Trajan midday. It's women bathing in the morning, men in the afternoon. I'd like you to catch the eye of the women who are regular visitors to the ludus...and especially of those who aren't. The men will notice a fine horse, and I want to get them curious about what I'm bringing to Ludus Bruti as soon as possible. A few conversations while I show you off should start the clients coming."

Otto looked away, trying to mask his thoughts. Unchained in a public bath. That would be the first time he wasn't tied or caged since Gundahar took him.

Brutus's laugh was more of a snort. "Don't think that will be an opportunity to escape. Rufus and Africanus will be right next to you the whole time."

As always, Africanus held the horse's lead rope while Otto mounted. Rufus clamped the shackle ring around his right ankle, then tossed the chain under the horse. But this was no tired, old mare. The stallion shied when the ring and chain hit the ground under its belly. It knocked Rufus to the ground, and he scrambled away to avoid the dancing hooves. Brutus stepped over and stroked the horse's neck. It calmed at his touch. He slipped the second ring around Otto's free ankle and locked it.

Otto's knees gripped the horse's sides, and the chain jingled. The stallion shied again, but this time the noise moved with him. His eyes flared, and his sideways dancing turned into hooves flailing the air.

Even with his hands shackled, Otto had no trouble staying mounted. When the stallion's hooves hit the ground again, he leaned forward to put his lips by the horse's ear.

"Calm, boy. Steady, boy." He gathered the chain between his wrists in one hand so it wouldn't jingle and stroked the horse's neck.

The lead rope was long, and Africanus had moved the full length of it away from the frightened animal.

Otto straightened, and the horse started fidgeting again as the chain links under its belly jingled every time it moved.

Brutus rubbed the back of his neck. "I bought the wrong horse."

Otto bent close to the horse's ear again. "That's a good boy. Calm down. Steady now."

The stallion shuddered, then relaxed.

Otto straightened and fixed his gaze on Brutus. "The horse will be a problem as long as my legs are shackled, but I can keep him calm if they aren't."

Brutus's head tipped as his gaze flipped between Otto and the horse. "Rufus, take the leg shackles off."

As the redhead moved to obey, Otto fought to suppress a smile. Wrist shackles alone wouldn't stop him from making a break for freedom. He sat on a horse at least as good as the one Brutus rode and better than the bodyguards' mounts.

Brutus's eyes narrowed. "I know what you're thinking, Bjorn." He rubbed his lip. "And I'm not giving you that chance." He turned to Ursus. "Get some rope. That's as good as a chain but without the noise."

The Roman's mouth curved into a smile, but the chill in his eyes left no doubt of his irritation. "Only a fool would risk losing the opportunity I'm giving you." He crossed his arms. "You told me your father raised no fools. This is your one chance to prove it. Do I leave you here to train to fight and die, or do you willingly come with me to Roma to train others and live?"

Otto's brow furrowed as he studied Brutus. Then he made his face relax. "I'm no fool. I'll go to Rome."

The lanista returned with a five-foot length of rope. He wrapped it several times around Otto's right ankle before tying a knot. Then he flipped it under the stallion's belly and tied his left ankle.

Brutus slapped Otto's thigh as he walked past to mount his own horse. "Good choice, Bjorn of the Langobardi. Keep making good ones, and we'll both be happier."

Luna, Day 23

The bed was soft and the covers warm as Adela drifted from sleep into drowsy wakefulness. She'd slept in the tunic Galen bought her in Octodurus. Today she would dress in the linen tunic with the flower garlands that matched the dark blue sash. A slow smile curved her lips. On the way back to the inn from the baths, he'd said the blue made her ice-blue eyes seem bigger and bluer than any he'd ever seen.

She would leave her hair down. Perhaps he'd liken it to rippling wheat again. Her smile broadened. He might even push a strand behind her ear to keep it off her face.

She swung her feet out of the bed, stood, and stretched. As she slipped the linen tunic over her head, the faint smell of roses teased her nostrils. Galen had said she smelled like the gardens of his childhood, and then his resting smile grew into a dancing one.

A soft knock on the door was followed by his deep voice. "Adela? Are you awake now?"

"Yes."

"We can get breakfast when you're ready."

"I'll only be a moment." She ran the comb he'd bought her in Argentorate through her thick, lustrous tresses to remove the tangles, then fluffed her hair with her fingers.

When she opened the door, he was leaning against the wall, eyes closed. They popped open as she stepped into the hall beside him, and then crinkled as a welcoming smile curved his lips.

"Grab what needs washing. The innkeeper will get that done for us." He scooped up a bundle of clothing he'd left just inside the door. "I've also talked with him about what we should see. It should be an interesting day."

He locked the door, hung the cord that held the key around his neck, and dropped the key inside his shirt. Then, with a wave of his hand, he invited her to go down the stairs ahead of him. With each step, her smile grew. Interesting was too vague a word to describe the day she expected. But what was the right word to describe a day with the man who could turn the dullest thing into laughter and delight?

The large gray and white birds with red bills, black heads, and webbed feet screamed overhead as Adela followed Galen along the road above the piers.

Her breath caught. Boats as wide as the houses in her village and at least four times as long rode on the waves in the harbor. Near the center was a pole as tall as the pine trees they'd ridden past between Octodurus and Augusta Praetoria. Another shorter pole stuck out the front at an angle. Crosswise with those poles were others that had bundles of cloth tied to them.

Galen's deep voice spoke beside her. "Those are merchant ships, *corbitae*, that carry cargo to different ports. They might go even farther than we've ridden before they unload."

She pointed to the one farthest out. "Look at the little boats pulling the big one."

She turned her face toward Galen and found him looking at her with the crooked smile that usually accompanied a surprise.

"Those are the rowboats that pulled it away from the pier after they loaded it. Keep your eyes on that one. We're about to see something special."

Her gaze locked on the ship. A man scampered up the pole. Then what had looked like a bundle opened into a sheet that looked big enough to cover a small house in her village. The wind caught the sheet and it billowed out.

Her fingers flew to her mouth. "It's beautiful!"

"That's the sail, *velum*. Watch and the smaller one at the front will open, too."

"The corbita's going faster and faster."

"The wind pushes against the sails. The sailors adjust them to control how fast they go. There's a pair of rudders that steer it."

"Have you ever been on one?

The crooked smile reappeared. "No, I've only read about them."

He took her hand. The warmth of his palm against hers and the security of his fingers wrapping around her own triggered heat that spread through her whole body. She looked away, hoping he wouldn't notice her blush.

His voice drew her eyes back toward his face. "I'd take you down on the pier, but we shouldn't get in the way of the slaves loading the cargo."

Adela scanned the faces of the line of men with bags on their shoulders. Like two streams of ants, they entered the ship loaded and came out with nothing.

Her mouth drooped as she turned her eyes back toward his. "They look sad."

His eyes chilled as he watched the men. "It's a hard life. No man should be treated like an animal by another man, but that's the Roman way."

The warmth returned as he turned his eyes back on her. "I'm sorry Otto got so drunk he got himself kidnapped, but I am glad he gambled and won you. No woman should be any man's slave."

Looking into his eyes started to heat her cheeks again, so she shifted her gaze to a block of white rock that swung from ropes over the other ship tied at the pier. "Why are they loading a rock?"

"That's marble. The block might be carved into a statue."

"That must take a long time."

"It does. Maybe we can find a sculptor and watch him carve for a while." He pushed the loose strand of hair back from his forehead. "But before we do that, I have a surprise."

He took her hand and led her along the road until they reached a spot where they could go down to the beach. Then he led her to the water's edge.

He squatted at the edge and scooped some water into his palm. The tip of his tongue touched the water he held. That drew a smile before he offered it to her.

She lowered her head so her tongue could reach the water. "It's salty!"

"Surprised?" He poured the water on the sand.

Her grin spread as she nodded.

Galen offered his hand, and she took it. "Let's see if we can find a sculptor to watch."

As he led her from the sand to the road, she intertwined her fingers with his. The perpetual smile that lurked on his lips grew broader.

When his fingers squeezed hers, she felt the pressure on her heart. Four weeks, and she'd be back with her father. But home was no longer four weeks away with the Hermunduri. It was anywhere Galen Crassus was. How could she bear to part from him when that time came?

Galen pushed back from the table and stretched out in the chair. He laced his fingers and rested his palms atop his head.

"Nothing tastes better than a good stew at day's end. My sister Val can take this and that and make something so good I want four or five bowls, but there's something in this one…I'm not sure what it is, but I'd like to take some back for her."

From the table next to them, the soft gurgles of a baby drew his gaze. "That little one looks like my niece Priscilla." The corner of his mouth pulled up. "Babies are cute, but I like them better when they can walk and talk. My nephews are four and six." His smile grew. "Those are good ages."

Adela's gaze locked on the cooing infant. The smile that had been dancing on her lips stiffened. Then she looked away.

"Adela?"

She turned her face toward him. Something about it seemed veiled.

"Is something wrong?"

Her mouth smiled, but not her eyes. "No. Nothing is wrong. I'm just tired."

"Then let's go to bed now. I'd like to get an early start tomorrow." His grin leaked out. "Tomorrow might be the day we find Otto."

He stood. "Why don't you go up first? I want to ask the cook what's in the stew. Then I'll join you."

As she climbed the stairs, he watched her. Something more than fatigue was wrong. But if she didn't want to tell him, he couldn't make her.

The bed was comfortable enough, but sleep eluded Adela. The soft sounds of Galen breathing reached her from where he'd placed his bedroll to block the door. Normally that soothed her, but not tonight.

The shining day exploring with Galen had been tarnished by the soft cries of the baby. Gundahar's words kept playing in her mind. Her days of a woman should have started more than a week ago.

If she were alone, she'd rise and go for a walk in the moonlight. In the days after Mother died, when her heart was bleeding, she crept out of her father's house and paced under the stars. A chieftain's daughter was supposed to be strong. Grief was something to be locked inside. But some things hurt too much to stay caged. The moon and stars would never tell anyone about the tears that wet her cheeks and the silent sobs that shook her body.

Maybe her days were late only because they'd travelled so far. So many hours in the saddle...surely that could change things from normal. Maybe that was all it was. But as she stared at the ceiling, a tear escaped and trickled down into her ear.

Then Adela forced her breathing to synchronize with Galen's, and sleep finally came.

Chapter 25

THE PRICE OF A MAN

Florentia, Day 26

Otto hadn't been in Luca, but Galen's smile grew when the wooden amphitheater of Florentia appeared in the distance.

He beamed at Adela as she rode close beside him. "The lanista in Luca said they never start a man out in Rome, so Otto must be here." His grin broadened. "The look on his face when I show up...that will be fun to see."

Adela's smile looked forced. "He'll be surprised you came so far."

Galen shook his head. "No. He would know I'd come for him, whatever it took. He'd do the same for me. It's his grin I'm looking forward to."

"I saw it when he won me."

Galen's head tilted. "You don't have to worry that he'll think he owns you. I'll set him straight on that." He rubbed his mouth. "After what he's been through, he'll never want to make someone else a slave."

When they reached the amphitheater, a heavily muscled, redheaded man sat under a spreading tree nearby. A carved stone bench had been set close, and the man sat with his arms crossed and eyes closed as he leaned against the trunk, relaxing in the dappled shade.

Galen turned Astrelo toward him and reined in just short of the tree's dripline.

The man's eyes opened.

"*Salve.* I'm looking for the ludus of Marcus Antonius Brutus."

The corner of the man's mouth pulled up. He uncrossed his arms. "Fortuna has smiled upon you. You have found the man in charge of it." He leaned forward. "Ursus Thrax."

Galen swung his leg over Astrelo's neck and slid off. "Galen Crassus."

Ursus's lips twitched as he scanned Galen head to foot. "Do you need to rent one of my men as a bodyguard? Or maybe you need a man big enough to take care of a problem for you."

"Neither. I'm looking for a particular man, one who might have just arrived."

Ursus's eyebrow rose. "Bjorn of the Langobardi?"

"Yes, but his real name is Otto—"

"Of the Vangiones." A chuckle rumbled up from deep within. "He told me so more than once."

Galen's couldn't stop the grin. "So he's here."

"No."

Galen's brow furrowed. "Not here?"

"Bjorn needs much training to be ready to fight in the arena. Brutus would have left him for me to train if he had not been so good with the gladius." Ursus rubbed the red stubble on his chin. "Marcus Brutus has a keen eye for this business, and he never misses an easy way to make money. Bjorn offers one."

"How?"

"Brutus can rent him out as a sparring partner and trainer. He can probably book him for at least five or six sessions a day, maybe more. Bjorn should earn as much or more in a year as a dead Class 1 with little risk of him dying. He could bring in good money for years."

Galen's stomach knotted. Otto could do an excellent job as a trainer, if he kept his disdain for Romans from showing. Would that make his owner refuse to sell?

God, don't let that happen. Let me buy him out of bondage.

Galen stroked the scar. "I've been told a Class 3 costs 2500 denarii, but what does a Class 1 cost?"

"They are 3750, but Class 1s are rare. Most games in Rome book Class 2 as their best fighters. Those are 3000 dead. There is a drop of 500 denarii between classes. Nothing lower than Class 6 is likely in the games there.

"Brutus never fights less than a Class 5 in Rome. He builds their rank here and in Luca before taking them to fight in the big shows. Dead, they bring 1500 denarii."

Galen's brow furrowed. "What do they cost alive?"

Ursus's mouth pulled sideways and up. "Whatever he can get for them. He is a shrewd trader."

Galen's jaw clenched. Would a live man cost more than twice a dead one? What remained of the horse money was less than 4000 denarii.

Ursus's red eyebrows bounced once. "Fortuna smiled on your friend when Brutus bought him. He will make him a trainer for young nobles, not a simple gladiator. Bjorn will train to use a shield so he can fight as *provocator* or *secutor*. But if he makes enough as a trainer, Brutus will never put him on the sand in real combat."

Galen drew a deep breath and blew it out. "That does sound better, but I would rather have found him here. Where in Rome is Brutus's ludus? How many days to ride there?"

"Just north of the Amphitheater off the Vicus Sandaliarius, on the edge of Subura."

Ursus rubbed the back of his neck. "For a man to ride there...four and a half, maybe five days." He scanned Galen's stallions, but his gaze settled on Adela. "You have good horses, but the girl could slow you down. If she is for sale, I would be interested."

Galen glanced at Adela. No indignation flamed in her eyes; she hadn't understood the lanista's words.

"My thanks to you, Ursus, but we'll both go on to Rome."

The lanista leaned back against the trunk. "Fortuna may smile on Bjorn a second time. If you can strike a deal with Brutus, he may become Otto again."

Galen jumped to lay his stomach on Astrelo's back, then swung his leg over his rump and settled into the saddle. He forced a smile. "I'm counting on it, Ursus."

◆

Adela caught a few words of Galen's conversation with the man under the tree, but not enough to know all they said. Lanista and ludus told her he was with the gladiator school they sought. Bjorn and Otto told her the man knew Galen's friend. Five days told her how long they would be riding before they reached Rome.

But she didn't need all the words to understand. She watched every twitch of Galen's mouth and tensing of his shoulders. His final smile was not the one that greeted her in the morning. Something was wrong.

As the horses started walking, she cleared her throat. "What's wrong?"

His lips tightened as he shook his head. "Maybe nothing. Otto has gone on to the ludus in Rome. He should be there whenever we arrive." He rubbed his chin. "But I'm not sure how much he's going to cost. Brutus has a scheme to make money with him as a trainer, and I have no idea how he's going to price him."

"You have a lot of money from the horses."

"Yes...and no. I have 3900 denarii, but from what Ursus told me, that might not be enough." A deep sigh escaped. "I hate the way they set a price on a man, as if he were nothing more than an ox for work or slaughter. Every man is precious in the eyes of God, and none of them should die for another man's afternoon entertainment."

"Because of you, Otto will not die."

Galen took a deep breath and forced it out through his nose. "No, he won't. Whatever it takes, I'll set him free."

The tension drained from his face. "I'm glad you're with me in the hunt. It makes all this easier."

"*Voluptas meus est.*" She grinned at him. "I knew that phrase would be good to remember. It truly is my pleasure to be in this hunt."

The smile that greeted her words was the smile of morning.

"Time to find a place for the night. I want an early start tomorrow."

He nudged his horse into a faster walk, and she did the same. A quick glance at his profile, and she knew one thing beyond any doubt. Being in the hunt with him wasn't just pleasure; it was delight.

Chapter 26

AN AUSPICIOUS BEGINNING

Roma, Day 27

In his head, Otto knew Rome was big, but that still didn't prepare him for the sight of a city that seemed to stretch forever.

Brutus led his party under a tree at the side of the road. "Before we go further, it's time for a change." His fingers snapped. "Rufus, the ropes."

Rufus slipped from his horse, and untied Otto's ankles. He gathered the rope in loops around his bent arm before handing it to Africanus. The key to the wrist shackles hung on a chain around Brutus's neck. Brutus lifted it over his head and tossed the key to Rufus. Otto extended his arms so Rufus could unlock them. Rufus handed the shackles to Africanus, who slipped them into the sack tied at the back of his saddle. Then Rufus remounted.

Otto's heart began to race. Hands and feet free, mounted on a quality horse...

Brutus reached over and unclipped the lead rope from Otto's horse.

Otto's head snapped back, which drew a chuckle from Brutus. "Don't think any of this means I'm setting you free. You'll ride next to me, and Africanus and Rufus will be right behind."

The corner of his mouth pulled up. "I think you're smart enough that you won't try to run. The better you cooperate, the better your life will be. You can live caged when you're not teaching, or you can have some freedom to move around the ludus. If you work hard and prove reliable, you'll get to go to the circus with an escort. The best horses in the Empire race at the Circus Maximus. Watching them is a suitable reward for a horseman like yourself."

His twisted smile grew. "You might someday earn the privileges of Rufus and Africanus. They have the freedom to go to the circus, the baths, anywhere else in Rome they want without being watched." His arm swept toward Rufus and Africanus and got two grins in response. "In fact, these men are my watchers."

Otto gave Brutus the smile he knew he wanted. "I'll stay right beside you today. I'm no fool."

Brutus slapped Otto's arm. "Then it's time to introduce Bjorn of the Langobardi to the people of Roma."

A cream-colored building the size of a small hill rose to the right. Several circular stories, each smaller than the one below it, rose to the height of at least 20 men. Bushes were planted on each level, with cypress trees on the top, surrounding the conical roof atop a circle of columns and a huge bronze statue of a Roman officer.

Brutus pointed at it. "The Mausoleum of Augustus."

Otto's mouth turned down before he could stop it. "I have no interest in a monument to the Roman general who led the legions against my ancestors."

Brutus choked back a laugh. "Not the response I want, Bjorn, but the one I expect. That was a long time ago. Now Germania Superior can boast that Trajan was governor there when he became emperor. And Emperor Hadrian is inspecting his legions on the Rhenus this year. You've missed seeing him there, but maybe you'll see him in the imperial box at the games sometime."

The corner of Otto's mouth lifted. "The chariot races sound worth watching. The Emperor...I don't care if I ever see him."

Brutus's mouth twitched. "*Ave, Imperator, morituri te salutant.* 'We who are about to die salute you.' To stand before the emperor is a great honor. But if you earn enough as a trainer, that honor won't have to be yours.

"Now ride proudly and stay right beside me. It's time to start showing Roma what a German chieftain from the Northlands looks like."

Otto's brow furrowed. "But I'm from Germania Superior, and it's my father who's the chieftain of the Vangiones."

Brutus chuckled, but his eyes chilled. "So you tell me, and between you and me, I admit it is a possibility. But the men of Roma never need to hear that, and you'd better not tell them. We're in the business of entertainment, and the truth of the matter is of no importance here."

Brutus cuffed Otto on the back of his head and urged his horse forward. Otto fought the urge to strike him back...and won. But he nudged his own horse to bring its head up even with Brutus's.

Then the corner of his mouth pulled up. Galen was a master at sloughing off the many insults his short stature drew from those who weren't even half the man Galen was. To win Brutus's trust, he needed to follow Galen's lead.

A man dressed in a tunic with two wide purple stripes that marked him as senatorial order rode toward them.

Brutus raised his hand. "*Salve*, Sabinus. It's been a month since I saw you last at the races. I trust all goes well with you."

Sabinus reined in beside Brutus. "It does. And with you?"

"Very well. I've just returned from Octodurus. I visited my estate to buy additional land, but when I went to the games there, I also found a unique addition for the *familia gladiatoria Bruti*."

He placed his hand on Otto's upper arm and squeezed. Otto tensed, and his bicep bulged. The corners of Brutus's eyes crinkled. "This is Bjorn of the Langobardi. He's a true master with the gladius. I watched him kill three men in a three-on-three like it was child's play. I bought him for Florentia, but he got a practice sword past an eight-year veteran of the games twenty times over at my ludus there. Such talent would be wasted anywhere but Roma herself."

Brutus's smile broadened. "I'll have Bjorn available as a sparring partner by tomorrow. His Latin is good, so he can serve as a personal trainer as well. I heard your nephew is soon to begin the *cursus honorum* with his first posting to one of the legions in Dacia. Some training with an expert before going could prove life-saving. Perhaps your brother would like to avail himself of the opportunity Bjorn can provide."

Sabinus's mouth first curved down, then up. "Gaius could certainly use some improvement in his swordsmanship. I'm on my way to my brother's villa now. I'll mention Bjorn to him."

Sabinus nudged his horse into a walk, then turned in the saddle to look back. "I'll probably try him out myself when I return. *Vale*, Brutus."

When the senator was out of earshot, Brutus turned to Otto and grinned. "An auspicious beginning, Bjorn. And except for where you came from, everything I said was truth. Even that agrees with the bill of sale. A good businessman never lies about the important things if he can avoid it."

An arched gate wide enough to let two wagons pass through at once loomed ahead, but before they reached it, Brutus reined in.

His hand swept toward the gate. "Porta Fontinalis...the gateway to life in Rome."

The arch of the city gate blocked the sun as they rode through, and Otto's jaw clenched. Cross-country trips selling horses, nights by a campfire laughing at Galen's jokes, feasts at his father's table when all the family gathered—one night of drinking and stupidity had swept it all away. Was going to the baths unescorted the best he could hope for now?

Despair nipped at his heels, but he kicked it in the teeth as he relaxed his jaw. Inside the walls of Rome or outside, life held possibilities. He needed to figure out how to get to them. Right now, that meant letting Brutus think he owned him and acting as if he thought so himself.

Galen always said his god would give him strength to do whatever was needed, but Galen's god was not Otto's god. He would have to find the strength on his own...somehow.

He glanced at Brutus. If he had to have an owner, he could do worse. Brutus held the power of life and death, and he wouldn't hesitate to exercise it. But at least he treated his slaves like the men they were, not brute animals.

Brutus nudged his horse, and they rode on toward the dense cluster of towering white buildings that proclaimed Rome's power and self-importance to all who saw them.

But Otto paid them scant attention. It was almost four weeks and more than five thousand *stadia* since Argentorate, and Galen hadn't found him. Maybe he never would. Maybe he'd given up, but that wasn't likely. Not Galen.

Maybe he was dead. If he caught up with Gundahar and Gerlach, that was a real possibility. Two against one when those two were snakes were bad odds, even for a man with Galen's quick thinking and quicker sword. Had his own stupidity cost his friend's life?

Otto slumped in his saddle.

Brutus's fist slammed into his ribs.

"Ride proudly, Bjorn of the Langobardi. No true Roman wants to fight with a man who acts defeated even before the contest."

Otto's lips tightened as he squared his shoulders. His gaze raked Brutus before he returned it to the monuments to Roman arrogance rising ahead of him.

Brutus chuckled. "That's better. A look of defiance is good...as long as it's only a look."

Otto turned his face away. Brutus was too good at reading his thoughts. It was time to start making Brutus think he'd reconciled himself to doing whatever he was told and making the best of it. Even if Galen never found him, the time would come when Brutus let down his guard. Then Bjorn of the Langobardi would walk out of Rome and vanish, leaving Otto of the Vangiones to make his way home.

Otto walked beside Brutus as they left the Baths of Trajan. Rufus and Africanus stayed close enough there'd be no chance to escape.

Brutus's whole face radiated smug satisfaction. "I'm pleased with this advertising campaign so far today. Ten friends met, and three sons or nephews will be coming to train. Three friends coming to spar as well. Word will spread quickly if you train and spar well. Then your position off the sand will be assured."

A smile tugged at his mouth. "The timing of our arrival was most fortunate. In that giggling group of girls who couldn't keep their eyes off you were two who often come to watch from the balcony." The corner of his mouth pulled up into a half grin. "I like to cultivate the appreciation of my fighters while they're young. Some return when they're grown women, and those can prove valuable."

After collecting their horses, they rode to the ludus. In the stable yard, a slave scurried over to take Brutus's horse first, then Otto's. Rufus and Africanus rode over to the stalls for their animals and dismounted to stable the horses themselves.

Brutus slapped Africanus's bicep as he walked past. "Good trip, men. You two can take tomorrow off."

His words were greeted with "thank you, master" and smiles.

Otto followed Brutus toward the sound of wood striking wood and entered the practice arena. A middle-aged man with a wicked-looking scar running from forehead to chin stood with fists on his hips. He slipped off his eyepatch and rubbed where his eye had once been. As he replaced the eyepatch, he caught sight of them.

"Master Brutus. It is good to see you back." A calculating eye took Otto's measure, and the growing frown declared Otto's failure to satisfy the lanista's expectations for a gladiator.

"What is this you brought to me?"

"Bjorn of the Langobardi. He's a special acquisition. Not a warrior, but his skill with the gladius is unusual. He should prove highly profitable training young men and sparring with more mature ones. I took him to the Baths on the way here. I have no doubt he'll draw the girls and women, too."

The lanista's gaze raked Otto from sole to hairline. "This one will run. He needs a collar first thing."

Brutus's eyes narrowed as he scanned Otto. "I'm certain he can imagine what some of the punishments for runaway slaves are." He rubbed his lower lip. "Most would make it hard for you to fight or train, and that's not something either of us want. The owner of the estate east of mine cuts off a runner's toes. Some brand with FUG, but that might make you less attractive to the women, so..." Brutus traced the three letters on Otto's forehead, "I'd rather not brand you. Is my lanista right that you're going to run at the first chance?"

Otto's lips tightened. "I keep telling you I'm no fool."

Laughter rumbled in Brutus's chest. "And that evasive response answers my question. If you'd told me no, I'd know you're a liar. Only a fool would lie to me, knowing I'll catch him in it. Betrayal of any trust I place in you will be punished. Your life here will be much better if you remain an honest man."

Brutus turned toward the lanista and tilted his head toward Otto. "Collar him."

Otto cringed when the lanista slipped the bronze band around his neck. It took all the willpower he had not to rip it off before the lanista pushed the copper pin through the holes in both ends and crimped it with heavy iron pliers so the pin could no longer be pulled out.

He wrapped his fingers around the bronze collar. It was loose enough, but it still felt like it was strangling him.

Brutus slipped his fingers into the space between the collar and Otto's neck. He slid them along the edge from ear to ear. "Smooth enough. It shouldn't cause you any problem." The crooked smile appeared. "I prefer a bronze design with the inscription on the collar instead of a tag on an iron ring. It doesn't say 'Seize me. I'm a runaway.' It only says you're the property of this ludus. Think of it as a torc with your tribal insignia, like some Britons wear. Even with the inscription, it looks good on a Langobardian chieftain."

Otto opened his mouth, but before he could speak, Brutus pushed up on his chin.

"I know. You're not Langobardian, and it's your father who's the chieftain. That might have been true in Germania, but in this ludus and anyplace else in Roma, I decide what's true about you. The sooner you accept that, the better."

The lanista lifted the three-cord whip from the hook on his belt. "I can adjust his thoughts."

Brutus rested his hand on the lanista's whip arm. "That won't be necessary. Bjorn understands his place here." His gaze locked on Otto. "Don't you."

Otto nodded. Brutus's gaze shifted to his lanista. "Take him to his cell. He could use some rest until dinner." His eyes swiveled back toward Otto. "And some time to think about making wise choices."

The lanista flicked the whip toward an open door. "You heard your master. Get moving."

As Otto started down the hallway to the cell block, his hand gripped the bronze collar. Whatever goes on can come off. If—no...when Galen came, he would find a way to set Otto free.

Chapter 27

Not the Same at All

Just north of Roma, Day 31

When Adela closed her eyes, she could once more see the sunlight dancing on Lacus Volsiniensis as the soaring white bird that Galen called a *larus* swooped down, skimmed the water, and rose again with a fish in its beak.

They'd passed so many farms and vineyards and orchards that she'd lost count, but Galen never seemed to tire of pointing out something new and teaching her the Latin name.

As they approached a sign post with an arrow pointing east, he reined in.

"Read that, and then tell me what's up that road."

"M Aug Veiens." Adela rubbed her chin. "Aug...is that Augustus or Augustum? It can't be Augusta because Veiens doesn't end in A."

His grin proclaimed his pleasure at her knowing.

"Augustum is correct. And the M?"

"*Mons?* There are mountains over there."

His eyes crinkled. "Good guess with a good reason for it...but it's wrong. *Municipium.* Town.

"More than five hundred years ago, Rome started expanding its control here. The first war for conquest was with Etruscan Veii. Wars, actually, since there were fourteen of them. The last one ended in a ten-year siege. The Roman army finally tunneled under the walls to take the city. They destroyed Veii, but it was rebuilt later as Municipium Augustum Veiens. Since then, Rome has conquered most of the world."

151

Adela raised her chin. "The Romans never conquered the Hermunduri. No Roman army could break the spirit of my people and take our land."

Galen's perpetual smile morphed into a grin. "If the Hermunduri warriors are anything like you, I'd hate to be in the legion that tried."

He nudged his horse, and they rode past the signpost.

Adela's gaze stayed fixed on his grin as it faded. No Roman legion could conquer her people, but there was one Roman who'd already captured her heart.

Maybe that was because she laughed more every day with him than she ever had before. Galen could take anything and turn it funny. The only time she saw her father and his friends laugh was when they'd been drinking too long.

Galen's head turned, and he caught her watching him. His smile broadened, and that shot heat to the tips of her ears. The smile turned into a grin before he looked back down the road.

As her ears cooled, she found herself mirroring his grin.

No, her father's laughter wasn't the same as Galen's. Not the same at all.

Roma, Day 31

Galen pulled a deep breath and blew it out as they approached Rome. Somewhere in that city, Otto waited for him. But it was late afternoon, and he needed to find a safe place to stable his horses and spend the night. That had been easy enough in the smaller towns where he could ask at a garrison or a shop where the proprietor seemed honest. But in a city of a million people, with "provincial" written all over him for any scoundrel to read, how could he find someone he could trust?

God, please protect us here in the belly of the beast. Guide me to one of Yours who can tell me where to go.

"Galen." The tension in Adela's voice echoed his own uncertainty. "It's too big. How will we ever find a safe place to stay?"

She moved her horse close enough for him to rest his hand on her arm. "Don't worry. My God will help us here."

Too many ears were close by for him to say more, but he felt her relax before he moved his hand back to his own thigh.

Galen led them along a street lined with raised walkways in front of shops on the first floor. Three or four stories rose above the shops. About every hundred feet, stepping stones spanned the roadway, spaced so wagon wheels could pass between them.

He scanned the shops as they rode, looking for the pair of curved lines, touching at one end and crossing near the other, that signaled a follower of the Way.

They had ridden several blocks when he saw what he was praying for. A woman who looked about thirty was selling vegetables to an older woman. He reined in and waited for the customer to leave before sliding off Astrelo and approaching the counter.

A pleasant smile greeted him. "What can I get for you today?"

His finger traced the fish on the counter. "I'm hoping for some information." He drew half a fish beside the first before raising his eyebrows to ask the question. Her finger completed the fish. Then the polite smile of a merchant was replaced by the warm smile of a sister.

Galen's sigh of relief accompanied his silent prayer of thanks. God had provided.

"I'm trying to rescue a friend, but I haven't been in Rome since I was a child. I know nothing about where a man with horses should stay. I also want a place that's safe for a woman while I go find the gladiator school where my friend is supposed to be. He was kidnapped and sold, and I'm here to free him."

Her voice dropped so those passing nearby wouldn't hear. "I buy my produce from a brother who runs a stable a short distance from here. My son can take you to him. As for a place to stay, he rents some rooms as well."

Galen glanced at Adela. She was listening too attentively. He dropped his voice to a near-whisper. "I need to ask you something where no one can overhear."

The shopkeeper swept her hand toward the door at the back of the shop.

Galen turned to Adela. "I'll be right back."

He followed the woman into the back room, where she waited for his question.

"Adela doesn't follow the Way, and she doesn't know I do. Will that be a problem?"

The shopkeeper's eyebrows rose. "She's not your wife?"

"No. I'm from Germania Superior. She was kidnapped past the imperial frontier before my friend won her throwing dice. He was kidnapped that night by the same men and sold as a gladiator. I was going to take her home before that happened, but it would have been six days before I followed his trail, and I would never have found him. I've been sleeping on the floor, blocking the door since so many inns aren't safe for a woman alone."

"If you explain to Quintus what you just told me, that shouldn't be a problem."

A boy of about ten entered the room. She summoned him with a flick of her fingers and wrapped her arm around his shoulders. "Titus, I want you to take this man to Quintus's inn."

The boy grinned and nodded.

"I'll pray for your success in finding your friend. What are your names?"

Galen rested his hand on his chest. "Galen Crassus, and my friend is Otto."

"And the girl?"

"Adela." The corner of his mouth lifted. "She doesn't follow the Way now, but I'm praying for the chance to change that."

Her friendly smile broadened into a knowing grin. "I'll join you in that prayer, Galen."

Galen's ears heated as his own grin grew. "Thank you for your help... and for your prayers."

◆

Adela fidgeted as she waited for Galen to appear. Too many of the men who passed by inspected her with hungry eyes. But when she rested her hand on her dagger and scowled, most looked away, and all moved on without trying anything.

A boy came out, followed by Galen with a smile on his lips. All the tension drained out of her.

Galen took his reins from her hand. "Titus is going to take us to a safe place to stay. It's only a short walk."

Adela slipped off her stallion and took her place at his side. "I'm glad you're back." Her shoulders twitched. "I don't like Roman men, the way they look at me."

"It isn't often they get to see someone as pretty as you."

The warmth in his eyes pushed aside any thought of the hungry ones.

They walked in silence until Galen ran his fingers through his hair.

"We're very close to finding Otto now, but I'm sorry it's taken so long. I know it's been more than four weeks since we left Argentorate, and it might be a few more days before we can leave Rome. Once we start back, it's going to be another three and a half, maybe four weeks to get you home."

Adela shrugged. "It doesn't matter how much longer it takes us to get your friend back. You can't leave him a slave. Besides, more time just means I get to learn more Latin. No one could have a better teacher."

"Or a better student."

"But I don't remember everything the first time. What was the word for "like?" I know you told me once, but that was days ago."

"*Amo, amas, amat...*It follows the first pattern." The corner of his mouth turned up. "But you better be careful how you use that in the I form. *Amo* means "I like" but *Te amo* can mean "I love you." You could give a man the message he wants, not the one you mean to give him. Don't use that one at a Roman garrison or any inn. To be safe, you shouldn't say that to anyone."

She nodded, and he turned his eyes back on Titus, who walked a few feet ahead of them.

Galen could tell her she should never say certain words, but he didn't know how wrong he was this time.

Her smiled broadened as she glanced at his profile. The scar she'd put on his cheek had done nothing to make him less handsome. Why had she ever thought a tall German warrior was more of a man than the short, kind, funny Roman walking beside her?

Te amo, Galen Crassus. Before she returned to the land of the Hermunduri, she would say that to him.

Then her smile dimmed. What if he didn't say it back?

Chapter 28

SO FAR BUT NOT ENOUGH

Day 32

When Galen headed back into Rome the next morning, nervous energy surged through him. Each step took him closer to finding Otto and setting him free. Quintus had given him clear directions to the amphitheater and how to find the Vicus Sandaliarius once he got there. The Ludus Bruti shouldn't be too hard to find after that.

As he walked through the area of the Forums, massive stone and concrete structures rose around him. They had seemed enormous the last time he came to the Basilica Julia with his father. He'd tried to look in some of the shops, but Father had ordered him to stay right beside him.

They'd gone into a room in the Basilica where a man in a tunic edged with purple had listened to Father and another man arguing about something. His father's face had frozen when the other man started yelling something about them being Christians and unfit to live in Rome.

The next day Father had loaded a few things into the cart a small horse could pull. Mother had taken Galen's toga and linen tunic and put him in a woolen tunic she got from one of the house slaves. She'd already changed her brightly colored tunic and *stola* for drab woolen ones.

Father had folded his toga and handed it to their steward. Galen had never seen the old man cry, but there were tears in his eyes that day. Rhoda wasn't even two, and her nurse was bawling as she handed his little sister to Mother. Then they headed north, never to return.

Even now, as a grown man, the Basilica and the temples towered over him. But much had changed between six and twenty-one. He was only a foot and a half taller, but many times wiser.

The trip to Germania had been hard as a child, but all things considered, he wouldn't choose to live anywhere else. He scanned the monuments to the gods of pagan Rome. White like the bones of something long dead, but the Roman gods had never been alive. He gave thanks that he needed no temple for his worship. His God was real, and He was everywhere Galen could ever go.

When he reached the Flavian Amphitheater, he got directions to the Vicus Patricias, which lead to the Porta Viminalis and on past the fortress of the Praetorian Guard. The headquarters of the personal legion of the emperor would be a good place to sell horses if he had any for sale, but it was not where a Christian man would normally want to go.

The Vicus Sandaliarius veered left off the Patricias two blocks from the amphitheater. Brutus's ludus filled a small block. Ludus Bruti was carved in stone above the door, and the words were flanked by intricate carvings showing the flexing muscles of men in combat. Everything about it proclaimed the wealth of its owner.

Galen's stomach tightened. The man who built this had money, and men with money knew what they wanted and held on to it once they got it.

God, don't let Otto be so important to this man that he won't sell him.

Galen waited for the peace that had often descended when he faced a hard choice on this trip. It didn't come.

He strode up to the door slave. "I'm looking for a particular gladiator, and I've been told he's here."

The doorman swept his hand toward a set of stairs that rose to the right just inside the entryway. "The viewing balcony is up there. If he's not among the fighters practicing, you'll have to talk to Lanista Felix."

As Galen climbed the stairs, the sound of wood striking wood grew louder. As he approached the balcony railing, his heart pounded. With jaw clenched, he focused on the sand below.

Tension flowed out of him like water through a sieve. There, swinging a long wooden sword at a practice post, was Otto.

Galen closed his eyes as a grin spread across his face. *All praise be to you, Lord God, for leading me here in time to save my friend.* His spirit soared, and he basked in the joy for a long moment. Then he opened his eyes and squared his shoulders. Time to negotiate the sale.

But before he did... "Otto."

He hadn't yelled it. He only spoke in a voice loud enough to be heard in a tavern, but Otto spun at the sound, and his head tipped back. As his gaze locked on Galen, the biggest grin Galen had ever seen split his face. He lowered the wooden sword to rest the tip on the ground.

"Bjorn. It's not break time." A heavily muscled man with an eyepatch stepped into view from beneath Galen. He strode across the arena and slapped the back of Otto's head. "You don't quit until I tell you."

Otto nodded and turned back to the post. Again, he struck it with the sword, but with greater force than he had before.

Hope could give a man power to do far beyond what seemed possible, and it was hope that flamed in Otto's eyes. Even after the rebuke, a trace of the grin had remained.

Galen's own grin stretched his face, but a grin was not the right way to start this negotiation. Dignity and the aura of confidence was required. He willed his face to relax until only his normal smile remained.

He descended the stairs and approached the door slave once more. "I found him. I want to speak with the man who owns him."

The doorkeeper stared at him without speaking.

Galen's forehead furrowed. "Marcus Antonius Brutus. Where would I find him?"

"You have to speak with Lanista Felix first. Master Brutus isn't usually here."

Galen summoned a smile. "Then where can I find Lanista Felix?"

"He's probably in the arena."

"And how do I get into the arena to talk with him?"

"There's a stairway down from the balcony, but he doesn't like people to come down." The corner of the door slave's mouth twitched.

Galen's forced smile turned into a real one. "I won't mention you told me how."

The relief flooding the slave's face was a bad sign. If Felix's slaves were that nervous about him, he couldn't be a reasonable man.

He climbed to the balcony and watched Otto for a moment. Still swinging the sword at the stake, more like a machine than a man. Galen's jaw clenched as his gaze locked on the stairway leading down to the sand.

Then, with shoulders squared, head high, and his friendliest trading face, he headed down.

The door opened into the arena to the left of the balcony. Felix stood across the sand, fingering the cords of the whip that hung from his belt as he watched a man with red hair striking a post.

Galen stepped close, but not within arm's reach. "Lanista Felix."

Felix's hands fisted as he spun, and Galen backed off with his hands raised, palms outward.

"I didn't mean to startle you."

Felix's scowl was a black as any Galen had seen. "What do you want here?"

Galen lowered his hands. "I'm interested in the German, Otto." He tipped his head toward his friend. "I understand Marcus Antonius Brutus bought him cheap in Octodurus, and I'm interested in buying him now. Do you have authority to sell him, or do I need to speak with Brutus?"

Galen sensed the motion behind him and turned. A tall, muscular man in the narrow-striped tunic of the equestrian order was leaning against the wall under the balcony.

As he scanned Galen, a dismissive smile tugged at the corner of the man's mouth. "Who is asking for Brutus?"

Galen straightened. "Gaius Crassus."

"I'm Marcus Brutus." His gaze swept Galen as Brutus straightened to his full height. Galen felt the silent laughter as Brutus took in his shirt and trousers...and his size. "Where do you come from, Crassus, and why do you want my gladiator?"

Galen kept his brow from furrowing. It was probably better if Brutus didn't realize he was scrutinizing Brutus at least as much as Brutus was surveying him. If he had to explain it, he couldn't, but something about Brutus said he was an honest man.

And an honest man valued the truth when another man spoke it.

Galen waved his hand toward Otto, who stood with his hand resting atop the practice post. "Otto is my friend. He was kidnapped in Argentorate. About four weeks ago, someone with whom he was gambling lured him from the gaming tables to look at a horse, knocked him out, and took him to sell into the arena. I've been tracking him since then. He was never anyone's to sell, and he should be freed."

Brutus's eyebrow popped up, then settled back into place. "I might be impressed by your story if I believed it was true. But I have a bill of sale certified by the questor in Octodurus, and I paid good money for Bjorn. I won't free my slave because someone claims he's a friend who rode more than 5000 stadia to set him free. That's beyond what I find believable, and I'm not one to be tricked by a sad story."

Galen's head tilted as he crossed his arms. "I understand you have some money invested in Otto, and I'm not asking you to lose it. I'll pay you what you paid for Otto in Octodurus."

Brutus's cynical laugh ended with his mouth twitching. "This is a business, Crassus, and I never pay more than I must or sell for less than I can get. I got an extraordinary bargain in Octodurus, and Bjorn is worth much more than I paid. I expect him to make me a great deal of money over an extended period of time."

Galen rubbed his chin. "I don't question your knowledge of your business, but I've been assured Otto will never fight better than a Class 3, and those are only 2500 denarii dead."

The corner of Brutus's mouth pulled up again. "That's not true. Bjorn's skill with a gladius is extraordinary. With a year's training to master the shield, he should become at least a Class 2. Those are worth 3000 denarii dead, and an ordinary live gladiator is worth at least two times a dead one.

"But Bjorn is not ordinary, and that drives up his price. He's good enough with the gladius to train my other men, and that raises the value of every fighter he trains."

Brutus took a step closer and crossed his arms. Galen stepped back to increase the distance between them. Standing too close to a tall man put a short one at a disadvantage in striking a bargain. The twitch of Brutus's mouth when Galen stepped back again and crossed his own arms revealed the ludus owner's own knowledge of the bargaining psychology Galen used selling horses.

"He has uses outside the arena as well. I've already lined up several men who want to train with him regularly at two denarii a half hour. As we build his clientele, I expect to make as much as ten times that a day. I'll make more money with him every year than with a Class 1 in the Imperial games.

"He's already a favorite with the girls who come to watch my men train. Several are bringing friends who didn't come before. I expect he'll appeal to the older women as well. And for the women who like to spar... with his good looks and command of Latin, he could become the most popular personal trainer in all Roma."

Brutus rubbed his chin, and Galen felt the disdain in the frowning smile directed at him. "But everything is for sale at the right price. If you offer me...9000 denarii, I would consider selling him."

Galen drew a deep breath. More than twice what he had from the sale of the horses. He stroked the scar with his middle finger, then glanced at Otto.

His best friend stood frozen on the sand. Otto had heard Brutus's price, and he knew how much the horses brought. It wasn't enough. As Otto's gaze remained locked on Galen, black despair filled his eyes.

Chapter 29

Galen bounced his head back before faking a wry smile. "I'd heard men in Rome enjoyed a good joke, but 9000 for a man who isn't even ranked yet?"

His gaze locked on Brutus's eyes. Cold calculation was all he saw. The words of his brother-in-law, who came from the highest circles of Roman power, played in his head. Mercy is not considered a virtue in Rome. But God could soften the hardest heart for a moment, and a moment was all he needed. *God, help me get the best deal of my life. Show me the way to Otto's freedom.*

He rubbed the back of his neck. "Otto's not worth 9000. He'll never be a Class 2. He is, as you say, exceptionally good with a gladius against someone who's never seen him fight before, but don't gladiators study their opponents? He's no warrior. The first time he ever killed was in the arena in Octodurus. You saw him fight there. It's all sword work and nothing else. He's never fought with a shield. He only knows how to spar close in with another fighter using a gladius. He knows nothing about fighting anyone who's expert at striking from a longer distance."

Galen tightened his lips as he shook his head. "Maybe some will pay two denarii a half hour now, but how many can there be and how long will they want to train with him once they learn his tricks? Even I beat him more than half the time when we spar, and look at me."

Brutus's eyebrow cocked and his mouth twisted as he fought back a laugh. "You've beaten him?"

"Many times. Do you want a demonstration? Or maybe you want to try me yourself. Real swords, of course, but I'll stop short of the kill. I don't want to be charged with your murder while I'm visiting Rome."

Laughter exploded from deep within Brutus. When it subsided, he covered his mouth with his hand and wiped a huge grin away.

Galen's head tipped as he gazed at Brutus. Proud and so sure of his superiority to a runt from Germania. God had just shown him the way to a price he could afford. Time to dangle the bait. "I'm not joking. I can beat him easily. He's not worth 9000. A dead Class 4 is worth 2000 denarii." He rubbed his chin. "The first time you fight him, that's the most you'll collect, but I'm willing to offer you the value of a dead Class 2. That's 3000 denarii...if you can beat me."

"That's an absurd offer. But...if you can best me sparring, I might lower the price to 7000."

One tweak of the pride of a sporting man, and the game was on.

"Too high. Even a Class 1 in the biggest Imperial games isn't worth 4000. No one will want to pay more than the Class 5 rate after they see him on the sand. Even though it's more than twice what he can earn you, I might go to 3800 if you give me a good fight before I win."

"Between what he cost and the time it took to get him here, I have more than that invested in him. I never sell at a loss." The arrogant grin leaked out again as he crossed his arms and looked down at Galen "But I've never fought a r...man of your stature, and it might be amusing."

Galen tilted his head and stroked his scar again. "I've fought men much bigger than you, and it is amusing."

Brutus almost choked trying not to laugh. "I'll give you credit for confidence. And for that, I'll split the difference. Say 5400." Brutus smirked as he looked down his nose at Galen. "That's my final price. If you can't pay it, no sale."

Galen glanced at Otto. "A moment alone with my friend."

Brutus waved him toward Otto and strolled across the arena to talk with his lanista.

Otto's eyes clouded as his shoulders drooped. "I know you can't pay that. Even if you could sell Astrelo and my stallion for top money, you'd still be short." He closed his eyes as he drew a deep breath. Then his eyes opened as he forced it out fast through his nostrils and squared his shoulders. "Brutus isn't planning to fight me in the arena any time soon. He knows I'll die in the first bout. He only plans to rent me out to spar with any Roman who wants to practice and to entertain the women who come to watch gladiators. It won't be so bad."

His shoulders drooped again. "I'm only here because I didn't listen to you. I had to get drunk and gamble. I told Brutus my father raised no fools, but I'm the biggest fool I've ever known."

Galen dropped his voice to a near-whisper. "Don't despair yet. I know I'm 1600 short right now, but I have a rich relative who should be here in Rome. I'm going to fight Brutus, and after I win, I'll get the extra money from him."

Otto's voice dropped as well. "But didn't your father barely get out of Rome ahead of the soldiers who came to arrest him? Will any Licinius Crassus be willing to help you after the scandal his faith caused?"

For Otto's sake, Galen made the corner of his mouth lift. "Roman family ties are stronger than most, even when someone is disowned for following the Way. After I beat Brutus, I'll go ask for the money."

The hope those words fired in Otto's eyes drew a genuine smile to Galen's lips. But if Otto knew which man Galen planned to ask, he'd tell Galen not to risk it. It could easily turn fatal.

The only rich man Galen knew in Rome was his sister's father-in-law, Tiberius Cornelius Lentulus. He'd hunted Christians as governor of Germania Superior and declared his only son dead when Dec chose Jesus over Rome. If Lentulus learned of Galen's faith, Otto wouldn't be the first one to die on the arena sand.

But Jesus had said there was no greater love than to lay down one's life for a friend. Otto was as good a friend as any man could have. Saving him was worth any risk.

The sound of sword on shield drew Galen's gaze. Brutus had a metal guard on his sword arm. He held gladius and shield and was warming up with one of his gladiators. Galen froze his face to block a frown. Like Otto, he knew nothing of shields, and he was too small for any of the armor a ludus would have, anyway.

Otto gripped his arm. "You can't go up against that. I don't want you dead as well as me."

Galen patted Otto's hand and lifted it off his arm. "I won't have to. Brutus will fight by our rules: no armor, no shield, only a gladius. He just doesn't know it yet."

He sauntered across the arena to join his opponent.

"I'm sure you want a fair contest. Like Otto, I've never used a shield or armor." He scanned the rack of shields sized for big, muscular men in mortal combat. "I see nothing my size. Besides, shields are for battle, and this is only a friendly contest to set a price. So...it's gladius only for us."

Brutus's brow furrowed. "I always fight fair, and it wouldn't be right to make you use a shield almost as big as you are."

He returned the shield to the rack and held out his arm for the gladiator to loosen the straps. When the arm guard fell away, he swept his hand toward the center of the arena.

"Gladius only. Let's begin."

Galen rubbed his hands together. "I'll have to use one of your gladii. I left mine at the inn where I stabled my stallion and Otto's horse. I assumed a dagger would be the most I'd need walking through Rome."

Brutus tightened his mouth to hide a grin. "You brought Bjorn's horse along? You were that sure you'd find him?"

"Of course. I wasn't going to quit until I did."

Brutus's eyebrows rose as his head pulled back. "Well, you found him. Now let's see if you can earn the right to buy him at the agreed price."

He waved his hand toward a man who was polishing the shields. "My armorer will show you some to choose among. You'll probably find them better than what you're used to. My men only fight with the best."

Galen followed the armorer into a storage room. Rack after rack of gleaming weapons lined one wall. On the other wall, polished steel helmets, metal and padded-leather arm guards, and greaves to protect the lower legs sat on shelves. The man led him to the gladius rack and stepped back.

He lifted a sword from the rack. The handle nestled in his hand like it was shaped for it. The blade was perfectly symmetrical, and the edge was sharp enough for shaving. The only sword he'd ever held of that quality was the custom gladius Dec had used when he was a tribune in the legion. After a few flicks and twists of his wrist and a couple of lunges to get the feel of it, he replaced it and selected the next one in the rack. Equally well crafted, perfectly balanced...Brutus was right about only giving his men the best.

After trying two more, he selected the first and returned to the sand.

Brutus stood, legs spread, arms crossed with the flat of his blade resting against his shoulder. "What rules?"

Galen rubbed the back of his neck. "Felix calls the start of each round. The round lasts until one touches the other with his sword. The touch has to be with the flat side of the sword so neither of us gets hurt. First to touch the other three times wins."

The corner of Brutus's mouth pulled up into a wry smile. "You're certain you want to do this with real swords, Crassus? We could use wooden ones and count any touch. Touching with the flat means getting in closer. My arms are much longer than yours. I have an unfair advantage."

Galen made his own mouth mirror Brutus's. "An unfair advantage? Perhaps not. Your arms aren't that much longer, and I'm a smaller target. I'll take my chances with steel."

"As you wish." Brutus assumed fighting stance. "Felix, begin it."

Galen relaxed into the focused state he always used fighting Otto and Dec. *God, give me victory...and freedom for Otto.*

Felix crossed his arms and scowled at Galen. "Begin."

The first thrust came at Galen faster than anything Otto had ever done. He swatted it aside as he sidestepped before dropping into a crouch and slapping Brutus's leg with the side of his blade. Then he jumped back out of range.

Brutus's eyes saucered. Then his mouth turned down. "Round one to you, Crassus. Not exactly conventional sparring, but not outside our rules."

He flexed his shoulders and settled back into fighting stance. Then he nodded at Felix.

Before Galen could prepare, Felix spoke, "Begin."

Brutus's attack was swift and fierce. Galen parried six thrusts and strikes before Brutus's blade touched his shoulder.

The smile that curved Brutus's mouth looked satisfied but not smug. "Round two to me. That's how we do it in Rome."

Galen drew a deep breath and slipped into the focused state again. Felix would time his word to Brutus's nod. *God, give me two more.* He locked his gaze on Brutus's head.

"Begin."

Brutus came at Galen the same way he had during the second round, but this time Galen was ready. He deflected a dozen thrusts and slashes before the opening came. As he pushed Brutus's blade aside with his own, he suddenly reversed the direction his arm was moving, swung his blade down, and tapped Brutus on the side.

Brutus stepped back and tipped his head toward Galen. "So you can spar like we do in Rome. Round three to you."

"I'm Roman-trained."

Brutus's mouth curved into a smiling frown. "Like Bjorn. You, too, would have walked from the sand in Octodurus." Then the smile overpowered the frown. "But I never would have bought you for my ludus. It's not enough for my fighters to win. They have to look like they can."

"Begin."

Felix spoke before his master's nod. Before Galen could raise his blade, Brutus's sword tapped his shoulder. "Round four to me. Looks like the next round will decide it."

Galen backed away. "And next round, Felix should wait until we both know he's about to speak."

Brutus turned his gaze on Felix, and his mouth turned down. "I neither want nor need your help to win this. Don't speak until Crassus is ready."

Brutus's knuckles whitened as he gripped the hilt of his sword. Galen's heart began to race...Otto's future hung on the next round.

God, focus me. Give me victory. His heart slowed, and he locked his gaze on Brutus once more.

A nod from his master, then Felix growled, "Begin."

Galen and Brutus both stepped forward, and each man slashed, thrusted, and parried. Galen lost count of the number of strikes before Brutus backed off and wiped the sweat from his brow.

Galen did the same and ran his fingers through his hair to push back the strand that fell onto his forehead. *One more touch, God, and then freedom.*

Brutus moved in, sword flashing. Galen leaped forward, catching Brutus's blade with his own. With all the strength he had, he shoved it upward. Then he ducked under Brutus's arm and spun to slap his opponent's side with the gladius as he slipped past.

◆

Silence hovered over the sand as Brutus's gladiators, who had been watching, froze. Then a string of curses erupted from Felix's mouth. All turned back to their posts, and the sound of wood striking wood returned.

The armorer took the gladius from Crassus. Brutus drove the tip of his own sword into the sand and crossed his arms. He should be sorry he lost, but he wasn't. For him, Bjorn was only a chance to make some money. The big German had great earning potential, but he'd already made a four-fold profit on him. For Gaius Crassus, Bjorn was a man worth dying for.

"Well done, Crassus. You can have him for 5400 denarii. Shall we retire to my office and sign the papers?"

Crassus stroked the scar on his cheek. "I don't have the full amount with me right now. I might need up to three days to get it all together."

The corner of Brutus's mouth lifted. "Three days? I can wait with some patience." He glanced at Bjorn. "But I'm not sure your German friend can."

"A word with Otto, and then I'll go arrange for the payment."

When Crassus got within reach, Bjorn wrapped him in a crushing hug and lifted him off the ground. He rocked his friend so his legs swung back and forth before returning his feet to the sand. The grin on his gladiator's face triggered a grin of his own until Brutus forced his mouth into the smiling frown.

Crassus started toward the door but turned back to face Brutus before stepping through. "I'll be back as soon as I can."

Brutus raised his hand to acknowledge the promise, but no promise was needed. Of course a man who'd crossed half the Empire to save his friend would be back.

He strolled over to stand beside his grinning gladiator. He rested his hand on Bjorn's shoulder, then fingered the bronze collar as the frowning smile played on his own lips.

His brow furrowed when his gaze shifted to the doorway through which Crassus left. "He tracked you all the way from Argentorate. Four weeks without knowing if you were alive or dead or if he'd ever find you, but he crossed half the Empire looking." Brutus shook his head. "Do you know how rare that kind of loyalty is? I can't name a single man who would do that." He crossed his arms. "He looks like a runt, but inside... he's a giant."

"He always has been. It's like he says, 'It's the heart, not the height that matters.'"

Brutus shifted his gaze to the tall German. "Soon you'll be Otto of the Vangiones, but until he actually pays me, you're still Bjorn of the Langobardi. I have two young men coming to spar with you this afternoon. I expect you to give them their money's worth."

A giggle floated down from the balcony that overlooked the training sand. Two young women draped with gold jewelry leaned over the railing. A seductive smile curved Brutus's lips as he raised his hand to wave. That triggered another round of giggles.

"We have some feminine visitors. Show them some muscles at the palus before your first customer arrives."

Bjorn swung the long wooden sword in a circle over his head before slashing the post. A gasp and a whispered "look at that big blond one" reached Brutus's ears as he turned away.

He circled the arena, pausing briefly to watch each of his gladiators at their posts. All were big men, muscled up and intimidating enough to rent out as "persuaders" whose mere presence ensured compliance.

His gaze drifted to the doorway through which Crassus had gone. Laughably unimpressive at first sight, but perhaps the most admirable man he'd ever met. It truly was the heart that mattered.

Chapter 30

It's Been a Good Life

When Galen walked into the courtyard of the inn, Quintus was brushing the back of a bay mare. Galen picked up another brush and began brushing her neck.

Quintus's eyebrows asked the question, and Galen's smile answered it. "So you found him."

"Yes, but there's a complication. The man who owns him wants more than I have. I sparred with him to get it down to where I almost have enough, but I still need 1600 denarii more." He paused mid-stroke. "I need your prayers, Quintus. The only way I can get the money is to go to an enemy of the faith."

"Who?"

"Tiberius Cornelius Lentulus."

Quintus rubbed his chin. "His reputation as an honorable man and loyal son of Rome is well known. But lately he seems to have stepped out of the group of men vying for top posts in the government."

"Loyal to Rome—I have no doubt of that. He hunted the followers of the Way when he governed Germania Superior. I hope he's still in Rome, not off somewhere serving. How would I find out where Lentulus lives?"

"In the Basilica Julia, there are offices that handle the court cases. Someone there should be able to give directions to the villa of a man so high in the circles of power." Quintus's brow furrowed. "But is there no other way? Why Lentulus?"

"He's the only one I know in Rome who has that much money and might give it to me. We're related by marriage, and that marriage might make him suspect I follow the Way. But Otto is a good friend of Lentulus's son, and that might make him willing to help even without him knowing my sister is the mother of his grandchildren."

Quintus ran his fingers through his hair. "I wish I had the money to spare you from the risk."

Galen rested his hand on Quintus's shoulder. "I know you'd help if you could, and I thank you, brother. But maybe the risk is not as great as I think. A father should be eager to hear about his only son and be grateful to the man who brings the news. I can tell him that Dec is happily married and has three children without revealing anything about myself. If Lentulus gives me the extra money I need to redeem his son's friend, all will be well. If not..."

Galen swept the brush along the mare's side. "I should trust that God will protect me from him discovering my faith. Sometimes I think I sense danger, and it turns out I'm wrong. I hope I'm wrong this time. But, to be on the safe side..."

He made two more sweeps with the brush. "I plan to take Adela with me and leave her holding the horses and all the money while I talk with Lentulus. I'll tell her to come back to you if I get taken. I've been training her to be able to find her way home alone for the last three weeks."

His lips tightened. "We've become good friends, and if something happens to me, it might tear her up. She's strong and smart, but I'm not sure she'll know how to start back without me. Please help her with that. And if she'll listen, please tell her I didn't really die. I've tried to tell her about Jesus several times, and she cuts me off. But if I'm killed for refusing to deny him...maybe she'll listen."

Quintus reached across the mare to rest his hand on Galen's shoulder. "If she comes back here alone, I'll take what you have and ask Brutus to free Otto for less so he can take her home. The worst he could do is say no."

"That's worth trying." Galen rubbed the back of his neck. Brutus made money feeding the Roman lust for blood and death, but at his core, he might be a good man. "Maybe he'll be willing to let Otto go if he learns I died before I could get the rest of the money. He tried hard to win, but he almost seemed glad when I did."

Quintus swept the brush down the mare's back once more. "I'll be praying for you. God will be with you, and His will shall be done."

As Adela followed Galen through the shadow cast by the great stone arch of the Porta Fontinalis into the heart of Rome, her eyes were drawn to the gleaming white buildings that towered just ahead.

Galen slipped off Astrelo and handed her the reins. "Stay here. I need directions to Tiberius Lentulus's villa." He pointed at a huge three-story building with rows of columns on the first two stories. "Basilica Julia. The courts are in there, and the clerks should know where he lives."

Adela watched him weave his way into the crowd of men in togas. His dark blue shirt stood out in the sea of white, but with his dark tan, aquiline nose, and wavy, dark brown hair, he looked just like them. A Roman among Romans…and yet there was something very different about him. Something special.

Her mouth curved at that thought. Then the word *pulchra* caught her ear, and she glanced down at the two Roman men leering at her as they stood nearby. A hand on her dagger and a glare were enough to make them move on.

When she turned her gaze back toward the basilica, Galen had vanished. But there was one thing she could count on. Galen would always return.

Long moments stretched into at least a half hour, and still Galen didn't reappear. In Hermunduri country, she would have gone to look for him, but no one would dare to take her horse there. The Romans who looked at the horses with a desire to have them were even greater in number than the ones who looked at her. Twice she'd started to unsheathe the dagger as she glared at one before he turned away and walked on.

The tension drained from her shoulders when she finally glimpsed Galen's dark, wavy hair and blue tunic weaving through the dense crowd.

The smile on his lips as he took his reins revealed his success.

"Tiberius Lentulus has several villas spread around Italia, but he was seen in Rome yesterday. They thought we'd find him at his villa that's a short way up the Via Tibertina. We need to skirt the Forums and ride northeast up the Clivus Suburanus. That takes us out the Porta Esquilina to the Via Tibertina."

Adela nodded. As long as Galen knew the way, that was enough.

"Now repeat what I just told you, only backward."

Her mouth fell open as she turned her head to stare at him.

"Trust me on this. Via Tiburtina through the Porta Esquilina. Then down the Clivus Suburanus to the Forum area before you go through the Porta Fontinalis in the city wall. Then the Via Flaminia, on past the Mausoleum of Augustus until you get to Quintus's inn."

As Adela recited the backward route until Galen pronounced it perfect, she fought a smile. It was odd what he wanted her to know sometimes, but she didn't mind learning. He waved his hand a little as she recited, almost like he was listening to music. He'd told her more than once that her voice was musical.

She glanced at his profile, with its trace of a smile. His deep voice was certainly music to her ears.

Vineyards and orchards lined the road that turned off the Via Tiburtina and led to the Lentulus villa. Adela preferred wilder country to the well-groomed farms around Rome. In Germania, a stag might leap from the brush in front of you, or the soft gurgle of a stream would accompany birdsong. In Italia, all seemed safe and peaceful, but tendrils of unease wrapped around her.

Galen had grown strangely silent. The trace of a smile was missing.

They came to a paddock where several gorgeous horses were chasing each other, and he reined in to watch. The corner of his mouth turned up a little, but there was something sad about his smile.

"That's a beautiful stallion. He reminds me of Dec's stallion at home." He patted Astrelo's neck. "Astro sired Astrelo. I wonder if these share the same bloodline." His smile broadened as he focused on her, but his eyes lacked the warmth she expected. "Val raises some of the most beautiful horses. I enjoy selling them to people who appreciate a fine mount. It's been a good life."

Been a good life? Those words sent a shiver through her. Those had been her mother's last words to her father. Father was not a man who let his feelings show, but he'd taken Mother's hand in both of his. When he raised it to his cheek and nodded, Mother's eyes had filled with love, and the smile she reserved for him alone broke free. Then her eyelids closed ...and she was gone.

Father had laid her hand on her chest and moved the other to lie on top of it. His jaw had clenched before he strode from the house without a word. He'd hurled himself onto his horse and galloped out of the village. Adela had watched him until he vanished into the woods, and then she'd returned to prepare the body that was no longer Mother for its funeral the next day.

But Galen was young and healthy. They had only come to the Lentulus villa to ask for some money to save the good friend of the rich Roman's son. Why those words?

He undid the belt that held his purse and dagger and draped it across the saddle in front of him. "Before we get to the villa, I want you to take all the horse money." He lifted his tunic to get to the two money belts containing his and Otto's horse money that he concealed underneath it.

"Here. Put these on." He faced away from her as she put both under her tunic and fastened her belt over them, just as he had always done.

"I'm through."

When he turned back toward her, his usual smile had returned...almost. There was something a little stiff about it, and something guarded in his eyes.

Her pulse ramped up. "Why did you give these to me? Is something wrong?"

"Probably not." He turned Astrelo's head toward the large white building surrounded by a matching wall that loomed ahead of them. "Let me do all the talking."

"I won't use my Latin and embarrass my teacher when I say something wrong."

His warmest smile accompanied the shake of his head. "Nothing you could ever do would embarrass me, Adela. Any man would be proud to have you at his side."

She felt the heat in her ears, but he didn't see her blush. His eyes were fixed on the villa ahead of them. What did he think awaited them there?

Galen had only been six when his father had abandoned the ancestral villa and carried his family to Germania Superior to avoid execution in the arena. That was fifteen years ago, but images of the beautiful white columns and colorful mosaics of his former home drifted through his mind as he led Adela through the gate into the stable yard of the Lentulus villa.

A burly slave immediately approached them. "You shouldn't be in here." He flicked his hand toward the gate. "Go around back and find the overseer."

It was the greeting Galen expected. He'd shaved that morning, but it had been almost two months since his last haircut, and his clothes were those of a rustic German, not the cultured attire of a Roman aristocrat. Adela bristled beside him, and he placed his hand on her arm to calm her.

"I'm Gaius Licinius Crassus. I've just arrived from Germania Superior, and I have an urgent personal message for Tiberius Cornelius Lentulus."

The stable slave's eyebrows popped up at his three-part Roman name. "Wait here. I'll see if the master is available to receive you."

When Galen turned to Adela, he almost laughed. Her eyebrows were as high as he'd seen them. "You're Gaius Licinius Crassus? I never heard that before."

Galen calmed his grin. "I told you outside Brigantium my full name had twenty letters. When seeking audience with a leading Roman citizen, I have to declare I'm a citizen to be worth his time. Only citizens can use the three-part name." He undid the purse from his belt and held it out to her. That shot her eyebrows up again. He shook it before she took it from his hand.

"Listen very carefully. When he comes back to take me into the house, you are not to get off your horse, no matter what anyone says or does to get you off." He slid off Astrelo and handed her the reins. "Do not let anyone take Astrelo for any reason. If I don't come back out, I want you to have him.

"If someone other than me comes out of the house and tells you to get off and come in, ride out immediately. If anyone tries to stop you, do whatever it takes to get away. Go back to Quintus. He'll explain what's happened and help you get home. I had you memorize the way...just in case."

◆

Adela's heart raced. "Why are you saying you might not come out? I'm not going to ride away and leave you. I need you...to get home."

His lips tightened. "No, you don't need me. I've been teaching you Latin this whole trip in case something happened to me when I tried to rescue Otto and you had to find your way home alone. You can do it. I've taught you how to ask how far to the next town and what road to take, where's a respectable place to stay that's safe for a woman alone. Don't forget that it's safest to ask directions from the Roman garrisons, and you know enough Latin now to do that. Take the roads we took and stay at the same places we stayed. When you get to Argentorate, ask for Centurion Silanus. Repeat his name."

Adela swallowed the lump in her throat. "Centurion Silanus."

"Good. Tell Silanus I died in Rome and ask him to help you figure out where to go when you cross the frontier to get home. He might be able to tell you what road to take and some of the larger villages that are on the way to your home village.

"If I don't come out, first go to Quintus, and he'll try to buy Otto with the horse money I gave you. Otto will take you home if Brutus agrees to sell him for less. If not, I know you can get home by yourself."

Adela fought the quaver in her voice. "But I don't want to leave you. Why do you think Lentulus might not let you come out?"

"You must leave. If I can't come out myself, it means Lentulus has taken me captive, and I'll be dying in the arena."

Her heart raced, but she shoved the surging emotions down. "But why would Lentulus do that? You've never done anything wrong."

Before he could answer, the slave emerged from the house and hurried over to join them. She understood enough of his Latin to know Lentulus had summoned Galen and wanted to know what a Roman from Germania could possibly have to tell him.

Galen rested his hand on her foot and squeezed. "Promise me you'll go to Quintus right away if I don't come for you and someone tries to get you off your horse."

"I promise."

As Galen followed the slave into the house, a single tear escaped and trickled down her cheek. It didn't remain alone for long. Her chest jumped, and she swallowed hard.

Oh, Galen. You have to come out. She flicked aside the tears and squared her shoulders. *Te amo, Galen Crassus. You can't die here.*

A Hermunduri woman was strong, able to face anything without showing emotion. But try as she might, she couldn't hold back the tears.

Chapter 31

THE ONLY RICH MAN

The stable slave led Galen past the Corinthian columns of the portico that ran the width of the stable yard. At the corner, he passed Galen off to a house slave who looked about ten. The boy led him half-way down the portico along the second side of the house. There, he was met by an older man with a gray fringe of curly hair encircling his head.

"I am Graecus, steward of the estates of Cornelius Lentulus. I understand you have an urgent message for Master Tiberius."

The smile he offered was reserved, and his crossed arms didn't encourage familiarity.

Galen tilted his head, as Brutus had done. "Yes, and I can give it only to Tiberius Lentulus himself. It is of a personal nature. I assure you he will be glad to receive it."

The steward's gaze swept Galen from head to foot and back again. "Gaius Licinius Crassus, you say? I thought I knew all the younger men of that family."

"I've been living in Germania since childhood. You would not have met me in Rome. But I'm not here to discuss my relatives. The message and associated request I bear are matters of some urgency."

The old steward's gaze settled on Galen's dagger.

Gallen slipped it from its scabbard and offered it handle-first to Graecus. "You may have this until I leave, if you wish."

Graecus took the handle, and his stiff smile relaxed into a subdued but genuine one. "I will take it, but I doubt that's necessary when it's so freely offered."

He looked over his shoulder as he turned to enter the house. "Follow me, Crassus."

As the steward led Galen through the peristyle's lush garden, brilliant with flowers, a sweet fragrance that Galen didn't recognize floated in the air. They passed into the atrium, and Graecus veered left to lead him into a room with a throne-like chair on a raised platform directly across from the arched doorway. A desk flanked by cupboards carved with hunting scenes stood against the left wall. A row of chairs lined the wall opposite the platform.

It seemed a lifetime since Galen had been in his father's *tablinum*, watching the many clients come to pay their respects during the morning salutation. White togas and tunics with purple stipes—all part of a life long gone. It was funny how memories that hadn't surfaced for years came back in this villa that was so much like their own.

But his life was in Germania, and that was the only place he wanted to be. Father and Mother had loved the freedom of simply being who they were, unshackled from their famous family name and all the social expectations. Father had said many times how much he thanked God for giving them Val as a new daughter and Germania as a new home where they could follow the Way without fear. But they had died before Tiberius Lentulus made following Jesus a capital crime.

Graecus dipped his head toward Galen and swept his hand toward the chairs. "Please be seated. Master Tiberius will be with you shortly."

The boy had followed them, and Graecus snapped his fingers to direct him to a corner of the room, where he became a statue with his eyes locked on Galen.

Galen settled into a chair and crossed his arms. If a room could be a window into its owner's soul, this one certainly was. The paintings on the walls portrayed great events in Roman history. The floor was an array of multicolored geometric tiles that formed an intricate pattern of interwoven lines. The masks of Tiberius's ancestors hung on the wall opposite the desk.

Everything about the room declared its owner's pride as a Roman and a Cornelius Lentulus and his passion for order and tradition. Tiberius had considered Dec's new faith a betrayal of his ancestors and of Rome. Would he still care enough about the disowned son who prayed for him every day to spend money he wouldn't even miss to redeem his son's friend?

He focused his eyes past the geometric patterns painted on the ceiling. *God, you gave me victory over Brutus. Please move Tiberius to give me the money so that victory means Otto's freedom.*

Galen's shoulders squared at the sound of sandals outside the door. With Dec and Val, he'd prayed for Tiberius's soul for eight years, but to what effect? Enemy or friend...he was about to find out.

The tall, gray-haired man who entered the room radiated authority and physical strength. Dec would look just like him in twenty years. Galen rose and straightened to his full height.

"Thank you for meeting with me. I have some information from Germania Superior that I believe you will be glad to receive and a request for assistance that only you can give."

"So Graecus has informed me. What is this personal information that you think might interest me?"

A movement in the corner drew Galen's glance. The boy who'd been left to watch him had turned his head to hear better. "It's for your ears only, and there are extra ears in this room."

Without even looking behind him, Lentulus snapped his fingers. His hand fisted, and he pointed to the door with his thumb. The boy bowed and left.

"Otto, son of Baldric of the Vangiones, and I were selling horses in Argentorate when he was kidnapped and sold as a gladiator. I've tracked him to Rome, but the man who owns him set his price higher than I can pay."

Tiberius's eyebrows dipped. "And why should this be important to me?"

"Otto is still alive because he trained for years in the use of a gladius with his good friend, a man to whom you were close when you were governor in Germania Superior. He was senatorial tribune of the XXII Primigenia while you were there."

Tiberius's head bounced back. "Decimus is in Germania?"

"Yes."

"When did you see him last? Is he well?"

"Four and a half weeks ago. He's very well. Happily married with two sons and a daughter. His horses were among those we were selling."

Tiberius said nothing, but the corners of his mouth turned up and his eyes started to crinkle.

"I have the money from selling the horses, but it's short by 1600 denarii. You're the only man in Rome with whom I have a connection who might have the resources to help me buy Otto out of the arena. I've come to ask you to help me redeem Otto by providing the funds I lack."

"What is the asking price for my son's friend?"

"His owner started at 9000 denarii, but I brought him down to 5400 by betting I could beat him sparring. I've trained for years with Dec as well."

Tiberius's brows rose, triggering Galen's grin. "Yes, I know I don't look like much of an opponent for a man who owns gladiators, but Brutus learned it's the heart, not the height, that matters. Plus years of training with one of the finest swordsmen who ever held a gladius."

Tiberius's mouth pulled sideways into a wry smile. "I'd wager being a horse trader helped as well."

Galen rubbed his lower lip. "No doubt. So, will you help me buy Dec's friend?"

"I'll provide the money you need."

Galen's grin broke free. "Thank you from Otto, from Dec, and from me."

Tiberius tipped his head once. "It will be my pleasure. You can make the purchase tomorrow." The corner of Tiberius's mouth twitched as amusement filled his eyes. "Graecus said you have an unusually pretty armed companion still mounted in the stable yard. Tonight, you both will stay here as my guests. I'd like to hear what Decimus has been doing these past eight years."

Tiberius scanned Galen from head to foot, and his mouth turned down. "You look like you've traveled halfway across the Empire. You'll both want to clean up before we dine. You should find the bath here as comfortable as any, and Graecus will provide suitable clothes for you both."

Galen kept his grin from turning into a chuckle. Tiberius wouldn't understand what was so funny. The warrior woman had never seen the inside of a Roman villa, and her reactions would be entertaining to behold. "That will be most welcome. I'll go tell Adela."

Tiberius tipped his head. "I have some matters to attend to, but I will join you for dinner. Relax and enjoy yourselves. There are gardens and a library, if you're so inclined."

"Dec told me about your library. I look forward to seeing it."

Galen followed Tiberius out of the tablinum and headed for the stable yard.

◆

Adela chewed her lip as she kept her gaze locked on the door through which Galen had disappeared. Would he ever come out? She blinked hard to push back the tears.

The stable man had come over to take the horses as soon as Galen left, but his eyes had saucered and he'd scurried away when she drew her dagger and glared at him.

"Adela."

Her head snapped sideways when his deep voice came from a different door. He walked toward her, a huge grin on his face.

All the tension drained from her body.

"Tiberius will provide the money, and he's invited us to use his bath, have dinner, and stay the night."

Galen summoned the stable man she'd scared away. She caught something about saddles going to their rooms and the horses being stabled and groomed. It would be a luxurious night for Astrelo and Otto's horse, too.

She swung her leg over her horse's neck and slipped off. She offered his purse, and Galen tied it back on his belt.

He held out his hand, and she slipped hers into it. As his fingers wrapped around hers, happiness wrapped around her heart.

"Dec said the gardens here were beautiful. Let's take a short walk, and then we'll get cleaned up for dinner."

He grinned at her. "I'm expecting a good night. I can sleep in a soft bed instead of on the floor to keep unwelcome night visitors out." His grin broadened. "But keeping you safe is worth all the cold, hard floors. And setting Otto free...nothing could make me happier."

Adela nodded. For Galen's sake, she wanted Otto free, but the greatest happiness she could imagine wasn't freeing Otto from bondage. It was binding herself to Galen Crassus as his wife.

But her days of a woman still hadn't come. If Gundahar had spoken the truth and she now carried his child, could a fine man like Galen want her?

Chapter 32

Still Not the Time

Adela felt her own smile grow as Galen led her toward an archway in the wall around the stable yard. Through it, she could see a patchwork of color. As they passed through, the scent of roses wrapped around her. A profusion of red and pink and white dotted the rows of bushes. Beds surrounded by low brick walls were filled with patterns of blue and pink, yellow and white. The blooms were so thick she could scarcely see any green between them.

Her breath caught at the large red flowers waving atop tall stalks with circles of silvery green leaves at their base. "What are those?"

"Poppies." Galen fingered a petal. "My mother loved them, and they grew everywhere around our villa. If you leave the blooms alone, they turn into brown seed pods. I used to like to turn them upside down and shake them to get the seeds out. Our cook used them on top of the little bread rolls that were my favorite part of lunch."

Galen led her toward a tower at the corner of the garden wall. "Looks like a watchtower, but what would Tiberius need one for? Let's go see."

He released her hand as they climbed the stairs. At the top, a panorama stretched out before them. Mountains rose in the distance past nearby fields and pastures. To their left, horses grazed in the long grass.

Galen's gaze settled there. "That's the pasture we rode by." His finger moved as he counted the horses. "I see at least two dozen horses. I wonder if this is where the tribune at the top of Summus Poeninus got his horse. He said Tiberius had the best stable in Rome."

Adela's gaze focused on the fields beyond the pasture. "The people working out there look like ants from here."

"Some owners treat them as if they were nothing more than that."

"Does Tiberius?"

"I don't know. Some men who treat their equals well treat their slaves like living tools that have no hearts and minds. They even call them *instrumentum vocalis*—talking instruments."

Adela's brow furrowed. "That's wrong. Even a slave is a man."

"And every man is precious in the eyes of God."

"But not in Roman eyes." A shudder passed through her. "I can still see that man on the cross in Octodurus. Let's not talk about this."

She led him back down the stairs.

A long, narrow pool stretched between the rows of flower beds. Along it stood several statues of men and women and animals, but Adela's eyes were drawn to the one at the end.

It was a warrior without clothes, sitting on his shield with his sword and a trumpet beside him. A sword wound in his chest dripped blood. He was dying.

Her gaze locked onto his face, and her hand covered her mouth. With his mustache and long hair and the torc around his neck, he looked exactly like her cousin. Brave in the face of death, but he looked so sad. Like he'd fought so hard, but he'd lost everything. Death was the enemy no man could defeat.

She'd seen that look on her father's face after Mother died, but only when he thought no one was looking. She wasn't as strong as he was, and she'd worn the look where others had seen. But even that was a mask. Only when she was alone under the stars had she let the deep pain show. Before she returned to the house, she always put on the mask again.

Galen's hand touched her arm. "Adela? Are you all right?"

She nodded and forced a smile as she turned her gaze back to Galen. "I hope I never see that look on your face. You were gone so long in the villa...I was afraid you weren't coming back. I couldn't bear it if you died here."

◆

Galen's heart leaped. Here was the opening he'd been praying for. "If I did die here, it wouldn't be death. Not like you're thinking of it. Life won't end for me when my body dies. My God has made certain of that."

A frown accompanied the shake of her head. "But that's not what I've seen. Life is over and gone when the body dies. I saw it with Mother. I saw it with my baby sister. She only lived a few hours, and I was holding her when she died."

"It only seems that way." He tapped his chest. "What you see dies and is buried, but we're much more than what you see. We're—"

The crunch of footsteps on the gravel behind him made him spin. Tiberius's man was too close. No time to explain and maybe too risky even if there was time. He exhaled without finishing his sentence.

The man bowed. "The bath now awaits you. I will escort you there."

Galen glanced at Adela. "Is there only one bathing area?"

"Yes."

Adela's eyes widened. Then a deep blush swept across her cheeks.

"I'll bathe quickly and leave it for you to enjoy alone. I'm eager to look at the library anyway, and this will give me more time there."

Tiberius's man made no move to leave, and Galen suppressed a sigh. The opportunity to talk with her about Jesus was blocked yet again.

"If you want to enjoy the garden longer or relax in your room, someone will come find you the moment I'm through."

Galen followed the man into the villa.

As they walked down a hall lined with mosaics, the man pointed to a door. "Your things have been placed in here." He pointed to the door next to it. "And your woman's things are here. All you should need is already in the bath, but a boy will be there to get anything else."

Galen's brow furrowed. "Is there a woman who can take care of Adela instead?

"Yes, I will arrange that."

"Good. We've been travelling a long time, and she doesn't have what she will need for a formal dinner."

"I will take care of that as well."

As they entered the bath, the man's hand swept toward the shelves. "You will find clean clothes there and towels. When you are through, send the boy to me, and I will see that your woman is summoned and has all the help she needs."

Galen let his grin leak out after the man left. A hot bath, a good dinner...a man couldn't ask for a better evening. Maybe having to come to an enemy of the faith wasn't a bad thing after all.

♦

After Galen left, Adela strolled back to the house and entered through the door where Galen had reappeared. Her breath caught as her gaze swept the interior of Tiberius's villa. Nothing she had seen in the public baths or respectable inns had prepared her for the elegant surroundings and luxurious lifestyle of a noble Roman.

The floor mosaics portrayed many kinds of animals, some engaged in mortal combat with people. The walls were painted with scenes of oceans, mountains, forests, and farms.

A woman walked up behind her. "Mistress, if it would please you, come with me to select what you wish to wear this evening for dinner."

Adela glanced down at Galen's clothes. "I have something Galen got me in my saddlebag."

The woman tightened her lips to fight off a laugh, and Adela felt her ears heat. "Steward Graecus told me to provide something suitable."

She swept her hand toward a hallway. "This way."

Adela followed her past the many wall mosaics to a room with a door carved with a floral garland. Inside, a wicker chair and a small table holding a polished silver mirror held by two dancing nymphs stood between two windows. A cabinet with a Roman goddess carved on the door and a matching trunk were on the opposite wall. A blanket striped with reds, oranges, and browns draped a bed. Adela pressed on it, and it was softer than any pillow she'd laid her head on.

The woman opened the chest and lifted out three tunics: one blue, one red, and one green. "Which do you prefer, mistress?"

Galen had picked blue for her in Luna. Adela touched the blue one, and the woman laid it on the bed before returning the others to the trunk. Then the woman opened the cabinet. She removed a cord of braided silver chains and placed it with the tunic. From a drawer in the small table, she selected eight silver pins and placed them in the small silver basket sitting on the table.

The woman's hand swept toward the door. "The oils and fragrances are already in the bath chamber, mistress. Please follow me."

Adela had enjoyed the baths Galen had taken them to, but they were nothing compared to the private bath of Tiberius Lentulus. The many different fragrances of cleansing oils left her trying to remember what Galen had said he liked best. She settled on roses. The woman had then washed her hair and rinsed it with water that smelled just like the oil.

The water for soaking had been perfect: hot, but not too hot. And the robe she'd been wrapped in when she rose from the tub was made of the same material as the towels.

After slipping her feet into a pair of slippers, she followed the woman back to her chamber. She stepped into the tunic and discovered it was nothing more than a tube. Then the woman pinned the top shut, and it turned into a tunic with openings that let her shoulders and arms peek out. After the cord was wrapped around her upper body, crossing in the middle, the curves of her body were obvious, yet somehow she didn't feel embarrassed by that. She glanced at herself in the mirror, and a slow smile formed. Galen would like the color.

Her hand rested on her belly, and the smile vanished.

"Sit, mistress, and I'll do your hair."

Adela settled into the wicker chair and forced herself to relax as the woman first dried her hair with a towel and then combed it to remove the tangles. She closed her eyes and savored the feeling of fingers running through her hair, dividing it into thick strands, and braiding it.

Her eyes popped open when she felt the braid being wrapped around her head. The woman pushed gold picks tipped with butterflies into the thick mass of hair to hold the braid in place.

The scent of roses wrapped around her again as the woman dabbed perfume into her hair, behind her ears, at her throat, and on her wrists.

She gazed at her reflection in the silver mirror. Was that beautiful woman really her? What would Galen say when he saw her in the soft tunic that draped her form so elegantly, drawn in at all the right places by the silver cord? Would admiration curve his lips into a grin and light up those laughing eyes?

The woman rested her hands on the back of the chair. "We're finished. You look lovely, mistress."

Adela turned in the chair to smile up at her. "Thank you. Can you take me to the library now? Galen is waiting for me."

Galen lifted another scroll from the library shelf and unrolled it. It had been a relaxing afternoon. He'd found history, poetry, and philosophy to choose among. Galen always thought Dec had embellished the description of the library at the Lentulus villa, but he'd understated how extensive it was. Tiberius had probably been adding to it during the last eight years.

His concern that Tiberius would kill him seemed rather foolish now. There'd been no need to reveal anything about his own relationship with Dec for Tiberius to be willing to help Otto.

Everything was turning out like he'd prayed for. After he freed Otto and they were heading back, surely the right time to tell Adela about his faith would present itself.

Adela.

His sigh escaped. If only she would let him tell her about Jesus, maybe she would choose to follow Him. Then his dear friend could become his wife...if she wanted him. She liked Romans even less now than she did when he first met her, but he considered himself more German than Roman. She'd said "those Romans" often enough that she must, too.

He suppressed the next sigh. He had no reason to think she didn't still want a German chieftain's son. And Otto would be traveling with them. What German woman in her right mind wouldn't want Otto? Tall, muscular, handsome, smart, good sense of humor, wealthy family...everything a Hermunduri chieftain's daughter would find appealing. And a truly good man, even if he did sometimes think with his eyes instead of his head. This trip may well have cured that problem.

Galen rubbed the back of his neck. Adela's father might insist she marry a Hermunduri, and then it wouldn't matter whether he or Otto were the richest, most handsome men inside or outside the Empire. German fathers had the power to choose, and Adela's father would never choose him. Otto, maybe, but never him.

But what her father would choose wasn't the only obstacle. Until she chose Jesus, he could never choose her. His own Father had rules about whom His children could marry, and a pagan woman, no matter how much he liked her, didn't fit those rules.

But if she decides to follow you, Lord, and if she puts Your choice for her over her earthly father's choice...maybe there is a way.

He turned at the soft sound of her sandals on the mosaic floor.

"Adela." His grin spread slowly. "I was right about my clothes not complimenting a pretty girl. I thought you looked good in what we got in Luna, but now..." His lips puckered as he blew out a long breath. The silver clips that closed the tunic at the top revealed her bare shoulders. The silver cord wrapped around her body emphasized her womanly curves. "You look just like a Roman lady. A very pretty Roman lady."

A flush of blood colored her cheeks. His grin skewed and broadened.

"Blue and pink together—I think I have a new favorite color combination."

"You look different, too. So...Roman."

His eyebrow arched. "Is that good or bad? I know you admire big Germanic warriors most." He ran a hand through his fresh-cropped hair and rubbed his clean-shaven chin. "Personally, I prefer shirts and pants to tunics and togas, but when in Rome..."

She walked over to stand close beside him. He inhaled the soft scent of roses that wafted from her hair. It was hard to keep his eyes off her. Such a pretty woman. So brave. So strong. The kind of woman any man would be proud to call his own. Proud to have love him. But she wanted a warrior, and he wanted a woman who loved Jesus like he did.

Every time he tried to tell her about Him, she turned the conversation another way.

But...God, I still wish she could be what you plan for me.

It was best not to think too much about that...about her.

She lifted one of the scrolls from its shelf and unrolled it enough to see the Greek letters. "All this...you could read it if you wanted. You could know everything the man who made this did." She waved her hand toward the wall. "What all these men knew."

He shrugged. "With enough time. But they aren't the ones who know the truth. Tiberius wouldn't have the scrolls that tell the real truth."

She turned toward him. "The real truth?" Those warm blue eyes held the question in their depths.

He took her hand in his and swept his thumb slowly across the back of it. His heart rate ramped up. Was this the opening he'd been praying for? She was asking, but would she listen this time? Would she understand? Would she feel God's call to her heart?

"Yes." He took her second hand. "Come sit with me, and I'll tell you."

He'd taken several steps back toward the couch, drawing her with him, when Tiberius's voice interrupted the opportune moment.

"Crassus. Dinner is ready." He was smiling that formal smile expected from a gracious host. "I trust you'll find it an improvement on what you've been eating. Follow me."

Adela withdrew her hands from his and turned to follow Tiberius. Galen heaved a sigh. Maybe it wasn't the right time after all.

Chapter 33

THE PERFECT HOST

The soft music of a lyre greeted Galen as he followed Adela and Tiberius into the dining room. Nine wide couches covered with red sheets were arranged in three sets of three, each set surrounding a low table. Centered under each table was an elaborate mosaic of servants delivering dishes of food. A row of living servants stood along the wall.

Tiberius's steward was already there, gazing into the garden just outside a wide window.

Tiberius waved his hand toward him. "This is Tiberius Cornelius Graecus." The formal smile that made Tiberius's mouth look stiff relaxed into a genuine one. "Graecus's service as steward has been invaluable during my many times away from Rome serving the Empire. He's also my good friend and a second father to Decimus. He will be dining with us."

Graecus tipped his head. "I've had the pleasure of meeting Crassus, but not this lovely young woman."

Galen stepped beside her. "This is Adela, daughter of Adalmar, chieftain of the Hermunduri."

Adela tipped her head and smiled. In her accented Latin, she replied, "It is my pleasure."

The corners of Galen's mouth curved. The warrior woman could do a fair job of passing herself off as a Roman lady, Latin and all.

Tiberius took the host's position at the head of the left couch, and Graecus took the right one.

189

Tiberius's hand swept toward the center couch. "I assume the two of you will recline together. You have, after all, been traveling together for a long time."

Their host's suggestive smile made Adela's eyes widen and her mouth straighten.

Galen shook his head. "It's not that way with us, and Adela has never reclined to eat before. We'll sit on the dining couch."

He settled on the edge as if it were a chair and patted the spot next to him. She sat down beside him, but her back stayed straight and her head erect with chin slightly raised.

Galen had to fight a smile. Tiberius was used to Roman noblewomen with their gracious manners and slaves who did what he wanted without question. Adela was neither.

A nod from Tiberius started the dinner service. As a boy of about ten filled the wine cups and handed one to each of them, the appetizer course consisting of a salad of mixed greens, boiled crabs, and hard-boiled eggs was placed on the table.

Galen ate each in turn, and Adela followed suit.

When the servants took that course away, water and towels were passed to the diners to prepare for the next course.

The main course included carrots in a white wine sauce and lamb in a cream sauce made with red wine, onions, mushrooms, and any number of spices that Galen was at a loss to identify. The silky richness exploded in his mouth with each bite. It would be much too easy to eat more than a man should at Tiberius's table.

Again, the water and towels appeared.

As the platters of pastries filled with fruit were placed before them, Adela placed her hand over her mouth and whispered in Germanic, "Do Romans always eat three meals for dinner?"

Galen whispered a reply. "Some do, but this is a dinner fit for company in a noble house."

◆

Tiberius kept his host's smile from turning into the one Adela's question deserved. A wise governor learned what he could of the local language, and no one would ever question his political wisdom.

There had been little conversation while they ate, but the time had come to answer the questions that had plagued him for years. He caught Graecus's eye. His steward would be his inquisitor. As host, it would be impolite for him to interrogate his guest. He wanted to know everything about Decimus, but he didn't want young Crassus to return to Germania and tell the son he banished how desperate he was for news of him.

Graecus took a sip of wine. "I've known Decimus since he was born. It's good to hear that life has gone well for him since he was last in Rome. How long have you known him?"

"He joined us eight years ago."

"Do you see him often?"

"We raise horses together."

"It was a pleasure to watch him as a boy. His own sons—I had hoped to see them. What are his boys like?"

That question brought a smile to Crassus's lips. "Publius is six. He's a smart one and eager to try anything new. Gaius is four, and whatever his brother is doing, he wants to join in."

"So far from Rome, are they learning Latin, history, and philosophy like every noble Roman should?"

"Dec has a small library, and the boys are learning Latin and Greek from Dec and their mother. She's an educated woman herself."

Publius and Gaius. Tiberius tightened his lips to suppress the frown. Why those names, not Decimus and his own? He caught Graecus's eye. A raised eyebrow was enough to tell him what to ask.

"Publius and Gaius? Not what I would expect. It's customary for the first son to share his father's name and common for the second to share his grandfather's."

"Publius was Dec's mentor growing up, and he preferred honoring his mentor over using his own first name."

"And why Gaius?"

"That's the name of the man who was father to his wife."

"What is her name?"

Crassus's smile broadened. "Valeria, and it suits her. She's a woman of strength in many ways. She and Dec are well matched and very happy together."

"From which family of the clan Valerius is his wife?"

Crassus's mouth twitched. "I never heard Dec speak of that."

"Near what city do you live?"

"The nearest legion town is almost two days away. The name of the nearest village wouldn't mean anything to you. It's in the hill country about halfway between Mogontiacum and Argentorate. I sell Dec's horses in both towns."

"Why did he choose to settle there?"

Crassus shrugged. "I never asked."

Tiberius considered himself a master at reading a man to see if he spoke truth. Nothing Crassus said seemed off, but his answers were short and to the point. He seemed relaxed and unperturbed by the questions. Still, a niggling feeling in the back of Tiberius's mind said there was more to the story.

His gaze settled on the German woman. It was harder to lie in a language that wasn't naturally your own, and a chieftain's daughter would be no match for a man who'd thrived no matter who the emperor and his favored subordinates were. Her eyes and body language were open and honest. She was ripe for interrogation, but not by Graecus.

"Adela, I hope you are not feeling left out of what we are talking about. Do you speak much Latin?"

Her face remained relaxed. "Some. Galen has been teaching me so I could get home alone if I had to."

Tiberius kept his face friendly. Galen? An odd name for a Roman who introduced himself as Gaius Licinius Crassus.

Tiberius slipped into Germanic. "That's very thoughtful of him. Why did he think that likely?"

Germanic words triggered a smile, just as he expected. "I'm not sure. His sister's husband taught him so well he's amazing with a sword. He could beat anyone I've ever seen."

He glanced at Crassus and detected a tension that hadn't been there. "What have you seen that's amazing?"

"He was sitting by the campfire when a man attacked him from behind with a dagger. He rolled forward to get out of the way, and when he stood, he'd drawn his sword. Then he knocked the man out with the handle. It would have been so easy to kill him then, but Galen didn't want to."

"That is impressive. It sounds like a trick my son sometimes used." He turned his eyes from Adela to Crassus. The hint of tension remained. "Well, Crassus, it's fortunate both you and Otto trained with my son."

Crassus's face relaxed into the slight smile that was his normal expression. "It is."

Tiberius scrutinized Crassus over the rim of his cup as he took another sip of wine. Without doubt, the young man knew more about Decimus than he'd revealed. What he'd spoken was not unreasonable for a good friend to know, but it was certain a brother-in-law would know it. If this Galen's sister was the mother of his grandsons, why hadn't he just said so from the beginning? And why was she not a Licinius like him?

As the remains of the final course were carried away, Tiberius turned to Adela. "So, what do you think of a Roman dinner prepared by a fine chef?"

"It tastes good. Some of it is like nothing I've ever had before. And there are so many different things on the table and so much of it. If I ate everything, I could get sick."

Tiberius tightened his lips, but that didn't stop his grin entirely.

Her blush heightened her beauty. "I shouldn't have said that."

Tiberius relaxed his grin into a friendly smile. "No, it's perfectly fine that you did. It's refreshing to have a woman at my table who speaks her thoughts instead of what she believes I want to hear."

He shifted his smile to Crassus. "You are a lucky man to be traveling with such a companion. The evening conversation must be most enjoyable."

Crassus smiled in return. "Not for the reason you imply, but for many others, I am."

A quick glance at Adela revealed no blush. That signaled either her lack of understanding of the hidden meaning of his words or the truth of Crassus's claim that it wasn't that way with them.

Tiberius appraised Adela over his drinking cup as he took another sip. The way the girl looked at Crassus...no Roman man could miss reading how much she was attracted to him. The way he looked back...the attraction was mutual. So, if it was true they didn't "recline together," why not?

As Galen and Adela strolled past the mural of alpine scenes on the way to their bedchambers, he glanced at the beautiful woman walking beside him.

"I'm sorry I had to bring you so far from home, but tomorrow we free Otto and can start back. It's been good having you with me on the hunt."

Adela's smile wrapped him in its warmth. "I'm glad you brought me. You've shown me so many wonderful things. Today was beyond what I ever imagined. It's so pretty here, and Tiberius has been so welcoming."

"I'd hoped he still cared enough for Dec that he'd help. I've no doubt now that he does. I'm glad I was able to tell him his son is married and happy."

"Eight years since they parted, and Tiberius hadn't heard anything. He must have thought Decimus was dead." Her smile dimmed. "Father probably thinks that about me."

"Another month and he'll know you're alive and well. It was a pleasure to see the smile on Tiberius's face. I'll enjoy seeing your father's smile, too." *Before I leave you with him.* Galen blocked a sigh.

"I hope so." Uncertainty colored her voice.

He took her hand and stroked the back with his thumb. "I'm sure of it. Don't believe anything Gundahar said. Dec left because his father ordered him to, and you saw how glad Tiberius was to know Dec was well and happy. Your father will be overjoyed to get you back."

Adela's eyebrows rose. "He told his own son to leave? Why?"

Galen lowered his voice. "Here is not the place to talk about it. After we're headed home, I'll tell you."

They had reached her door, and he pushed it open for her.

Adela released his hand. "I still have the horse money, but I'd rather you did. Wait here."

She dug to the bottom of the bag tied to her saddle and returned with the belts.

Galen draped them over his shoulder. "Tiberius said breakfast would be ready shortly after dawn. He'll send someone to fetch us. Until then, rest in peace."

She leaned her head against the edge of the door. "It seems strange, you not sleeping by the door. The sound of you breathing...it makes the room feel safer."

Galen's mouth curved into a near grin. "It's good to be spending the night where I don't have to worry about someone breaking in. I expect the best night's sleep I've had since I left home."

Adela's eyes warmed as she stepped back into the room. "Good night, Galen." She closed the door, and he heard the latching rod slide into place.

As he pushed open his own door, his mouth pulled sideways into a wry smile. It was ironic. The place he thought might be the most dangerous had turned out to be the safest of all.

Chapter 34

Not the Same Mistake

Crassus and the girl had retired to their chambers, but Tiberius sat at the desk in his library. He drummed on its surface with a stylus while his old friend lounged in the chair opposite his own.

"An interesting day, Graecus. After eight years of silence, I never expected to hear anything about Decimus. To have this young man suddenly appear with the news that my son is not only alive but married with two sons of his own...If I believed in the gods, I'd say the goddess Fortuna smiled on me when Crassus's friend was kidnapped."

Graecus's smile was as big as Tiberius's own. "The only thing that would give me more pleasure would be to see him again myself."

"I might go to Germania again...to meet my grandsons." Tiberius's smile dimmed. "When I spoke to Adela in Germanic, she let it slip that Decimus's wife is Crassus's sister. Odd. If I needed help from a stranger, I'd use that as the reason he should help me, not because the stranger's son was a friend of the one needing help."

Graecus's smile dimmed as well. "That is an odd choice. But are you sure that's what she said? His wife's a Valerius, and he's a Licinius."

"Assuming he spoke the truth about her." Tiberius rubbed his chin. "His relaxed demeanor during your questioning suggests he's honest, but he tensed when his pretty friend said that."

Graecus's brow furrowed. "So where does the truth lie? He requested a large sum to buy Decimus's friend. A suspicious man might think the tale is a story made up to cheat you out of 1600 denarii."

Tiberius stood. "The simple way to find out is to ask him."

As he approached the door to Crassus's bedchamber, light was visible along the thin crack between the door and the floor. Crassus was still up, and that drew a satisfied smile. A good host wouldn't awaken a sleeping guest, but he didn't want to wait until morning to settle his doubts.

Tiberius pushed lightly on the door. Crassus had failed to slide the latching rod across. The well-oiled hinges let the door swing open soundlessly, and Tiberius stepped into the room.

Crassus sat on the edge of the bed, elbows resting on his knees and forehead against his clasped hands. A peaceful smile curved his mouth.

Tiberius crossed his arms and watched that smile broaden, relax, and broaden again. A peaceful aura surrounded his guest. Tiberius's jaw clenched as the meaning of what he saw struck home.

♦

Galen sensed a presence in the room and opened his eyes. Tiberius stood just inside the door, arms crossed and a deep scowl dragging his mouth down.

"Are you praying to the Christian god?" Cold anger colored the voice. Hostility simmered in his eyes.

Galen's heart dropped into his stomach as he stood. He'd let his guard down in the presence of his enemy, and he was trapped. He straightened to his full height.

God, give me courage and strength to face what's coming.

With shoulders squared, he took a deep breath. "Yes."

"And yet you dare to enter my house, receive my hospitality, and ask for my money?"

"To save my friend...yes."

"Do you really know my son?"

"He's lived with us the past eight years."

"Licinius Crassus...I should have made the connection, but it's been fifteen years. Is your father the Licinius Crassus who fled Rome just ahead of the troops sent to arrest him?"

"Yes."

"Is he the one who corrupted my son and took him from me?"

Galen shook his head. "No. Father died three years before I met Dec. My sister found him near death after an ambush and brought him home to heal."

"My son knew Christians were enemies of the Empire until that ambush. He was never the same afterward." Tiberius's jaw clenched, then relaxed. "Was your sister responsible for my son becoming one?"

Again, Galen shook his head. "No. Dec didn't follow the Way when he left us after healing from his wounds. It was in Rome that God himself led Dec to faith."

◆

Tiberius advanced three steps. A flicker of light by the saddle just to his left caught his eye. The polished brass of a scabbard reflected the flame of the lamp. He gripped it and drew the sword. When he tossed the scabbard aside, it clattered against the wall.

Crassus made no move to escape. "If you plan to kill me, I won't fight you. If it's to be a public execution, I hope the fact that I'm a citizen will be considered when choosing how I die."

He pressed his hands against his thighs as he drew a deep breath. "But Adela and Otto are not Christians. Adela doesn't even know I am. Neither of them should suffer any punishment you choose for me merely because they are my friends. Please let her take my horses and leave."

Crassus's blink seemed too long. Then his hands fell away from his thighs as his shoulders relaxed. "Regardless of what you do with me, please don't change your mind about freeing Otto. He's at the Ludus Bruti on the Vicus Sandaliarius. Marcus Antonius Brutus agreed to a price of 5400 denarii. The 3800 from the horses are in two money belts in the sack tied to my saddle. Once he's free, please ask him to take Adela home to her father. I promised her I would after we rescued him, and I know he'll fulfill my promise."

"I said I'd help him. I keep my word."

Tiberius's breaths came faster as his jaw clenched. His grip on the gladius tightened. As he took another step toward Crassus, his gaze locked on the young Christian's face.

Then he froze.

Eight years earlier, that same calm determination had radiated from the face of his own son as he stood in the dining room, declaring his decision to die before he would deny the Jesus he'd chosen to follow.

Tiberius's anger that day had cost him his only son. He wouldn't make that mistake twice. For eight years, he'd ached to know if Decimus was dead or alive, miserable or satisfied with his new life. That uncertainty was gone, thanks to the young man standing before him. And if he spared Crassus, he could see Decimus again.

Tiberius picked up the scabbard and slid the sword back into it. "I have no intention of killing you. Your death would serve no purpose for the Empire, and I'm not a man who kills without good reason. Tomorrow, we'll go together to buy my son's friend."

Crassus's eyebrows shot up, and his mouth dropped open. That pulled a wry smile from Tiberius. "You needn't look so surprised, Crassus. You are my son's brother-in-law and friend. Sparing your life is my gift to him."

Tiberius rubbed the back of his neck. "You being a Christian from a family that fled Rome to avoid execution for that faith...that poses a problem for you performing the manumission. A man must be twenty to free a slave. With your youth and small stature, proof will be required. I'll pay the entire cost and take possession of him. When I free him, no dangerous questions will be raised."

The smile that lit the young man's face was one of the happiest Tiberius had ever seen.

The corners of his own mouth turned up. "But I'm not going to take a bedraggled German around Rome with me. You're a citizen, and you should be in a toga. Tomorrow one of my slaves will find a toga and an equestrian tunic in your size."

"A toga is fine, but the tunic should be plain. Father was equestrian before leaving Rome, but he walked away from his wealth when he left. I don't qualify for narrow stripes."

Tiberius's eyebrow rose at his candor. "Very well. A plain tunic, but it will be high quality so it won't embarrass me."

Both eyebrows lowered. The Licinius Crassus family had extreme wealth, yet a son of that family had abandoned it for the Christian faith. Simply walking away, taking almost nothing, disappearing into the northern provinces... his son had done the same. Had Decimus had any regrets? From all Crassus had said, it would appear not.

Decimus had served as this young man's father for several years. If there had been regrets, a son should know. But his own son never knew what he was thinking, so maybe not.

"You use your real name. Does my son?"

"Mostly I'm known as Galen Crassus or just Galen. It's not often I need to use the three-part name. Dec doesn't use his real name. Too many people would recognize it since you were governor."

"What name does he use?"

"Only his first name." The corner of Galen's mouth turned up. "Otto's father still just calls him Roman."

"His sons. What name?"

"They're only six and four, so nothing yet."

"Will their other grandfather let them use their mother's name?"

"That's a complicated story. Valeria was born Alba of the Vangiones. She was twelve when she became my sister. Father named her Valeria then. I guess they could be Licinius Crassus, except under Roman law, a peregrine girl can't be adopted. I'm the *paterfamilias* now, so I suppose I could claim them. But in Germania, none of that really matters."

"Of course it matters." Tiberius closed his eyes and rubbed his forehead. When he opened them, he spread his arms to encompass all around them. "All this should be theirs someday."

Galen shrugged. "I'm just a man from the provinces. The intricacies of Roman inheritance law are far beyond me."

Tiberius rolled his eyes. Even in the provinces, inheritance law prevailed. But it was a problem for which he would find the solution.

He replaced the scabbard by the saddle. "I've learned more than enough for this evening. You can go back to praying to your god, but make sure you let no one else here know you're a Christian."

The corners of Galen's mouth rose as his whole body relaxed. "I'll be careful. Thank you...for everything."

Tiberius tipped his head in response. "It's my pleasure."

That was the automatic response in proper society, but though it seemed strange, as he left the room, it was true.

Chapter 35

Gifts for His Son

Day 33

The last traces of pink had barely faded from the morning clouds when Adela entered the dining room with Galen, but Tiberius was already there, looking out the window into the garden.

He turned as they approached. "*Salve.* I trust you slept well."

"The whole bed is softer than my pillow at home." Adela joined him by the window. "It's a beautiful morning." She drew a deep breath. "You can smell the roses from here."

"I noticed you smelled of roses last night. Many women place that scent among their favorites." His eyes shifted toward Galen. "And many men seem to prefer it on their women."

When his eyes turned back to her, they were laughing. Try as she might, she couldn't keep her cheeks from heating.

"And they like the color of roses on their women's cheeks."

The heat spread to Adela's ears.

Galen moved into the space between her and Tiberius. "The roses in your garden reminded me yesterday of my mother's garden. Roses smell good cut, but most things are better when left as God created them."

Adela could have hugged Galen for diverting Tiberius, but that would only have given him a different subject for his teasing. Only Galen was welcome to read her thoughts and turn them into a tease against her.

Tiberius's head tilted as his gaze shifted between Adela and Galen. "The natural way of things is often the best, and I, for one, enjoy watching it."

The blush had started to fade, but his words warmed her cheeks again.

His mouth pulled sideways into a crooked smile before he turned to sweep his hand toward the couches. "My chef has prepared a breakfast for us. I suggest we eat now. My clients and others will be coming shortly for the salutation, and I want to deal with them promptly so we can go purchase your friend."

When Tiberius reclined where he had the night before, Galen sat on the couch they'd used. On the table before them was an assortment of fruit, honey for dipping, bite-sized chunks of cheese, rolls, and sliced hard-boiled eggs beside a sauce bowl.

Tiberius selected an egg slice and dipped it into the sauce before placing it on his tongue. "Try the sauce first, Adela. It should be quite unlike anything you've tasted before."

As he had done, she picked up a slice and dipped it. As she raised it to her mouth, its powerful odor assaulted her nostrils. She froze with it close to her lips. To set it down without eating would insult her host. Besides, it might taste better than it smelled.

She placed it in her mouth and suddenly found herself fighting a heaving stomach. She forced herself to swallow. The sauce-covered egg did go down, but it didn't want to stay there.

She took a sip of the watered wine that the slave boy had set out for each of them. Her stomach settled, but her mind was like a churning stream rushing toward the lip of a waterfall.

Gundahar hadn't lied. Or had he? Maybe her upset stomach was only because Tiberius's food last night was too rich and too much. She'd eaten more than usual, and much of it was strange. Her stomach had felt much too full before she went to sleep, and she'd felt queasy when she first swung her feet out of the bed. Maybe this was just more of the same.

Her stomach churned again.

The healer who'd tried to help Mother always gave her cheese and bread when Mother's stomach had been upset.

She took two pieces of each of the three kinds of cheese plus a fresh roll. Alternating the cheese and roll, she ate it all, taking small bites and swallowing quickly.

The crashing breakers in her stomach calmed into gentle waves, then stilled. Maybe it was only last night's food.

She peeked at Galen as he sat beside her, starting on his fourth egg. He hadn't noticed her distress, but why should she expect a man to notice?

Her gaze switched to Tiberius. The man who seemed to notice everything was watching her, but he said nothing. His gaze settled on her stomach before returning to her eyes. Then he smiled that smile that made him look like he knew as much as the gods himself and turned his attention back to Galen.

She selected another roll and nibbled at it. The mighty Roman man of the world suspected what she feared, but at least he didn't comment on it. If the worst had truly happened, what would the future hold?

She rested her hand on her stomach. All seemed quiet there. But only one thing could quiet her fears, and it was almost three weeks late.

Tiberius had gone to meet with his visitors, and Adela strolled with Galen through the villa. Most of the floors were mosaics, with ornate patterns in the hallways and scenes ranging from peaceful landscapes to fighting men in the rooms. Paintings of mountains and rivers and oceans adorned the walls. In the room Galen called an atrium, a pool sat directly under an opening in the roof. In the middle of it, statues like she'd seen in the sculptor's shop in Luna stood on pedestals.

Her eyes were drawn to the small child reaching down to touch the water. His mirror-self reached up from below, their fingers meeting at the surface.

Adela knelt on the wall beside the pool and leaned over to see her reflection. But it wasn't her own face that caught and held her attention.

It was Galen's happy smile and laughing eyes. He was looking at her like a man appreciating what he saw.

A familiar warmth spread across her cheeks as she stood. Father used to look at Mother that way.

But Galen didn't know what she now suspected. She held back the sigh. Could he still look at her that way if he did?

Galen rode next to Tiberius as they left the Lentulus estate. Two mounted slaves followed, leading Otto's horse. The thought of Otto astride that horse again triggered a grin.

More than once, Galen had tripped on his toga as a child. It was beyond imagining how a man could mount a horse in one, but Tiberius had solved that problem by placing their togas in special saddle bags and bringing the manservant who traveled with him whenever he went anywhere on business, imperial or otherwise. It was a relief that he wouldn't have to try to wrap one around his own body without help.

His host radiated authority as he sat on a prancing gray stallion, dressed in a brilliant white tunic with the wide purple stripes that marked him as a senator. But the plain tunic his man had found for Galen was just as white, and Astrelo was as fine a stallion as any he'd seen around Rome. He couldn't look less like a bedraggled German, as Tiberius had styled him, but it was the man inside, not the outer trappings, that mattered.

Tiberius led them through the Esquiline gate and veered off the Clivus Suburanus that Galen had taken from Quintus's inn. As they continued west on the hilltop, a massive building rose before them.

Tiberius tipped his head toward it. "Trajan's Baths. Only the Circus Maximus and the Amphitheater are more popular destinations for all of Rome."

They skirted the north side of the building and continued west into a residential area.

"I prefer a rural estate myself, but many choose to live in the city, at least part of the year. We'll leave the horses at a friend's town house in Carinae. It overlooks the heart of Rome, and it's a short walk down to the Amphitheater and the Ludus Bruti."

A gatekeeper swung open the stable gate as their party approached. Before the slaves had entered behind them, four stable boys started toward them. Galen had barely reined in when one stood beside him, awaiting his pleasure.

Tiberius swung his leg over his horse's neck and slid off. "Is your master home?"

The boy who took his reins dipped his head. "No, Master Lentulus."

The manservant had already dismounted and stood with the saddlebags slung across his shoulder.

Tiberius turned his gaze on Galen. "Come." Then he strode into the house as if he owned it.

Galen followed him under the portico and into the lush garden surrounding a pool in the center of the peristyle. A woman knelt on the wall of a flower bed. She snipped a stem and placed the blossom in a basket. As Tiberius approached, she rose and bowed her head.

"How can I help you, Master Lentulus?"

"I only need a place to robe. I have business in town."

Her hand swept toward the door into the atrium. "Please follow me."

She led them into a small room off the atrium that contained a bed. After bowing, she vanished.

Tiberius's manservant pulled a toga edged with a wide purple stripe from the saddle bag and laid the semicircular fabric on the bed in all its ten-foot by sixteen-foot glory. He folded it in half, and Tiberius stood before him, arms outstretched. After placing the straight edge over Tiberius's left shoulder, the servant wrapped it around him. Elegant pleats formed as if by magic, and a large pocket appeared under his right arm. When he finished, Tiberius's left arm supported the extra fabric, but his right arm was free for whatever was needed.

Then the manservant extracted the plain toga from the saddle bag, placed it on the bed, and folded it. Expectant eyes turned on Galen.

Galen's mouth pulled sideways as he stepped forward. "One big advantage of living in Germania is never having to wear one of these. I was only six when we left our estate, but I still remember hating my toga as a child."

Tiberius's mouth twitched. "It is sometimes inconvenient, but wearing one is a small price to pay for the honor of being a citizen of Rome. Get used to it. I plan to take you to the chariot races, and citizens are required to wear them there. They are required at the games as well, but since your kind don't participate in the games from the spectator seating, you won't be needing one there."

Galen's breath caught at those words, and that triggered a short laugh from his host.

"You needn't worry, Crassus. I already told you I'm freeing Otto as a gift to my son. Your life is a gift to my son as well, and I've decided to deliver the gifts personally."

Galen's mouth settled into a smile. "That's something Dec will really like."

Tiberius frowned, and his eyes narrowed. "I have my doubts of that. My son has never tried to let me know where he is, so I don't expect a warm reception. But I am his father, and he will respect that even if he has no affection for me."

"But he prays for you every night, and nothing could please Dec more than seeing you again."

Tiberius's head bounced back. "I don't like flattery or lies, Crassus."

"I'm not lying. I've prayed for you with Dec since I was thirteen."

Silence was Tiberius's response, but his eyes had turned thoughtful.

The servant finished wrapping Galen and stepped back to appraise his handiwork.

Tiberius nodded his approval. "Keep your arm up and bent so you don't drop the folds."

Galen's smile leaked out. "I know. Roman citizen, not bedraggled German."

He rubbed the back of his neck with his free right hand. "If we're going to the chariot races, Adela would probably like to watch them, too. I don't know if she drives a team, but she knows horses. She rides as well as any man I know."

"That can be arranged, but she'll go dressed as a decent Roman woman, not in the men's clothes she arrived in."

Galen sucked air between his teeth. "Those were my fault. I gave her my spares when we started after Otto. We had to ride far and fast to catch up, and she said it was easier if she was dressed that way. I did buy her a woman's tunic in Luna."

The memory of her walking at his side in the blue tunic that matched her eyes drew a smile.

◆

Tiberius shook his head at the light in the young man's eyes. It bespoke more than a traveling companion. "Her beauty could tempt any man, even when dressed as a man herself. Since you claim she's not your woman, how is it you brought her along with you?"

"Otto won her from the kidnapper just before they took him. It wouldn't have been safe to leave her behind."

"So, she's Otto's slave."

"No, she's a free woman. She'd been kidnapped outside the Empire, just like Otto, and the kidnapper had no right to use her to cover his bet. It's not like Otto's case, where someone faked papers to show they owned him. Brutus bought him from the man who was cheated with the forgery and supports his claim of ownership with a certified bill of sale."

"Taken outside the Empire? Then she is legally a slave. There's no reason your friend can't take possession of her when he's freed."

"He won't do that."

"Because you tell him not to? What makes you so certain you have that much influence over him? She's beautiful enough to make any man want her."

"That's true, but Otto's father has made it very clear what he thinks of slavery and treating people like animals. Otto will do the right thing. It never takes more than a reminder of what's right from me."

Tiberius's laugh was more of a snort. "So, you are your friend's conscience? The best of men sometimes ignore their consciences, even when that conscience takes the form of a faithful friend."

His mouth pulled sideways as he shook his head. Crassus was either very naïve in the ways of the world, or the people he lived with didn't act like those in his own circle of acquaintances.

But his own son had believed the unbelievable and done the unimaginable when he decided to follow the Christian god. Young Crassus had made the same foolish decision. It was unreasonable to expect wisdom from such men.

Chapter 36

CHANGING OWNERS

A short walk took Galen, Tiberius, and his two slaves to the edge of the wealthy Fagutal district, where a view of the city stretched out before them. Looming just in front of Galen was the amphitheater.

Tiberius's hand swept the length of it. "The Flavian Amphitheater. Started by Vespasian and finished by Titus with the spoils from the Jewish war. The roar of the crowd can be heard from here."

Galen massaged his neck. "Dec has spoken of it. That's where Publius died."

Tiberius's hand dropped to his side. "Yes." His voice was almost a whisper, and Galen's head snapped sideways toward him.

Almost instantly, Tiberius masked the sadness in his eyes. His mouth curved up. "Your friend will never get a chance to test his courage and training there."

"For which I'm very grateful."

"It's time to set him free." Tiberius strode toward the staircase that descended to the valley below.

Galen started to lower his left arm, and the toga dragged on the ground. He jerked it back into place against his stomach. He'd broken his arm when one of Baldric's horses threw him when he was ten. He'd never forget having it trapped in a sling for weeks, pressed against his stomach. Wearing a toga made him a one-armed man again. It would be good to get back to Germania, where a man could wear whatever he wanted and no one would tell him otherwise.

As they turned off the Vicus Patricias and walked up the Vicus Sandaliarius, Galen's gaze locked onto the carvings of fighting men above the door of the Ludus Bruti. But this time, the anticipation surging through him wasn't tempered by fear that he would not find Otto or would find him dead. Tiberius Lentulus walked beside him, and the slave behind them both carried the 5400 denarii that would set Otto free.

The same doorkeeper greeted them. "Welcome to the Ludus Bruti."

Before Galen could speak, Tiberius took charge. "I'm looking for Marcus Brutus."

"Master Brutus isn't here at the moment, but he is expected to return soon." He swept his hand toward the stairs to the balcony. "The viewing balcony is up there. You can watch our gladiators practice while you wait."

Tiberius crossed his arms. "Do you know where Brutus has gone?"

"Yes, and he should return shortly."

A slight tip of Tiberius's head let his eyelids partly close as he looked down his nose at the slave. "Shortly is not soon enough. Send someone to fetch him. I don't have time to waste waiting."

The door slave's eyes saucered, and he took a step back. "Yes, senator."

"Send him to the balcony as soon as he arrives." Tiberius swept through the door and disappeared into the stairwell.

Galen shrugged and offered the slave an apologetic smile before following the man in control up the stairs.

When he reached the balcony, he strode to the railing and scanned the array of posts. No Otto. His hands fisted. It had only been two days since the swordfight. Brutus had agreed to three days for him to return with the money...but had he waited? If someone came and offered more...

"Otto isn't here."

Tiberius stepped up beside him, and a hand settled on his shoulder. "That's not a matter for concern. There are only twenty posts, and this school would own many more fighters than that. They switch between this arena and other training stations."

A quick squeeze, and then Tiberius's hand was gone. The worry drained away, but not the intense anticipation. Galen paced the depth of the balcony, returning to the edge after each lap to see if Otto had come into the arena.

The corner of his mouth pulled up into a crooked smile. Otto would do a double take when he caught sight of his best friend in a toga, looking for the first time like the Romans Otto despised.

A mixture of curiosity and irritation swirled within Brutus as he strode down the street. A pleasant conversation with his friend had been interrupted by the arrival of one of his kitchen slaves. What man would come to his ludus who thought his time was so important he could summon Brutus from anywhere?

He stopped at the door, and his doorman dropped his eyes. "I beg pardon, master. The senator insisted I send for you."

"Where is he?"

"On the balcony, master."

"Lepus didn't know his name. Do you?"

"Cocinus took some cheese and bread up, and his manservant called him Master Lentulus."

"Lentulus? As in Cornelius Lentulus?"

"I don't know, master."

"Tall, silver hair, still looks fit enough for combat?"

His doorman nodded. "Yes, master, and he said he didn't have time to wait. I was afraid not to send for you."

Irritation faded, and curiosity grew. Tiberius Lentulus on his balcony, waiting impatiently. Lentulus was well known for breeding champion horses, but he seldom attended the games.

Brutus adjusted the folds of his toga where it draped his left arm and headed up the stairs.

His head bounced back when he saw Gaius Crassus, dressed in a toga and tunic of whitest wool, standing beside Lentulus at the balcony railing.

How was a young horse trader from the provinces able to get a man of Lentulus's stature to cover what he didn't have? Brutus would have bet the 3800 was all Gaius Crassus had when he didn't make the purchase right after the fight. He'd half expected Crassus to return in three days to report he couldn't raise the rest of the 5400. And if he had, a special discount would have lowered the price to match whatever Crassus did have.

"Crassus. I presume you've returned to complete the purchase."

The young man spun at his voice, and the smile that lit his face was almost as broad the grin that accompanied his victory.

Brutus let a smile curve his own lips. "Who is your friend?"

Crassus started to sweep his left hand toward the stately figure standing beside him, but he stopped before the toga shifted too much. "This is Tiberius Cornelius Lentulus."

He turned toward Lentulus, and his right hand swept toward Brutus as the senator turned from the railing. "And this is Marcus Antonius Brutus."

Brutus tipped his head before locking his gaze on Lentulus. "I haven't had the pleasure before, but your reputation precedes you, Lentulus." He raised an eyebrow. "How is it you've come to help one of the finest young swordsmen of my acquaintance?"

Lentulus donned a formal smile, but his eyes were cool. "I governed Germania Superior for the better part of three years. A wise governor knows more of his province than the governor's residence and administrative offices. Some men are worthy of my help."

Brutus glanced at Crassus, and his smile broadened. "On that point, we agree. I have the bill of sale already prepared. It only lacks the sale price and final signatures."

His hand swept toward the stairwell. "After you."

The senator took a step, then paused. "You will need to make some changes in the documents. My name should be on the bill of sale. I will be paying, not Crassus, and I will take possession."

Brutus's eyebrow rose at that. "Are you going to set Bjorn free, like Crassus was?"

Tiberius's mouth curved down. "Why is that any of your business?"

Brutus crossed his arms. "Because the 5400-denarii price is for a man who risked dying to set his friend free. For anyone who plans to keep Bjorn a slave, the price is 9000."

Crassus stepped forward. "He's paying the 5400 for me. He's going to free Otto."

Brutus tilted his head and raised his eyebrows as his gaze locked on the senator. "Are you?"

◆

Tiberius's frown deepened. An equestrian gladiator owner had no right to question his intentions. Then his mouth relaxed. Brutus was willing to sell to Crassus at a cost far below what he thought Otto was worth. A man who valued courage and faithfulness that much deserved an answer.

"I am." He rested his hand on Crassus's shoulder. "Some men are worth helping."

Brutus's smile grew as he uncrossed his arms. "Then follow me to my office, and we'll put it in writing."

A sack of sand hung from each end of the yoke resting on Otto's shoulders. For what seemed like the five-hundredth time, he squatted to let the bags that weighed almost as much as Galen rest on the ground, then stood. He'd thought about telling Lanista Felix he shouldn't have to do this because his friend was buying him. But that would only have drawn a lash from Felix's three-cord whip, and then he'd be lifting the sand with a sore back as well as tired legs.

And what if Galen's relative refused to help?

As he squatted and lifted the bags once more, his jaw clenched, but it wasn't from exertion.

The boy who usually served the food scurried into the room and spoke to Felix. His voice was too soft to catch the words, but he cast several furtive glances in Otto's direction. Was that a good sign or bad?

Felix's scowl was blacker than normal when he glared at Otto. He tipped his head toward the door. "Your master wants you in his office. Now."

Otto followed the boy down a hallway and across a courtyard where men with nets were trying to trip each other.

When he stepped through the doorway into a waiting room lined with chairs, Galen stood before him, wrapped in a toga and grinning.

Brutus stood beside him, arms crossed, with a grin that matched. "Well, Otto of the Vangiones, it's time for us to part company. You're going with Tiberius Cornelius Lentulus, senator of Roma." His hand swept toward the tall, silver-haired man with broad purple stripes on his toga and tunic.

Otto's breath caught, and his gaze bounced between Galen and the governor of Germania Superior who'd declared all Christians should die.

Brutus snapped his fingers. A man with heavy clippers gripped the brass collar around Otto's neck and wriggled the tips between the two ends of the collar. The shearing of the copper pin was announced by a snap, and he lifted the collar away.

"It's been a pleasure owning you, Otto, and an even greater pleasure meeting your friend Crassus." The familiar smiling frown curved his lips. "Feel free to come visit any time."

Brutus slapped Otto's shoulder and tipped his head first to Galen, then to Tiberius. "Now, since we're through here, I'll return to the business from which I was summoned."

Galen offered his arm. "I won't forget you, Marcus Brutus."

The frowning smile relaxed into a grin, and Brutus's eyes crinkled as he gripped Galen's arm. "I can say the same, Gaius Crassus. *Vale.*"

After a final nod toward Tiberius, he strode into the courtyard and disappeared through the door on the other side.

Tiberius handed the bill of sale to the man carrying a leather pouch. "You're the first gladiator I've owned, but I'm always open to something new. This should prove interesting."

"You own me?" Otto's stomach clenched. "But I thought Galen was only getting enough extra to free me."

Tiberius chuckled. "Calm down. You are now the property of a Roman citizen who will have no one question his citizenship, his age, or his right to do whatever he wants with you...with no complicating personal history." The corner of his mouth pulled up as he glanced at Galen.

"Crassus tells me you're only twenty-one, so you would normally become a Junian Latin rather than a full citizen. But I have a ready solution to that since your family breeds and sells horses."

Otto squared his shoulders. "The best in Germania."

"I've seen your stallion. Not the best in the entire province, but he is a quality animal."

Tiberius tapped his chin with his fist. "That presents a business opportunity I consider worth pursuing. I breed some of the finest chariot horses in Italia. All four factions race my animals in the Circus Maximus, mares on the shafts, stallions in the outer traces. They have many wins to their credit.

"I'm ready to expand beyond Italia. If I make you my business agent for a new racing stable in Germania Superior, I can request special approval for you to become a Roman citizen immediately. Does that interest you?"

Otto rubbed his mouth. "A Roman citizen and raising good horses? I'd be a fool to say no."

The corner of Tiberius's mouth curved up. "Yes, you would, and that would disqualify you for becoming my agent. You only need to choose what you want for your third name after the Tiberius Cornelius part."

Tiberius summoned the man carrying the pouch with a flick of his finger and pantomimed writing on his hand. The man withdrew a hinged wax tablet and stylus and stood ready to write what Tiberius spoke.

"Address it to Quintus Flavius Albus as *praetor*. Request time in his court as soon as possible this week for obtaining full citizenship for an underage man being freed to operate as my business agent in Germania Superior. Then deliver it and wait for a response. Return to the villa as soon as you have the date and time."

"Yes, master."

As the scribe drew letters in the wax with the stylus, Tiberius turned back to Otto. "If the court date is not tomorrow, we'll go to the races so you can watch some of my horses compete."

Tiberius's gaze shifted to Galen, then back to Otto. "Perhaps you should hope for a delay. As soon as you're freed, you'll have to wear a toga like Crassus. He's already informed me of the advantage of living in Germania that spares him from dressing like the citizen he is."

Otto rested his hand on Galen's arm and gave a light shove. "Wearing a toga is a price I'm more than willing to pay, even if Galen does complain about it." He got a grin in return.

Otto fixed his gaze on Tiberius...governor of Germania Superior who'd wanted to kill his friends for their faith, senator of Rome who could command instant responses from men in power. Reeking of the Roman arrogance that he'd always hated, but also the man willing to spend his own money to buy Otto's freedom and to make him a business partner so he could be a Roman citizen.

"I want to thank you, Tiberius...can I call you that?"

Tiberius tipped his head, giving permission. A slight smile curved his lips as he turned his face toward Galen. "You may also use that name. You can tell me later why I'm calling Gaius Licinius Crassus 'Galen.'"

"I want to thank you first for helping Galen rescue me and also for giving me Roman citizenship. I've seen the value of that many times."

A flick of Tiberius's hand swept his words away. "I need no thanks. My own son would have asked me to do it if he were still alive, and what father would refuse what he knew would be the request of his son to rescue one of his friends?"

Otto's brow furrowed. "But Decimus isn't—"

"My son died eight years ago, murdered by robbers just outside Rome and his body never found."

"But I—"

Galen rammed an elbow into his side. "I want to offer my deepest condolences on having your only son disappear eight years ago, never to return. I remember my own grief when my father was murdered."

Otto opened his mouth, then shut it. He'd find out what was going on later when he could talk with Galen in private. "Please let me join in offering my condolences as well."

Tiberius nodded his acceptance. "We'll head back to my estate now. There should be time to look at the horses I have there before dinner. I may want to use one of the stallions for founding the new herd."

When Tiberius led the party into the courtyard, Otto tipped his head back to gaze at the sky. It seemed a much brighter blue now he was a free man again.

Chapter 37

STILL MORE TO LEARN

Lentulus estate outside Rome, Day 33

Adela chewed her lip as she sat at the table under the portico off the stable yard. She tried to keep her attention focused on the young stallion as the stable man brushed him, but her gaze kept returning to the gate.

Galen and Tiberius should be back soon, and Galen's friend should be with them. Traveling with Galen had turned into pure delight. How would his friend change that? Would Galen's jokes and laughter and general conversation all be directed at his friend and no longer at her? Would his friend insist she was his slave and take advantage of that? If he tried, would Galen protect her or let his friend do as he pleased?

The friend of a lifetime must be more important to Galen than she was. That thought drew a deep sigh.

The thuds of nearby hooves snapped her gaze back on the gate. Tiberius came through first, riding alone on his gray stallion. Then Galen appeared, riding beside his friend and talking. But his eyes sought her out the moment they came inside the wall. His hand shot straight out to point at her, then lifted into a wave.

Relief flooded through her as she raised her hand in response.

Seeing Galen beside his giant friend made him look small. Funny how she'd stopped noticing that. With his beard shaved and hair cut short like a Roman, Otto was even more handsome than she'd remembered. Funny how she'd come to like Roman hair and a clean-shaven face better than the long hair and trimmed beards of the Hermunduri.

But Galen was much more attractive. The cut she gave him had scarred, but no woman would think it made him less handsome. The laughing eyes and the permanent smile that flipped so quickly to a grin would delight any woman, Roman or otherwise.

The stable slaves took the horses, and Galen led Otto toward her. She rose and braced herself for meeting the man who might try to claim her as his slave.

Otto stopped right in front of her, and he was tall enough she had to tip her head back to look into his eyes. Those eyes seemed friendly, not lecherous, but a man's looks could be deceiving.

"It's good to see you again, Adela. Galen told me how good it was to have you as company coming here. I'm glad we were able to free you before I got taken so he wasn't lonely."

Those words released the tension that had her tighter than a bowstring. "We caught Gundahar and Gerlach, and we found you. A successful hunt is always good."

Otto grinned. "I'm glad I won a horsewoman. You two rode a long way to find me."

"I enjoyed riding your stallion, even if Galen did have to lift me up when there was nothing to stand on to make me a little taller."

Galen's mouth was curved in his broadest smile when she shifted her gaze down from the giant. "I'll get you a horse that's more your size for the ride back."

Otto rested his elbow on Galen's shoulder. "You might not have to. We'll be taking some of Tiberius's horses back to Germania. Maybe one will be broken to saddle enough that I can ride it. Then you can keep riding mine. You helped Galen catch the men who sold me. Letting you ride my stallion is the least I can do to thank you."

"I'd like that. Gratias tibi."

Otto's eyebrows shot up.

That triggered her laugh. "The proper reply is 'Voluptas meus est.' Galen has been teaching me Latin in case I needed it to get back to Germania alone."

Otto's mouth twitched. "I learned a few new Latin words in the ludus, but you don't need to know them. With three men taking you back, you won't even need what you've learned."

She glanced at Galen, and he was watching her, too. "Even if I don't need it, I'd like to keep learning. Galen is such a good teacher. Who knows how much he can teach me in four more weeks?"

But maybe that wouldn't be the end of what he'd teach her. If they married, she could also learn Greek, like his sisters. *Te amo.* How would she say that in Greek?

Te amo, Galen Crassus. She'd been practicing different ways to say it, and she knew the exact one to use when he said it first.

Otto had thoroughly enjoyed the hot soak in Tiberius's private bath, and it felt good to wear a tunic of softest wool instead of the rough slave tunics at the ludus. Dinner had been delicious, and even the ever-hungry Galen left food on his plate.

The scribe who'd been at the ludus followed the final tray of pastries into the room. He waited for Tiberius to nod before speaking.

"Master, the manumission is scheduled midmorning day after tomorrow."

Tiberius smiled and waved him away. After a quick bow, the man withdrew from the dining room.

"That's good timing, Otto. Tomorrow I'll take you all to the chariot races at the Circus Maximus. Some of my horses are always running there, and it will be good for you to see them race at the greatest racetrack in the Empire. You'll be able to tell our customers that horses from the same bloodlines are winning at the Circus in Rome, and you've seen it yourself. That should be persuasive for anyone who's ever visited Rome.

"The races will take most of the day. After we complete your manumission the next morning, we can visit my stables here and select the stallion and mares we'll be taking to found the herd in Germania."

One corner of Tiberius's mouth turned up. "Too many horse traders twist the facts to make a sale, but I never have to lie about my animals." His gaze shifted to Galen. "What does the Christian god think of one of his followers lying to make a living?"

Galen opened his mouth to respond, but Otto beat him to it. "I've never heard Galen say anything that wasn't true. We have good horses to sell, and he only has to let someone ride to know the horse is worth what he's asking. The Romans in Argentorate almost fight over who gets to buy from him. The asking price is always what it should be, but sometimes they bid it up higher. That's not Galen's fault. Who are we to tell someone a horse they just bid for isn't worth what the other man was almost willing to pay?"

Tiberius's lips curved into a wry smile. "And do you do as well?"

Otto bristled. "No. I'm honest, too, but the Romans don't trade with a German like they do with a Roman."

Tiberius's eyebrow rose. "That never influences me. You can try to sell me something later, and I'll tell you what the real problem is so you can change before you start trying to sell my horses."

Otto glanced at Galen, whose gaze had shifted to the pastry tray. Everything inside him wanted to argue with Tiberius, but the echo of Galen's words about trying to pick a fight when making a deal rang in his head. "That might help."

Galen's gaze turned back on him, but his partner's eyes weren't laughing at him. They looked happy that he was finally ready to work on his real problem.

◆

After Tiberius excused himself at the end of dinner, Galen escorted Adela and Otto to their rooms. Otto's room was on one side of Adela's, Galen's on the other.

Ornate metal brackets cradled oil lamps like leaves around a flower bud. The pools of light below each overlapped, making a chain of circles leading to their rooms. The golden glow that filled the hallway mirrored the glow in Galen's heart.

He could remember only one day when he'd been happier: the day Dec married Val, giving her the finest husband and him the best brother and friend a man could want.

Adela walked between Otto and him. The scent of roses that lingered in her hair teased his nostrils. The music of her voice tickled his ears. A profile that could inspired any sculptor fired his imagination. It was a pleasure just being close to her.

His quest to rescue Otto was over. But as much as he'd wanted his friend by his side, he wanted her more. *God, open her heart to what I can tell her. Make her want to be yours, and then make her want to be mine.*

They reached her door, and Galen opened it.

Otto smiled down on her as he rested his hand against her doorpost. "After so many meals with ugly gladiators, eating with a pretty woman this evening was the best part of dinner. It's good to hear Germanic spoken again. I'd grown tired of using only Latin."

Adela tilted her head as a smile lit her eyes. "I like using Latin. I've enjoyed every moment of Galen teaching me."

Galen basked in the warmth of the smile she directed at him as she spoke those words. "Voluptas meus est."

She grinned. "I like that saying best. Nothing could describe our trip better."

"Adela." Otto pulled her gaze back to him. "I've watched some chariot races before, but never with the finest horses on the most famous race track in the world. Tiberius knows how to treat guests well."

Adela's gaze flipped between Otto and Galen. "I'm looking forward to it." Her gaze settled on Galen. "Rest well."

She closed the door, and Galen grinned at Otto. "You're definitely going to rest well. Tiberius's beds are softer than any pillow I've ever laid my head on."

Otto dropped his hand from her door and straightened. "I can't thank you enough for everything you did to set me free. You shouldn't have risked Tiberius killing you just to get the money, but I'm glad you did. I'm going to be a citizen and you're still alive, even though he knows about your faith. How did he find out?"

"He caught me praying. He was going to kill me; then he decided our lives would be his gifts to Dec. I'm glad he decided to go to Germania. God truly protected me, and Dec is going to be thrilled when his father comes back with us."

"Maybe your god protected us both. One thing is certain." Otto rubbed the back of his neck as his eyes narrowed. "I've learned not to go blindly ahead and do stupid things when you point out the danger. It's not real men who drink until they can't defend themselves. It's stupid ones."

"I'm glad to hear that. It might not turn out so well next time. I tried to get you back for myself as much as for you. I promised Val we wouldn't do anything stupid. She would have skinned me alive for breaking my word to her. And then I would have had to face Baldric for not bringing his young stallion home."

Galen would never say it to his face, but Otto was as good a friend as any man could have. It would break his heart to lose him. "Some good came of the whole affair, anyway. At least you managed to rescue Adela."

Otto shook his head. "No, that wasn't me. It was you. I would have gambled her away that night. What she needed wasn't a big fool like me but a wise man like you who took her away before I lost her again."

Galen shrugged. "God took care of us all." He slapped Otto's arm. "Sleep well, big man."

Otto grinned. "You, too." He walked into his room and closed the door.

Galen rested his hand on Adela's door and closed his eyes. *God, give her a good night's sleep, but don't let her be so comfortable that she doesn't think she needs you. Give me the chance to tell her all she needs to hear.*

He drew a breath and blew it out. Four weeks left. Surely that was long enough for her to learn the truth and choose to believe.

Chapter 38

Day 34

Adela awoke to the sun streaming through the window and waves crashing in her stomach. She'd been careful what she ate at dinner. No rich Roman food was to blame.

She swung her legs out of bed and pressed her hands against her belly. What were all the things she'd heard would help?

Her gaze settled on the food sack tied to her saddle. Bread and cheese and some dried apples were in there. Bread and cheese had helped yesterday.

She took a deep breath and held it as she walked the few steps and knelt. She pulled out a roll before hurrying to the window. If the nausea won, at least she could empty her stomach into the garden.

Slow deep breaths and many small bites...gradually her stomach settled. Tomorrow she would put the food sack by the bed, or maybe she'd ask for some bread and cheese before she went to her bedchamber.

The room blurred, but she won the battle against the tears.

She had no doubt she was with child, but sometimes a pregnancy ended quickly. That happened to her mother several times. Maybe she'd be like Mother, and all the worry would be for nothing. If there was no baby, no one ever needed to know what Gundahar had done.

When Adela stepped into the stable yard, Tiberius's gray stallion, Astrelo, and Otto's horse were saddled and waiting. Her brow furrowed. Where was her mount?

At the sound of her footsteps, Tiberius turned from his stable master. "As soon as the young men join us, we'll go into Rome for the races."

"I only see three horses. Who isn't going?"

The twitch of his mouth betrayed that he was laughing at her. His hand swept toward a team of mules hitched to a small cart. A seat wide enough for three sat directly above the single axle, and a man sat on one side, fingering the reins.

Adela glanced down at her ankle length tunic and the ten feet of *palla* the lady's maid had wrapped around her. "I guess it would be easier to drive in this than ride. I do know how to handle a team."

"Somehow, I'm not surprised." Tiberius tightened his lips, but she still saw the start of his grin. "No Roman lady would ever sit astride a horse or drive herself, and neither will you while you're my guest. Galen may let you dress and ride like a man, but I won't."

Her eyebrows dipped as she straightened to her full height. "I do think this tunic is pretty, and I thank you for letting me wear it. But I'll dress however I want when we ride back to Germania."

His eyes rolled, but the smile remained. "That, my dear Adela, will be between you and Galen. But while we are still in Rome, you'll dress and act like a proper Roman maiden." His smile broadened. "Except for speaking your mind when it's just the four of us. That I find quite entertaining."

"I'm not a Roman maiden, and I like to drive. I don't need anyone to help me."

She jumped when Galen's hand rested on her crossed arms.

"Just relax and enjoy the ride. Then you can spend all your time looking. There are many things to see. Let me help you in."

He called the driver by flexing his fingers. When the cart stopped beside them, he lifted her into it. Before he stepped away, he took her hand and squeezed.

Tiberius mounted and led the party toward the gate. Galen and Otto fell in behind him, riding side-by-side. The driver flicked the reins, and the cart jerked her back as it started forward.

Galen turned in the saddle, and his eyes met hers. His perpetual smile broadened before he faced forward again.

He was right that there was much to be seen, but a ride in a cart had no appeal...unless Galen held the reins.

When they reached the stable yard of Tiberius's friend near the city, Adela was more than ready to get out of the cart. The jostling from the wheels rolling across paving stones was much harder to bear than a comfortable saddle.

Galen was by the cart before the stable boy could bring over the mounting stool. She stood and let him place his hands on her waist to swing her out and down to the ground.

"We walk from here, but Tiberius said it's not far."

Tiberius walked up behind Galen as he was adjusting his toga, which had shifted during the lift. "We'll walk, Galen, but I have a sedan chair for Adela."

Adela craned her neck to look past him. Four men carried a chair mounted on poles.

"I have two good legs, and I can walk as fast as any man. I don't need the chair."

Tiberius rubbed his lips, but she saw the start of the smile he was trying to wipe away. "As you wish. The crowds will grow thick as we get near the circus, so stay close to me." He looked past her to Galen and Otto. "But you have two bodyguards, so I don't have to worry about your safety."

Otto's gaze swept Adela from head to foot. "To guard you is a pleasure, Adela. You remind me of the wild daffodils in Germania dancing beneath a blue spring sky."

Adela fingered her yellow tunic and blue shawl as heat crept to her ears.

Otto's hand rested on Galen's shoulder. "I'm glad we're here today and not tomorrow, or I'd be in a toga like Galen." He grinned down at his friend. "The gatekeepers might let me into the races without it, but you look so Roman, they'd tell you to leave without one."

Galen made his final adjustments of the yards of fabric. "I'll be glad when we head home and I can wear a shirt and trousers again."

Tiberius shook his head as his lips tightened. Then they curved up at the corners. "Clothes don't make the man, but they identify the citizen. Of that, you should be proud. Stop complaining." His reprimand lost its effect as the full smile leaked out.

The walk had not been long, and the views were spectacular. Adela tipped her head back to stare at the three stories of arches and columns that towered over her as they approached the curved end of the Circus Maximus. Four giant bronze horses with flaring nostrils and flowing manes pulled a chariot over an arched entrance wide enough for two chariots to race abreast.

"It's huge!"

Tiberius's hand swept the length of it. "Almost two thousand feet long, more than six hundred feet wide. Built of marble, a fitting display of the magnificence of the greatest empire the world has ever known. It will seat more than a quarter million people."

"How many is that?"

Galen spoke beside her. "The whole town of Argentorate could fit in it more than ten times over."

Adela drew a deep breath. "I would hate to have so many watching me race."

"But, as you will see, the men who race here love it." Tiberius turned and walked on.

They walked the length of the building, passing many doorways through which thousands of spectators were entering. When they reached the far end, Tiberius knocked on a door and was admitted to the area behind the starting gates.

As they walked past a row of stalls, Tiberius paused. "This stallion is from my estate near Ticinum. We'll be spending a night there."

A man dressed in a short green tunic, laced around his body with leather thongs, came over. "Lentulus, it's good to see you here. The new stallion performed beautifully in his first race last week. I won easily."

"I'm glad to hear it. I'm about to start another stable in a province I once governed. The founding stallion will share his bloodline."

"The provincials will soon be grateful to have Lentulus horses setting the pace there."

Tiberius offered a gracious smile. "The races start soon, and I'm taking my visitors to the sponsor's box."

The charioteer scanned their group, but his gaze settled on Adela. "Cheer for me, and I'll drive a race like you've never seen before. Nothing inspires me more than the support of a rare beauty."

Something in the smile he flashed made Adela move closer to Galen.

Tiberius spread his arms as if to shoo them along like chickens. "Time to take our seats. We'll be joining the sponsor of today's races in the state box above the starting gates."

A narrow set of stone steps led to a canopied balcony with several small sections divided by stone walls. Tiberius led them to the largest one in the middle and entered.

As they walked past a table laden with fruit, cheeses, and pastries, he paused to select two plain wheat rolls. As he raised one to his lips, he handed the other to Adela.

The slightest smile lifted a corner of his mouth as his eyes held hers. "If you feel hungry any time, feel free to get something here."

She felt her cheeks heat. He knew, but he was a friend who would help, not a man who would betray her secret.

The man seated in a throne-like chair by the front railing turned his head. "*Salve*, Lentulus. I see you brought your guests from Germania."

Tiberius placed his hand on Otto's shoulder. "I have, Secundus, and Otto of the Vangiones will be my business agent for a new stable I'm starting there."

Secundus's eyebrow rose. "An interesting choice."

"He is young, but he already raises horses and sells them in Mogontiacum and Argentorate, so there's wisdom in it." His smile turned wry. "You know I never do anything without a good reason."

Secundus's formal smile relaxed into a genuine one. "True. In forty years, I've never seen you act without thinking. Always the level head. Rome has been fortunate to have your service."

"And yours." Tiberius turned and reached back toward Adela. "Come up here to the front where you can see better. Secundus will start the race when he waves that flag."

She moved to his side. He raised his roll for a bite and offered her a smile. As she nibbled on her own roll, she glanced at the stately man of power. Who would have thought he'd be an understanding friend?

◆

The roar of the crowd was deafening when Secundus waved the flag and the twelve chariots burst from the gates below. With horses at a fast gallop, they fought to be first to get the position closest to the wall that stretched at least a quarter mile before them.

Adela's hands flew to her mouth. "They're beautiful! What power!"

Tiberius's smile broadened. "Yes, and the horses love it. The charioteers have to hold them back at the start, or they'd tire themselves out before they finish the seven laps."

When the chariots rounded the wall directly in front of them the first time, Adela gasped. "That was too close. Those two almost hooked wheels."

"The goal is to win, whatever it takes. Some days a charioteer dies, but it's a life of glory. Men often die young with no one to remember them, but a winner here will have a monument erected in his memory. Most start as slaves, but no one wants to stop even after they're freed. Some become very wealthy if they win often enough. The man we spoke with downstairs has won over a thousand times." He pointed at the rows of men with purple-striped togas along the track's edge. "He's made enough to buy out many of the senators sitting down there. His wealth may someday surpass mine, if he doesn't die first. But there's more to life than money."

Adela pulled her eyes from the horses to smile into his. "That's what Galen says."

Tiberius's wry smile was accompanied by a soft snort. "He would say that. Many might say it, but he would truly mean it."

She hadn't thought it possible, but the yelling grew even louder. For the last time, the chariots rounded the posts at the far end of the wall and sprinted toward the white line in the dirt that marked the finish.

Adela found herself bouncing on her toes as the two lead teams crossed the line less than a horse's head apart.

The winning team pulled up directly below them. The driver was the man who'd spoken to them. Secundus stood and tossed a bag of coins down to him.

He caught it and raised it over his head. Then his eyes caught hers. He placed his fingers on his lips, then raised them to her.

She felt Galen's eyes, and for no reason she could say, her cheeks warmed. When her gaze returned to Tiberius, she found him smiling.

"It's a delight to have you here. One can take beauty for granted until he sees the joy it brings to fresh eyes. Your excitement reminds me of Decimus when he was a small boy and watched from here."

Galen's chuckle came from beside her. "I can picture Dec like a stretched bowstring just before the release. His own sons are just like that when waiting for something they want. Whenever I return from a trip, they're all over me like ants on a honey jar the moment I'm off Astrelo."

Otto stepped to the rail and rested his elbow on Galen's shoulder. "I won't have Roman ants on me, but Father will nearly crush me with a hug when I come home safe after so long."

Adela's smile faded, and Galen wrapped his hand around hers. "Your father will be delighted to see you home, too."

A gentle squeeze, and then he withdrew his hand much too soon. She forced a happier smile, for Galen's sake. Would her father be glad, like Galen said? Like Otto is certain his father will be? And even if he is when she first arrives, what will he say if she has to tell him she carries a kidnapper's child?

Otto had been a slave, but tomorrow morning he'd be free again. The nightmare of slavery was over for him...but not for her. Otto had agreed she was free when he gave her to Galen, but her kidnapper had chained her to him even after his death.

Chapter 39

The Roman Forum, Day 35

As Otto, Galen, and Tiberius emerged from the Basilica Julia, Otto rubbed his shoulder again.

"Why did that judge whack me so hard with the rod when he pronounced me free? You said it would be a light tap."

Tiberius wiped the start of the smile off his lips. "Did your father never tell you about the rebellion of Antonius Saturninus a little over thirty years ago? He was governor of Germania Superior with two legions stationed in Mogontiacum, and he allied with some Germans from across the Rhenus against Emperor Domitian. But he hadn't expected an early melt of the river ice. The Germans never got across the river, and Saturninus was defeated and executed.

"Quintus Albus's mother was Saturninus's niece. She blamed his death on the deliberate betrayal of his German allies rather than the ice melting. She encouraged her son to hate Germans for causing that family disgrace."

Otto's brow furrowed as Tiberius's smile grew. "Did you know he was going to hit so hard?"

Tiberius shrugged. "I haven't seen him actually hit a German in court before..."

Galen chuckled. "He didn't hit as hard as you hit your sparring partners at Ludus Bruti. Besides, wasn't it worth it to become Tiberius Cornelius Baldricus?"

Otto's frown shifted into a smile. "Yes. It's even worth wearing this stupid-looking liberty cap until we head home."

Tiberius gripped the yellow felt cone and lifted it from Otto's head. "As your patron, I can solve that. Don't wear it in my presence unless I tell you to. I don't need you following me around in it to make me look more important."

He slapped the hat against Otto's chest, and Otto took it.

Tiberius looked first at Galen, then Otto. The corner of his mouth pulled up in a wry smile. "Now that we've created the newest citizen of Rome, we'll go select the horses for the newest racing stable in Germania Superior."

As they rode through the gate at Tiberius's villa, Galen scanned the portico for Adela. Each time he'd gone off with Tiberius, she'd been sitting at the table when they returned. And each time it felt like she was watching for him.

She was there again, but her elbows rested on the table, and her face rested in her hands.

"Adela!" Otto kicked his horse into a trot and headed for her. He swung the liberty cap in a circle over his head. "You're looking at Tiberius Cornelius Baldricus now. But to my friends...still Otto."

Adela lowered her hands and turned her smile on. But it wasn't the same bright smile that she'd worn in Luna. And though her eyes focused first on Galen, they shifted to Otto as soon as Galen waved. Otto rode over to her and dismounted.

Tiberius swung his leg over the gray's neck and slipped off. "Galen, you're welcome to join us as we select the horses that will accompany us to Germania."

Galen slid off Astrelo, and the stable slave led him away. "Adela might like to join us as well. It's boring to stay here alone for hours."

"We'll be riding."

"If you lend her a horse, that won't be a problem. As she's told me more than once, she's the daughter of a Hermunduri chieftain and can ride anything I can. And I can ride anything."

"No proper Roman maiden rides like a man."

"But a proper German one does." He raised his eyebrows and left his request hanging.

Tiberius's gaze shifted to Adela where she stood holding Otto's liberty cap. With a grin, Otto lifted it from her hands and plunked it on his head. When he bounced his eyes at her, her giggle brightened the courtyard.

"Very well. I suppose it is asking too much for a chieftain's daughter to become a demure Roman maiden, but you'll all be in tunics, not trousers."

Silent laughter lit Tiberius's eyes. "Go tell her now."

Galen couldn't stop the smile Tiberius's words spawned. The two Tiberius Corneliuses could ride together. He'd make sure Adela rode by his side.

It took no maneuvering to get Adela to ride beside him. She took her usual place even before Tiberius told Otto to ride beside him.

As he spoke with Otto, Tiberius's voice drifted back to Galen. "First, we'll select the stock we'll be taking, but there's much more to running a racing stable than breeding and selling the horses. Do you know anything about tracking bloodlines?"

"Yes. My father has done that for years. Our regular customers know which bloodlines they want to buy. I'm skilled in keeping the kinds of records that satisfy in Germania, but if there's anything else I should be doing, I want to learn."

Tiberius leaned over and slapped his shoulder. "Admitting you might not know everything is the beginning of wisdom. I'll have my own stable master prepare a stable codex for the horses we'll be taking. He'll show you what is required."

Tiberius turned in his saddle and rested his hand on the stallion's rump. "Galen, do you track your bloodlines?"

"Dec brought three fine Spanish mares as his bride price, and Val used Astro as the stallion to found the herd. Val keeps records like he showed her, so I think we do what you do."

"Tiberius?" His gaze shifted to Adela when she spoke. "Can I learn how to do a stable codex, too?"

Her question drew Tiberius's smile. "Of course. Perhaps your future husband will need you to understand how to help with this."

Adela's smile grew. "Good. I like to learn." She turned toward Galen. "I want to keep learning to read and write Latin and maybe someday Greek, like your sisters did."

"Teaching you made the trip to Rome more enjoyable than I ever expected."

"I need lots of practice, and you're the best teacher." She squared her shoulders and raised her head. "*Voluptas meus est* for Latin and many other things. I hope I get to use what I've learned for years."

Tiberius nudged his stallion into a trot, and all conversation ended.

Galen's gaze drifted toward Adela. Tiberius had mounted her on a gentle chestnut mare, but a horsewoman like her could have ridden his most spirited stallion.

Did she want to learn the stable codex because she thought she might become Otto's wife? He obviously admired her, and his attentions seemed to delight her. She'd told him from the start that a chieftain's daughter expected to marry a chieftain's son. Did she realize that stirred an emotion he'd never felt before? Envy was a sin, but for the first time, comparisons between himself and Otto fed it.

He'd never spoken of his feelings for her because he couldn't do anything about them unless she followed the Way. No, that's until, not unless. How could it not be God's will for her to give her heart to Jesus before they reached Hermunduri country?

But even if it was, maybe it wasn't God's will for her to give a short Roman her heart as well.

Galen had just finished dressing after a relaxing soak in the hot tub of the villa's bath when Graecus appeared at the doorway. "Tiberius would like to speak with you in the library."

He followed the steward down the hall. Tiberius stood by the library window, contemplating the garden, but he turned with a smile the moment Galen entered. He waved his hand toward a cluster of three wicker chairs. Graecus settled into one, so Galen took another.

Tiberius lowered himself onto the blue cushion embroidered with a silver laurel wreath and leaned back. He draped his arms across the back of the chair.

"We need to discuss some financial matters so Graecus can get the necessary papers prepared before we leave."

Galen cocked his head. "Financial matters?"

"Decimus probably told you we had to fake his death to prevent his execution when he decided to worship the Christian god. That presents a serious problem for transferring the Lentulus property to him when I die." The corner of his mouth pulled up. "Roman law doesn't define how a paterfamilias can pass his rights and property to an already-dead son." A full smile appeared. "I suspect the issue hasn't been raised before."

He glanced at Graecus. "Graecus and I are the only people in Rome who know he's still alive. Before you came, we had no idea where Decimus was so how to make the transfer was a pointless question. But now that you've come, I can see a way forward. I recognize an honest man once I get to know him, and I believe you to be as honest as any man can be."

"I try to be. What do you want me to do to help?" Galen tensed when Tiberius leaned toward him.

"I want to formally adopt you so you will inherit with the understanding that you will find a way to transfer at least half my wealth to Decimus. You will still have a few million denarii after the transfer."

Galen's head drew back. "Adopt me?"

"Yes. It's a common solution to the problem of a man having no male heir. With Decimus's sons, I actually have three, but no one in Rome knows that. If you become my heir, you can adopt your sister's children and make a clean line of inheritance for them."

Galen rubbed the back of his neck. "I see the logic of the plan, and I'm honored that you consider me a trustworthy partner in it. But I can't dishonor my own father's memory that way. I'm content to be paterfamilias with what I have rather than erasing my father's lineage by accepting your offer. Besides, doesn't that require special approval that would draw attention to who I am and who my father was? There might still be an arrest warrant for us, and I don't want to put my sister at risk by revealing where we're living."

Tiberius frowned as he settled back in the chair. "I understand your reluctance." He looked at Graecus with raised eyebrows.

Graecus rubbed his chin. "There might be a different way that avoids that. The estates will revert to your known living relatives, but there's nothing that prevents you from bequeathing Galen a large sum of money." The steward's eyes warmed as he fixed his gaze on Galen. "I believe you can trust him to make certain most of it is passed on to Decimus and his children."

Tiberius nodded. "And I can start the transfer by taking a sizable sum with me on this trip."

Galen straightened. "How many guards will travel with us?"

Tiberius shook his head. "None. No one but Graecus knows the real reason I'm going. Even my household thinks it's for the pleasure of the trip and to participate in starting the new stable with Otto."

Galen blew his breath out through pursed lips. "Then I have some suggestions. I travel often with a few thousand denarii on me, but I try to look like I don't have much. We'll need to do the same. Your tunic with the senatorial stripes—that has to go. You shouldn't even wear one like this one you gave me. It looks too expensive. Anything that suggests wealth is an invitation to robbers. We'll already draw attention with the horses we'll be leading. We need to look like your servants, not like men with money."

Tiberius tipped his head. "The roads are safe enough this side of the Alpes, and we'll be sleeping at the villas of men I know. After we cross the pass, that would be wise. We'll also ride with swords in plain sight so no one will doubt that we're ready for trouble. That usually prevents it ever starting. I'll supply Otto with a gladius from my own collection."

"I'd like to arm Adela, too. Hermunduri women learn to fight. She can use a gladius as well as a dagger." Galen touched the scar on his cheek. "I know from personal experience.

"Otto is intimidating, but even though I'm a good fighter, I don't look like it. Your gray hair makes you look like an easier target than you are. Adela looks like she's only a girl, even though she's a warrior woman. But dressed in men's clothes and wearing a sword, that should make her look as threatening as a Roman of sixteen or so."

Tiberius's eyes crinkled. "Adela looks like no Roman girl I've known. Even when she's dressed Roman, only a fool could fail to see she's no helpless maiden. She's like a statue of Diana with an arrow nocked in her bow and a glare that says she's ready to fire."

Galen chuckled. "I've never seen her draw a bow, but give her a little while to set snares, and we'll be eating roast rabbit for dinner."

Tiberius stood. "Graecus will attend to preparing the will so I can sign it before we leave. You and I have other business in this room. Decimus will need a good library to educate his sons. I don't want to duplicate anything he has, and you can help there."

His hand swept toward two boxes by the wall of scrolls. "He will need my scrolls of Pliny's *Natural History*. Also, Tacitus's *Annals* and *Histories*.

"He always liked history best. We both thought he would make history himself." Tiberius's eyes focused on Galen. They seemed sad, then they hardened. "But the Christian god put an end to that."

Tiberius shoulders squared. "But even a Christian father needs a good library to educate his sons. The scrolls he read as a boy will serve my grandsons as well."

As Tiberius handed each scroll to Galen to roll tightly and pack, Galen avoided looking at his face. Tiberius might read the pity written on his own.

Decimus's father had so much to give by the world's standards, yet he lacked the one thing most worth giving. Galen's own father had given up what Tiberius treasured to gain what Tiberius thought worthless. But of the two, his father was the only rich man.

Chapter 40

Three Germans and a Roman

Tiberius's villa outside Roma, Day 37

Tiberius leaned against the portico column, watching the tents and cots being strapped to the last of three pack mules. When Graecus stepped through the doorway, he waved him over.

"It's been more than ten years since I headed out to govern Germania Superior." He directed a wry smile at his best friend. "I took more baggage and a much larger party then. But traveling with these three is likely to be a more enjoyable experience. They make me feel almost young again."

Graecus pressed his lips together to control his smile. "Galen Crassus could make any trip enjoyable. That young man's humor never seems to stop."

"Adela certainly finds him amusing, and she amuses me." He swept his hand toward the German beauty. "Look at her. It took some persuading to keep her in that tunic instead of the men's clothes she likes for riding. I told her she could switch when we left Augusta Praetoria to head over the pass."

His new stable would start with nine chestnut mares and a chestnut stallion from the Rome estate. Many preferred a color-matched team, and an unusual color could increase the price. The nine mares were linked in three chains of three, but a stallion was easier to control being ridden instead of led. Adela stood with her fists on her hips, watching as he was saddled.

Otto strolled over to her. "He's a fine animal, but he's small compared to the ones Father breeds."

He stood close, and Adela's head tipped back as she looked up at him. "I'll ride him. He's more my size."

She took the reins from the stable slave and stroked the stallion's nose. He jerked back and shook his mane. But as she spoke softly to him in Germanic and stroked his neck, he settled. His head turned to watch her, and he let her rub his blaze.

With a firm grip on the base of his mane, she jumped to lay her stomach across the saddle, then twisted to swing herself into it. The chestnut danced as she settled in. She leaned forward and crooned more Germanic in his ear. His ears twitched, and then he stood calmly as she straightened. Two pats to his neck, and she nudged him into a walk toward Otto's horse. When she drew alongside, she untied a sack from Otto's saddle and attached it to her own.

Tiberius stroked his jaw. "She has unusual skill in calming a spirited animal."

That drew a soft snort from Graecus. "She'll make a good wife for a Germanic chieftain. Spirited animal is a good description of many of them."

"True, but if I were to bet, I'd put my money on a short Roman, not a giant German."

Graecus's brow furrowed. "Why?"

"Because there's more to her than meets the eye, and Galen is the kind of man she needs, whether the two of them realize it yet or not."

Graecus shrugged. "She probably won't marry either. A Hermunduri chieftain would never choose a Roman over one of his own tribe. Otto might have a chance, but will a Hermunduri consider a Vangiones too long under the Roman yoke to be worthy of a daughter like her?"

Tiberius's amused smile faded. "She needs something a man of her own tribe might refuse to give. Otto might give it, but Galen would for certain. It's three weeks to Argentorate, maybe four days past that to take her back to her father. Much can happen in that time. For her sake, I hope it does."

Graecus's gaze switched to Galen. "It's regrettable that young man declined your offer to adopt."

Tiberius crossed his arms. "Indeed. Were it not for his faith, any true Roman would be proud to call him son."

Graecus mirrored his movement. "Perhaps it's that very faith that makes him the man he is."

Tiberius's head snapped sideways, and he frowned at his friend. "That faith leads men to make foolish choices." The frown softened. "But any father who would make the choice his did would be proud of him.

"Did he give you the letter for Decimus telling him I was returning with them?"

"Yes. I'll send that off by horse relay today. It should reach Decimus in about a week."

Tiberius straightened and slapped Graecus's arm. "Time to head north and find what awaits in Germania."

Graecus's smile broadened. "Give him my warmest greetings."

Tiberius grinned. "I will. May the gods guard your safety until I return, old friend."

"And yours as well."

Tiberius mounted his favorite gray stallion and took the lead of the first string of mares from his stable slave. Galen and Otto took the other two strings, leaving the string of three mules for Adela. With a flick of his hand, Tiberius started them forward.

As Tiberius led the troop through the gate, he twisted in the saddle to look back. Graecus raised an arm in farewell. Tiberius responded in kind, then set his face toward the future.

The pack mules followed willingly enough, but Adela was still sorry she was leading them. For some reason not obvious to her, their party had spread out along the Via Cassia, with each rider alone, followed by the string of three animals. Tiberius rode first, then Otto. Galen had stationed her between him and Otto. He said he didn't want her riding last, but with him behind her, she couldn't even watch him without turning too far in the saddle for comfort. The few times she did, he raised a hand and smiled.

He was watching over her. That thought triggered the start of a smile. But that also meant he saw the many times she took the roll from the food bag and nibbled a little when her stomach started feeling uneasy.

A short stop for a lunch of cheese and fruit had been refreshing, but Tiberius didn't let them rest long. His goal was to reach the villa of a friend just north of Sutrium by midafternoon. He didn't want to surprise them by arriving too late to be easily added to the dinner service.

Adela rested her hand on her belly. Dinner didn't sound that appealing, but at least her stomach stopped at queasy instead of launching its contents. As long as she nibbled the rolls, she was fine.

Tiberius turned off the cobble-stone road onto a graveled track and reined in. Otto stopped beside him, and she rode to his other side before stopping. Galen chose to stop beside her instead of Otto.

Tiberius swept his hand toward a clump of trees rising past a vineyard. "My cousin, Gaius Cornelius Cinna, lives here. He'll be glad to host us for the night, as I have hosted him many times when he's come to Rome. His wife loves to entertain, and she'll expect us all to recline. Have any of you done that before?"

Three heads shook in unison.

Adela felt the warmth in his eyes as his gaze turned on her. "Very well. Adela, I'll have her place you beside me. Follow my lead, and you'll be fine." He pressed his lips together to keep the smile from turning into a grin as he shifted to Galen and Otto. "I'll also warn her that my Roman companion is really a German and not to expect elegant manners from either of you. She's a gracious hostess who will enjoy feeding you well anyway."

"Adela, ride beside me." He nudged his horse into a walk, and she guided the chestnut to his side.

Tiberius dropped his voice. "Are you feeling well enough for a Roman dinner?"

Her ears heated. "I think so."

"Good. The way you're dressed will raise some eyebrows when we arrive, but don't let that bother you. Come to dinner in one of the long tunics I had you pack, and you'll fit in fine."

He turned his eyes forward, and Adela took a deep breath.

"Tiberius?"

"Yes?" His smile invited her words.

"Thank you for understanding... and saying nothing. And for helping me. I don't want to be a burden."

"It's not a burden. No, that's not quite right. As you're so fond of saying, *voluptas meus est.*"

South of Ticinum, Day 49

It was twelve days since they left Rome, and Galen was frustrated. Each night, they stayed at the villa of a friend of Tiberius. It was a luxurious way to travel, with private baths, soft beds, and sumptuous food. He didn't have to sleep on rocky ground or stand guard half the night to make certain no one stole the horses.

But the dinner conversations revolved around the politics of the Empire, and neither he nor Otto had much to say about that. He'd learned far more about political intrigues and social indiscretions than he ever wanted. Tiberius mostly listened after asking a leading question that got his host and any other guest talking.

Most of the hostesses had been gracious, but a few had found their German guests terribly amusing and made no effort to conceal it. More than once Adela's cheeks had flushed when she tried to use her Latin and was mocked for it. His jaw clenched at the memory. But at least the rudeness of one hostess never kept her from trying to talk with the next one.

He'd hoped for the right opportunity to talk with Adela about Jesus, but Tiberius had her ride beside him most of the time. He and Otto rode together after they'd found the strings of mares were content so close to each other. Otto was good company, but time was slipping away. In less than two weeks, they'd be back at Argentorate.

But tonight, they'd be at Tiberius's own estate near Ticinum, and he planned to stay at least three nights to let the horses rest before crossing the high pass through the Alpes.

With just the four of them in the privacy of Tiberius's own home, maybe the chance he'd been praying for would finally come.

Chapter 41

Not Worth Dying For

Tiberius's estate near Ticinum, Day 49

A flurry of motion greeted them when Tiberius led their party into the stable yard at his estate. Galen had scarcely reined in when one stable slave appeared at Astrelo's head and another stood beside him, waiting for the rope tied to the first mare.

A middle-aged man hurried out the closest door under the portico and strode to Tiberius's side. "Welcome, master. Graecus sent a courier to tell us you were coming."

Tiberius slipped from his saddle and tossed his reins to the stable boy. "I expected he would. We'll be here three nights to rest the horses before proceeding to Germania."

"Very good, master. I have already spoken with the chef about tonight's dinner, but if you have special requests for the next two nights, I will arrange that."

Tiberius glanced toward Adela. "Tell him I leave the menu to him, but nothing too rich." The corner of his mouth turned up. "My German traveling companions enjoy simpler fare." A full smile appeared. "And I must admit, my own stomach has come to prefer the same."

Tiberius turned to Galen. "Feel free to enjoy anything you find here: library, bath, gardens. There are some fine horses to ride as well. Let yours rest if you decide to tour the countryside. I'll be inspecting the estate and visiting some neighbors, but I'll join you each day for breakfast and dinner."

His gaze settled on Adela as she stood beside Otto, taking in everything and pointing Otto's attention toward his garden.

"I suggest you spend some time with Adela. I'm certain she's missed your long conversations and Latin lessons since you reached Rome." His mouth twitched. "A man has a duty to take care of the one he's mentoring. Otto being with us shouldn't change that...if you're wise."

Galen fought a grin. "I'll work on that."

As Tiberius walked away with his steward, Galen's gaze shifted to Adela. She and Otto were already looking at a flowering vine that climbed the end column of the portico.

Tiberius was right. A man shouldn't neglect the woman who'd ensnared his heart. Especially when she might be only one conversation away from opening her own heart to God, if she'd just let him tell her why she should.

Day 51

It had been a relaxing day: a short ride around Tiberius's estate, a visit to the market in Ticinum, time in the library showing Adela some Latin scrolls and having her read from a volume of Pliny's *Natural History*.

The day would have been perfect, except for two things. Almost every time he started to talk about God, Adela changed the subject. The only two times she didn't, Otto did.

In fact, Otto had stayed beside them the whole day, and that was the second problem. It normally wouldn't have bothered Galen. Otto was as good a company as any man could be. But today, he wasn't wanting the company of a man. He wanted time alone with Adela, and it hadn't happened.

Otto even followed them into the library, but he wasn't content to select a scroll and read himself. He had to keep drifting over to join them. He'd start reading aloud over Galen's shoulder, with wild mispronunciations and flamboyant hand gestures. Before Galen could say anything, he'd have Adela laughing so hard she'd be wiping tears from her eyes. It was funny, but laughing with Otto was a poor substitute for talking with Adela.

Galen stood in the hallway outside her room, waiting to escort her to dinner. Just as her door opened, Otto came bounding out of his own room.

He rested his elbow on Galen's shoulder. "Ready for another good dinner? Tiberius keeps the best cooks, and there's even enough to fill you up."

Otto grinned at Adela when she stepped into the hall, a vision of loveliness in the blue tunic Tiberius had provided. "Don't you wonder where Galen puts all the food? He eats more than me, but look at us. A pony and a war horse. How can he do it?"

Adela giggled. "Maybe he needs that much because he works so hard trying to teach me." The warmth in her eyes fired his heart, and her smile took the sting from her laughing at Otto's words. "He's the best teacher in the Empire. Besides, it's the heart, not the height, that matters. Any time I'm with him, *voluptas meus est.*"

Otto slapped his shoulder. "Maybe you are the best teacher after all. There's no doubt you're the very best friend."

As the three of them strolled down the hallway toward the dining room, Galen's irritation faded. The heart, not the height—Otto towered over him, but Adela knew what really mattered.

Any day with his best friend and the woman he wanted to marry was a good day, and they were still at least two weeks from her home. When Adela was ready to listen, nothing would keep God from opening the door.

After dinner, Galen leaned against the fluted column supporting the portico roof. Adela and Otto had left him conversing with Tiberius to explore the gardens near the main house of the villa.

She was leaning over the edge of the man-made pond where the fish they'd eaten were raised. When Otto stepped up behind her, he placed his hands on her upper arms. A small shriek when he pushed her toward the water was replaced by the music of her laughter when he pulled her back at the last moment.

A sigh welled up from deep within Galen. They looked like the perfect couple: Otto so tall and muscular, Adela so graceful and beautiful. Both children of chieftains. Many would say they were a perfect match. As much as he hated to admit it, they looked like they might be.

When Tiberius joined him on the other side of the column, Galen masked his thoughts, but the man who played high-stakes politics missed almost nothing.

"You'd better tell Adela you want her before Otto pushes you aside."

"I know she'd make a fine wife, but I can't ask her now. She doesn't follow the Way. My sister told Dec no for the same reason when he asked her to be his wife before returning to the legion."

◆

Tiberius straightened. The Decimus that returned from the dead was not the man who'd left Mogontiacum for a surprise inspection of the legion in Argentorate. He'd given up nights with strange women and getting drunk with his friends. He'd remained aloof and brooding every evening on the way back to Rome. Decimus told him it was his conversation with Publius that shifted his loyalty from Rome to Jesus. That conversation and the ridiculous claims that the Christian god had healed him with miracles and met him in his bedchamber.

But was that all? Who'd told him it was miracles? Tiberius clenched his jaw. Galen's sister was to blame. The change had started long before that talk with Publius, and he'd married the woman who started it after he'd become what she wanted.

Tiberius turned a frown on Galen. "If that's the case, you might as well give up now. She stops you every time you start to talk about religion."

Galen massaged his neck. "That's no reason to give up. God wants to claim every heart, and I've been praying for Adela to want to listen. If she'll just let me talk with her about Jesus, she'll see the truth in what I say."

"Truth?" Tiberius snorted. "Can any man really know what's true? Philosophers try. My closest friend Publius tried, and when he decided the ridiculous story about a Jewish carpenter being god and redeeming him from sin was the truth, it got him killed."

Galen tipped his head and raised one shoulder. "Yes and no. Publius's body died, but he's not dead. He's alive with Jesus right now. So are my parents. Someday I'll join them." His gaze shifted to Adela, now talking and smiling with Otto. "Even if Adela and Otto marry, I still want Adela to know what I've found following Jesus."

Tiberius's eyes narrowed. "What you've found?"

"Yes. Contentment, peace, joy. Knowing God's love here and now and knowing that life will only get better when I join Him after my body dies." The slight smile that Galen wore most of the time appeared. "That makes anything life throws at me tolerable and even lets me find the good in the bad."

Tiberius tightened his lips. Galen spoke like a fool. "Good in the bad? That sounds like a game the philosophers play. Fooling themselves into believing what isn't true so they can claim to understand everything."

Galen rubbed his lower lip. "Maybe philosophers do that, but that's not what I'm talking about. My faith isn't just philosophy. It's based on what's real, and I often see God bring good out of bad."

"So you say, but I've mostly seen bad come from bad, not good. Mere words aren't proof."

"But the things that happen are." Galen raised one finger. "Look at Adela. If Otto hadn't decided to gamble with her kidnappers, she'd have ended up someone's slave." Galen rubbed the back of his neck. "You know what many owners do to their female slaves. But he did win her, and now she's free to go home."

A second finger rose. "And Otto. He drank so much he didn't see the danger of going off with a man who covered a bet with a woman who claimed she wasn't his slave. But if he hadn't been taken, I would never have come to Rome. Otto wouldn't be a Roman citizen, and you wouldn't be on your way to visit Dec."

A third finger joined the first two. "And then there's Dec. If he hadn't almost been killed in that ambush, Val would never have brought him home to heal. He wouldn't have become my brother-in-law. Otto and I wouldn't have learned how to use a gladius so well that Otto didn't die in his first fight. Then a good man like Brutus bought him, and I fought well enough to beat Brutus to get Otto freed. But if Brutus had set the price low enough that I hadn't been forced to come to you for help, you wouldn't be going home with me to make Dec a very happy man when he sees you again."

What Galen said almost made sense. But wishful thinking could fool a man, and he was no fool. "Make Decimus happy? I'm probably dead as far as he's concerned. It's been eight years."

Galen shook his head "I'm not lying when I tell you Dec has prayed every day since he came back to us for this chance to reconcile.

"But the biggest proof of good from bad was in Judaea almost 90 years ago, when Pontius Pilatus crucified Jesus to satisfy the Jewish leaders after they said Pilatus was no friend of Caesar if he didn't."

Tiberius's head snapped back. "We've both seen what a man suffers on a cross. How could that possibly be good?"

Galen stroked the scar on his cheek. "The physical torture wasn't the worst part." His eyes saddened. "It was taking on all the sin that separated him from God the Father." His mouth drooped. "Taking on my sin."

Then his perpetual smile returned. "Jesus's death changed everything. Pilate didn't know it, but he was fulfilling the prophesies of how Jesus would die to be the final blood sacrifice that paid for the sins of all men for all time. Then Jesus rose from the dead and proved that everything He'd said about having power over death itself was true. The good that came from that horror includes me being a child of God who will live with Him forever."

Tiberius faced Galen straight on and crossed his arms. "I've heard the claims that Jesus is the son of a god and even a god himself. That delusion took both my son and my best friend."

His eyebrows lowered. "The gods aren't real. They're just stories people tell to make sense of a world that truly makes no sense. All you've described are just strings of coincidences. No god would die to save any man, and no god is worth dying for, like Publius did.

"And no god who lives only in your imagination is worth denying yourself the woman who might make you happy. If you want Adela, you're a fool to let your religion keep you from her." Adela's laugh drew his attention to the pair by the pond. "If you wait too long, she may change her mind and not want you."

Tiberius moved away, but he hadn't taken three steps before he turned back. "Tomorrow, Otto rides beside me, and you teach her more Latin. You should be able to slip *te amo* in there somewhere, and make sure she knows you mean it."

◆

Those words triggered a noncommittal tilt of Galen's head, but Tiberius's satisfied smile revealed his assumption that Galen would do as he said.

"Sleep well, Galen. Tomorrow offers another chance." Tiberius stepped inside.

Another chance. That was what he needed. *God, give me another chance to tell Adela about you. Let her listen and decide to follow the Way. Let it be your will that she becomes my wife.* A sigh welled up from deep within him. *But if it isn't, let her marry a truly good man...like Otto.*

He dragged his gaze away from the laughing pair to focus on the door through which Tiberius had gone. Every new day offered another chance, but some things were a long time coming. *God, please let our years of prayer bear fruit. Claim Tiberius as your own.*

Chapter 42

Road to Reunion

An estate outside Augusta Praetoria, Day 57

Scattered clouds framed the mountains that rose past the elegant villa just ahead. Tiberius turned in his saddle to face Galen and Otto as they rode behind his string of mares.

"This will be our last stop before we cross the pass. The estate belongs to Aulus Flavius Rutilus, the oldest brother of my cousin's son's wife."

Otto placed his hand on top of his head. "Is there any estate owner in Italia who isn't related to you by blood or marriage or both?"

Tiberius shrugged, but what his young German friend said was almost true. "Family ties are important to Romans, and the slightest connection is cause to welcome a traveler as an overnight guest. That includes you now, as my freedman and business agent."

Otto placed his hand on his chest and raised his chin. "As Tiberius Cornelius Baldricus, allow me to extend an invitation to come stay at my father's house anytime." He tightened his lips to squash the grin. "Of course, you won't have a room of your own, and you'll have to sit on a chair to eat. My little brother can eat standing while you're with us." He wrinkled his nose. "And it might not be wise to mention to Father that you were once provincial governor."

The grin leaked out. "I can guarantee we'll take good care of your stallion. He's almost as big as one of our best studs and fine enough to produce foals I wouldn't be ashamed to sell to the tribunes in Argentorate."

Tiberius chuckled. "I can see I've chosen the right man to partner in my new stable. A horse trader to the bone."

He pointed at the mountains. "There's a mansio at the summit of the pass for those on Imperial business. As a former governor, I can stay there. The horses can be stabled under guard. After that—" He shrugged. "You'll soon see why we have three pack mules. We may be camping until Argentorate, and you'll be on night watch."

As Tiberius turned to face forward again, Adela reached into her sack and pulled out a roll. He raised his eyebrows to ask the question, and she smiled to tell him it wasn't a problem.

His lips relaxed into a contented smile. These young men were worthwhile additions to his extended network of family and friends. He couldn't have chosen a better brother-in-law for his son or a man more worthy of becoming his freedman.

He glanced at Adela. One of them should marry her and pull her into his network as well. In Rome, he would have bet any amount on Galen. But after almost three weeks on the road together, a wise gambler would have to split his bets.

Their party had arrived at the villa in the early afternoon, leaving time to relax before gathering for dinner. As Adela strolled through the garden with Tiberius, they walked through an arch in a rose hedge.

She froze. A young woman was removing the spent flowers while a baby slept in a basket beside her. The world swirled down into a tunnel with the baby at the end and started sucking her into it.

"Adela." Tiberius's voice pulled her back. "You should tell Galen you're carrying his child. He'll do the right thing and marry you."

"I can't say that." She bit her lip. "Galen never touched me that way. He's always treated me with respect. It was the kidnapper. I was knocked out when he pulled me off the horse, and he…" Her chest jumped, but a few hard blinks stopped the tears. "We caught up with him in Brigantium. The soldiers crucified him, but his death didn't change what he's done to me."

She squeezed her lips together in a futile effort to stop her chin quivering. "I don't know what will happen when I go home carrying his child. Father was going to arrange my marriage with another chieftain's son. Mother lost several babies early, so maybe I will. But if I don't lose the baby soon…I'm scared, Tiberius. A woman of my tribe who carries a baby before her marriage...sometimes her family kills her to end the shame."

Tiberius wrapped his arm around her shoulders and pulled her against his side. "I won't allow that. Before we leave you there, I'll talk with your father to make certain he understands what happened. He should take my word that Galen wouldn't have touched you and Otto's had no chance to."

"But Father hates Romans. He might kill you just for being one, and he'd kill you for certain if he knew who you are." She dropped her gaze to the ground. "You shouldn't even go with us across the border."

He took her chin in his hand and lifted until their gazes met. "If he doesn't welcome you back, we won't leave you there. I don't think it will be necessary, but if you have nowhere else to go, you can come home with me."

A single tear escaped, and he smiled at her as he wiped it away. "Don't. There's no need to worry before you must." He glanced over the low wall into the stable yard where Galen was brushing Astrelo, even though a slave would have done it. "Galen will ask what's wrong, and you don't need that question right now."

Adela flicked away the second tear and forced a smile. If only Father could be as understanding as Tiberius, but that wasn't the Hermunduri way.

Day 58

Galen stood by the window in the dining room, waiting for the rest to appear for breakfast. As he scanned the mountains before him, he smiled. It would be good to return to the wilder country. Pillow-soft beds and exotic foods with aromas that made a man's mouth water were luxuries he didn't even have at home, but staying in a stranger's house left no opportunity for long talks with Adela.

Something about dancing flames and glowing coals fueled deep conversations. Maybe it was how the deep shadows of the night made someone feel less exposed while sharing private thoughts. Maybe it was how flames seemed to burn away attacks of shyness like dried leaves tossed on a fire.

Tiberius entered wearing his wide-stripe tunic, and Galen's eyebrow rose. They were entering wild country, and advertising his rank and wealth was not wise.

"I'm not a fool, Galen. One more day in senatorial splendor, and then I'll wear the plain tunic, as you advised. I need to look the senator for admittance to the mansio tonight. Tomorrow is soon enough for servant's clothes."

Adela entered in her short riding tunic, and Tiberius smiled as if she were the sun rising. "Today's the day I promised you. Before we start the climb, you can change back into your Germanic attire."

She rested her hand on her chest as she looked down at what she was wearing. When her eyes turned back on his face, her grin lit the room.

Tiberius settled onto the couch as Otto entered. "I hope you enjoyed last night's meal. It may be your last good one for a while. The food at a mansio is often…edible but not much more. And what we'll take for the trail…" He shrugged.

He patted his couch, and Adela sat as if it were a chair. He swung his legs over the edge and joined her. "When in Germania, do as the Germans do. I might as well start this morning."

He picked a plain roll from the basket on the table and handed it to her.

She took a small bite. "I won't miss the food as much as the beds. I've been spoiled for sleeping on rocky ground."

Tiberius took some dates for himself. "Soon you'll see why we have three pack mules. They carry more than a library and some money for my son and grandsons. Three tents, three cots, bedding including pillows. We only need three because someone will be on watch all night. Perhaps best of all, the folding chair I used when I commanded a legion."

His eyes crinkled. "It took Graecus some time to find where it had been stored more than fifteen years ago."

"When I was governor, I had a friend from my legion days in Octodurus. If he's still there, we'll have another night of luxury." He turned his gaze on Galen. "You can ask your Christian god for that tonight."

The skepticism in Tiberius's eyes reinforced the sarcasm dripping from his words.

Galen fought a smile. "Since you suggest it, I will."

Tiberius rose. "Time to head out. It's a long climb, and we'll take some breaks to rest the horses." As he passed, he rested his hand on Otto's shoulder and squeezed. "But I think this time you all might enjoy it."

Summus Poeninus, Day 58

Galen scraped the last of the stew from his bowl. Tiberius was right. The food at the mansio wasn't terrible, but the quality made even him think twice before asking for a third serving.

The weather was warmer than before. No vicious wind, no snow-flakes—a definite improvement, but he'd welcome the coldest winter storm to have Adela snuggled against him to stay warm.

The horses were secure in the garrison stable. Tiberius and Otto had already gone to bed. A little longer, and he'd join Adela. With so many men watching her with too much interest, he'd decided she should share his room. But at least he wouldn't be on the hard stone floor.

He handed his bowl to the boy cleaning the tables and strolled across the courtyard to his room in the two-story building made of local stone. He knocked with the agreed-upon pattern.

"Who is it?

"Galen."

"Come in." She lay on the bed, smiling at him.

He loosened the straps around the folded cot and set it up. As he placed it across the door, he glanced over his shoulder. "Traveling with Tiberius certainly has advantages. This cot is much softer than the floors at the inns."

Adela rolled on her side and propped her head on her elbow. "Nothing could be better than Tiberius's beds. They're like sleeping on pillows."

"Traveling with a senator has many benefits. I'm glad he's coming back with us."

Galen sat on the cot and rested his elbows on his knees. With his forehead supported by clasped hands, he closed his eyes. His breathing slowed. *God, I thank You for this day. For—*

"Galen."

He opened his eyes.

"You sit like that every night. What are you doing?"

"Talking with God."

Her eyes saucered. "Talking? Like two people talk?" She lowered her eyes and fingered the blanket. When she looked at him again...was that longing? "What does your god's voice sound like?"

"Most of the time, it's not so much a voice as it's thoughts that I know aren't my own that come to me. When I'm faced with a hard decision, I ask Him about it, and then I know what to choose."

"But that doesn't always work. We went to Brigantium when Otto went to Octodurus."

"Yes, but that sidetrack brought justice to Gundahar and Gerlach. Now they'll never take another person's freedom and sell them into misery." He straightened and placed his hands on his thighs. "If we hadn't added those seven days to our trip, we'd have caught up with Otto in Octodurus. Then we wouldn't have gone to Rome, and Tiberius wouldn't be going home with us to see Dec again." Her first real question about God...he'd prayed for this for weeks. "So, I really did make the right decision when you look at everything."

"And I wouldn't have learned so much Latin or seen so many new things. Getting to know Tiberius and Otto has been wonderful, too. Tiberius treats me almost like a father would. And Otto's such a nice man and so much fun. It's easy to see why you would do anything to save him. I'm glad that decision made us go all the way to Rome. This journey...it's been the best time of my life."

She lowered her cheek to the pillow. "Tiberius said we should leave as early as we can tomorrow. He's not sure where we'll be able to stay near Octodurus until we get there."

She pulled the blanket up to her chin. "I'm so tired. Coming up this side of the pass seemed harder."

"At least it's warmer here in the mansio."

"I didn't mind sleeping in the stable. It wasn't cold with you there. It's good Otto's so big that his blankets covered us both."

Galen watched her eyes close. "I wasn't cold, either." Her breathing slowed; she'd drifted off before he could tell her he felt blessed by God to have her along.

The best time of her life. It had been the best time of his life, too. But was getting to know Otto the thing that made it so special for her?

She never failed to laugh when she talked with him. Otto was a tall, Germanic chieftain's son, like she'd always admired. And he really was a good man. It would be hard to find a better man than Otto.

Any woman judging with only her eyes would choose Otto over him. But it really was the heart, not the height, that mattered, and if she would just let him lead her to Jesus...That was a barrier he could never cross.

Please, God, bring that barrier down. Claim her as yours so I can ask her to be mine.

Chapter 43

Everything He Wanted

Octodurus, Day 59

As Tiberius led them off the main road toward the estate that once belonged to his friend, he heard galloping hoofbeats behind them. With his hand on his sword, he turned in the saddle.

"Tiberius! Is that you?" A gray-haired man reached him and reined in. "What are you doing here?"

"I'm on my way to Germania Superior to start a new racing stable. It's good to see you, Quintus."

"Fortuna has smiled on us. I'm just returning from Aventicum, and I'm leaving for Lugdunum day after tomorrow. I had planned to stay another day with my brother. We would have missed this meeting after so many years." He slapped Tiberius's shoulder. "It's time to celebrate. You will, of course, stay the night with me. I'll ride ahead to start the dinner preparations."

As his friend cantered away, Galen rode up beside Tiberius. Tiberius's frown stopped any words, but Galen's smile and shrug said it all.

South of Aventicum, Day 60

It had been another luxurious night with Tiberius's friend outside Octodurus. But it was a two-day ride to Aventicum, and the only roof over them tonight held the stars. The horses stirred on the picket line, and Galen scanned the edge of the woods. An owl appeared against the moon before swooping down to the grass. Its talon gripped a mouse when it rose into the sky.

Otto had been asleep for some time since he was taking the second watch. Tiberius was in his tent as well. Adela had won her short argument with him over who would take the third watch. Now she sat across the fire in Tiberius's field chair. She'd seemed too quiet since supper, and she sat poking at the coals with a long stick.

Galen closed his eyes, and peace swept over him. *God, I thank You for this day. For Adela and Otto and Tiberius. For—*

"Galen?" Thick tension coated her voice.

He opened his eyes to find her staring at him with eyes that looked too moist.

"Is something wrong?"

She bit her lip. "Yes."

He straightened. "Can I help?"

"I don't know if anyone can."

"Tell me what it is, and I'll try."

She took a deep breath, and it turned into a sigh. "Everything is so... uncertain. I used to know what I wanted, what the future held, how to get there. But now, since Gundahar took me and after this trip with you...I don't know what to do anymore. But you always seem to, no matter what happens. Why is that?"

She pulled at the edge of her eye, and he could have sworn that was a tear she wiped away. His heart rate ramped up. *God, is this the time? Give me the words.*

"Remember in the mansio, when you asked me about talking with God?"

"Yes. You said your god guides you when you don't know what to do. I'd never heard of any god who talks to people like us. Mother said the high priestess of Nerthus got messages from her during the sacrifices, but plain people like us, just talking with her by a campfire...I don't think that works."

"Tiberius would tell you that's because the gods aren't real. He'd say they're just stories made up by people trying to make sense of the world around them. For the most part, he's right, but in one case, he's totally wrong. There is one God who is real, and He's the one I talk with."

"The god of the Christians?"

"First of the Jews and now of the Christians, too."

"Why is he different from the others?"

Galen's hand swept toward the clearing and forest around them. "You see all this? It didn't just happen. Someone made it. That someone is God. He made people, too, but He made us different from the animals. He made us in His own image. We can think and dream and plan...things no animal does. He made us that way so He could enjoy being with us, but we ruined that with our sins."

Her head tilted. "Sins?"

"The things we do that are wrong, and the things we don't do that we ought to. The problem is that God is holy but we never can be because we keep committing sins, even when we're trying our best not to. That puts a barrier between us and God, one we could never cross on our own. But He loves us so much he wants us with Him. So, when our sins built that barrier, He decided to give us a way across it. God came as a man, as Jesus, and made Himself the sacrifice to remove our sins.

"Jesus was crucified in Judaea ninety years ago and paid the penalty we couldn't pay ourselves. His suffering and death paid the price to redeem us, like buying a slave and setting him free. All we have to do is admit the truth of what He did and accept His gift of forgiveness. Then our sins are erased, and the barrier is gone. Believing Jesus did that is what makes me a child of God. It's why I can talk with Him like I do."

Adela's brow furrowed. "How can you be sure Jesus wasn't just a man? Anyone could say he's a god. If he really was, how could the Romans have killed him?"

"He let them do it. That's why God came to earth as a man in the first place. His death was the sacrifice for the sins that separate us from God."

"That man in Octodurus..." She shuddered. "It's such a horrible way to die. How could he ever let them do that?"

"Because He loves us enough to pay that price."

"But how do you know his death did anything?"

"He explained it all to His followers before it happened. He didn't just claim He would die to be the sacrifice for sin. He proved He had the power to do whatever He said by rising from the dead three days later.

"And He really was dead. A soldier drove a spear into His side to make sure. The governor of Judaea himself asked the centurion who crucified Him if Jesus was dead before he let them take the body. They put Him in a tomb sealed with a stone slab too heavy for one man to move, but that tomb opened when He rose from the dead.

"Jesus told His followers before He died that He had the power to give up His life and take it back again, and that's exactly what He did.

That was the proof that He was the true Son of God, not just some man claiming to be God."

Adela rubbed her cheekbone. "Are you sure he came back to life? Couldn't his body have disappeared because several men opened the tomb and took it?"

"Jesus met with His followers many times between His death and when He returned to God the Father in heaven. They spread out across the Empire to tell any who would listen about what Jesus had done. Some came to Rome, and that's how my father came to believe."

Adela nibbled her lip. "Just believing in Jesus makes you a child of your god?"

"Yes, and it means I don't have to fear death myself."

Adela raised her chin. "A Germanic warrior doesn't fear death." Her gaze dropped to the ground, then rose to meet his again. "At least, they say they don't. Shame is feared more." Her eyes lowered and raised again. "A Germanic woman feels the same. Better dead than shamed."

She cleared her throat, and Galen's brow furrowed. Adela's voice had caught as she said 'shamed,' but why? He opened his mouth to ask, but she cut him off.

"So, if you're a child of God, does the son of God love you like a brother? Like you love Otto? You would have died to free him."

"Jesus said, 'Greater love has no man than this, to lay down his life for a friend.' And then He said, 'You are my friends if you obey what I command.' And what He commanded was for us to love God and each other.

"Out of love, He sacrificed Himself to save me. The truest test of love is what I'm willing to sacrifice for someone, even if it's my own life."

"You could have died fighting Brutus. Otto's lucky you love him so much."

"That wasn't the most dangerous thing I did. Going to Tiberius was."

"I don't understand why you thought Tiberius might kill you. He's such a nice man."

"Rome has decided Christians should die because we won't worship the old Roman gods or the dead emperors it claims are gods or the genius of the emperor before he dies. When Tiberius was governor of Germania Superior, he hunted Christians because he thought we were enemies of Rome. We're not, but if I love God, how could I ever betray Him by pretending the other gods are real and offering sacrifices to them? One thing

He forbids is having any other God but Him. But why would I ever want to trade the God who made everything for a story made up by men?"

"He hunted Christians?" She drew a breath and blew it out. "But he doesn't want to kill you now. Maybe the rest of the Romans will change, too."

Galen shrugged. "Maybe, but even if they don't, it's better to know Jesus and risk dying that to never know Him."

Adela frowned. "I would die for someone in my family or someone I loved, but not for a god. Death is forever."

"It doesn't have to be. Jesus had a good friend named Lazarus who died. Four days later, he raised his friend from the dead."

Adela's eyebrows shot up. "Jesus brought a dead man back to life?"

"Yes. Just before He did that, He made a promise to His friend's sister. 'Whoever believes in Me, though he die, yet shall he live, and everyone who lives and believes in Me shall never die.' He asked if she believed that, and she said, 'Yes, Lord; I believe that you are the Christ, the Son of God, who is coming into the world.'"

Adela's head tipped. "He actually brought a dead man back to life?"

"Yes, and a girl of twelve and the only son of a widow. That's three we know of, and there were probably more that weren't written down. And then He raised Himself after His crucifixion. The Latin for that is *resurrectio*, rising again."

She bit her lip and dropped her head. When she raised it, the corners of her mouth rose. "Only a real god could do that."

"That's right."

Silence hung between them as she stirred the coals. Then her gaze lifted from the fire and locked on his eyes.

"If I believed in your god, would he talk to me like he does to you?"

"Yes. That's the best part of following the Way. I'm never alone, and I'm never lost. The answer to a prayer doesn't always come right away, but it always comes. And sometimes the answer is so much better than what I wanted when I asked. When someone loves you, they always want what's best for you, even when what's best seems hard at the moment."

The fire snapped, and an ember jumped out of the fire pit. Adela slipped her stick under it and flipped it back into the flames.

"For him to listen and answer, do I have to be good, like you?"

"I'm not that good. The best parts of me come from loving and following Him. He's forgiven me, and He's told me I must forgive others if I follow Him. That's not always easy, but when I try, He helps me. He knows every thought from the softest whisper to the loudest shout to the voice that's only inside my head. And no matter what, He loves me as His child."

"Like Mother did."

"Yes, and so far beyond a parent's love, we can't even imagine it. Whenever we tell Him the bad things we've done and the ones we've wanted to do but didn't and ask Him to forgive us, He does. That's called confessing, and when we do, He wipes all those sins away, as if they'd never happened."

Adela poked at the coals with her stick, and the soft crackles of the fire broke the silence. Her mouth curved into a deep frown. "You have to forgive others? What if someone did something horrible to you? Something they deserved to die for. Something that changed your life forever."

Galen drew a deep breath and blew it out slowly. "Someone did. When I was ten, Father and Mother went to our market town. I wanted to go, too, because I thought Otto might be there, but Father told me to stay and help Val in the garden. I was so mad at him that I didn't even tell him goodbye." He stroked his scar. "My last words to him were words of anger."

His lips tightened. "Some men from across the frontier raided the village that day. They killed both my parents.

"Val was sixteen, but Rhoda was only six—too little to help with much. With just me and Val, it was a struggle to do everything on the farm. Otto's father brought us meat sometimes, and Val made a little money as a physician because Father had been training her. But it wasn't until I was thirteen, when Dec came back and married Val, that things got easier. He brought the mares that started our herd. I'd wanted to be a physician, like Father, but that ended with his death, so I'm a horse trader and farmer instead."

He rubbed the back of his neck. "I've struggled with forgiving the men who murdered my parents. I hated them with every fiber of my being when it happened. I can't say I've totally forgiven them now, and I'll never forget, but God has taken the hatred and anger that was eating me up. And when the old feelings flare, I ask Him to help me forgive again. He always does.

"So when I say we have to forgive, what I really mean is we have to try. He understands when it's hard. I'm still His child, and children sometimes take a long time before they do things right."

The corner of his mouth lifted. "I can tell you one thing. Something changes inside me when I try to set aside that anger and forgive. I can find peace with what's happened, and losing my parents hurts less. That might not make sense to you, but it's true."

Adela had been staring at him as he spoke. Her gaze dropped to the fire, and she resumed stirring the coals.

Galen closed his eyes. *God, please let my words reach her.*

"Galen."

His eyes popped open.

"If I wanted to be a child of God, what would I do?"

"Believe Jesus died to save you, confess your sins, and ask forgiveness. Then thank God for making you His child."

"If I confess, can I tell only God? I don't have to say it aloud, do I?"

"Of course not. Only God needs to know your heart. When you're through, tell Him you believe Jesus paid for your sins and thank Him for forgiving everything. Tell Him you want to follow Jesus and ask Him to accept you as His own child forever."

Adela closed her eyes, and the first tear escaped. Her chin quivered until she pressed her palm against it.

She rested her other hand on her belly and began to rock. First a trickle, then a rivulet, and finally a torrent of teardrops washed over her cheeks. Then, as the tears slowed, a peaceful smile appeared. As her head tipped back, the smile broadened until she was beaming. Her eyes popped open.

"Oh, Galen!" Her gaze locked with his as she swept the old tears from her cheeks. "I understand now. When I was little, whenever I felt bad, all it took was Mother's arms around me to make it better. She'd whisper in my ear how much she loved me, and I'd feel warm inside. But this...it was like all the love in the world wrapped around me, and He whispered, 'I love you, My child. Come and find peace in Me.' And then the brightness faded, but I still feel Him with me."

Galen's smile matched hers as he rose from the stump. "I know exactly what you mean. He'll always be there, and you'll always be His child, just like me. You and I are more than friends now. As children of God, we're brother and sister in Christ. We will be forever."

She rushed past the fire and threw her arms around him. He closed his eyes as he encircled her in his arms. "God loves you, Adela." *And so do I.*

As she rested her cheek on his shoulder, her lips brushed his ear. "Thank you for telling me...and for everything." Her whisper triggered his silent shout of joy.

Their breathing synchronized. Could her desires for the future blend with his as well?

God, thank you for making her my sister. Now, please make her want to be my wife.

Too soon, her arms relaxed and she stepped back.

"Oh, Galen. I feel so...I don't know how to describe it."

He pushed a strand of hair behind her ear. "You don't have to. I know."

A beaming smile lit her eyes. "Does Otto know how wonderful this feels?"

He froze his smile. "No. He hasn't wanted to listen yet."

"Somehow, you have to tell him. I want to share this with him, too."

He nodded, even though he'd already tried many times.

She took his hand and swung their arms. "I think I'll go to bed now. I feel so at peace...like you." She held his hand as she took a step, then let it slip from her grasp.

"Rest in peace, Adela."

"Oh, I will. Like I never have before. Good night."

She entered her tent, and he heard the cot creak as she lay down.

The deepest sigh escaped him. Adela had just become everything he wanted in a wife, but would he ever be what she wanted? He wasn't the son of a chieftain like Otto, he was a Roman, which her father despised, and he was short. Well, maybe the last wouldn't matter that much to her. It was the heart, not the height, that mattered.

He picked up her stick and moved a half-burned log over the glowing coals. Some wood smoldered a long time before catching fire.

Until the day she announced her betrothal to another, God might still give him the way to win her heart.

◆

Tiberius lay on his cot, but his heart raced as if he'd just run a mile in battle armor. What had started as a quiet conversation between Galen and Adela had turned into a torrent of words and surging emotions that threatened to drown him.

He'd hated the Christians all his life. They were troublemakers and rebels, threatening the Empire with their refusals to yield to the simple requirement of a meaningless sacrifice.

Their claim that their god was somehow special, the only real god in a multitude of false ones, was absurd. He'd found that so easy to reject as a foolish delusion that needed to be purged from the Empire.

And then his own son had turned traitor and become one. For eight years, that decision had haunted him. How could a brilliant man like Decimus be so deceived?

But tonight, in the quiet darkness, he'd heard another young man whom he'd grown to respect explain it.

And it almost made sense.

But what sounded logical wasn't always true. A gifted orator could twist words enough to make the grossest falsehood sound like the noblest truth.

But that wasn't what Galen had done. He was no philosopher or politician playing with words. In Ticinum, Galen had claimed it was events, not words, that proved the truth of something. He'd willingly risked his own death at Tiberius's hands to rescue his friend, and he claimed it was because his god had done far more to save him.

To hear him tell Adela about being a child of the Christian god—that was beyond what was believable. And yet...

The joy in her voice as she claimed that god told her he loved her— what was a man of logic to do with that?

Eight years earlier, Decimus had declared he'd met his god in his own bedchamber. His words described impossibilities: surrounded by light, wrapped in love, filled with his god's presence.

He'd rejected Decimus's claim that his god was right there with him as the ravings of a madman, but what about Adela's words? Galen hadn't told her that would happen, so she wasn't saying it just to please him. And to hear Galen say he knew what she experienced, that his god would always be present with them both?

He'd thought his son had abandoned everything for a delusion, but was there a reality here that he'd never let himself consider before?

He willed his body to relax, and his heart rate slowed. The silence of the forest wrapped around him. But try as he might, he couldn't silence Adela's voice as she echoed Decimus's words.

Chapter 44

A Fight He Can't Win

Near Argentorate, Day 66

Except for the occasional conversation between Galen and Adela about the Christian god, Tiberius had found much of the six-day ride from Octodurus to Argentorate quite amusing. Somehow, it was always Galen who finished packing the mules when they broke camp, and that gave Otto a chance to ask Adela to walk with him alone. The big German had a rare gift for making her laugh, and he paid her enough attention the rest of the day that any woman would think he might be courting her. She giggled and blushed at all the appropriate times, so it was clear she was very aware of him as a man.

Galen's response was not what his own would have been, had he been a young man who wanted Adela himself. Galen was at least as funny as his tall friend, and by far the smarter of the two. He was just as handsome and strong for his size, even if he was short. Why didn't he tell Otto it was his turn to pack and take Adela for a walk himself?

Galen had admitted he liked Adela in Ticinum as they watched the others by the fish pond. His reason for not telling her made no sense, not then and much less now.

Tiberius almost snorted as he remembered Galen saying he couldn't marry a woman who didn't worship the Christian god. That excuse was gone, and he still hadn't told her he wanted her.

It was only a few hours to the estate of a friend from his time as governor, and time was running out. Tonight, before Tiberius let Galen sleep, he'd teach the boy an important political and military principle.

The contest didn't always go to the strongest or smartest or richest. It often went to the one who made the first move.

Tiberius took his last sip of wine. The dinner hosted by his friend had been up to the standards of Rome, and his stomach was content. His three Germans had acquitted themselves well as they reclined at dinner, with Adela chatting in passable Latin with their hostess and both Galen and Otto listening attentively as he and Septimus discussed the changes in the province since he'd left.

He rose from the couch. "An exceptional dinner after so long on the trail, but we have always enjoyed a good meal together." He flexed his shoulders. "My young companions will be heading across the frontier early tomorrow, but such trips are meant for younger men who haven't experienced the wilder parts of Germania like we have. I shall enjoy a few days of relaxation as my horses rest."

Septimus's smile was more than gracious as he stood. "Since we'll have several days together, I'll bid you goodnight. Those who plan to travel early need to retire early as well." He offered his hand to his wife to help her rise, and they left the dining room.

Otto swung his legs off the couch. "A man can't do better than the food in a Roman dining room, but I still like chairs better." He held his hand out to Adela.

She gripped it, and he pulled her to her feet. "What I like about the villas is their flower gardens. So many different blossoms, such lovely smells."

Otto didn't release her hand after she stood. "Let's walk in one for a while."

Adela flashed him a smile and pointed out the window that over-looked a pool with statues on pedestals down the center. "There are roses by the wall over there." She held out her hand to Galen. "Come with us."

Tiberius raised his hand. "He'll be with you shortly. I need to speak with Galen first."

As soon as they left the room, Tiberius turned on Galen. "You do realize how little time you have left with Adela? When are you going to tell her you want her and ask if she wants you?"

Galen walked to the window. "Never." A sigh escaped as Adela leaned over a rosebush and inhaled. "Look at her. She's the extraordinary daughter of a Germanic chieftain. He'd planned to marry her to the son of one of his fellow chieftains, and when she goes home, he'll still expect to do that. She'd never marry without her father's approval."

He ran both hands through his hair. "Look at me. I couldn't look more Roman if I tried. Her father respects Roman warriors, but he hates Romans. He'll never let her marry one. If I were to ask, he'd probably take my head off with a battle ax. What I want isn't even a remote possibility, even if she wanted me, too.

"She likes Otto a great deal. Who wouldn't? He's a good man. He'll be a good husband and father. His father's a chieftain of the Vangiones. Even though he lives in a Roman province, a Hermunduri chieftain might just say yes if Otto asked for her.

"Three or four days from now, I'll have to say goodbye to her. It's the last thing I want to do, but I can't put what I want over what's best for her."

"She deserves to know how you feel. She might persuade him if she tries." The corner of Tiberius's mouth curved. "I'd have a hard time saying no to a daughter like her."

"Don't tell her. If she feels the same as I do, I don't want to make it harder for her by making her think we might have married if it weren't for her father. Anger at someone who takes away someone you love can destroy affection. I don't want to make her resent him. She might say or do something he'll never forgive. Forgive the unforgivable—that's a command from our God, but very few can do it without His help, and even then, it's hard."

"So you're giving up without a fight?"

"A wise man never enters a fight he knows he can't win."

Tiberius rolled his eyes. "I respect your desire to protect her, but I think you're a fool. At sixteen, I married the girl my father selected for me. She fulfilled her duty and gave me two sons. She watched over my house while I served as tribune, but we were nothing to each other. You and Adela have a chance for so much more, if you'll only take it." He flicked his hand toward the garden. "But if you won't reach for that future, go enjoy what little of the present remains."

Day 67

Tiberius stood beside Adela, watching his chariot horses in the corral while Galen and Otto saddled their mounts and loaded the pack mule with two tents, bedrolls, and supplies for ten days. It was the last time she'd be beside him, and that punched a hole in his heart.

She leaned one elbow on the rail and rested her chin in her hand. "Thank you for letting me ride your stallion. He was even better than Otto's horse."

"He is more your size." He'd never look at that horse again without remembering her, but he forced a slight smile. "The only thing more amusing than watching you ride such a spirited animal as if he were a child's mount is watching Galen ride that big brute of Otto's."

"I rode Otto's horse over five thousand stadia, and he's a lovely animal."

"It's good you gave him back to Otto. I wouldn't want a man of his size riding my stallion this far." He let his full smile appear. "Having you ride beside me shortened the distance."

Her gaze dropped to the ground. "It's going to seem strange not having you with us." When she turned her eyes back on him, they were clouded.

"Is something wrong?"

She bit her lip. "Maybe not...but I'm afraid of what Father is going to do when I come home. It's been so long; I'm sure he thinks I'm dead. When I suddenly show up, he's going to ask about everything that's happened to me."

Her lips tightened. "He listens too much to that woman he married after Mother died. He didn't even wait four months, and she's meaner than a weasel. She hates me, maybe because I told him he shouldn't marry again so soon."

Tiberius's eyebrow rose. "I'm not surprised she'd dislike you for that."

"If my stepsister Gunda got killed when they took me, she's going to blame me, even though I did everything I could to save her. But it really was Hildegard's own fault. If she hadn't insisted we pick strawberries that day, nothing would have happened to Gunda, and I wouldn't be here."

She gripped the rail with both hands, and Tiberius rested his on one of them. "She has no right to do that. As you say, you tried to protect her daughter. It's not your fault you weren't able to."

"That won't matter. She always blames me for anything she's not happy about. And she jumps at any chance to do something to make me miserable. Now that I follow Jesus, I know I have to try to forgive her for that, but it's not easy.

"It's not the Germanic way to forgive anything. It's remembrance and revenge." She drew a circle in the dirt with her toe. "Galen says forgiveness is what gives peace. He says what looks like a bad thing sometimes turns out not to be. We need to look to find the good in the bad and give thanks for it. Then it gets easier to forgive. I'm trying to forgive the things Hildegard did to me. When I do, it's like a weight lifts off me."

She erased the circle with the sole of her shoe. "He's right about finding good in the bad. Being kidnapped was horrible, but being with Galen is good. Following Jesus is good. Meeting you is good. I can give thanks for all those, but…"

Her hand covered her mouth. She glanced at Galen, then rested her hand on the rail again. "What Gundahar did…how could that ever be good? I know I should try to forgive him, but I can't. Galen says he's mostly forgiven the men who murdered his parents, but every time my stomach feels queasy, I see that ugly, leering face in Brigantium as he bragged about what he'd done. How can anyone forgive someone for something like that when he wasn't sorry at all? He was proud of what he did to me."

Tiberius shrugged. "I can't tell you. It's not the Roman way to forgive."

"Galen says Dec has forgiven you for disowning him, and they're both Roman. He's sure Dec will be happy to see you."

"I'll be glad to see him again, but I haven't forgiven him for deciding to become a Christian and abandon all our plans for him rising in the service of Rome, like I did. Like my father and grandfather did before me." His teeth clenched. "That was a betrayal of everything I'd taught him. A betrayal of me. Nothing he can do will change that."

Adela's head tilted. "But it's been eight years. Being angry so long… hasn't that made you unhappy?"

"Why do you think I'm unhappy?"

She lowered her eyes and looked away. "It's just a feeling. Maybe I'm wrong."

He gripped her chin and raised it until her eyes met his. "There have been times, but this isn't one of them. I'm happy to have met you and Galen and Otto. This trip has been pure pleasure."

He gave it a gentle shake before dropping his hand. "If there's going to be any problem staying with your father, come back to me." His smile broadened as he gazed into her ice-blue eyes. "I never had a daughter, but if I did, I'd want her to be just like you."

She slipped her arms around him. "I'm going to miss you so much."

As her cheek rested against his chest, his heart clenched. He wrapped one arm around her and rested his other hand on the back of her head.

"And I'll miss you."

He would have held her longer, but Galen and Otto rode up, leading the horse Galen had bought for her in Argentorate.

With a final squeeze, Adela released him and walked to her horse.

Galen's face mirrored his own well-concealed regret. "We'll stop at the legion fortress before we leave town. One of the centurions who buys our horses should know something that will help us find her village. It will probably be about a week before we return."

"Perhaps I should go with you. A party of four is safer than three."

Galen glanced at Adela and lowered his voice. "You look too much like a senator. That's an invitation to trouble that might get us killed before we even reach her father. It's bad enough I look Roman, but anyone we meet is more likely to laugh at me than anything else. Otto and Adela are so obviously Germanic we should be able to pass through Hermunduri country safely."

Tiberius opened his mouth to argue, but Galen's logic was irrefutable. "I know you're right." His jaw clenched as he watched her mount. "Keep her safe."

Galen's eyes sought Adela. "I'll do my best." His voice dropped even lower. "If we don't come back, go to Borbetomagus and take the road west into the hill country. It joins the road between Mogontiacum and Argentorate at our village. If it's market day, ask for Valeria. She'll take you to Dec. Ask at the inn if it's not. Someone will help you find our farm."

Tiberius rested his hand on Astrelo's neck and gripped a handful of mane. "You'll be back. If her father doesn't welcome her, don't leave her there."

Otto rode up beside them and spoke before Galen could. "We'll make sure she's safe before we leave. But I can't see any reason why there should be a problem. My own father would be overjoyed to get one of my sisters back after he thought she'd been killed." He turned a smile toward Adela before his gaze returned to Tiberius. "Adela's better than any of my sisters."

Adela rode close and reached out her hand. Tiberius took it.

Her eyes looked moist. "Thank you for everything. I'll never forget you."

He squeezed her hand and nodded.

Otto reined his horse away from Tiberius. "Let's go."

Adela moved next to him. With a pack mule trailing behind him, Galen nudged his horse to Adela's side. Three abreast, they headed out.

Tiberius's couldn't stop the sigh as she rode through the gate. Was it wrong to hope her father would reject her? After eight years of loneliness, was it too selfish to want her and her child to fill his life with laughter and love again?

Chapter 45

Argentorate, Day 67

The gray stone walls of the legion fortress rose above them as Otto, Galen, and Adela approached the gate.

Galen rode forward and held his hands away from his body as the legionary guard eyed him with suspicion. "State your business."

In perfect, unaccented Latin, he replied. "Gaius Crassus would like to speak with Centurion Silanus. I'm seeking information."

A young legionary headed into the camp to fetch Silanus.

Otto's mouth turned down. Roman-to-Roman made everything easier.

When Silanus strode through the gate, his head snapped back as his gaze settled on Otto. "So Crassus's hunt was successful. It's been so long I thought he must have failed. It's good to see you, Otto."

Otto blanked his face to conceal his surprise that Silanus spoke to him instead of Galen and even knew his name. "The kidnappers were caught in Brigantium, and Galen followed me to Rome to free me. That took a few weeks."

"I'm glad Roman justice was served and gladder still to see you back. I'd miss you coming with your horses."

"I'll be back often. I'm starting a racing stable with prime chariot horses from Rome."

Silanus tipped his head. "Whose horses?"

"Tiberius Lentulus."

"The former governor?"

"Yes."

Silanus gave Otto a tight-lipped nod. "I didn't know he bred horses."

"His racers are famous. They often win in the Circus Maximus. I watched four of them run for the Greens and the Blues while I was in Rome, and they won every race."

"I was new in the VIII Augusta when he was governor here. How did you meet him?"

"He bought me out of the ludus in Rome.

Silanus's eyebrows shot up. "And made you his agent?"

"Yes."

"So, you're a citizen now. That almost makes it worth being kidnapped. What should I call you?"

"Otto son of Baldric, Tiberius Cornelius Baldricus. Whichever you choose. I'm the same man either way."

"I hope you'll bring your horses to the fortress as well as the circus. I'd like to see them."

"I plan to. Adela rode the stallion here from Rome, and she found him pure pleasure to ride. I'll train all my horses for saddle as well as harness."

Silanus stroked the neck of Otto's horse. "Some want a smaller horse than the giants you need to ride." The corner of his mouth turned up. "I'll let Vitellus and the tribunes know there will be more fine animals coming when you get your stable going, but I want first chance to see them."

He stepped back, and his gaze shifted to Galen. "Crassus, I was told you needed some information. What do you need?"

"We're taking Adela back to her father, but we need to figure out where to go. She was blindfolded the first day, but I'm hoping someone here might know enough about Hermunduri country to advise us."

Silanus rubbed his chin. "One of our centurions served in the *auxilia* with some Hermunduri. Bring your pretty friend, and we can ask him what he knows." Silanus took a step, then turned back. "Baldricus, you come, too."

◆

As the trio rode out the fortress gate, Galen scanned the wax tablet filled with notes about villages and trails and streams in Hermunduri country.

"I think we have enough here to guide us." He offered an encouraging smile to Adela. "We should be able to get you home."

She dropped her gaze. "Maybe."

Otto guided his horse between them. "With me and Galen working on it, we will." He twisted in the saddle to face Galen. "I noticed something back there."

Galen's head tipped. "What?"

"Silanus talked with me, not just you. Is it because I'm Roman now?"

Galen tightened his lips to stop the grin. "No. It's because he can tell you're a friendly man wanting to help him find a good horse."

He slapped Otto's arm and nudged Astrelo into a trot. The days of Baldric needing him to negotiate all the prices were over.

Hermunduri country, Day 69

The flickering light from the campfire pushed the darkness back to the edge of the clearing, but nothing could push back Adela's dread of tomorrow.

Otto already slept in one of the tents. He'd be taking second watch. She should be sleeping, too, but she couldn't. Fatigue dulled her thoughts and penetrated to her bones, but this last night with Galen was too precious to waste in sleep.

She poked at the fire with a stick and watched the orange sparks fly upward and fade to black. Just like her life.

What waited for her in her home village? She glanced at Galen as he sat across from her, staring into the fire. Then she focused once more on the shifting shades of yellow and orange in the coals under the burning logs. Life with him was filled with laughter and Latin and the love of a friend, but not the love of a man.

Was there anything she could do or say to make him see how much he meant to her? That she never wanted to leave him?

She left the stick in the coals long enough to catch fire, then beat it out on the rock Otto sat on during dinner.

Otto. She glanced at his tent. He'd become a dear friend since they left Rome.

She was glad they'd rescued him, but he'd changed something between her and Galen. Every time Otto tried to slip his horse between them, Galen let him. When Otto suggested they walk together, Galen found some reason to let them walk alone. Every time she tried to make Galen jealous by paying Otto more attention, he seemed to withdraw a little more.

And then there was Gundahar's child. She clenched her teeth to stop the quiver. Only Tiberius knew, but maybe Galen suspected and didn't want her because of it.

Or maybe he just didn't want her.

And tomorrow, when she stood before Father and told him the ugly truth, would he not want her as well?

◆

Galen kept his eyes focused on the flames. Each time he looked at Adela, the dagger of regret pushed deeper into his heart. Regret that this was their last night together. Regret that he was taking her back to her father. Regret that he was only a short Roman horse trader instead of a Germanic chieftain's son from a wealthy family, like Otto. If he was, he could ask Adela's father for her hand and take her home with him.

Otto was the tall, proud chieftain's son, afraid of nothing and no one, that she'd said she wanted. He was a much better man in the eyes of most fathers. He obviously liked her, and the attraction between them was growing every day. Otto would have to be blind not to see what a fine wife she'd make, and he'd be a good husband, too.

Could he convince Otto to ask for her hand before they left her? Would a Hermunduri chieftain say yes if he did?

And there was another problem. Adela was a believer now. What would happen if she was left there alone? Would the Hermunduri punish her for following the Way? Would she stand firm? She was so new to the faith; could she bear it when the pressure was on? With no one to encourage her, no one to guide her, no one to love her as a sister…and as a woman, like he already did.

He lifted his eyes from the coals. Her jaw was clenched, and her eyes looked too moist.

"Adela?" She raised her gaze from the fire to his face. "Are you all right?"

When she relaxed her jaw to speak, he saw the quiver. "I'm afraid. I've been gone so long. Father must think I'm dead. What if he doesn't want me anymore, like Gundahar said?"

"Come over here." He patted the log he sat on. "Let's talk."

She walked around the fire and settled beside him. He took her hand and held it between both of his.

"Don't believe anything Gundahar said. He only wanted to hurt you. I'll swear to your father I've protected you ever since Otto won you. It's the truth, so he should believe me."

"Maybe, but it was three days from when Gundahar took me to when you started taking care of me. You can't swear to what happened then."

"True, but your father will believe you. Remember how you ordered me to take you back and he'd pay me? You were sure he wanted you home then."

Her grip on his hand tightened. "But that was two months ago. Things can change."

"They can if you want them to. I know taking you back has been the plan since I met you, but you don't have to stay. Not if you don't want to. Tiberius told me not to leave you if it doesn't seem safe, and I won't."

And I hope you won't want to. I'd never see you again. Never know if life was going well for you. Never know if you were happy. And that's what I want for you, even if you aren't with me.

"Promise me you won't?"

"I promise, and I never break faith with a friend." He pointed at Otto's tent. "The proof is right there." He stroked the back of her hand with his thumb. "Feel better?"

"Some." Her eyes still looked too moist. "But I don't think I can sleep yet. Can we just sit here and watch the fire together?"

"For as long as you want."

Adela slumped and rested her head against his shoulder. "*Gratia tibi.*"

Her voice broke on the *tibi*, and another crack opened in his own heart.

Chapter 46

No Longer Home

Adela's home village, Day 70

Adela led their party through the maze of small cottages, sheds, and corrals. Her father's house was the largest in the village and near the center, befitting his rank as chieftain. Quiet gasps and murmurs spread out behind them, like ripples from a rock tossed into a still lake at dawn.

Each step of the horse stretched her nerves tighter. As she passed the last house before the large open space in front of Father's house, her head snapped toward the garden between the corrals and house. There in the garden was Gunda.

Relief surged through her, and the depth of it surprised her. She'd always thought Hildegard's daughter an irritating pest, but she'd grieved when she though Gundahar had killed her.

Gunda would have told Father what happened, and Hildegard should be grateful for Adela saving her daughter.

Then Gunda looked up, and her hand shot to her mouth. Her eyes saucered, and she dashed into the house.

Odd. That looked like fear, not delight, before she turned and ran. And why would she run, anyway?

She slowed her horse, and Otto and Galen rode up on either side of her.

Otto rested his hand on his gladius. "Did that seem strange to you?"

"Gunda's always been a cowardly little thing, but...yes, that was odd. The kidnappers tried to take her, too, but I drew them off so she could get away. She should be glad to see me."

Galen shifted his gladius where he could draw it quickly. "Stay close to us."

Her body stiffened, and her stomach churned. *God, please don't let me be sick. Not until after I talk with Father.* Several deep breaths, and her stomach settled. *Thank you, God. Now give me courage.*

Hildegard came through the doorway frowning, followed by her almost-grown son. Humbert always wore a dagger, but why did his hand rest on the handle?

Adela dismounted and handed her reins to Galen. He tied them to Astrelo's saddle, like he always had Otto's reins, but he ran them under his leg so they wouldn't slow him dismounting.

Her pulse pounded in her ears as she walked toward the pair. Maybe they should just leave...but maybe they shouldn't. Father would never understand.

Hildegard braced her fists on her hips. "What are you doing here?"

Adela raised her chin. Stupid question. "I've come home. Where is Father?"

"At the council of chieftains enrolling your brother as his heir." Hildegard's lip twitched. "Three months ago, he'd planned to arrange your marriage at this council, too." The twitch settled into a sneer. "That will never happen now."

Adela crossed her arms. "Now that I'm back, he can do it at the next one."

The sneer turned into a snort. "He won't even try. You've been a slave, and Adalmar knows what that means." Her eyebrow rose. "You've been gone two and a half months. Why so long?"

"The kidnapper took Galen's friend, and we had to go to Rome to free him. I came back as soon as I could."

Hildegard's gaze raked Galen. "You traveled with a Roman for two months, and you want me to believe nothing happened? Everyone knows how they treat Germanic women, given half a chance. I bet you've given this one more than that, and I'll tell Adalmar there's no way you haven't lain with him."

Her eyes focused on Otto, and her eyebrows rose in appreciation. Then the sneer returned. "And a month with this one? He'd be impossible to resist, if you even tried."

"These men are only my friends who've helped me get home. We've done nothing wrong."

"Friends? Young men are never just friends. You've lain with both of them. Two in one night or did they trade you back and forth?"

Adela stepped toward her, fists clenched. "That's a filthy lie."

Hildegard tipped her head to look down her nose. "It doesn't matter if it is. I only have to tell my brother to warn the other chieftains that you're unfit to marry their sons. First a slave, then two months with a Roman. The shame of that is so great your father will have to cast you out, no matter how he feels about doing it." The sneer blossomed into a grin. "He'll never put you ahead of me again."

Humbert drew his knife and felt the sharpened edge. "I should kill her now. That's the punishment for a woman like her who'll lie with any man. Her father might blame you if he has to do it himself."

Adela recoiled as she drew her own dagger. She heard thuds behind her as Otto and Galen slid from their horses. Before Humbert took another step, she spun and ran to Otto. He shoved her behind him.

His gladius made tight arcs as he flexed his wrist. "If anyone tries to touch her, you'll get a taste of gladiator steel."

Humbert froze. When he glanced at Hildegard, she called him back with a flip of her fingers.

Adela jumped when Galen's left arm wrapped around her shoulders.

His right hand held his gladius, ready for an attack. "Get on your horse. We're leaving."

Her gaze swept the men and women standing around them. She'd once called them kinsmen and friends, but their faces showed nothing more than curiosity, hostility, or amusement.

Galen kept his arm around her as they backed up to the horses. She untied her reins and mounted as he stood guard. Then he mounted himself.

A feral chuckle accompanied Hildegard's smirk. "Yes, leave with your Roman, and never come back."

Galen led Otto's horse to him. As soon as Otto settled into his saddle, Adela leaned sideways and spat.

"These are men of honor, worth ten of you or your children, but a snake like you can't recognize honor when she sees it."

She straightened in the saddle and raised her chin. "You're not what Father should want, and I pity him. But if you truly *are* what he wants, he deserves you."

She reined away from Hildegard. Then she drove her heels into her horse's ribs and trotted past the corrals and staring eyes into the forest.

As the trees closed around them, she kept her back straight and her chin high. Tears trickled down her cheeks, but she didn't try to flick them away. Someone might be watching, and she couldn't let them tell Hildegard they'd seen her cry.

Adela had circled the village and paralleled the road for almost a mile to be sure no one was chasing them before they left the sheltering trees. When they were back on the road, Galen came up beside her.

"I'm sorry about what happened back there."

She nodded without speaking. It had taken half a mile for her tears to dry. Words might unplug the barrel she'd crammed her emotions into and almost sealed.

"It might have gone differently if I hadn't been along looking so Roman."

The concern in his eyes made her risk it. "That wasn't the problem. She hated me before I was kidnapped. Nothing you did made that worse. Even before Gundahar, I'd been counting the weeks until I could marry and get away from her. I'd have left Father then, anyway. This just made it quicker."

His normal slight smile returned. "Remember, there's almost always some good that comes with the bad. You won't see your father again, but you're coming back with us. Tiberius never wanted you to leave. You'll be very welcome among the Vangiones." He glanced at Otto. "You'll have no trouble finding a good man to marry there."

"Tiberius has been kinder to me than Father ever was. I would have missed him." She managed a fleeting smile.

Tribe and family were gone, and no young man would want her when the baby began to show. But Tiberius was a dear friend; she wouldn't be alone. *Thank you for that, God. And for Galen and Otto.*

Men of honor and true friends. She glanced at Galen as he rode close enough to touch. If only he wanted to be more.

The hoofbeats of a cantering horse echoed behind them. Galen placed his hand on his sword and turned in his saddle.

"Who is that?"

Adela twisted to see, and her breath caught. "Hildegard's daughter."

"The one you rescued?"

"Yes."

Otto drew his sword and turned his horse to face her.

She slowed to a walk before she reached him. "I don't want to hurt Adela. I only want to talk."

Otto didn't take his eyes from her. "Adela, do you want to talk to her?

Adela reined in. "Let her pass."

Gunda guided her horse to Adela's side. "I'm so sorry for what happened back there." She swept a tear from her cheek. "It was all my fault." Another tear swept, and a sniff followed.

Adela's lips tightened. "No, it wasn't. It was that weasel you call mother who told your brother to attack. I saw her call him off."

Gunda's hand covered her mouth, and it looked like a cloudburst was coming. "Not for that. For everything else."

Adela's brow furrowed. "Everything else?"

"I lured you out to the strawberry patch. Mother hates you because you were too important to your father." Gunda swallowed hard. "She hired the kidnappers and told me to take you where they were waiting." She closed her eyes and dropped her head. "I was too afraid of her not to obey." When she raised her head again, she stared past Adela. "And then when you tried so hard to protect me, even when I was betraying you..."

Gunda's voice broke as tears flooded down her cheeks. "It's all my fault, and I'm so sorry. I should have been braver and said no. But she said I'd be sorry if I didn't do it." Her voice dropped to a whisper. "She broke my arm the last time, and she promised something worse if I didn't help."

Adela closed her eyes to stop the world spinning. Gunda's sobs faded into the distance. Her shoulders slumped...and then she felt Galen's hand gripping her arm, steadying her, like always.

Galen, her protector. Always ready with a joke or a song or some funny Latin saying. She opened her eyes and found his smile gone as concern flooded his eyes.

Galen, the man she never would have met if Gunda hadn't feared her mother too much to disobey. And maybe he still might come to love her like she loved him.

"Gunda." Gunda's head dropped lower. "Gunda, look at me." She raised her eyes faster than she lifted her head.

"You were right to fear her. I don't blame you for that. All things considered, what just happened isn't bad. Something better waits for me back inside the Empire." Adela pulled a deep breath. "I forgive you."

She glanced at Galen. His smile declared how proud he was of her. It was the hardest thing she'd ever said, but for the most part, she meant it.

Gunda bit her trembling lip. "You forgive me?"

"Yes. But it's not enough for you to be sorry. You need to do something about it. Not for me, but for you."

"For me?" Gunda's eyes widened.

"Yes. You can't let her hurt you again. When Father gets back from the council, I want you to go to him and tell him everything that you did and why. Tell him everything that just happened. And tell him I'm going to be fine. I have friends who will welcome me, and I'll have a good life with them.

"Tell him I'm asking one last thing of him as my father. I want him to protect you from her now and free you from her forever. You're a chieftain's granddaughter. Father can find you a good husband." She looked at Otto and smiled. "There are chieftain's sons who are very good men and will make fine husbands. Tell him I want him to find you one, just like he'd planned to do for me."

"But Mother might—"

"Forget your mother. Go back and don't tell her we talked. Try to act as if nothing's changed. Then, when Father gets back, go to him right away. Promise me you will. That's the only way you can make up for betraying me. Find your freedom, like I have."

Gunda cradled her cheeks in both hands. Then a slow smile formed. She straightened in the saddle. "I promise."

Adela managed a smile that looked genuine, and Gunda brightened. "I promise, Adela."

"Good. Now go home, but circle the compound so it doesn't look like you took the road. A few more days, and you can be free."

Adela reached out her arm, and Gunda maneuvered her horse close for a one-arm embrace. Then she nudged her horse into a fast walk up the slope by the road.

A kick to her horse's side moved Adela into a trot.

Life as a Hermunduri was over. But what would she now become?

◆

Otto moved up beside Adela, but Galen hung back. She mustn't see him until he could conceal his disappointment. Chieftain's sons who are good men and will make fine husbands. Adela's gaze and smile rested on Otto as she spoke those words.

He couldn't fool himself any longer. She wanted to marry Otto, not him. A Germanic warrior was still her ideal for a husband, and her actions just proved it. When her stepbrother started toward her with his dagger drawn, she ran to Otto, not him.

And what woman wouldn't prefer Otto? He was the tall, handsome son of a Germanic chieftain with wealth and power among his tribe. When Otto talked with Adela, she brightened, at least as much as she ever did with him. Otto was the logical choice for a smart woman, and she was as smart as they came.

Galen sighed. He was only a Roman with enough to be content, and he always had been before Adela. But Otto had more to offer.

Adela cared for him as a friend, but that was all he should let himself expect. She could be happy with Otto, and he would always pray for life to go well for his two best friends.

Soft night sounds surrounded Galen as he sat by the fire. Adela sat opposite him. On the outside, all seemed quiet, but the human ear couldn't hear the silent cries of a man who knew the woman he loved preferred another.

Adela stared into the fire, as she had the night before. How could she do otherwise? Disappointed after months of anticipation, losing someone dear to her...that he could understand. But it was time to cheer her up, even if regret dragged him down.

He stirred the coals with a long stick. "Today didn't go like we planned, but I think you coming home with us will work out well." He whacked the orange-and-yellow coal that was shaped like his cottage, and it split in three. "Your father was going to arrange a marriage, but you won't need that. Otto thinks you're very pretty, and he likes you very much. You're a lot like my sister, and his father wanted Val to marry his brother Adolf. I know he'll approve of you. After Otto gets Baldric's permission, I wouldn't be surprised if he asks you."

He stirred the coals again as an excuse not to look at her. Her pleasure over the prospect of marrying Otto wasn't something he wanted to watch.

"I don't want to think about that right now." Her voice sounded strained.

"There's no hurry. You can stay with us as long as you want. And if Otto doesn't work out, no man in his right mind could help wanting you for his wife. My sister Val will find a good husband for you. Otto's father is rich enough you wouldn't need a dowry with him. But I'll provide one if you do."

◆

His sister would find her a husband? Adela's heart shattered into a hundred jagged pieces, like the marble chips littering the floor at the sculptor's shop in Luna, something to sweep up and throw away.

It was bad enough that he expected her to marry Otto. At least Otto made her laugh, and she liked to talk with him as a friend. But he'd never be more than that. Galen owned her heart.

And how could he even suggest she'd want just any man his sister could find?

But Galen only saw her as a friend, not as a woman to marry. And with Gundahar's baby, Otto wouldn't want her either.

"I'm tired. I think I'll go to bed now."

He didn't look up from the coals. "Goodnight. Rest in peace."

She blinked hard, but that didn't stop the tears building. "Good night."

At least she'd kept her voice steady, and she didn't have to face his eyes that too often saw past her mask. Before the dam cracked and all the pain came spilling out, she entered her tent. There, the flood broke free. She sank onto the cot and buried her face in the pillow as silent sobs shook her.

She fought to dam the torrent and finally won. Maybe no one would notice her puffy eyes come morning. Or if they did, maybe they'd think she'd cried over losing Father. She'd put on a brave front for Gunda, but leaving him forever did tear at her heart every time she thought about it.

Galen always said God could bring good from bad, and He had. She did have somewhere to go. Tiberius was a good friend, closer than her own father had ever been. He was generous, and he probably meant what he said about staying with him. But if something happened that he couldn't take care of her and the baby ...*God, please bring good from all this.*

The firelight cast Galen's shadow on the wall of her tent, and her heart clenched.

She rolled on her side where she wouldn't see it. It wasn't time to give up. God could change any heart, if only He would.

And please let Galen be part of it.

Chapter 47

A Better Place to Be

Estate outside Argentorate, Day 74

Tiberius leaned on the fence post, watching the chestnut stallion drink. Its head shot up, water dribbling from its mouth.

He turned to see what had caught its attention. Three horses with riders and a pack mule came through the gate, and his lips twitched as he fought a smile. He shouldn't be happy the reunion with her father had gone badly. But he couldn't quench the satisfaction that surged when he saw Adela riding between Galen and Otto.

As he strode toward the trio, Adela dismounted and handed her reins to Galen. The young men rode on toward the stable, and Tiberius opened his arms. She ran to him and slipped her arms around him. Strange how that seemed the most natural thing in the world. His own encircled her, like they had before she left.

"He didn't welcome you?"

"I never saw him. He was at a council of chieftains. But Hildegard wouldn't let me stay. She was going to tell everyone lies about what I did with Galen and Otto so Father would have to cast me out. Her smile when she said that…" The small jerk betrayed her. "She said he'd have to let them kill me to erase the shame." Another jerk. "And I'm not sure he'd have any choice, even if he wanted to save me. Her son wanted to kill me right away, but Otto stopped him."

Adela's arms tightened. Her chin lowered. "And then Gunda told me it was her mother who hired the kidnappers." She tipped her head back to look at his face, and the pain there slammed into him. "Did she even tell Gundahar to rape me? How could she hate me that much?"

He rested his palm on her cheek. "She can't hurt you anymore. You're safe now, and you have a home with me for as long as you want."

He stepped back a little, but he left his hands on her arms. A quivering smile accompanied moist eyes. "Are you sure?" Her hand rested on her belly.

"Very sure. As Galen is so fond of saying, if we look hard enough, we can see the good in the bad. Having both of you with me will be a good thing."

Adela pressed her palms against her cheeks. "I need to keep reminding myself God can bring good from the bad."

"I wouldn't say it's God, but Galen seems to find the good in anything. He's got me doing it, too. At least your stepmother revealed her intentions when he and Otto were still there. If they'd already left, you'd have had no one to protect you. You're safe with us."

"I'm safe for now, but what lies ahead?" Her hand settled on her stomach again.

"Wait and see. Battles are often won or lost when the unexpected happens."

"Galen would ask God to tell him what to do. I have been, but I don't hear an answer."

"Time will give you an answer."

"I know God can do it. We took the wrong road to Brigantium, but it turned out to be the right road after all, because we had to go to Rome. And going to you, even when Galen was afraid you might kill him, that was the right road, too. Galen says it's turned into the answer to many years of prayers by his whole family."

Her voice quavered. "But I'm afraid of where this road leads. Galen tells me it will lead to good because God wants the best for me. I know staying with Father wouldn't have been the best.

"But he doesn't know what we do. He says his sister will find me a good husband. But what man will want me with another man's child?"

Tiberius wrapped his arm around her shoulder and drew her to his side. When a single tear escaped, his fingers swept it away.

"Time will make it clear."

What man, indeed? He followed her gaze toward the stable. Galen's words, too soft to hear, drew Otto's laugh.

Her shuddering sigh triggered his frown. How could a father let someone kill a daughter like her when she'd done nothing wrong? And if he did, how could he live with that choice?

The memories a man tried to kill and bury — sometimes they wouldn't stay dead.

Eight years earlier, he'd banished his own son. He'd done it to save Decimus's life after he rejected everything Tiberius had taught him. He'd had no choice if Decimus was to live, but the way he'd done it—how much pain had that caused? No matter what Galen said, it was too hard to believe Decimus could forgive that. He hadn't forgiven Decimus for his betrayal, either...but should he try?

Will time make it clear for me?

Galen's family farm, Day 77

Tiberius and the rest of his party left Otto and his three mares when the wagon track to Galen's farm turned off the road. The leaves overhead made dancing dappled patterns on the road, and Tiberius's own heart danced with them.

As they rode along a steep ravine, tendrils of uncertainty wrapped around his mind. What if Galen was wrong? What if Decimus refused to see him?

His mouth twitched. Galen could take him to Otto's home. They still had to get the stable started, even if his son banished him from his house, as he once had Decimus.

Galen and Adela rode ahead of him, with Galen pointing out things he'd known since his childhood, still telling her the Latin word whenever it was something new.

But Tiberius could read the tension in her body. She was as nervous as he was about what lay at the end of this tree-lined track.

The leafy canopy opened above them as they rode into the farm yard, but the sunlight washing over him couldn't sweep away his dread of a rejection he deserved.

Adela reined in and dropped back beside Tiberius as Galen rode ahead. Her eyes widened as she bit her lip. He reached out his hand, and she gripped it as if it were all that kept her from sinking into deep water to drown. After a gentle squeeze, he donned a self-assured smile that concealed his own fears.

"You don't have to be afraid. You're under my protection."

Her shoulders squared as she released his hand. When Galen teased her about being a warrior woman, he hit the mark. A warrior wasn't brave because he had no fear. He was brave because he could act as though he had none, even as fear tried to take him down.

Galen trotted ahead to the corral and dismounted. As he tied the first mare's lead to the rail, two small boys came running. They stopped a short distance from Galen and bounced as they waited for him to move away from the horses.

Tiberius's heart rate ratcheted up. Publius and Gaius, the grandsons he'd never known existed and never expected to see.

Tiberius and Adela dismounted and tied their mounts and lead ropes to the railings as well.

As soon as Galen was ten feet from the horses, the boys tackled him.

With the arms of the larger wrapped around his waist and the shorter one's arms around his leg, he put one arm around each. "This is how I like to end a trip. Where's Dec? I have a surprise for him."

The older boy spoke, "Father's at Adolf's helping him build a shed."

Galen released them. "I guess the surprise will have to wait, but sometimes surprises only get better when they do."

Publius tugged on Galen's sleeve, and Galen bent over. The boy's lips brushed his ear, but the soft words reached Tiberius. "Who's the Roman?"

Galen lowered his voice to answer. "He's your grandfather."

Gaius slipped behind him, but Publius stood bravely at Galen's side. As Tiberius moved closer, Galen rested his hand on Publius head. "Tiberius, this is Publius."

He reached behind him and drew Gaius forward, only to have Gaius wrap his arms around his leg again. Galen's other hand settled on his second nephew's head. "And this is Gaius."

Tiberius dropped to one knee to reach their level. "It's my great pleasure to meet you." He'd never spoken truer words.

Publius squared his shoulders. "*Voluptus meus est.*" He poked Gaius, and their voices blended. "*Voluptus meus est.*"

Galen tousled Publius's hair. "Run fetch Val."

With a giggle, the two darted toward the cottage.

Tiberius rose, his heart near bursting with happiness. "Handsome boys, like their father at that age."

A short, pretty woman with hair more gold than brown stepped through the cottage doorway with a baby balanced on her hip. The two boys bounced at her side as they pointed at Tiberius.

Joy radiated from her eyes and smile as she hurried toward them. Still holding the baby, she wrapped Galen in a one-armed hug. "Praise be to God you're finally home safe!"

When she turned the smile on Tiberius, it didn't dim at all.

"Tiberius, welcome! My brother has probably told you already, but I'm Valeria, Decimus's wife. We were so delighted to receive Galen's letter telling us you'd be returning with him and Otto." Her eyes warmed with her soft chuckle. "Decimus has been counting the days since it arrived. It's ironic he's off helping our neighbor when you do get here. But he'll be home for dinner."

Her gaze moved past him to the horses tied to the rail. "They're beautiful. Such a long way to bring them, but these look worth the effort." Her eyes focused back on Tiberius. "My father raised horses when I was a child. There's nothing I enjoy more myself." She slapped her brother's arm and got a grin in response. "Galen was supposed to keep himself and Otto out of trouble while they were selling them in Argentorate, but it's God's blessing that he failed at that long enough to reach Rome and bring you back to us."

The warmth of her greeting, as if they were long acquaintances, was a surprise both pleasant and disturbing. Had Decimus told her the circumstances of their last parting? Had he told her he was the governor who wanted all the Christians like her killed? Surely not, or she couldn't be so open and friendly with her greeting.

"I thank you for the warm welcome. The opportunity to accompany Galen back from Rome was too good to let pass. To see Decimus again and meet his family is more than I ever expected."

◆

Adela stood back from the family group until Galen turned and reached out his hand. When she came forward, his eyes crinkled. "Val, this is Adela. She's come to stay with us."

Valeria's eyebrows rose as she questioned Galen without a word.

His ears reddened. "She's a sister now."

Valeria offered her free hand and a smile that could drive away anyone's shyness. "Come with me into the cottage, Adela. I'm working on dinner. The men can finish putting up the horses. It's going to be pure delight having another woman around. With Decimus and Galen and my two sons, and now with Tiberius as well, Priscilla and I have been outnumbered far too long. It will be good to have three against five for a while."

Adela looked over her shoulder as she followed Valeria toward the cottage. Galen was watching her with smiling eyes and matching lips. But did his eyes only see a friend and sister instead of the woman he might want to marry?

He raised a hand before turning back to help Tiberius put the mares into the corral and unsaddle the horses.

As she stepped across the threshold of Galen's home, a cold hand gripped her heart and squeezed.

She could stay as long as Tiberius did, but what then?

God, please make Galen want me. Make this last forever, not just for a while.

Tiberius sat at the table, watching Valeria stir a stew whose aroma rivaled any from his chef in Rome. When footsteps pounded across the wooden porch, his eyes flipped toward the sound. The large frame of the son he'd longed to see for eight years filled the doorway.

He rose from the table as Decimus strode toward him, a huge smile lighting his son's face.

"Welcome, Father. I've prayed for this for a long time." Strong hands gripped Tiberius's upper arms.

"It's good to see you again, son."

At the word 'son,' Decimus pulled him into a quick, manly embrace. With a slap to Tiberius's back, Decimus stepped back, still grinning.

Then his eyes settled on Adela, who sat in the chair next to Tiberius. "And who is this young lady gracing our table?"

Tiberius rested his hand on her shoulder. "This is Adela, daughter of Adalmar, chieftain of the Hermunduri. She's my ward. She'll be staying with me until we find a better place for her to be."

His eyebrow rose as he focused on Galen, who sat on the other side of Adela. He froze his face to stop a grin as Galen's ears reddened. Adela's ears would be flaming, too, if she had only seen.

"It's been too long, Father. I hope you both can stay for a long while."

Tiberius shifted his gaze from Galen to the son he once rejected. What a fool he'd been.

"Since I came out to Germania Superior to start a racing stable with Otto as my agent, I might be here for some time."

"You're welcome to stay with us for as long as you wish. The longer the better. I'd like my boys to get to know their grandfather."

Tiberius couldn't keep his own smile from growing into a grin. "I came out here for that as well."

Valeria's silken voice came from behind him. "Speaking of the boys... Galen, would you please call them in for dinner now? And make sure they wash their hands first."

As the man who made the reunion possible headed out the door, Tiberius's gaze followed. His heart swelled with a happiness so great it might burst. There might be a finer young man in the Empire, but he doubted that. Galen had managed to bring good out of bad for all of them.

The beauty of his estates, the luxurious life his fortune could buy, the power he'd wielded in the service of Rome—it was all worth nothing compared to being in this rough cottage with the son he thought he'd lost, the grandsons he never knew existed, and the young man he'd almost killed for his faith.

In the entire Empire, there was no better place to be.

Chapter 48

WHAT SISTERS ARE FOR

It was snug with seven around a table that usually held five, but no one seemed to mind. With Tiberius on one side and Galen on the other, Adela couldn't have chosen a better seat.

Valeria handed out bowls brimming with a lentil stew that smelled of onions and garlic with chunks of carrots adding color. Adela stirred it, and the aroma drifting around her didn't seem too nauseating.

She selected a wheat roll to nibble first. Her stomach felt calm, but that could change quickly if she didn't eat soon. The small piece she tore off should be safe enough. The mild yeasty flavor was no problem, and when she swallowed it, it went down easy and settled comfortably.

"Adela." Galen seated himself beside her after filling his bowl a second time. "Try some of Val's stew. It's tastier than anything we ate on the way to Rome and at least as good as some of the dishes Tiberius's chef made."

She stirred it, postponing that first bite. "I was letting it cool a little first." As she raised a spoonful to her lips, the smell made her stomach swirl. But she still placed it on her tongue and forced herself to swallow it. It tried to come back up, but she managed to swallow it again. A drink of water got it back into her stomach.

Valeria's eyes triggered an inner shiver as they probed her, and Adela forced a smile to deflect the questioning gaze. "The stew is delicious, just as Galen promised it would be. He says you're the best cook he knows."

Valeria's light laugh was musical. "He's told me that for years, but I know the truth. Whatever cook gives him the largest portions, that's the one who'll be his favorite as long as the taste isn't so horrible he can't gag it down." She shifted her focus to Galen, who tried to hide his grin by taking a drink.

"That's not true, Val. You are a good cook. I'd stop at seconds instead of thirds if you weren't."

Adela took another bite. It did taste delicious, as long as it was on her tongue. Another swallow, another churn, another sip of water. Soon she'd eaten half, but how was she ever to finish it? And how was she to explain it if she didn't?

Then Decimus spoke to Valeria, and her eyes and smile turned toward the man who obviously owned her heart.

Tiberius's empty bowl took the place of Adela's, and he began eating what she hadn't been able to. A roll moved from his plate to hers, and the exchange was complete.

She hugged him with her eyes and received a wink in return.

Adela sat at the table, watching the fire. For the first time, she'd shared in Christian worship. Galen had read from a codex written by one of Jesus's closest followers, and the family had shared many prayers. Even Tiberius had remained at the table, his arms crossed and his head tipped as he observed them all. It was a glorious way to end an evening.

Valeria was in the loft, putting the boys to bed and setting up one of Tiberius's cots for her. Decimus had gone with Tiberius and Galen to the second cottage for more conversation.

After the sweet childish voices spoke their goodnights, Valeria climbed down the ladder. She joined Adela at the table, leaned on her elbows, and rested her chin in her hands.

"Adela." Valeria's voice was gentle. "How far along are you?"

Adela's heart dropped into the pit of her stomach. "What do you mean?"

"I'm a physician and a woman with three children. I know the signs."

Adela buried her face in her hands and closed her eyes. "Not quite three months." She swallowed hard. "It was the man who kidnapped me."

She squeezed her eyes tighter, trying to stop the tears, but one trickled down each cheek anyway. "Galen keeps telling me you can find me a husband among the Vangiones, but with this child, no man is going to want me."

Her eyes opened when Valeria's hand touched her arm. "I'm not so sure of that. I see how my brother looks at you. I think you've already won his heart. Does he know?"

"No. Only Tiberius. He figured it out the first morning in Rome when my stomach didn't feel good. He's watched over me ever since, as if he were my real father. Actually, more than Father ever did. He's such a kind man."

"I can see you love Tiberius, and he loves you. How do you feel toward Galen?"

"He's the finest friend anyone could ever have. Nothing stopped him from rescuing Otto, and he's taken such good care of me from the moment Otto won me from the kidnappers."

Valeria's head tipped. "Is that all?"

"Yes...no. I mean, he's such a wonderful man. So kind and funny and smart and brave and..." Her voice tapered off. How could she tell his sister that she loved him and longed to be with him when she carried another man's child?

"And he's won your heart, too." Valeria's statement sounded so certain that there was no point in trying to deny it. "I see how you look at him."

"He deserves the finest, and I'm not that. Not anymore."

Valeria leaned across the table and rested her hand on Adela's. "You're a child of God, precious and of infinite value in His eyes. Nothing done by any man can make you less than that."

Adela traced the letters of Galen's name on the table, then covered them with her palm. "In my head, I can tell myself that, but in my heart, I can't believe it. I keep asking God to change this, but it's like He's not listening." She rested her forehead on her hands and closed her eyes. "Galen says He always hears, but sometimes He doesn't answer right away." She turned sad eyes back on Valeria. "But this hurts so much, and I'm afraid." She bit her lip. "I really need Him to answer right now."

"I've always found that God's answer comes at exactly the right time, even though my heart might break while I'm waiting for it. The way I came to marry Decimus was like that."

Valeria stood. "It's late, and you've had a long day. Take some rolls to the loft so you'll have something to eat when you first awaken."

She walked behind Adela and massaged her shoulders. "I'll join you in praying for God to give you His answer soon. He can bring good out of bad, and sometimes the result is more wonderful than anything we ever expected."

Decimus's footsteps on the porch ended the conversation. After he stepped into the cottage, he closed and bolted the door. Then he walked to Valeria's side and leaned down to kiss her cheek.

Valeria's head tipped back as her eyes caressed the man who towered over her. "Is your father comfortable in Galen's cottage?"

"Yes. He seems as happy about him being here as I am. It's good to have you here as well, Adela. We're glad you came."

"I'm glad I'm here, too."

Decimus's arm wrapped around Valeria, and Adela placed her foot on the bottom rung of the ladder.

"Good night, Adela. Rest in peace." His words were barely spoken before his eyes turned on his wife. His other arm encircled Valeria.

Adela's heart ached for Galen to do the same. To be his wife...She fought the sigh. Each night his deep voice had spoken those words. Rest in peace—would that ever be possible again?

"Good night." She climbed the ladder and laid down on the cot.

The soft murmurings of husband and wife drifted up to her.

God, please let Galen be your answer to my prayer. She rolled on her back, and a tear trickled across her temple and into her ear. *But if he can't be, please guide me to what is.*

It was barely sunrise when Galen heard the light tapping on the door. He opened it to find Valeria, wrapped in her shawl to ward off the cool dawn air. She gripped his wrist and pulled him onto the porch before closing the door behind them.

"Good morning, Val. Do you need me to do something?"

"No, but there's something important I need to know. It can't wait, and it's not something the others should hear. I watched you and Adela last night. What's going on between the two of you?"

"Nothing."

"Is that the way you want it to be?"

"Well, no." He rubbed his neck. "But Otto's been courting her. They talk a lot, and he makes her laugh all the time. She told me at the start that she expected to marry a chieftain's son. I'm almost certain he's going to ask her after he gets Baldric's permission."

"You're wrong about her wanting Otto. Don't you see how she looks at you? She's in love with you. She even admitted it when I asked her last night."

Galen's head bounced back. "Are you sure? What woman would choose me when she could have Otto?"

"Any smart one, especially if she also follows the Way." She pushed the stray lock of hair off his forehead. "She'll say yes the moment you ask and be thrilled with her choice."

His nose scrunched. "That's hard to believe. I tried not to show how I felt before she decided to follow Jesus, and by then she and Otto seemed like they belonged together. I've even encouraged them because I thought he was what she wanted."

Valeria's eyes rolled. "You men are so clueless when it comes to a woman's heart. She was probably trying to make you think Otto was a rival so you'd say something before he did."

"But if that's true, what about Otto? I think he'll want to marry her in a few months."

"That's too late, and it's not likely, either. Baldric won't give his permission."

"Of course he will. He wants the best kind of woman for his sons, and Adela truly is the best kind."

Val drew a deep breath. "She might be, but he'll never say yes with her carrying another man's child."

Galen's hand flew to his mouth, and he dragged it down his chin. "Gundahar." His jaw clenched. "He kidnapped her north of the frontier before he kidnapped Otto. Her stepmother hired him. We caught up with him in Brigantium, and he was crucified. As they were hauling him away, he told Adela he'd taken more than she knew and her father wouldn't want her back."

He rubbed his lower lip. "This changes everything." His normal smile reappeared. "I won't be at breakfast. I need to talk with Otto." The smile grew. "When I come back, I hope she'll become your sister in more ways than one."

He kissed her cheek. "Thank you for telling me, Val."

Val pushed his stray hair back again. "That's what sisters are for. I'll be praying for all of you."

"If anyone asks, I've gone to discuss when he'll get the rest of the horses."

As he strode toward the shed to get his saddle, his usual slight smile grew. What was a problem for Otto was no problem for him, and he would do his best to make it no problem for her. His heart would gladly welcome any child, no matter how he or she started in this world. And to the right woman, it really was the heart, not the height, that mattered.

Chapter 49

THE PERFECT MAN

Galen rode into Baldric's compound just as his family was drifting out of the main house after breakfast. Otto came out with a nephew clinging to his back, arms around his neck and legs around his waist. When he spotted Galen, he squatted so the little boy could slip to the ground and scurry off.

He sauntered over to join Galen under the tree where he'd tied Astrelo. "I didn't expect you this early. I thought you'd be stuffing yourself on Valeria's breakfast porridge." He glanced back at the main house. "Olga's a good cook, but it's not the same."

"I needed to talk with you alone about something."

Otto tipped his head toward a shed. "Behind there should be private."

When they were behind the shed, Otto leaned against the wall. "So, what is it?"

"It's about Adela. I know you like her, but is it more than that?"

"What man wouldn't like her? She's probably the most beautiful woman I've ever seen. She's not afraid of anything." The corner of his mouth pulled up in a twisted smile. "She laughs at all my jokes, so she has a good sense of humor." He scrunched one eye. "But she laughs at all your jokes, too, so maybe she'll laugh at anything."

"I was really asking what your intentions are."

"Intentions?"

"Yes. Do you want to marry her right away?"

Otto's eyebrows shot up. "Marry her? I think she'd make a fine wife, but I'm not planning to marry anyone soon. I like her as a friend, but I hadn't thought past that."

Galen squared his shoulders. "I have. I love her, and I'd like to marry her as soon as possible."

Otto straightened. "Then I think that's exactly what you should do. Having my best friend marry my good friend...I approve." He slapped Galen's shoulder. "I thought it might come to this after she decided to follow your Way. You don't need my blessing for anything, but you have it anyway."

Galen closed his eyelids as he released a deep breath. When he opened them, a smile lit his best friend's eyes. "Almost forgot. When do you think you'll get the rest of the horses?"

"Later this week. Father has to decide what land I'll use for them, and we'll need to make corrals." Otto's grin leaked out. "I haven't told him yet that Tiberius made me a Roman citizen. He doesn't like Romans, but he won't disown me over it. Besides, Baldricus doesn't sound that different from 'son of Baldric.'"

Otto draped his arm across Galen's shoulders and started them back toward Astrelo. "You keep saying good can come from bad. When her stepmother tried to kill her, that was as bad as it gets. But getting you as husband, I can't name anything better."

Galen mounted Astrelo and grinned down at the best friend in the Empire. "Time to go see if she agrees with you."

When Galen rode out of the dappled shade of the wagon track into the bright light of the farm yard, Adela was sitting on the porch with Tiberius. Her hand raised in greeting, as if she'd been watching for him.

He pulled a deep breath through clenched teeth and blew it out through puckered lips. Then he reined Astrelo toward the porch and the future he hoped for.

When he reached her, he swung his leg over the horse's neck and slid off. "Adela, would you come with me to the corral?"

He held out his hand. When she stepped off the porch, she placed her palm on his. He interlaced their fingers and squeezed. When she squeezed back, warmth flooded through him. The future was only one question away.

Galen glanced at Tiberius in time to see his lips twitch. The noble Roman crossed his arms and raised one eyebrow. Her guardian was on duty, but he'd already told Galen he should marry Adela. He wouldn't object to the topic of their conversation or to the result if it went the way Galen hoped. But Galen's heart rate ramped up anyway.

He led them to the corral where Astrelo usually stayed. Adela stroked the horse's neck as Galen uncinched the saddle, lifted it off, and placed it on the railing. She stepped back when he opened the gate. After removing Astrelo's bridle, Galen sent him in with a swat on the rump.

One quick glance at the sky, and he was ready. *God, let this be your will for us. Let her say yes.*

◆

Adela's stomach had swirled when she took Galen's hand, but that had nothing to do with the coming baby. The determined look in his eye and the question that felt more like a command caused it.

He closed the corral gate and focused serious eyes on her. "I've wanted to ask you this since the camp before Aventicum, but I don't want to wait any longer." He scooped up both her hands. "Adela, will you be my wife?"

Her breath stopped as his words sunk in. Then it returned, rapid like something was chasing her.

"You won't want me...after you know. I'm not a good match for you."

A smile played at the corners of his mouth. "Is there something about me you couldn't learn to love, or at least overlook? I can work on it. I am a short Roman, and that's not what you told me you want. I can't change the Roman part, but I was hoping you might agree it's the heart, not the height, that matters.

"Val has to stand on tiptoes and stretch up to kiss Dec. That can't be easy on her neck. It should be easier to lower your head for a kiss from me than to stretch up to reach some tall German."

His hand swept toward the second cottage. "I already have a place, so we can marry right away. The winter nights won't be so cold with you snuggled against me, like at the top of the pass...only better." His smile blossomed into a full-blown grin.

She bit her lip. If she told him about the baby, it would drive away the man she loved. But she couldn't lie to him just so he would marry her. Better her own pain than his when he found out.

"You're the perfect man who would fulfill any woman's dreams. The problem isn't you. It's me." She closed her eyes to stop the tears, but some escaped anyway. "I'm carrying Gundahar's child."

Her eyes popped open when his fingertip swept the tear away.

"Then I'll be getting a true bargain. I don't have to pay anyone a bride price, but even if I did, I'd be getting two for the price of one. And I won't even have to wait as long as most for my first child." He wiped the tears from her other cheek. "I love children."

Her eyes saucered as she stared at his smiling face. She'd never seen him lie, but could he really mean what he'd said?

"Don't look so surprised. I'll love our first as much as any others God might give us in the years to come. The blood father doesn't matter to me. Every child you have will be my child, too."

Her lips tightened as she shook her head. "You say that now, but that's not how it works. No man can love a child who isn't his own. Even a woman can't. Just look at what Hildegard did."

"What she did...that sprang from her own black heart. It doesn't have to be that way. My father and mother loved Val as much as me and Rhoda, and she didn't even become my sister until she was twelve."

Her hand flew to her chest. "Valeria's not your sister?"

"Of course she is. She just had different parents before we met her."

He slipped his hand around hers again. "Now that's clear, will you be my wife?"

The love in his eyes wrapped her in warmth like a leaping fire while a winter storm raged outside. He truly wanted her.

"Yes. Nothing on earth could make me happier...if you're sure it will make you happy."

Her words drew his arms around her. "Wise choice. From the evening I met you, I knew you were no fool."

A sudden thought pierced her bubble of joy. She'd be a fool to refuse him, but why had he really asked her? No one was kinder or more willing to sacrifice himself for others. Was that all it was? She couldn't let him marry her just because she needed someone.

"You knew I carried a baby before you asked."

His smiling shrug answered better than words could have. Her stomach dropped, and she fought to keep breakfast down. She didn't want to ask the next question, but she had to know.

"Are you sure you want me? Did you only ask because I need someone?" Her gaze dropped from his eyes to their feet. "I don't want you to marry me for that reason. I don't want to be your wife because I have no other choice."

Her gaze rose to meet his, and her finger traced the scar on his cheek. "I know I tried to kill you the day we met, but *te amo*, Galen Crassus. *Te amo*, and I always will."

He rested his palm on her cheek and stroked it with his thumb. "I know, and it's good to hear you using the Latin I taught you the right way. Just remember I'm the only man you can say that to."

The curve of his mouth grew until a grin lit his whole face. "Actually, I hope what you said before *te amo* isn't true. I hope you have no other choice. My own heart wants no other, and I hope yours feels the same."

His arms slipped around her and drew her to him. She melted against him as she lowered her lips to his, and their first lingering kiss sealed the promise of a future together blessed by God.

Chapter 50

READY TO LISTEN

Tiberius watched from the porch bench as Adela and Galen talked by the corral. Her surprise, then sorrow, then sheer delight revealed the ebb and flow of their conversation. When Galen drew her into his arms and she lowered her lips to his, a satisfied sigh accompanied Tiberius's broadest smile.

All would be well for the three of them.

Their lips no sooner parted than Adela grabbed Galen's hand and led him toward Tiberius, joy radiating from every feature of her beautiful face.

When they stopped at the edge of the porch, he couldn't decide who looked happier.

With fingers entwined, she placed Galen's hand above her heart. "I won't be going back to Rome with you."

Tiberius rose and stepped to the edge of the porch. "I hoped Galen would be smart enough to take you as his wife so you wouldn't have to. From the day I met you, it was obvious you would do well together."

He stroked her cheek with his thumb. "I look on you as a daughter, and I approve of your choice to marry one of the finest men I've ever met." A wry smile tugged at his mouth. "Even if he is a Christian." He shook his head. "But since you've become one yourself, perhaps only a Christian man will do." He stroked her hair before taking his hand away. "You two deserve each other."

She threw her arms around him and burrowed into his chest. "We plan to call our first boy Tiberius."

His arms encircled her and held her tight. "I'm honored."

No words could tell her how much the love that inspired that choice meant to him. A senator of Rome didn't wear his heart where others could see, but sometimes the hidden heart burned brightest with love.

She made no move to release him, so he fixed his gaze on Galen.

"If you had agreed to let me adopt you, your child would officially be my grandson. But perhaps there are ties more important than those recognized in Roman law. Your children will be grandchildren to me, anyway."

Three from Decimus, one from Adela, and who knew how many more to come. Tiberius had never expected to be a patriarch in fact, even if not in name.

When Adela released him and slipped her arm around Galen again, Tiberius couldn't stop his smile.

After lunch, Tiberius leaned on the post supporting the porch roof and watched his mares in the corral. He needed to focus his mind on something real, something his eyes could see and his hands could touch.

The food had been tasty, but the conversations left a queasy feeling in Tiberius's stomach. Too much talk about the hand of their god and how he'd guided Galen in his quest to rescue Otto. Even more about how the Christian god had brought Galen and Adela together and all the blessings that would come because of that.

Tiberius was a man of logic, and all the things they talked about could be explained as coincidences...except there were far too many of them, and they meshed together in just the right way to make something that seemed destined to end badly turn out well.

He could try to discount it all as superstitious thinking by childish people of limited intelligence...except Decimus was one of the smartest men he knew. Galen was an acute observer of people and as wise in the ways of the world as any young man could expect to be. And Valeria missed nothing going on around her.

The gods were merely stories made up to control weak-minded people, and yet...if no god was real, why did these intelligent people keep claiming they knew one?

Adela's words in the darkness, when she told Galen she felt their god with her. His response like that was the most natural thing in the world to expect. And Decimus's words from years ago, claiming he met his god in his bedchamber and his god was in the dining room while they argued.

And then there was Tiberius's best friend Publius, widely acknowledged as brilliant, a man who always wanted to know the truth. Yet his allegiance to the Christian god put him in the arena to die when a meaningless sacrifice would have saved him. Sacrificing to the emperor only said you were loyal to Rome, not that you thought he was a god. Why hadn't Publius understood that and chosen to live?

But Publius wasn't the only one willing to die for that god. Galen and Decimus were ready to do the same. Without hesitation.

To make matters worse, he felt strangely attracted to what they said. Even while everything he valued argued against listening to them, something compelled him to listen.

He shook his head to dislodge the nagging thoughts and focused back on the horses.

Galen came out and leaned on the other side of the post. "They're beautiful animals. Otto thought it would be about a week before he's ready to take them. His father is giving him some land, and they need to build corrals."

His young friend crossed his arms and showed no sign of leaving. The thoughts Tiberius was trying to banish wormed their way into his head once more.

"That story you read last night, the one about one lost sheep, why did you pick that?"

Galen's eyes shifted from the horses to him. "It reminded me of Adela and Otto."

Dipped eyebrows accompanied Tiberius's frown. "Otto I can see, but Adela? She wasn't someone you'd lost and had to find."

"She was lost, not to me but to God. We're all lost until we hear the Shepherd's call and follow Him home."

"The shepherd?"

"Jesus. He was talking about Himself in that story."

Tiberius deepened his frown. "But wasn't he a carpenter? When did he ever risk losing everything to find one lost sheep?"

"Ninety years ago. I was that sheep, and He did more than risk. He paid for me with His blood when Pilatus crucified Him, and He proved what He'd done when He rose from the dead."

Tiberius's bicep flexed when Galen rested his hand on it. Why did it feel so warm? "We're all lost sheep, and He won't stop calling your name until you finally come, too."

Galen's eyes bored into him. Could he see the turmoil beneath Tiberius's veneer of confidence? The river out of its banks, eating away at the foundations of everything he'd believed?

Questions tumbled in his mind, but before he could form them into words, a big German about his own age cantered into the farmyard.

"It's Otto's father, Baldric." Galen stepped off the porch with his hand raised in greeting, and the big man reined in beside him.

"It's good to see you, Baldric." Galen's teasing grin appeared as he spoke Germanic. "I got good money for your horses this time, like I promised Val. Sorry about taking so long, but there were...complications."

The big man swung his leg over his massive stallion's neck and slid off. "I did not expect you to bring back a Roman citizen, but it is good to have Otto home, even if he is one." The grin that accompanied those Germanic words relaxed into a grateful smile. "I came to thank you for that, for everything you risked to rescue him."

"No thanks needed. I did it for me as much as for him. Who'd be my bodyguard if we didn't trade together? He's even gladiator-trained now. I learned what those cost in Rome, and they're too expensive for me to hire."

The German's eyes shifted toward Tiberius. "Is this the Roman's father?"

"This is Tiberius."

Baldric switched to heavily accented Latin. "It is good to meet the father of Valeria's husband. I used to think all Romans belonged in a grave or back in Italia, but he changed my mind. At least some of them are decent men."

The wry smile took the bite out of Baldric's words.

"I've known a few Germans who deserve my full respect as well."

Baldric's hearty laugh brought Decimus onto the porch. "Welcome, Baldric."

The big German tipped his head. "I am glad you are here, Roman. I have come to offer my thanks for you teaching Otto so well." The wry smile broadened. "I do not think you knew you were training a gladiator. It is good you trained him well enough to be a good one."

Baldric's large hand settled on Galen's shoulder. "It is also good you raised Galen to be a man of courage who would never abandon a friend."

Decimus's headshake accompanied his smile. "I taught Otto to handle a sword, but Galen gets his courage from God. God himself protected Otto until he could be redeemed. Give God the thanks, not me."

Baldric shrugged. "Perhaps your god had something to do with it. Valeria has been telling me so for years."

His gaze shifted to Tiberius. "I also came to offer you my thanks for buying my son out of the arena. I will repay you for that. How much?"

Tiberius swept the question away with his hand. "Nothing. It gave me pleasure to ransom the friend of my son. I won't accept repayment."

Baldric's mouth opened, as if to insist. Instead, a twisted smile appeared. "The two of you make it hard for me to question Roman honor. But I am sure some other Roman will make it easy again."

Valeria appeared in the doorway, wiping flour off her hands. Her welcoming smile warmed Baldric's eyes.

"I thought I heard you. We just finished lunch, but I have some left, if you'd like it." She focused laughing eyes on Galen. "My brother didn't eat every last morsel today." She rested her hand on Baldric's arm. "We always love to have you join us."

Baldric patted first her hand, then his stomach. "Another time, Valeria. Olga is preparing a special meal for all my family to celebrate Otto's safe return. I need to be hungry to eat enough to make her happy. She is the finest wife, but your Roman married a better cook."

He mounted his horse and leaned on its withers. "Do not tell her I said that." He straightened. "Tiberius, have Galen bring you to my compound. A horseman like you will appreciate what we raise, and since my son is now your agent, we should know each other."

He reined away and nudged his horse into a walk.

Valeria wrapped her arm around Decimus's and laid her head against his shoulder. "Farewell, Baldric. Come again soon."

A backhanded wave acknowledged her invitation, and he kicked his horse into a trot.

Tiberius remained on the porch, watching until Baldric disappeared into the trees. Decimus had walked over to the corral to watch his main stallion with a black mare. Galen and Adela had strolled into the woods for some time alone. Valeria had gone back into the cottage, and he heard her humming and talking to their baby girl. His gaze was drawn by childish laughter. His two grandsons were digging in the dirt with a couple of sticks.

He rubbed his chin, took a step off the porch, then stopped. His mouth turned down. His own life had been spent in pursuit of power in the service of Rome. His son had chosen a better life. Filled with the love of his family. Filled with love for his god...for Galen's god...for Publius's god.

When faced with too much evidence, sometimes a man had to change. Only a fool would cling to the past without weighing the facts before him.

He took a deep breath, then blew it out before striding to the corral where his son was leaning on the rail.

He moved into place beside Decimus, who turned his eyes on Tiberius and smiled. A smile of contentment. Of peace.

Tiberius cleared his throat. "Son." He swallowed.

Decimus tilted his head, but the peaceful smile remained. "Yes, Father?"

A second chance was a precious thing. Only a fool would waste it... and he was no fool.

"I might have been wrong in condemning your decision to turn from Rome to the Christian god." He rubbed his neck. "Perhaps you and Publius made the wiser choice after all. Tell me why you follow this Jesus...I'm ready to listen."

Finis

I'd Love to Hear from You!

If you enjoyed this book, it would be a real gift to me if you would post a review at the retailer you purchased it from. A good review is like a jewel set in gold for an author. Other great places to share reviews are Goodreads and BookBub. If you've read others in the series, it would be great if you post a review of those, too.

I'd also love to hear from you at carol-ashby.com or directly at carolashbyauthor@gmail.com.

Want to hear about upcoming releases in the Light in the Empire series and free gifts only for newsletter subscribers?

For free gifts and other special offers, advance notices of upcoming releases, and info about my latest writing adventures, I hope you'll sign up for my newsletter at carol-ashby.com.

Carol Ashby

Faithful is the fourth volume in the Light in the Empire series, which follows the interconnected lives of the members of three Roman families during the reigns of Trajan and Hadrian. The eight novels of the series will take you around the Empire, from Germania and Britannia to Thracia, Dacia, and Judaea and, of course, to Rome itself.

For a preview of the opening chapters of the sixth volume in the series, coming in May 2019, read on!

True Freedom

The chains we cannot see can be the hardest ones to break.

When Aulus runs up a gambling debt to his father's political enemy, he's desperate to pay it off before his father returns to Rome. His best friend Marcus suggests they fake the kidnapping of Aulus's sister Julia and use the ransom money. But when the man they hired kidnaps her for real, Aulus is catapulted into a desperate search to find her.

Torn from his childhood home by Rome's conquering armies and sold as a farm slave to labor until he dies, Dacius's faith gives him strength to bear what he must and serve without complaining. After a deadly accident makes him one of Julia's litter bearers, he overhears Marcus advising her brother to kidnap her. When Dacius almost dies thwarting the kidnapping, a Christian couple pretend Julia and Dacius are their children to keep her brother from finding them before her father returns.

But pretending to be free again makes returning to slavery more than Dacius can bear, while acting like a common woman opens Julia's eyes to dreams and destinies she never knew existed. With her brother closing in and her father almost home, can she find a way around Roman law and custom to free them both for the future they long for?

TRUE FREEDOM

Chapter 1

READY TO HELP

The woman's scream ripped into Dacius. He dropped his shovel of manure and sprinted into the stable yard.

Flames danced in a pile of straw three feet from the grindstone. The fire was small, but it transformed the skittery young stallion the master's son had just bought into a thousand pounds of lunging, rearing, kicking terror. The horse had ripped its lead rope from the stable boy's hand and run for the open gate in the ten-foot masonry wall—just as the young mistress returned on her litter.

She blocked its escape, and the stallion was determined to get out, even if it had to go through the litter where Mistress Julia sat screaming. The flailing hooves knocked the right rear bearer to the ground. As the stallion's full weight came down on his head, it crushed the man's skull.

Dacius stripped off his tunic as he ran toward the stallion. The horse reared, pummeling the top of the litter with its hooves—right above the mistress's head. The curtain bar splintered, then snapped before the hooves returned to the ground.

Her shrieks fueled the stallion's panic. It started to rear once more. Dacius leaped, caught the lead at the halter, and pulled its head down and sideways before it could strike the litter again.

As the hooves came back to earth, he flipped his tunic across the horse's face and pulled it snug around its eyes. The stallion froze, trembling, when the fire disappeared from view.

He led the horse into its stall and stood with it, stroking its neck. "Calm, boy. Steady, boy."

The fear drained from the trembling stallion as Dacius's voice and hand caressed him. When the last was gone, Dacius released his tunic and lifted it from the horse's eyes.

"Good boy." Two soft slaps to the horse's shoulder, and he left the stall.

The litter escort, a tall, muscular German, carried the limp form of Mistress Julia into the house. Dacius's brows rose. He would have sworn he'd pulled the horse away before he struck her.

A boy of about eleven stood with his back pressed against the wall, his eyes flicking toward the overseer like he was hoping not to be noticed.

Dacius slipped along the wall to stand beside him. "Is the mistress hurt?"

The boy shook his head. "No. She fainted. She can't stand blood."

"Well, I don't really like it myself." Dacius tousled the boy's hair and smiled at his worried face.

The boy tipped his head to look up at Dacius. "You ran up to that horse. Why weren't you afraid?"

Dacius shrugged. "He was only panicked by the fire. I knew he'd calm down as soon as he couldn't see it anymore."

The boy's eyes shifted from Dacius to the overseer, and Dacius's followed. The overseer strode over to the slave who'd been sharpening the hoes and swung the bronze knob on the handle of his three-cord whip into the side of his head, knocking him to the ground.

"Stupid son of a donkey! Didn't you see the sparks going into the straw? Move the grindstone over there." He pointed to the wall farthest from the straw and hay.

The slave stood, rubbing the side of his head. He bowed. "Yes, overseer."

Dacius stared at the whip as the overseer hung it back on his belt. The bronze was polished, the leather supple, as if frequently oiled. The overseer was proud of that whip, and that could only mean one thing. He liked to use it.

The overseer nudged the trampled bearer with his foot to make sure he was dead. "Move this litter out of the gate." He turned to one of the other bearers. "You. Get this body out of here."

The man bowed. "Yes, overseer."

The overseer swung and pointed at Dacius. "You. Clean up that blood so the mistress won't see it again."

Dacius dipped his head. "Yes, overseer."

He drew a bucket of water from the cistern and poured it on the blood that had pooled on the paving stone where the man's head had been. The red diluted and faded in the expanding circle of water, but some had soaked into the stone.

He'd seen war, and he knew too much about cleaning up blood. It would take soap and hot water and scrubbing to remove most of it. And even then, a faint shadow would remain. The water had washed away enough that the mistress shouldn't notice it, but he would always know a man had died there.

Dacius sucked a breath between his teeth and shook his head as he released it. In Roman eyes, not a man. A slave had died there, his body now gone, tossed aside like a piece of broken furniture and just as easy to replace.

The steward had gone to the slave market yesterday to buy Dacius for stable work. He'd be going tomorrow to get another slave for the mistress's litter.

He replaced the bucket by the cistern and returned to the dirty stall. As he scooped up one more shovelful of manure and straw, he sighed. *Slaves, obey your earthly masters with respect and fear and sincerity of heart, just as you would obey Christ.* That was what Apostle Paul had commanded. *Serve with your whole heart, as if you were serving the Lord, not men.*

He hadn't even been in this household a full day, and it was already clear it would be a place to sorely test him as he tried to serve Jesus, his Lord.

Julia awoke in her bed chamber as her lady's maid wiped her cheeks and forehead with a cloth dampened with rose water. Her eyelids drifted open as she threw up her arm to rest the back of her hand on her forehead.

Apicula dropped the cloth in the blown glass bowl. Its blue and green swirls caught the light to make a dancing pattern on the wall as she set it aside on the small table by the bed. She pushed an escaped strand of graying hair behind her ear. "Are you revived now, mistress? What happened?"

Julia started to sit up, then flopped back on the bed. "Not quite. The room is still spinning. That horrible horse my brother just bought—it killed one of my bearers and almost killed me. Someone pulled it away, and then I saw the crushed head. All the blood—you know what that does to me."

She tried to sit up again, and this time she succeeded. "Am I ever going to grow out of this? I feel so stupid when I faint over the smallest amount of blood. A Roman woman shouldn't be so squeamish." She touched Apicula's arm. "I'm glad you weren't walking beside the litter today. You might have been killed, too."

Apicula offered her hand to help Julia back to her feet. "I'm glad, too. Who did the stallion kill, mistress?"

"I don't know. Whoever was standing at the right rear. I didn't notice who was there earlier, and I couldn't bear to look at him all bloody."

"It's a good thing, mistress, that someone reached that horse before it hurt you. Who was it? Perhaps he would like something extra to eat tonight. You could have some of the leftovers sent out to him."

Julia raised her shoulders and arched her back after she stood. Her dizziness was gone. "I like that idea. It was one of the stable slaves, but I don't know which one. I didn't look at him before I saw all the blood and then... Gallio can find the right one. I would think our steward knows all the slaves, even if I don't."

Julia pressed her palms to her cheeks and pulled them off sideways. "I'm planning to go to my sister's house tomorrow morning. It's been almost a week since I went there and played with her little girls."

Five steps took her to the dressing table. Her hair was still tidy, and the reflection in the polished silver mirror showed her color had returned to normal. "I promised Flavia I would do her hair up pretty like mine the next time I came, and I don't want to disappoint her. I need a box to take some of my hair ornaments. I'd better take enough to do Sabina's as well, since she's three now and likes to mimic her older sister."

"Shall I get the box now, mistress? Do you feel well enough for me to leave you?"

"Yes. That's over. Let's pack now so I have everything ready. They're such precious children, and I want to go early."

Apicula smiled her agreement. "You'll make a wonderful mother yourself, mistress. When your betrothed returns from Britannia, perhaps the gods will smile on you and give you a child during your wedding week."

"Wouldn't that be wonderful? I don't remember much about Metilius Nepos, except he's handsome. I was only twelve when we celebrated the betrothal at Metilia's town house, and we didn't talk alone."

Her stomach fluttered. In a few months, she'd marry the man her father had chosen. But that was the Roman way, and Father loved her too much to pick someone unsuitable.

"Metilia says he's such a dear, kind brother. If she thinks he'll be a wonderful husband and father, I'm sure he will. In only a few more months, I'll find out."

As Apicula left the room to find a box, Julia began selecting the ornaments she was sure the little girls would love.

Aulus walked up the marble steps of the cold-water pool at the Baths of Trajan. The bath slave handed him a towel, and he wiped his face. He moved away from the pool edge before toweling his hair. His eyes were closed when something hard rammed into his stomach.

"What the—" He stepped back as he tossed the towel aside. A man muscled like an ox stood before him with a hinged wax tablet clutched in a hand large enough to crush a melon.

"Aulus Julius Secundus?" His voice was a low growl.

A shiver ran up Aulus's spine. "Yes."

The man thrust the wooden frame of the wax tablet into his stomach again. "Take it."

Aulus snatched it from his hand and stepped back again.

With spread legs and crossed arms, the thug glared at him. "Your brother-in-law's cousin, Sextus Sabinus, let you continue to gamble on promise of prompt payment. Four months paying nothing is too long, and his father is calling in the debt." He dipped his head toward the tablet and held out a stylus. "Read and sign."

Aulus flipped the tablet open and scanned the text.

> Marcus Julius Secundus owes Quintus Flavius Sabi-
> nus 10,000 denarii for debts incurred by his son, Aulus
> Julius Secundus. Unless other arrangements are made,
> M. Julius Secundus will pay in full within thirty days

of his return to Roma at the end of his governorship of
Sicilia.

A wide finger tapped the wax below the text. "Sign." Two more taps.
"Now."

Aulus rolled the stylus between his fingers as his stomach churned.
He'd lost money that wasn't his to lose. Everything he treated as his
own was legally Father's as *paterfamilias.* And every debt he owed was a
claim against his father.

Father's red face on the pier in Portus swirled in his memory. Father's anger at him betting too much on the Red faction to win in the
Circus Maximus was seared into Aulus's brain. He'd promised Father he
wouldn't do that again while his father was away from Rome. And he
hadn't...he'd bet on the Greens, and they almost always won.

He'd been money ahead until that dinner party at his step-sister's
house.

He planned to pay the debt, but to sign a legal promise committing
Father to pay as soon as he returned...

The thug's mouth turned down. "If you don't sign now, I will come
back." His scowl turned into a cruel smile. "But you don't want me to."

His fist hit his open palm, then twisted slowly.

Aulus's clenched his jaw and hoped that was enough to hide his fear.
Better another tongue-lashing from Father than a beating from a gladiator.

He pressed the stylus into the wax, concentrating on keeping his
letters from wiggling and betraying him.

With a snap, he closed the tablet and handed it back to the brute.

"Wise choice." The thug smirked as his gaze raked Aulus from head to
foot and back. Then he spun on his heal and disappeared into the crowd.

"What was that about?"

Aulus jerked at the quiet voice of his best friend, Marcus Drusus.

He ran shaky fingers through his hair. "I'm in big trouble. I was at
my step-sister's villa a few months ago, and I gambled with her husband's cousin. I lost 10,000 denarii, and I don't have the money to pay."
He rubbed the back of his neck. "Sextus said that wasn't a problem, that
he'd give me time to pay him. But now he's told his father, and his father
is demanding the money...from Father."

"Your father's rich. He can pay that without even noticing it."

"That's not the problem. Sabinus and Father have been political enemies for years. Sabinus will try to use this to hurt him."

Marcus's brow furrowed. "Your father seems more than a match for anyone."

"But I wasn't supposed to be gambling. Not at that level, anyway. I hadn't planned to, but they had this great Falerian wine. I drank too much of it before we started. "His shoulders drooped. "Father's going to kill me when he comes back to find I've exposed him to his enemy like this. Sextus's father is Quintus Sabinus."

"Quintus Sabinus?" Marcus sucked air through his teeth. "He wanted to marry my aunt Claudia right after Grandfather died. Mother fought with Father for saying yes before Sabinus married someone else."

His brows lowered, then relaxed. "I can ask Father to give me the money. Ten thousand isn't much for him. He'd do anything for his best friend." Marcus nudged Aulus's arm. "He'll let me help mine."

Some tension drained from Aulus's shoulders, but not all. "But what if he won't?"

"Then we'll figure out another way to get it." A twisted smile curved Marcus's lips. "I know. We can fake your kidnapping to get enough ransom money to pay the debt." The smile turned into a chuckle. "But Gallio already took away your key to the strongbox after you bought that stallion that's too jumpy to ride. Maybe he won't want to pay that much for you."

Marcus slapped Aulus's shoulder. "We can fake Julia's kidnapping instead. Gallio would pay any amount to get her back."

Aulus chuckled. "He would." He punched Marcus's arm. "I can always count on you to come up with a good plan." The last of the tension vanished. Marcus's father would help, and his own father would never know.

Chapter 2

A Bad Idea

Dacius had almost finished feeding and watering the horses the next morning when the steward entered the stable yard with the overseer.

The overseer nodded as the steward spoke. "The young master's stallion created a problem, Vilicus. She wants to go as soon as she finishes her breakfast, so I need one the same height. There isn't time to go to the market. Do you have one you can spare?"

Dacius emptied his bucket into Niger's water trough. The steward's request shouldn't affect him. He was the only slave working in the stable. There had been another, but yesterday Vilicus sent him into the garden to help dig a new reflecting pond. No sign of him this morning, so Dacius had to do the feeding, grooming, and cleaning alone. He couldn't be spared from the horses.

He patted the young stallion's neck before fetching another bucket of water from the cistern.

Vilicus didn't like a slave to look directly at him, so Dacius kept his eyes down. Since he tried to serve as unto the Lord, he never avoided work. But it was obvious why the other slaves tried to be invisible when this overseer came near. He'd jerk a man off one task to do another. Later, he'd curse and sometimes strike him for not completing the first task. It was a chaotic place to serve.

As Dacius poured the last bucket into the stallion's trough, he heard the guttural voice. "You."

He turned and bowed his head. "Yes, overseer."

"Go stand by the litter."

He froze his eyebrows to hide his shock. Was Vilicus planning to leave the horses untended? But no matter how foolish the command, he had to obey.

Three bearers already stood by the litter, so he joined them.

Satisfaction lifted the corners of the steward's mouth. "He's the right size. I'll take that one for today. Have him wash to get rid of the stable smell and put him in the litter tunic. She'll be wanting to leave in perhaps half an hour."

Vilicus tipped his head. "Yes, steward." He watched the steward enter the house before spinning on Dacius. "You. Wash that stench off, then dress for litter work."

Dacius lowered his eyes. "Yes, overseer."

The overseer strode through the small archway that connected the stable yard to the garden, and Dacius sighed. It was a good thing he'd risen early. Otherwise, the poor animals would have gone without. He'd barely finished placing the feed and water in the last stall, but Vilicus didn't know that when he ordered him to litter duty.

He scanned the stable yard as he headed to the cistern to draw some water. The horses needed grooming. The stalls needed cleaning. If he were a betting man, he'd bet the work would still be waiting for him when he returned, and Vilicus would yell at him because he hadn't finished.

Slaves, obey your earthly masters with respect and fear and sincerity of heart, just as you would obey Christ. He'd reminded himself at least ten times yesterday. Another sigh escaped. He'd probably hit twenty today.

When Marcus entered his father's library, Lucius Drusus Fidelis had a hinged wax tablet open before him.

"Good morning, Father." Marcus lowered himself into the second chair by the desk.

His father closed the tablet. "A letter from your brother."

Marcus raised his eyebrows to feign interest. "How is he?"

"You know your brother. It's impossible to tell. He never complains, no matter what his situation." Father's lips tightened. "I went to some trouble to get him a good tribune posting near Rome, but he's decided to apply for a posting in a frontier province. He going to ask for Britannia, Dacia, or Judaea. He hasn't decided which."

Marcus pasted on a smile. "That sounds like Lucius. He'll want to go to the most dangerous place where no one else would volunteer to serve, so I'd bet on Judaea."

Father drummed on the tablet with a silver-tipped ivory stylus. "You're probably right. Your brother would put the needs of Rome above his own self-interest. Someone needs to serve there, but I'd rather it wasn't my son."

Marcus picked up a brass stylus and rolled it between his fingers. "There's glory to be found in battle. Lucius probably wants some excitement while he's tribune."

"Judaea isn't like Germania before it was pacified. The Germans fought you like warriors. They didn't stick a knife into you as you were going down the street and then keep walking as if they'd done nothing. Lucius might get himself killed by some zealot and left like the bodies the urban cohorts gather after they were murdered during the night. There's no glory in that." Father rolled his eyes. "But Lucius is too much like his grandfather, so he'll probably volunteer for the most dangerous place."

Father placed the stylus atop the closed tablet and leaned back in his chair. "But you didn't come to discuss your brother." His eyes warmed as they rested on Marcus. "So, why have you sought me out so early?"

Marcus stopped rolling the stylus. "I need 10,000 denarii."

Father rested his elbows on the desk and steepled his fingers. "What for?"

"To help a friend."

"Aulus Secundus? What sort of trouble has he gotten himself into this time?"

"He was gambling when he'd drunk too much, and he lost more than he realized."

His father laughed. "I'm not surprised. Aulus tends to act without thinking, and when the wine flows in, his sense leaks out. I'm glad my own sons are smart enough to keep their drinking and gambling separate."

Father's eyes narrowed. "Why didn't you stop him before he lost too much? He always follows your lead."

"I wasn't there, or I would have. You've taught me what a man should do for his best friend. His father told Aulus not to gamble to excess while he was governor in Sicilia, and except for that night, he hasn't."

Marcus leaned forward. "Will you give me the money so I can help him before his father finds out?"

"Of course. My best friend helped me more than once so your grandfather wouldn't know. Marcus Corvinus and I were closer than brothers at your age. We still are. That's why you carry his name."

"Thank you, Father. Sabinus sent a gladiator to the baths yesterday to make Aulus sign a document committing his father to pay the debt within a month of his return. If Aulus clears the debt now, his father will never know."

Father's head pulled back. "Why would Aulus's brother-in-law use a gladiator?"

"He didn't lose to Antonia's husband. It was her husband's cousin, Sextus."

"Quintus Sabinus's son?"

The edge on Father's voice raised Marcus's heart rate. "Yes."

"Did it say Secundus owed Quintus?"

"Yes. Why?"

His father rubbed his mouth. "That changes things. Secundus and Quintus Sabinus have been political enemies for as long as I can remember. Secundus is an honorable man, but Sabinus...Let's just say he's not a man to cross."

Father rested his elbow on the desk as he rubbed his forehead. "You were only fourteen and living with your mother when he wanted to marry your aunt Claudia. She ran off to Titus in Thracia to avoid that, and Sabinus was ready to kill me over the embarrassment that caused him.

"He spared our family because he found another girl to marry with better political connections. It's been four years, but I still feel the venom in his gaze."

He tightened his lips until they vanished. "If it were anyone else, I'd give you the money, but I'm not going to get between the crocodile and his prey."

"But—"

Father held up his hand. "This discussion is over."

Marcus froze his face to stop the frown. "As you wish, Father." While he could still control his irritation, he turned and left the room.

Aulus was waiting for him in the peristyle garden, sitting on the low wall by the pool.

When Marcus entered, he shot to his feet, smiling. "So, do we go to Sextus or his father to settle the debt?"

"Neither. Father said he'd give me the money; then he backed out when he heard you owed Quintus Sabinus." He spat. "I never took Father for a coward before."

The blood drained from Aulus's face. "What am I going to do?"

Marcus placed his hand on Aulus's bicep and squeezed. "I'll think of something." A slow smile crept across his face. "I guess we need to plan a kidnapping."

"I thought that was a joke." Aulus bit his lip. "We can't actually do it."

Marcus rubbed his chin before the half-shrug. "Why not?"

Historical Note

THE DAILY LIFE OF GLADIATORS:
CELEBRITIES YET SOCIAL OUTCASTS IN THE ROMAN WORLD

Perhaps the most widely recognized symbol of ancient Rome is the Colosseum, started by the first Flavian emperor, Vespasian, in AD 72 and finished by his son and successor, Titus, in AD 80. During the Imperial era, Romans called it the Flavian Amphitheater after the dynasty that built it. Nothing epitomizes the Roman attitude toward the value of human life better than this marvel of Roman architecture that let up to 85,000 people watch as men fought and died, urged on by the roar of the blood-thirsty crowd. Perhaps as many as four hundred amphitheaters were spread across the Empire, ranging from wooden structures, which might seat one to ten thousand, to stone or concrete marvels that are still in use today for bull fights, concerts, and film festivals in Arles and Nimes in France and Pula in Croatia.

The typical schedule for the Roman games involved more than gladiatorial contests. The morning was filled with animal events, ranging from hunts to *damnatio ad bestias*, the feeding of condemned criminals to beasts. Irenaeus (AD 130-202, Bishop of Lugdunum in Gaul) reported that Ignatius of Antioch was fed to the lions in Rome in AD 107 for the crime of refusing to worship the Roman gods. Condemned criminals or prisoners of war might be forced to fight each other until only one remained to be killed by a gladiator. But the real excitement came in the afternoon, when professional gladiators met in one-on-one combat, fighting until one was dead or so badly injured he was forced to admit defeat.

A loser who fought well enough was often spared to fight again, so the odds of surviving a single fight were about five to one. The typical gladiator fought only two or three times a year. Half died during their first year in the arena, but for those who survived their "rookie year," life after the arena was a real possibility. That life might even be long; a memorial stone in a gladiator cemetery in Ephesus was erected by the family of a retired gladiator who died at age 99.

But how did someone become a gladiator, and what was life like during the 360-plus days of the year when a gladiator wasn't entertaining the masses in mortal combat?

While gladiators were admired for their courage and fighting skills, they were social outcasts. Like a prostitute, a gladiator was an *infamis*, a person of low repute. He couldn't vote or hold public office, and many burial grounds refused to accept a gladiator's remains.

Many became gladiators through no choice of their own. Over half of the fighters in a gladiatorial school (*ludus*) were slaves. Many were taken as prisoners of war and sold into the arena with some fighting skills. Some were slaves who had proven too hard to handle. Some were condemned criminals. These came in two categories: condemned to the sword (*damnatio ad gladium*) and condemned to the games (*damnatio ad ludos*). While those condemned to the sword would be killed during their first appearance in the arena, men condemned to the games could survive as long as they fought well enough and might even hope to be freed someday. If the sponsor hosting the games decided to free a gladiator, he could pay the purchase price to the owner and award a wooden sword to the fighter as the symbol of his freedom.

Some gladiators were free men who were paid a sizable sum of money to sign a contract with a ludus for a fixed period of time, typically four or five years. During the term of the contract, they belonged to the ludus as if they were slaves, swearing the gladiator oath to submit to anything the ludus owner wanted, including having them killed. These voluntary gladiators were called *auctoratii*.

Some auctoratii needed the money to pay debts before they were sold into permanent slavery to pay them. Sometimes former soldiers, especially those who had been dishonorably discharged and were already *infames*, chose to become gladiators if they had no other job prospects. Some were gladiator slaves who had been freed and chose to continue in their profession after receiving their freedom.

While the vast majority of gladiators were men, women gladiators have been pictured in mosaics and listed as special attractions. Whether these were slaves or auctoratii isn't known.

The head trainer of a ludus was the *lanista*, a man who had been a successful gladiator himself. While the lanista was an infamis at the bottom of society, the wealthy Roman who owned the ludus was usually a well-respected member of Roman society. A large ludus might have several hundred fighters, and the money to be made feeding the Roman lust for bloodshed was attractive to many businessmen in the equestrian order. A sponsor of the games hired the gladiators through the schools. For every fighter who died, the sponsor payed a fixed fee based on the ranking of the gladiator, so win or lose, the owner of a ludus made money on every match.

The training regimen for a gladiator was vigorous. Many hours were spent daily practicing with wooden swords weighted to be twice as heavy as real metal ones and shields heavier than those used in combat. Muscles were built up to a level that bones were deformed. Attack and counter-attack were practiced until responses were reflexive and instantaneous. Stamina, strength, and intimate knowledge of how an opponent would fight could make the difference between life and death. Bouts seldom lasted 30 minutes and might be over in a minute, but a longer, fiercer fight might impress the crowd enough that the loser might be spared to fight again. A new gladiator usually trained for a year or more before his first appearance in a professional bout.

The intense training burned many calories, so gladiators were fed large quantities of a mostly vegetarian diet. The gladiator diet differed from the civilian diet in several ways. While wheat bread was a staple for most Romans, gladiators ate mostly barley. Some fruit and vegetables were combined with ample servings of barley porridge (*polenta*). The goal was to have a layer of fat overlying vulnerable blood vessels and nerves so a shallow cut wouldn't prove disastrous. Fat tissue can bleed impressively, making spectators marvel at the fighter's ability to continue the battle, while not being a crippling injury. To build strong bones, a drink made from the ashes of bones and charred wood was served.

Gladiators and former gladiators worked outside the arena as bodyguards, debt collectors, and enforcers to settle disputes. They also served as sparring partners and personal trainers for men and for women who wanted to fight privately.

Memorial stones in gladiator cemeteries provide ample evidence that many gladiators married and raised families. The stones usually list the names of the relatives erecting the stones and the number of fights, the number of wins, and the age at death. Many died in battle in their twenties or early thirties, but others lived to die a natural death.

In *Faithful*, Marcus Brutus is a wealthy equestrian who includes three gladiator schools among his business enterprises. He's an honest businessman in a brutal business, callous but not cruel, a man who treats his gladiator slaves like the men they are but is perfectly comfortable making money off them when they kill or are killed in the arena. But Brutus is a man of his times and culture. The popularity of the games didn't wane until Christianity became the dominant religion. Emperor Constantine replaced sentences that condemned a criminal to die in the arena with condemnation to work in the mines, and Emperor Valentinian III banned gladiatorial contests in AD 438.

For more about life in the Roman Empire at its peak, please go to carolashby.com.

1) Adela's world is turned upside down through no fault of her own, first by her mother's death and father's immediate remarriage, then by the kidnapping and its aftermath. At the beginning of the novel, how does she deal with upheavals in her life? How and why does that change during the course of the story?

2) Otto's foolish choices led to personal disaster when he failed to listen to Galen's sound advice. Otto's bad choices dragged his friend into danger as Galen tried to rescue him. Have you ever had someone like Otto in your circle of friends? How do you deal with that?

3) Galen is the conscience and calm head for a friend who doesn't think through the consequences before acting. Could Galen have done more than he did to protect Otto from himself? Should he have tried? If you have friends who seem to drift into dangerous waters with the slightest temptation, what can you do to help?

4) Each time Galen almost catches up with Otto to free him, something prevents it. Yet each setback is met with a willingness to go on trying and a firm hope that he will ultimately succeed in the rescue. Why? Do you know people like that?

5) Galen's sense of responsibility for Adela grows first into friendship and then into love. But he doesn't act on his feelings because he knows they aren't aligned with God's commands as long as Adela has no interest in God. He risks losing her to his best friend because he puts his faith above his feelings. Could you have made the same choice?

6) The only way Galen can get the money to save Otto is to go to Tiberius, with every expectation that Tiberius will kill him if Galen's faith in Jesus is discovered. When Tiberius accidentally discovers what Galen is, how does Galen respond? How did Tiberius respond to Galen's commitment and courage?

7) Marcus Antonius Brutus is an honest businessman in a brutal business. He's a man of his times who is callous but not cruel. He treats his gladiator slaves like the men they are, but he leaves no doubt that he owns them and has no qualms about sending them into the arena to kill or

die. Brutus admires Galen for his perseverance and courage in trying to free Otto at any cost. What do you think would be his response if he learned Galen followed Jesus? Do you have people in your life who are like Brutus? What do you think would reach them?

8) At the end of *Blind Ambition*, Tiberius disowned his only son for becoming a Christian and told him to leave and never return. Yet he protected his son from being executed for his faith. What had changed in the 8 years between the two stories? Do you know anyone in the same situation as Tiberius and his son, Decimus?

9) Tiberius is forced to question his prejudice against Christians when people he cares about and respects have chosen to follow Jesus. His best friend chose to die for the Christian god when a meaningless sacrifice would have set him free. His only son walked away from everything he'd ever wanted and was willing to die for that god. Eight years later, Tiberius meets Galen, whose loyalty to that same invisible god was even greater than his loyalty to the friends he would do anything to save. When Tiberius returns to Germania for a reunion with the son he banished for his faith, will Tiberius change his own course? Why? Do you know someone like Tiberius? What would reach them?

10) *Faithful* tells a story of loyalty and perseverance, of faith that God wants what is best for us and that good can come from the worst situations, of being open to the second chances God gives us. What touched you most? What made you think about what your own choices would be?

What should the future hold for Marcus Brutus?

In a militaristic society where it was considered a good afternoon's entertainment to watch men fight to the death, Marcus Brutus is an honorable man in a brutal business, callous but not cruel, a man who treats his slaves like the men they are but is perfectly comfortable with making money off their deaths. Brutus will return in an important role in Spring of 2019 in *True Freedom*, a story set four years before *Faithful*. But I haven't yet decided what Brutus's ultimate end will be. Will he continue on his present path, or choose a different way? I'd love to hear your thoughts about that. Please go to Contact Carol at carol-ashby.com (my blog) or carolashby.com (my Roman history site) and share your thoughts in the comment box. I hope I hear from you!

Glossary

Aureus: gold coin worth 25 *denarii*

Auxilia: large military units of soldiers who were not Roman citizens

Ave, Imperator, morituri te salutant: "Hail, Emperor, we who are about to die salute you."

Bireme: Roman naval vessel, a galley with two rows of oars

Caldarium: the hot bath room in a Roman bath complex

Caupona: inn, canteen, tavern; sometimes a place to find prostitutes

Centurion: 1st level officer over 80 men; rises through the ranks based on merit

Corbita: merchant sailing ship

Cursus honorum: the sequence of military and political offices held by men of the senatorial order

Denarius: (plural *denarii*) silver coin worth about one day's living wage

Diversorium: lodging house, inn, usually respectable

Doctor: teacher; in gladiatorial schools, a trainer who assists the lanista

Dupondius: brass coin worth 1/8 *denarius*

Equestrian order: 2nd highest class of Roman citizens; required personal wealth greater than 100,000 *denarii*

Flumen: river

Familia gladiatoria Bruti: members of the gladiatorial schools *(ludi)* of Brutus

Gladius: short thrusting sword used by the Roman military and some gladiators *(secutors)*

Gratias tibi (tam): Thank you (so much)

Gregarius: a semi-skilled gladiator who fights in a group; often a prisoner of war

Honestus: reputable, honorable, decent

Hordearius: "of barley," slang term for a gladiator, whose diet was mostly barley

Lanista: the head trainer of a gladiatorial school

Ludi: "games," especially public spectacles like gladiatorial contests

Ludus: (pural *ludi*) training school for gladiators

Mansio: roadside guest quarters for travelling Roman officials

Paenula: semicircular woolen cloak with hood

Palus: wooden stake struck with a sword during gladiatorial practice

Palla: rectangular cloth wrap worn by Roman women

Paterfamilias: oldest living male of an extended Roman family; the patriarch who owns everything

Peregrine: a person who is not a Roman citizen

Polenta: barley porridge

Provocator: gladiator who fights another provocator with short sword and shield

Questor: Roman magistrate who oversees markets and financial matters

Retiarius: a gladiator who fights with a net and trident

Salutation: daily ritual during which prominent citizens received clients and others seeking favors

Salve: Latin greeting, "hello"

Secutor: a gladiator who fights with sword and shield, often fights retiarius

Senatorial order: highest class of Roman citizens; required personal wealth greater than 250,000 *denarii*

Stadia: Roman units for distances: 1 mile = 8.7 stadia; 1 km = 5.4 stadia

Stola: a long robe worn by married women fastened by clasps at the shoulder and worn over a tunic

Taberna: tavern or shop selling prepared food

Tablinum: the main office and reception room for the Roman master of the house

Tabula: popular Roman board game, often played with betting

Te amo: I like you; I love you

Thermae: Roman bathhouse

Ubi honestum diversorium?: Where is a reputable lodging house?

Vale: Latin farewell, "goodbye"

Voluptas meus est: It is my pleasure or my delight

Scripture References

Scripture quotations marked (ESV) are from the Holy Bible, English Standard Version, copyright © 2001, 2007, 2011, 2016 by Crossway Bibles, a division of Good News Publishers. Used by permission. All rights reserved.

Chapter 43: John 11:25-27 (ESV)

Jesus said to her, "I am the resurrection and the life. Whoever believes in me, though he die, yet shall he live, and everyone who lives and believes in me shall never die. Do you believe this?" She said to him, "Yes, Lord; I believe that you are the Christ, the Son of God, who is coming into the world."

Chapter 50: Matthew 18:12-14 (ESV)

What do you think? If a man has a hundred sheep, and one of them has gone astray, does he not leave the ninety-nine on the mountains and go in search of the one that went astray? And if he finds it, truly, I say to you, he rejoices over it more than over the ninety-nine that never went astray. So it is not the will of my Father who is in heaven that one of these little ones should perish.

Acknowledgements

I'm so thankful that God has given me another opportunity to tell a story about the faithfulness of one person who tries his best to follow God's command that we love one another, no matter the cost, and how that changes the lives of those around him. The hundreds of hours spent writing this story of transformation and love flew by, and it's hard to say goodbye to these characters who feel like my dear friends.

No author could write the best book she can without the help of many others. Special thanks go to my critique partner, Katie Powner, who's an award-winning author herself and read every line as if she were an editor. Many thanks also to Andrew Budek-Schmeisser, my New Mexico compatriot and fellow author, who gave tirelessly of his time critiquing both *Faithful* and *True Freedom*, number six in the series that will be out next year. He's also been my expert consultant on combat and medical details for this novel and for *True Freedom*. What a blessing when the answer to a question I didn't even know to ask is only an email away! I'm especially thankful for the deep wisdom and spiritual insight of my beta readers: alpha beta Regina Fujitani, who gets so many things tried out on her more than once, and my kindred spirit Lisa Garcia, who also read *Blind Ambition* and told me more than once that teenager Galen had to have his own novel when he grew up. She was right.

Many thanks also to my wonderful friends who read draft versions and gave me many helpful comments. My deepest thanks go out to Patti Stouter and Brennan McPherson for their wise comments on the deep spiritual sections. Their insights and suggestions made the characters more real and the situations more authentic.

It's been a delight to work yet again with my line editor, Wendy Chorot. I especially treasure her spiritual wisdom as we refine the deep spiritual conversations to mirror real life. Her skill as editor is everything a writer could want. It's a true blessing to work with her. If you're looking for an editor, call Wendy!

Roseanna White has created another gorgeous cover that captures the theme of the series, the Light in the Empire. No one could do a better job designing the cover of a historical novel about spiritual transformations with a romantic subplot that draws ooohs from women and wows from men. I feel the smiles coming every time I think about what she'll come up with for the next two in the series.

I especially want to thank my wonderful family. I love talking books with my son Paul, who's been writing himself since 8th grade. My daughter Lydia gives me the best reasons to shut off the computer and enjoy a day with her. God truly blessed me with them!

Nothing tops being married to a man who is kind, smart, funny, and so patient he even smiles as he listens to my umpteenth variation on a scene. Jim has been a true blessing for two thirds of my life now, and that's a record I look forward to beating for years to come.

Carol Ashby has been a professional writer for most of her life, but her articles and books were about lasers and compound semiconductors (the electronics that make cell phones, laser pointers, and LED displays work). She still writes about light, but her Light in the Empire series tells stories of difficult friendships and life-changing decisions in dangerous times, where forgiveness and love open hearts to discover their own faith in Christ. Her fascination with the Roman Empire was born during her first middle-school Latin class. A research career in New Mexico inspires her to get every historical detail right so she can spin stories that make her readers feel like they're living under the Caesars themselves.

Read her articles about many facets of life in the Roman Empire at carolashby.com, or join her at her blog, The Beauty of Truth, at carol-ashby.com.

LIGHT *in the* EMPIRE SERIES

Dangerous times, difficult friendships,
lives transformed by forgiveness and love.

The Light in the Empire Series follows the interconnected lives of four Roman families during the reigns of Trajan and Hadrian. Join them as they travel the Empire, from Germania and Britannia to Thracia, Dacia, and Judaea and, of course, to Rome itself.

NOW AVAILABLE

Forgiven

Are some wounds too deep to forgive?

With a ruthless father who murdered for the family inheritance, Marcus Drusus plans to do the same. In AD 122, Marcus follows his brother Lucius to Judaea and plots to frame a zealot for his older brother's death. But the plan goes awry, and Lucius is rescued by a Messianic Jewish woman. Her oldest brother is a zealot and a Roman soldier killed her twin, but Rachel still persuades her father Joseph to put his love for Jesus above his anger with Rome and hide Lucius until he heals.

Rachel cares for the enemy, and more than broken bones heal as duty turns to love. Lucius embraces Joseph's faith in Jesus, but sharing a faith doesn't heal all wounds. Even before revealed secrets slice open old scars, Joseph wants no Roman son-in-law. With Rachel's zealot brother suspecting he's a Roman officer and his own brother planning to kill him when he returns, can Lucius survive long enough to change Joseph's mind?

Blind Ambition

Sometimes you have to almost die to discover how you want to live.

It's AD 114 in the Roman province of Germania Superior, and being a Christian carries a death sentence. Tribune Decimus Lentulus is on the fast track for a stellar political career back in Rome. When he's robbed, blinded, and left for dead, a young German woman who follows the Way finds him. Valeria knows it's his duty to have her and her family killed, but she chooses to obey Jesus's command to love her enemy and takes him home to care for him.

It's not his miraculous recovery that shakes Decimus to his core. It's the way they love him like family and their unconcealed love for Jesus. In spite of himself, he falls in love with the Christian woman Rome wants him to kill. Can Valeria hide her faith to follow him into the circles of Roman power? Or should he abandon his ambition to help rule the Empire and choose to follow a different way?

The Legacy

When Rome has taken everything, what's left for a man to give?

Betrayed by a ruthless son who'll do anything for power and wealth, Publius Drusus faces death with an unanswered prayer—that his treasured daughter, Claudia, and honorable son, Titus, will someday share his faith. But who will lead them to the truth once he's gone?

Claudia's oldest brother Lucius arranged their father's execution to inherit everything, and now he's forcing her to marry a cruel Roman power broker. If only she could get to Titus—a thousand miles away in Thracia. Then the man who secretly told her father about Jesus arranges for his son Philip to sneak her out of Rome and take her to the brother she can trust.

A childhood accident scarred Philip's face. A woman's rejection scarred his heart. Claudia's gratitude grows into love, but what can Philip do when the first woman who returns his love hates the God he loves even more?

Titus and Claudia hunger for revenge on their brother and the Christians they blame for their father's deadly conversion. When Titus buys Miriam, a secret Christian, to serve his sister, he starts them all down a path of conflicting loyalties and dangerous decisions. His father's final letter commands the forgiveness Titus refuses to give. What will it take to free him from the hatred poisoning his own heart?

Join the people you met in *Second Chances* eight years earlier in this tale of betrayal, hatred, love, and forgiveness, where even bad things can work together for good.

Second Chances

*Must the shadows of the past destroy
the hope of the future?*

In AD 122, Cornelia Scipia, proud daughter of one of Rome's noblest families, learns her adulterous husband plans to betroth their daughter to the vicious son of his best friend. Over her dead body! Cornelia divorces him, reclaims her enormous dowry, and kidnaps her own daughter. She plans to start over with Drusilla a thousand miles away. No more husbands for her. But she didn't count on meeting Hector, the widowed Greek captain of the ship carrying her to her new life.

Devastated by the loss of his wife and daughter, Hector's heart begins to heal as he befriends Drusilla. Cornelia's sacrificial love for Drusilla and her courage and humor in the face of the unknown earn his admiration...as a friend. Is he ready for more?

Marriage to the kind, honest sea captain would give Drusilla the father she deserves...and Cornelia the faithful husband she's always longed for. But while her ex-husband hunts them to drag Drusilla back to Rome, secrets in Hector's past and the chasms between their social classes and different faiths erect complicated barriers to any future together. Will God give two lonely hearts a second chance at happiness?

Join the people you met in *The Legacy* eight years later in this tale of hope and a future never imagined until God opens the door.

True Freedom

*The chains we cannot see
can be the hardest ones to break.*

When Aulus runs up a gambling debt to his father's political enemy, he's desperate to pay it off before his father returns to Rome. His best friend Marcus suggests they fake the kidnapping of Aulus's sister Julia and use the ransom money. But when the man they hired kidnaps her for real, Aulus is catapulted into a desperate search to find her.

Torn from his childhood home by Rome's conquering armies and sold as a farm slave to labor until he dies, Dacius's faith gives him strength to bear what he must and serve without complaining. After a deadly accident makes him one of Julia's litter bearers, he overhears Marcus advising her brother to kidnap her. When Dacius almost dies thwarting the kidnapping, a Christian couple pretend Julia and Dacius are their children to keep her brother from finding them before her father returns.

But pretending to be free again makes returning to slavery more than Dacius can bear, while acting like a common woman opens Julia's eyes to dreams and destinies she never knew existed. With her brother closing in and her father almost home, can she find a way around Roman law and custom to free them both for the future they long for?

Find out what happens to Ariana's brother Diegis twelve years later in this tale of hope and a future never imagined until God opens the door.

Hope Unchained

Can the deepest loss bring the greatest gain?

Rome's conquering army took Ariana's family and freedom, but nothing can take her faith in Jesus. When she rescues a tribune's wife from certain death, her reward is freedom and a chance to free her brother and sister. But first she must catch up with the slave caravan before they vanish forever, and tracking them from Dacia to the coast seems impossible for one woman alone.

Discharged from the legion with a hand crippled by a Dacian knife, Donatus faces a future without hope. When the tribune asks him to escort Ariana on her quest, it's the only work he can find. It means four weeks with a Dacian woman and a gladiator bodyguard, but it takes money to eat. A man without options must take what he can get.

But a lot can happen in four weeks. Even battle-hardened men can be touched by love and forgiveness, and it's easier to face an enemy with a sword than to face the truth. When his moment of truth comes, what will Donatus choose, and what will that mean for both of them?

Honor Bound

When the honorable path isn't clear, how do you find your way?

Marcus Brutus owns estates, ships, and gladiator schools that increase his fortune daily, but his greatest treasures are his honor and his wife. When she reveals her faith in Jesus before dying after the birth of their son, he's consumed by hatred for the unnamed Christian woman who led his beloved to abandon the Roman gods, making him lose her in this life and the next.

For fifteen years, Licinia's father hid her Christian faith. But now her father is dead, and a ruthless political enemy is hunting for anything to destroy her brother's career. When she becomes the target, her brother sends her to their estate in Germania. But is that far enough to protect her from an evil man who will stop at nothing?

When a carriage accident leaves Brutus injured and his best friend near death after rescuing Brutus's son, Licinia welcomes and cares for them. But her strange habits and his friend's unexpected recovery make Brutus suspect she's the Christian who corrupted his wife. When her brother's enemies come for her, does honor require him to protect her or turn her over as an enemy of Rome? And when Licinia's heart is drawn toward the pagan man who makes money off death, can she reconcile her growing affection with her love for Christ?

Join some of the people you met in *True Freedom* four years later in this tale of loss and discovery, anger and forgiveness, and the truth that sets people free.

I'd Love to Hear from You!

If you enjoyed this book, it would be a real gift to me if you would post a review at the retailer you purchased it from. A good review is like a jewel set in gold for an author. Other great places to share reviews are Goodreads and BookBub. If you've read others in the series, it would be great if you post a review of those, too.

I'd also love to hear from you at carol-ashby.com or directly at carolashbyauthor@gmail.com.

Want to hear about upcoming releases in the Light in the Empire series and free gifts only for newsletter subscribers?

For free gifts and other special offers, advance notices of upcoming releases, and info about my latest writing adventures, I hope you'll sign up for my newsletter at carol-ashby.com.

Carol Ashby

www.ingramcontent.com/pod-product-compliance
Lightning Source LLC
Chambersburg PA
CBHW030527190726

48283CB00006B/1805